Raising Limbo

RAISING LIMBO

Book 1

W. L. CAROL

Acknowledgments

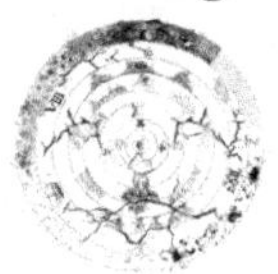

I would like to show gratitude to "The Man Upstairs" for protecting me throughout my life's journey and leading me to my purpose. To my mother and father, I am forever grateful for your love, support, and belief in me especially when I doubted myself. Ms. Wright, I greatly appreciate you for taking the time out of your busy schedule to read and do the foreword of my novel. And, a special thank you to Dr. Brown and Samone Publishing for giving me a chance to realize my dream.

Foreword

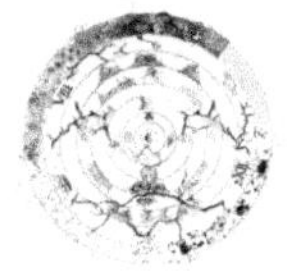

Nostalgia-a sentimental longing or wistful affection for the past, typically for a period or place with happy personal associations. The idea of one's childhood home evokes and awakens senses of earlier days and times.

Raising Limbo is a work of astonishing imagination and breathtaking descriptions of Trina, from the Valley of Ancestors, as she travels through her memories and emotions of another place and time as she journeys through Limbo to another place and time. Slices of her past life are filled with exquisitely crafted characters you truly care about as you go along with her on this fantastical adventure. Set in a captivating, unique world rich with details, Limbo was unlike anything I've ever experienced. I ventured into my own nostalgic journey to my childhood as Trina described hers.

I met W. L. Carol about 15 years ago while teaching Gifted and Talented middle school students. Her mother was my principal. W. L. would come up to the school in the afternoons to do her homework, write papers and keep her mom company since she often put in late hours at school. Many days when I would see her in the office, we would exchange stories and talk about her passions-writing, fantasy, science fiction, and Super Heroes! Oftentimes, her mom would join in on our conversations and before we knew it darkness had set in outside. Most days we would miss dinner because we were enthralled in old memories and storytelling of people and days gone by.

As W. L. worked on her graduate studies, she would ask me to read and sometimes proofread her papers or critique something she had written. That's when I learned about her incredible knowledge of comic book heroes, villains, and plot twists. I used to invite her to my classes to visit with some of my students who had the same passion and interests in fantasy and comic book characters. I would sit in awe watching her interact with these kids-most of them boys. They could talk for hours!

Eventually, W. L. would share some of her book ideas and even some chapters with me. I was so impressed with her vast vocabulary and ability to develop creatures, characters and worlds from her imagination. She could turn her words into magical descriptions of people, places, and fantastic beings. She has always been a storyteller of both grace and power.

From world to world and character to character, W. L. Carol displays her signature handiwork for worldbuilding and, above all else, compassion for people. She spins a mesmerizing tale that made me want to stay lost in its pages, wandering deeper into the maze of the beguiling, imagined intricate world of Limbo.

Raising Limbo is heartwarming and reveals compelling and necessary truths as souls are at stake as they transition and come to terms with memories as the story unfolds that endangers not only Trina's soul, but the very souls of everyone in The Valley, her family included.

—**Beth Wright**

Chapter 1

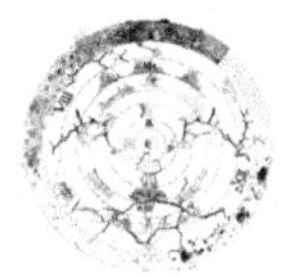

Travel—going from point A. to point B. by various means. There are places where travel is a simple thing to do and understand. To go to the movies or take a trip to the grocery store, one could walk, run, take the bus, or drive a car there. For outings much farther from home, there are planes to take to the skies or boats to set sail across the ocean. Where Trina was from, traveling was even easier. She was from the Valley of Ancestors, the home of the Egun. In the heavenly realm, a mere thought could take her to any place or anyone she wished to see. Outside of that domain, Trina's inner light gave her powerful wings to fly fast and far. In the realm she had entered, however, getting from one place to the next was nothing like traveling in the world of the living or the spiritual plane of the Egun. To journey through Limbo, memories, and emotions were the only ways travelers could reach their destination. For Trina, nostalgia and hope took her to her childhood home.

Until the age of eight, Trina lived in one of the suburbs littering Wyndal Park, Texas. She could recall the maze of thoroughfares, houses, and mailboxes posted at the front of small, square cut lawns. Penmark Lane was a cul-de-sac, a street where straight concrete led from access to the edge of the woods. On the right side of this dead end, was a one-story house with a forward-facing mailbox, a modest sward, and an inclined driveway leading to a garage door. The size and turf design were like the neighboring houses save for the sapling planted in the front yard. Trina's childhood home was manifested so vividly it absorbed her. Memories of foot races from the driveway's incline to the door had overtaken her to where she scarcely noticed her surroundings. The memory drew her in and moved her from the street and up the meandering walkway. Before Trina realized it, she faced the Cherrywood door, and then followed its beckoning through the other side to glimpse the past of the Finley family.

The den was as Trina remembered it. On the opposite side of the room, there was an enormous sliding window slightly to the right. The long curtains covered the view of the back yard, but natural light from the other side gave the semblance of day. Around the den, three sofas faced inward towards the mahogany coffee table in the middle. With the long couches placed on three sides of the room, the VCR set and shelf completed the rest of the square. Everything was still and deserted at first, but as her steps met the carpet, the room came alive with ghosts. These apparitions moved fast and were oblivious to her presence. They were blurs that disturbed and reordered furniture, danced across floors and swept on and off of couches. Sometimes, Trina caught sight of plates and cups, newspapers and coffee mugs, plastic castles and Barbie dolls, and other items, as they settled in place before a blur swept them away. Trina's prompting steps or her wish to see the genuine nature of these ghosts, caused the hazy shapes to slow their movements, and for the first time, she clearly saw the apparitions.

In one instance, a trim yet strong figure emerged from a door to the far-right corner of the den. The door was the only entrance and exit from the master bedroom, her parents' room. The person who stepped beyond the door's threshold was a man, clean shaven with only the slightest hint of facial hair shadow on his even, dark brown skin. He shaped his afro short and neat. His shoulders shifted as he straightened out the heavy belt of his uniform. Trina smiled at the living memory of the lean man who, over the years, had grown broader, but muscular from years of strength training. He was Aaron Finley, her father. The image of her then 35-year-old father disappeared under the blur again, as though someone had pressed fast-forward on the memory that played out before her.

In the next slowdown, Trina heard the front door open and shut, the jingling of keys, and the familiar clicking of heels. She moved aside and swiveled towards the noise. A woman with soft blushes of wine-colored rouge on the honey brown complexion of her high cheekbones entered the room. She wore a plaid dress jacket with colors that coordinated with her black blouse and emerald, knee-high dress. A vibrant green hair band kept her permed curls in place as her earrings dangled and swayed with her every move. One shoulder holstered her purse and stuffed carrier bag while her arms cradled three notebooks. Trina watched the youthful woman who was as occupied and effortless with the items she carried as she always was with being an educator and a mother. At the time of the memory, Trina's mother was an assistant principal at an elementary school. Since then, she had worked her way up the administrative ladder and was now the head principal of a high school in Cedar Hill. Trina continued to watch her mother. She knew her winding down ritual. She would place her things on the sofa and coffee table, kick off her shoes to relieve the aches of her feet, and then call the grandparents, her husband or the school. The image of Deborah Finley only managed a step or two towards the nearest phone before it vanished into another blur.

There was another fast-forwarding of hazy shadows that zipped in and out. Doors opened and closed, furniture and items shifted places until the flurry of motion crawled to normal. In this memory episode, Trina's mother wore different office attire. She had arrived home from work again. This time the house wasn't empty. Another woman, weathered and gray-haired, hugged her in greeting. For a moment, Trina caught her breath. The older woman was Mayva Lee Jettis or Granny May as she called her. At that time, Granny May was 63. She looked much younger now that she was part of the spirit world.

Two little girls interrupted the noiseless chatter between mother and daughter as they scurried onto the scene. Trina's insides leapt as she watched her mother beam as she knelt to greet the clamoring children with open arms. The image that played before her was mute, yet Trina could still hear a gleeful "Heeey!" of her mother's high-pitched voice. Transfixed, Trina watched the brief embrace and the four as they chatted about their day. When the two children broke away from the huddle, Trina's eyes followed them. In the lead was a girl in shorts and a shirt with frilly edges. From the jumbo beads of her ponytail holder to her flip-flops, she coordinated with the color of watermelon. Her semi-coarse hair, although combed and tied in a high ponytail, bounced as she ran.

Following behind was another girl who was younger and shorter. Her yellow shirt, composed of white stripes, topped her sunny and solid shorts. Neat braids striped her scalp and ended in small beads that clattered when she moved. The lead girl stopped for a second, grabbed hold of the younger girl's hand as she reached and the two hurried off to the room they shared.

Trina wistfully reminisced. The older girl was Trina at age seven. The smaller one was her little sister, June. Seeing herself and her younger sibling brought back many feelings and memories. Being at this particular place and time was like experiencing a home video. Deep down, she wanted to roam through the old memories of when times were happier. Urgency and that awful burrowing at the pit of her stomach would not let her. Now was not the time to reminisce. She would have to make the most of the precious time it gave her. This room in their childhood home was an excellent place to start her search.

Trina followed the shadows of her younger self and her sister. She entered the door that they had closed seconds before and found that the apparitions had vanished. Now all alone, the room looked as though someone had used it. Pillows and stuffed animals were strewn about the disturbed sheets of a queen-sized bed. Light emanated from the white sphere-bodied lamp on the nightstand. Coloring books, crayons, and paper scattered atop a small desk in the far corner of the room. On the dresser was a plastic bust. Long strands of a doll's hair sprouted from a dotted scalp, bound into a top-seated ponytail. Weighted down by clips and its heaviness, the hair bowed over and partially hid a rouge-covered face. Trina approached the dresser to comb through the soft fibers with her fingers. It was her hairstyling *Barbie* set. She was more liberal with braiding, with dyes, and clasps before she practiced on June's hair. Other times, she used the bust to teach her little sister a thing or two about experimenting with cosmetics and fashion. Her lips tremored upward a little in remembrance, but then dimmed. Nothing happened. She turned her attention to the long wooden box between the clothing dresser and room door. She opened one of the red sliding doors and rummaged through figurines, dolls, toy ponies and knick-knack instruments. There wasn't any resonating spark, nor altering of the surrounding shadows, nothing. She moved through the closet and tore through costumes and clothes. The results were the same. When she thought about doubling back to the desk to look through the loose papers, a noise startled her. A brief electric scrambling introduced a familiar melody and song of a woman who longed to go beyond her home under the sea. It came from the den area.

Trina rushed back to the den and hoped to catch June or whoever turned on the television. The room was empty. She moved to face the TV and saw that it was *The Little Mermaid* that played on VHS. Trina smiled and her mind nostalgically drifted. She remembered her fairytale phase when her mother would read to them. June used to love fairytales. *The Little Mermaid* was her most favorite of all. Trina remembered her little sister watched the *Disney* movie at least a thousand times. It was always something she talked about during lunch and at recess. Then, one day a boy at lunch had gotten annoyed and, in jeer, told her the tragic life and death of the sea princess in the original tale of *The Little Mermaid*. Distraught, June sought reassurance when she made it home. The thoughtfulness and reluctance on her mother's face when she broke the news was clear in Trina's mind. Even more vivid was her sister's sadness. That day, June found out not every ending was a happy one. That painful moment seemed to foreshadow what would happen a year later when June would know the more profound tragedies of loss.

Wind rustled through the curtains of the sliding doors. Trina followed the whisper of the breeze. She slipped through the door's threshold and expected to step into her back yard. Instead, a sepia landscape met her. The sky above was clear and, judging by the shine of the sun, it looked to be noon. Before her was a gravel yard complete with swings, slides, monkey bars, and other equipment that created a playset. The pebbled platform was an island among a sea of old anemones. Trina could smell their stale perfume. Now and then, a breeze made the anemones chatter like hollow chips. Stray petals brushed her hand, and it felt brittle and dry. This place was their elementary school's playground, or at least some semblance of it. She remembered low grass and sparse patches of sunny weeds, not a flowery field. Treading among dead flowers, Trina made her way to the gravel pit. She neared the wooden crop, and she realized that the faded wash of sepia receded and return some of the scenery's original color. She also noticed something else as she approached, something that drew her to the playset's crawl tube. It was the blurry image of a grade school girl who wore a dress dotted in sunflowers. The mirage hurried to the mouth of the playset's tunnel. The figure knelt at the crawl tube turned makeshift shrine, tilted her head to unfasten a barrette from one thick plait, and added the item as another tribute.

"June!" Trina shouted. She ran into gliding skips and covered a lot of ground. When she arrived, however, the mirage melted away. Aside from the illusion that disappeared, everything else at the shrine stayed intact. Trina remembered this spot that seemed to be June's sanctuary in grade school. Stickers of stars and cartoons dotted the edge of the roof and walls. On the floor of the opening was a white paper bag, the butterfly-shaped hair clip, and a book. Trina paused for a moment, first to peer into the darkness of the playset's tunnel. When nothing happened, she turned to examine the items. At once, she recognized the book as Hans Christian's tale of *The Little Mermaid*. It was her sister's book. She bent down, took hold of the book, and the vivid deluge was instantaneous.

The first wave of memories showed the young Trina as she led June by the hand and roamed their grandparent's farm. Twilight approached dusk. Both stopped mid-scurry when June lingered behind as they passed the old tool shed. She didn't hear any words, but she felt them. Trina could perceive her younger self as she wondered and asked June why she stared into the dark space? June turned to her with an odd, distant expression. Her pupils dilated to where the browns of her eyes turned a solid black. The lining of the black iris expanded beyond its normal size. The vision brought up an old eeriness, a familiar cold bristling of the skin that Trina almost forgot as a spirit. A blur of colors settled into the view of a funeral. Tearful relatives and friends populated pews. Her mother, father, and sister sat in the front row across from a child's casket. Watching them weep made Trina's heart ache.

In the next scene, June was alone in their room. Halfway curled under a mess of covers, she clasped the painful bulge in her throat where tears could not escape. Suddenly, the stress on her face relaxed as her dry sobs stopped. June quickly sat up on the bed, her gaze fell where the moon casts its light on the dark pool on the floor. As Trina continued to observe the vision, she noticed that the shadow on the floor grew denser. At one point, it glittered like the shuffling of water that reflected the moonlight. A bump rose from the shadow's center. Before the shape fully emerged from the black, Trina's body lurched, her trance broken.

Trina blinked and tried to gather her bearings. During her visions, she stood without realizing it. She recalled the rude shove of tiny hands at her shins.

"Give it back!" came the shrill demand of a child. Trina's eyes instantly fell on the tiny figure in front of her. He or she stood in a defensive stance and kept enough distance to get a pace or two heads start should the small spirit flee. The child scowled and glared at Trina with solid black eyes vaguely reminiscent of June's strange stigmatism.

"That's mine!" The child barked once again. "She gave that book to me!"

"She gave you this book?" Trina repeated and mulled over the child's words. In doing so, she studied the little ghost. The apparition took on the guise of a child that was six or seven years of age. Despite zeir petulance, Trina could tell sadness enveloped the specter. The blue glow that emanated from zem seemed to affect her. A sinking feeling at the pit of her stomach evoked pity. She wanted to approach the child but hesitated. The child's knee-length shirt rippled, and zeir legs shifted as though any movement would send the ghost into flight. Trina stayed her steps and instead continued her scrutiny. Growing more impatient and nervous, the ghost fiddled with the butterfly clip that dangling on the few strands leaning from zeir thick forest of curls. The blue glow deepened the child's already dark complexion and hair, but there was something eerily familiar about the specter.

"June!" Trina murmured. Her memory pieced things together. She recalled her little sister's claim of someone watching them or sometimes walking with them in the dark. She remembered her ritual at the playground shrine, the imaginary friend she would add in her doodles of family portraits, and maybe even the strange vision of the thing emerging from the shadow in the moonlight. The more she examined the child, the more she realized this was the lost soul.

Trina's eyes lit up with hope when she recalled the name she remembered from the drawings. "You were a friend of my sister's, weren't you? The one no one else could see, but her."

The child's head jerked back, somewhat taken off guard. "She was my yana before she was ever your sister." The lost soul's correction came out in a low, wary growl. "I knew her before you did."

"Alex, right?" Trina asked with a smile. Creases of the black eyes softened as the child gave a hesitant nod. Alex's posture relaxed slightly, not as apt to fight or flee. Trina knelt to the small spirit's level. She planned to engage in small talk to put the lost soul at ease. Then came the abrupt updraft of chilly wind. The gust was rough enough that they both shielded themselves from the flailing of hair, clothing, and debris. Dry petals of the anemones rattled more harshly in alarm. When there was a slight break in the draft, Alex's arms lowered and eyes lifted. The child gasped, zeir face twisted in horror before zeir body swayed, swiveled and swam in escape through the field. Trina stood up and called out to Alex and thought of going in pursuit of the lost soul until she heard something else under the clatter of petals and whir of the gust.

It was a cacophony of hissing, twitters, and buzzing, like a locust plague. The noise behind Trina was distant. Still, it made her shiver even more so than the chill of the air. She barely turned to see the source of the sound before three blurs zipped past. The black shapes seemed to ignore her and instead wavered along the path of the fading streams of blue light. They were after the child. Trina knew she would have to stop them somehow. Raising one arm, she spread her fingers and daggers of light sprouted from the webs of her hand. Poised to fling the daggers, she focused in on the fleeting shapes. The buzzing things were quick. She would have to expect their pauses. Luckily, the lost soul had gotten a bit of a head start and took to the cover of the anemones. Some distance off, Trina caught a winking of blue light. The shapes paused as they caught sight of the glow and Trina could make out their insect-like outlines. She wouldn't give them a chance to pursue. The instant they lagged, she flung the daggers, and the trio exploded into nothing as the projectiles hit their mark.

Loud buzzing at her back startled Trina from her watch of the lost soul's escape. Wings, bulbous bodies, and flailing limbs surrounded her before she could react in defense. Four more black shapes made their assault, only this time she was the target. The creatures were malign. Some were twisted hybrids of bird and insect. One had a vespoid body covered with jet black feathers, sported a stinger and a serrated beak of a crow. Another had a bulky body of an enormous owl with the back and wings of a beetle, bulging eyes, mandibles and pincers. A third, armed with a scorpion's tail, hovered on membraned wings—a gaping mouth of thorns—the only facial feature on its dreadful body. The fourth member of the hideous quartet was different in that it was a severed head that was upside down with bat wings that were outstretched and flapped the air.

Their erratic flight and thrashing obstructed Trina's vision and threw her off-kilter. She fell backward and used her arms to shield herself from harassment. Suddenly, she glimpsed a snaking sliver of flashing mist, saw the creatures stall in movement, and heard their shrieks before it vaporized them.

"Stay behind me, young Egun." The woman's voice carried both assurance and strength. Trina obeyed the command.

In her panic, at first, Trina did not recognize the woman's voice. But, as she stood up on shaking legs, her eyes widened at the sight of her savior. The woman was tall, dark, and sleek. A stem of a mark ran up from the back of her neck and ended in a spiral on her smooth, evenly shaved scalp. Usually, anyone could find the woman liberally adorned with jewelry and dressed in elegant clothing that shimmered with the colors of rubies, violets, and copper. Today, however, she wore a moonlit battle garb, bangles, and a beaded necklace. Trina had glimpsed her from time to time, but heard a great deal about her from her fellow Egun. She was a fierce warrior, a powerful being that guarded and oversaw the Valley of Ancestors and its inhabitants. She was the Orisha titled the Warrior of Wind and Thunder, Oya.

The Orisha's wielding of the crackling lash was swift and precise. The weapon rested in a protective curl around Trina, then leapt to life when more evil spirits attacked. As many as seven creatures dove at them at once, but Oya made quick work of them. The thunderous whip whirled, its curve sliced, its tip stung—the lash's prick paralyzed the flying assailants—before it disintegrated them into shadowy ash. Trina couldn't help but be both in awe and fearful of Oya. The whispers of the Orisha being a fearsome warrior were very true. Someone as formidable in battle would be even more stringent as the watcher of the ancestors. Trina had left her home realm without permission and that made her dread that fact.

At the moment, the prospect of punishment was the least of her worries. A dark billow moved quickly past the sky's horizon. At first, Trina assumed them to be clouds. The longer she stared at the clouds, however, the more she made out the distorted shapes within them. Crooked limbs writhed in the murky bulk, reached out, and tumbled forward from the mass with gnarled claws. Infernal colors blinked from the opening of sockets and maws of the smog's gaunt, lulling pates. It was then that Trina realized with horror that the source of the evil spirits was the monstrous mass that rumbled towards them.

Seeing the dark mass that rolled swiftly across the sky was enough to make anyone run. Sensing Trina's fear, Oya looked over her shoulder at her ward with a smirk. The inquiry of the gesture barely entered Trina's mind before she heard a loud boom. Thunder accompanied the white streak that tore across the dark mass. Strangely enough, the mass halted its travel. Its shape bubbled each time lightning danced within it. Trina watched the lightning agitate the clouds to the point of churning. She glimpsed a slight shape, a man's shape, within the streaks of light. Thunder overtook wails, and the chill dissipated as a warm gale came opposite the spirit horde. The gale softened to a breeze that brought with it a drizzle and an ocean fragrance that intermingled with the scent of anemones.

Among the calamity of the storm came the silhouette of another giant. A lady titan was a distant, dark shadow against the gray. As the lightning stalled the mass, the lady's shadow swayed. Then in one quick and graceful movement, the lady shadow took hold of the hem of her dress, extended the cloth, swept forward, and cast the dress' train over the mass like a net. In an instant, the spirit horde vanished.

Soon after the giant shadow's robe swallowed the mass, the upheaval calmed, and the sky cleared.

Trina exhaled, and her lungs released the corset of tension. When she remembered the rule she broke, a jolt of fear shattered her brief moment of relief. Trina's heart raced, her head and eyes fell to the sea of shriveled petals as she heard the shuffling of the Orisha's sandals. "Forgive me, Lady Oya," Trina stammered. "I know they forbid coming here, but I had to. It's an emergency."

"We know, young one. We've all been expecting this for some time, and it appears that you were the one chosen to save them."

The voice that answered was gentle, motherly, and different from Oya's bold tenor. Trina's eyes lifted. Two other Orishas arrived, but she barely noticed. The one who spoke was a woman dressed in a silken fabric of sea foam. Her headdress glistened with pearls and cockle shells. Like Oya, she was beautiful, her strength was quiet, and her demeanor nurturing. It was both the air that the Orisha gave off and what she heard from others that led her to believe the woman was the oldest of her two companions. She was an elder of the Orishas and mother of the oceans, Yemoja.

"Then you know about my sister?" Trina inquired, a little relieved, yet there was something in Yemoja's voice that worried her.

"It's no easy feat to leave Oya's realm." The third Orisha was a tall, well-chiseled man with broad shoulders. He too, dressed for battle and in one hand held a double-headed ax. He was a handsome man, but his impressive stature and hardened expression were intimidating until he flashed Trina a friendly beam. "The fact you're here is permission enough. No worries, girl," he assured.

"What Shango says is true," Oya agreed and simpered a little as she glanced over at the man. "I'm glad we caught up to you in time."

"Yes," Yemoja nodded. "And we must wisely use the little time we have."

As Trina scanned the surrounding faces, the sinking feeling in her stomach returned. "What else do you know about what June is going through? I know she's in danger, but there's something else, isn't it?"

"There is little time to explain. Just know that when the time comes, you must unite the lost soul with that of your sister's and return them to the living. Should they surrender to oblivion, the impact would be a terrible one." As Yemoja spoke these words, her hands held open to receive the book. Trina recognized the gesture at once and relinquished the item. "Travel through purgatory can daunt anyone, but if you follow the fragments of June's memories, the lost soul will be close by."

After Yemoja's instruction, it was Oya's turn to offer her help. Her arms reached behind the clasp of her beaded necklace. She unfastened it and placed the trinket around Trina's neck. The centerpiece of the ornament was a pendant in the form of a square-jawed face fashioned from some petrified wood or stone. Oya introduced the ornament. "His name is Ori. Should there be an opportunity to check your sister's progress, he can provide you with a window to the living world. You will not be alone in your search. Others of our kind will be there to assist you."

"You might want to hurry, now," Shango chimed in. "The lost soul got quite a lead on you."

Trina nodded and took a deep breath. Every nerve of her being was charged with urgency, especially after the information the Orishas shared. Even their heartfelt farewells and encouragement failed to mask their apprehension. It made her wonder about the true direness of the situation and the dangers that lay ahead. Despite her questions, Trina flew to her search.

The Orishas lingered in silence for a moment. Shango's gaze found the place in the sky where his lightning dance herded the billows for consumption by Yemoja's cloth. "Another sluagh." Shango spoke, the mask of optimism discarded. "This is the fifth cluster I've encountered today."

Oya's expression also grew grim. She knew the anguish of the most vulnerable souls were delicacies to the more malign denizens of purgatory. "Before long, the legion will be after them. And to have someone so young take on such a burden."

"We must believe in Trina's resolve as she has faith in our protection." Yemoja affirmed. She studied the worn cover and noted the young mermaid perched on the rock. The moon hung in the sky above and shimmered over the murky sea. Since the beginning, she came to know all the oceans that existed. The illustration, the circumstance in its entirety, reminded her of her visits to one primordial domain, a shadowy scape where the cloudy swirls of its watery expanses stretched from shore and past a spacious fissure to the horizon beyond. It was a place since sealed and forgotten until now. She placed her hand on the book's surface and steeled herself for the reading. Yemoja's grim focus extended to Shango and Oya. The two exchanged wary glances before they gravitated towards their elder. All eyes fixed on the book as Yemoja opened it, or rather, pried the pages loose from the substance that pasted its contents together. There was a loud tearing as dark, viscous strings stretched and fell apart. The low seething of murmurs her keen senses felt underneath now bubbled to the surface in harsh, inaudible rasps for all to hear.

"Eeeeeh! What is that?" Shango groaned with a mixture of startle and disgust. His eyes flitted to Oya when he heard her gasp. The look of shock and, dare he fathom, horror on her face was enough to give him chills. He followed her gaze to what a solemn Yemoja held open. It was the last page of the book. On it was a crude altering of the tragic tale's ending, a child's drawing that evoked as much disquiet as the substance and the seething.

"Residue from the Black Dive," Yemoja spoke, answering the lightning dancer's inquiry from earlier. "Tears shed still bear the remnants of that place and it's beginning to churn."

Chapter 2

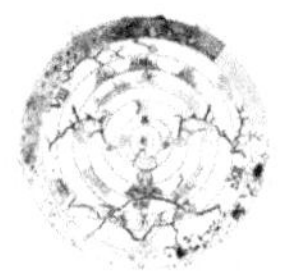

The Processor was a little piece of Sheol in Limbo. The place was an immobile prison of weighty darkness fashioned from the realm of shades. For such a being who relished the dark, Narakai never thought that a sliver of Sheol's blackness would drive him mad. He was sure that millennia had passed since the imposed torpor, stuck in a suffocating stasis of no movement or breathing. This inert force of overwhelming oppression robbed him of seeing, of hearing, of touch, of taste. All of his senses and freedoms were taken away, except the acute awareness, and his episodes of the running and lulling of the mind and, worst of all, the hunger. Left to himself and the weighted nothingness was torture. Narakai's only relief was what he entertained in his thoughts of his final placement in the Inferno. At this point, the Inferno was preferable to the Processor. A demon of top tier, he was powerful enough that he could take a place of high standing in the deepest parts of the underworld. Then again, by the time his sentence was done, Narakai was convinced the darkness would have gnawed him down into a dim husk like the gaunts of Sheol.

"Despondency does not suit you, Narakai, Favored Noose of Argath." a woman's voice broke into his mind.

Narakai flinched, surprised at the telepathic utterance. *Who knew his name and dared to speak it?* With such sensitive knowledge of his name, the person who called was no mere dabbler in magic. Perhaps, it was some occultist well-versed in goetic arts who wished to summon him. Normally, he considered the transaction of being summoned to be a brazen disregard. Though an incubus, he held power that rivaled that of most archfiends. For a demon of his caliber, being called to serve and to have his true name thrown around casually, would warrant immediate theft of the summoner's tongue. However, the sudden intrusion could present a window of opportunity. There was something unusual about this transaction. Aside from the summoner's knowledge, Narakai sensed an energy from the voice. Both the energy and the sound of a woman's voice piqued his interest and appetite. For the sake of promising prospects, he would entertain it.

"Does the one who knows my name wish a favor?" Narakai purred. In answer to his inquiry, a slight, shuddering fuzz of color broke the monotony of the dark. Gradually, the haze became clearer and clearer until the scene before his mind's eye was as sure as sight. Blackness was replaced with a narrow view of a winding path edged with dull yet strange plants. Hidden among the vegetation and scattered along the line where weeds met rutted trail were archaic fragments of what might have been a building.

What stood out the most in the tapering vision was the small specter traveling the meandering path. It was a child, or at least had the appearance of one. For a few steps or so, ze walked, now and then scanning zeir surroundings. Eventually, a single wing sprouted from the middle of zeir back. The odd appendage was more a feathered fin than a wing for it propelled the child-like apparition just above the road in a slow, swimming glide.

The blue glow of grief radiated from zem. Even as a vision, Narakai could sense sadness exuding from the phantom as clearly as one would feel the warmth of heat or smell the aroma of a meal simmering on a stove.

"Do you see the soul, incubus?" The woman's voice broke through in another telepathic transfer.

"I see zem," Narakai answered.

"Bring the lost soul to us," the lady summoner ordered. "Succeed and you may one day reign as ruler of Avadon."

Narakai's nerves jumped, this time in delight. He scarcely had a moment to contemplate the genuineness of the reward that the lady summoner had offered before feeling a tingling sensation. There was a strange pulling at his lungs that was gradual, at first. The drawing of a heavy weight from his body quickened until, eventually, it yielded him space for his lungs to expand. Narakai gasped, and for the first time in forever, he could breathe. As the weight that held him in place gave way, the blackness did also. His ears that knew nothing but silence, suddenly came alive with the stretch and tears of phlegm and the groan of some thick rind that fell away. Narakai reached out, pushed his hands through slime until he broke beyond the wet and gooey surface. Soon, the rest of his body dropped from the compartment and on to a hard, cold surface.

Narakai could breathe, but his insides bubbled, heavily congested with gunk. He gave way to fits of gags and harsh coughs to clear his airways. He tried to stretch his back and his wings sprouted involuntarily from his shoulder blades. The cramping was intense and he gasped from the pain. He was weak. Every time his body shook when he voided his lungs, the faintness he felt in each break made him acutely aware of his fragile state. His limbs still tried to wake up and he could barely stand, let alone fly. Awareness of his present infirmity made him more conscious of his surroundings. Sounds of unearthly wailing, roars, and gibberish filled his ears. Echoes of the noises surrounded him. He quickly wiped away the phlegm that obstructed his vision. For a while, he stared at the back of his hands. Next, he examined the rest of the area and found that the prison outside the compartment was a cavern-like space. He surveyed the area further and spotted a nearby puddle. Narakai crawled toward the small pool and leaned in to dunk his face under to gulp the water, but paused when he saw his reflection.

Bright green eyes flashed as they studied his sleek, ebony skin and chiseled features. One hand swept across spiked quills of hair on his scalp. Then, with both hands raised, he brushed his fingers along his high cheekbones, smiled, and showed vampiric teeth. Narakai then flexed the sinews of his left arm. His eyes left the reflection briefly to catch a short, soured gleam of a coiling mark, the portrayal of a meandering beast that signified the crest of his clan. Narakai returned his gaze to the reflection and chuckled. Being in the Processor had drained him to the point where he was malnourished, but he was still handsome and youthful. The shade of Sheol had almost made the incubus forget what he looked like, but thankfully, the darkness had not completely stolen his beauty. After dealing with the absence of sight for so long, Narakai would have stayed at that puddle for another century or so, but there was the matter of the summoner's proposition and the even more pressing issue of his hunger.

Narakai noticed movement above him. He raised his head and gazed upward. The ceiling was alive, and it wriggled as though it were made of worms. Slowly, he stood on unsteady feet and turned to what used to be his prison. On the floor where he fell was the dense crust of the compartment's door, which left gelatin membrane exposed. Other outer regions of the prison made of the same coating were wedged between a low place in the ceiling and the ground. The color of the cell's interior was a mixture of reddish orange with thin pink veins strung across it. The compartment was three times bigger than he was and could surely fit more than two prisoners. Narakai wondered if there were other creatures imprisoned with him all those years without his knowledge. He tottered towards the crusted pen, thought to touch it, but recoiled his wandering hand when being sucked back in the cell crossed his mind.

He stepped away from his prison, took another survey of his surroundings and made an additional discovery. There were other membraned cages around the area. They were spaced from each other in misshaped stalactites and stalagmites. All of them were empty now, the inner flesh of their compartments exposed. Their crusted flaps in whole forms slid to the ground while other doors littered the Processor's floor in pieces as the inmates within shattered through to freedom. As soon as Narakai made the revelation, a powerful force lifted him from floor to air, sent him to a hurtle across the chamber and smashed him into a rocky wall.

The rude impact rattled Narakai's senses. An acrid taste exploded in his mouth. There was pain in his jaw, around his head, and in his right shoulder. The fiery sting and numbness were especially around his right shoulder, and he was sure he felt a snap. First, he slowly shifted under the rubble of rocks to assess the nature of his injuries. He pushed some of the boulders with his left hand as he moved to stand. His wings twitched to remove some of the light rubble before they fully retracted into his shoulder blades. There were bruises, scrapes, and soreness. The break he expected in his right shoulder was nothing more than a dislocation of joints. Aside from minor damage to his right shoulder, the knock seemed to do more of service to him than harm. The tingle of atrophy that numbed his limbs and joints were gone. He was fully awake now, and once the drumming in his head ceased, his mind was clear. In spite of his new-found alertness, there was still the light haze of faintness that threatened his wakefulness with a sudden blackout. Hunger pangs made the inside of his stomach twist from its awful burn. He needed to feed and soon.

Narakai had barely popped his right shoulder back in place when some fat appendage arrested him. He quickly found the huge extremity to be a tail. The owner of the tail hoisted Narakai from the ground until his face was level with a swine's broad snout. It was another demon. As to what kind of demon it was, Narakai did not know nor did he care to know. He was more wrapped up in the tug of war of his emotions and grimaced at the fact that its tail belted his arms and waist. Disgust churned his stomach at the offensive sight and odor of the beast. The demon was a grotesque behemoth with the flushed, perspiring flesh of a pig. As its skin stretched towards the demon's rear, its pinkness tapered into swampy speckles and disappeared into a solid, mossy hue at its posterior and tail. On either side of its head were thick horns that curved in sharp pointed ends. Its long, muscled arms and bouldering fists, its large thighs and bowing knees, and its flabby gut, were humanoid. Its three-digit hooves, snout and thick face complete with tusks was that of a boar.

The swine hulk had company—its entourage—a pair of demons that were scrawnier and significantly dwarfed the swine hulk in height. The one perched on the giant swine's shoulder had tightly drawn skin that was a sickly green. As it squatted, the green thing's skinny legs were like puny, jutting columns tucked around a distended belly. The green demon's claws strummed eagerly, and its sharp elbows pointed outward with its bat-like wings. Yellow teeth spread in an upward arch around most of its bauble head, and awaited the tasty crumbs it would scavenge from their latest hunt. The third demon stood at the swine hulk's feet. Its visage was that of a warped skeleton with dry, black skin that hung to bones. On the top of its knobbed head were sparse strands of hair. Its eye sockets and ribs smoldered like embers on blackened wood and like its accomplice perched on the giant's shoulder, the dark imp's skull grinned in anticipation.

Confident in securing their meal, it didn't take long for the three to bicker among themselves. The green one's grubby reach prompted the argument, and before long, there were bewildered shrieks from the smaller demons amid barks of the giant to reinforce the pecking order. As the inaudible row went on, Narakai's eyes searched the cavern even as he swayed in the unbalanced motion of his attacker's tail. The glimmer of hope he had was to see some lady thing or a demoness appear from the recess of the Processor. Any woman would do; beautiful lilim, a banshee, or a murderess's ghost.

Narakai kept looking until his hope soured. Hunger was at a point where survival took precedence over preference. His aching stomach turned in disgust. Incense, humor, and a spurned craving soon bubbled to the surface, as he thought of the irony that his first meal of freedom would be two runts and a brute.

"Two runts and a brute." Narakai repeated out loud as he rolled his eyes. The words had made the bickering between the trio falter. His chuckle turned into outright laughter and drew his captors' full attention.

The inflamed eyes from the swine hulk settled on its prey. The brute puffed a cloud of breath from snout to silence the laughter and was painfully surprised when sharp quills ejected from Narakai's back. The incubus dropped from sight, and left the swine hulk to roar in agony and anger. Though starved of much of the vitality meant to sustain him, Narakai was still swift. His in-and out-darts were even fast enough to keep them blind to his whereabouts as his laughter echoed throughout the cavern. There was a wild search. The swine hulk trumped around in circles, and the green runt fluttered overhead in search for their lost prey.

"Forget something?" Narakai teased. The swine hulk and green runt slowed down when they heard the taunt. It was then that the two noticed the other runt was missing. The mystery of the sudden disappearance confounded them further. The incubus chuckled, amused at his play of turning the tables.

"Here," Narakai's disembodied voice spoke. The withered corpse of the soot-skinned imp seemed to drop to the swine hulk's feet out of nowhere. Its face was further distorted by the expression of fear. Its life essence drained; the orange smolder of its eyes and rib cage dimmed to ash.

The green imp shrieked in surprise. For a brief moment, the swine hulk's ferocious grimace dropped. Narakai could sense the onset of fear that the brute struggled not to show. From the dark, the incubus smiled and enjoyed the mischief.

He swooped in again. The swine hulk froze. Its warier eyes were still not quick enough to catch even a glimpse of the prey turned predator. Still, the brute did not need its eyes to know that the incubus had carried off the other runt. Its ears could hear shrieks and frantic flaps of wings that trailed off somewhere in the distance before there was silence. The swine hulk was alone.

After having his fill of the green imp and the soot demon, Narakai felt a little generous. He waited in his hiding place and allowed the brute its last moments to indulge in a meaningless search before he stepped out from behind a nearby stalagmite. The instant the piggish demon's eyes found him, it charged. Narakai stood his ground. He was composed in the path of the swine hulk's frenzied stampede. He waited until the brute was only seconds away from trampling him before he disappeared out of sight again. The swine hulk thundered to a halt as fast as its lumbering body would allow. The beast was off balance as it turned and even as it whirled around to defend itself, however, the brute was too slow. Narakai's movements were so fast that the brute did not know how or when it had been struck. There was only a sharp pain that ran across its stomach, the snap of a clean slice through spine, paralysis, and then fog.

Black blood pooled around the giant heap of a demon as Narakai approached. There was no way the brute could protect itself, much less lift a finger to prevent the incubus from inhaling the last of its dwindling life-force. After the feeding, Narakai was invigorated somewhat, but not nearly as satisfied or enlivened with energy as he would have been had he eaten his usual meal. Still, running on bottom feeders was far better than nothing, especially when he considered the circumstances. Standing next to the husk,

Narakai stared into the darkness of the cave. He could hear the growls and wailing of the other inmates from the dark recesses of the Processor, and from the reverberations, he could tell they were closing in. Likely, the other prisoners of the Processor had been freed from their cells as Narakai had. It was also more than likely that they too had received the same message from that summoner or sorceress who had propositioned him. Narakai tittered to himself, intrigued that the invitation came under the condition that he prove himself in surviving a game of battle royale. He smiled, amused at the sport he had to play and felt his confidence grow even as the dark twinkled with the hungry eyes of a legion.

Chapter 3

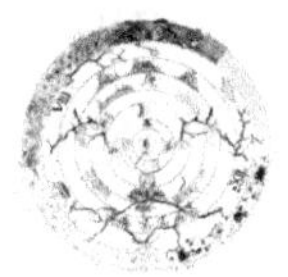

Ori was the Orisha of consciousness and of the mind. All thinking, all evocation of the emotions, all dreams, all deep recesses hidden in the subconscious was his domain. At least, that was what Trina understood and why the other Orisha had left her under his guidance and care. In a shifting realm of spirits, memories, and forgotten things, Ori would surely be of great help. She desperately needed his help now. She had spent what seemed like hours flying and searching the land below. Thus far, she saw no signs of a lonely blue spark on its speedy travel. For miles, there had only been the seemingly endless plain of dead anemones. The forever of the long stretch of pale purple only interrupted by the dull gold of weeds.

In a place like Limbo with its odd sense of time, Trina hoped her long stint of an aerial search had equaled a mere minute and not the passing of days.

"Please!" Trina's growing urgency made the whisper of her prayer more of a forced rasp. "Please! Where are you?"

Her eyes strained at the sea of tall, swaying gold. The sun, or maybe something with the likeness of the sun, shone from somewhere. Its light glistened from the collective gathering of stems of tilting weeds. Trina's scouring was so concentrated she was sure that her eyes would set a spark. Her prolonged staring into the light that glinted from the grass made her eyes ache a little. The glint reflecting from the sunlight seemed to grow more vibrant with each interval of shining light. Trina was forced to squint as the light stung her. Then, Ori moved. Trina heard the hollow jangling of links and felt the lifting of her medallions' weight. She saw Ori before her, his small form outstretched as his opaque color lightened into bright traces of the inside of a mask. For a moment, his eyes became her eyes, and then his face stretched even more. His face traced in white light and expanded further until his mouth was the size of a cave. As the cavernous opening of white moved towards Trina, she was enveloped in blinding light.

Trina felt as though she had been swallowed by the sun. It was warm in the light and quiet at first. Then she heard the movement of air, a labored yet steady inhale and exhale. As she recognized the sound of breathing and the clip-clopping of shoes that followed the same rhythm, Trina knew without seeing the jogger that someone was in the middle of a long-distance run. Although still enveloped in hot white and yellow, Trina began to develop a clear feeling along with the growing clarity of sound. She could feel her lungs expand, then constrict, along with the runner's steady rhythm as if she and the jogger were one.

The lungs were strong and healthy, yet there was a slight ache with each draw of breath. The sensation was not the kind of pain developed from short-windiness, cramping, or lack of fitness. Initially, what she felt seemed to be a phantom impression of hollowness. But with each drawing of breath, the persistent hollow became a sinking of the diaphragm. Trina could feel what the runner felt as the sinking grew heavier, and burdened her lungs which felt weighted and as though they burned. The breathing gradually fell to a struggling rasp. Scorched tingling spread through arms and legs. Tears that could never escape clogged the runner's throat with a fiery knot. The runner tried to regain pace, and struggled against the dam of tears, the fatigue, the anxiety, and all of the thoughts that sapped the runner of vigor to carry on the race. It was a grueling feeling to fight to regain the illusion of wellness while struggling against the metastasizing of mental anguish. Eventually, the clopping of shoes stopped, the lungs gave out.

"Can't," a girl's shaking whisper soon choked under airy sobs.

"June?" Trina reached out as soon as she broke free from the link and her hands searched blindly through the white to find her sister. Surprisingly, she felt the hard surface of glass, metal, and laminate wood give way. The whiteout faded away and revealed a door that opened into a space that looked like a lobby or a waiting room. There was a line of five chairs. Their backs faced a sectioned, full plexiglass window. There was another door on the far side of the small office that led to the exit. From the feel of the air, the lighting and the mundaneness of her new surroundings, Trina knew that Ori had somehow taken her, or at least, presented to her, the here and now of the living world. She happened to be in the front office of Dixie Grove High School.

The principal's secretary sat behind the receptionist desk. Her hands worked on the office computer and her head was crooked to nestle the phone between shoulder and ear. Standing silent on the other side was a girl whose cornrows striped her even brown scalp and black braids that fell over sharp ears and cheekbones. Her letterman jacket and loose jeans cloaked her slender frame. Badges for basketball, track, and cross country sports, decorated the girl's wool and leather coat. A varsity level athlete, June had earned her jacket and ornaments as a junior. Trina knew this year would be the start of her senior year. It was supposed to be the start of new things. It was supposed to be a time of making fun memories with friends and looking forward to the future. It was supposed to be a time where Trina would share in the excitement June would experience. Instead, however, as her sister stood waiting in front of the reception's desk, the only thing Trina felt was dread.

"June!" Trina called out once more. As she expected, there wasn't a response. She had a half hope that her sister could at least feel her presence. Trina studied June with a sad gaze as she approached. Though built like a sprinter, June seemed much thinner than usual. When Trina stood next to her sister, she even noticed the sharpness of her collar bone. What made her more uneasy were the blank eyes that stared down at the desk. There was an eerie sereneness about them, a finality.

Trina's gaze fell on one of June's hands that held a white piece of paper between her fingers. Her phantom hand gently clasped hers and instantly she felt the awful sensation of a heart that seemed to sink into the hollow pit of her stomach. In turn, Trina's attempt at contact seemed to bring an upsurge of anxiousness that made the paper shudder between June's trembling fingers. Trina's eyes fixed on June, desperately willing her presence to be felt.

"I'm right here, okay? I'm right here so, please don't shut me out."

"Good morning!" The greeting from the receptionist interrupted the possible link and made June's eyes light up with a mild start.

"Oh! Hello, Ms. Scarborough."

June smiled weakly and offered the white slip to the secretary for her to inspect. Ms. Scarborough suddenly gave a worried frown as she gave a quick read of the nurse's note.

"Not a fun way to start the senior year, is it?"

June shrugged, and gave a small, conceding smile. "Can't seem to keep anything down, I guess. I called my mom. She should be here soon."

Ms. Scarborough paused. Her eyes were concerned as she scrutinized the girl in front of her. "Is everything okay?"

Trina's eyes traveled from the steady wavering of June's calm façade to the secretary's soft yet troubled glower. This invitation was a crucial moment. Perhaps a chance to stall, or at the very best, prevent what was about to happen.

"Talk," Trina urged. "Say something." She hoped her heartfelt emotions would provoke some admission or at least break through her sister's self-imposed numbness.

"I'm fine," June replied.

"You're not!" Trina protested, her strained voice never reached either party of the gathering.

"Are you sure?" Ms. Scarborough asked once more.

"Tell her. Please, tell her what's wrong!" Trina wished June could feel the intensity of her eyes or the grip of her hand. She wished that her urging voice could reach June's ears or move her heart to transcend the stigmatism that prevented tears from falling.

June nodded. "Just need to get some rest and stay hydrated, that's all."

Ms. Scarborough's reluctance dwindling under June's mask of reassurance made Trina's heart plummet further. And then, June swayed backward from the desk. "Just going to the restroom for a minute."

Ms. Scarborough's head turned at the sound of her name being called from the recesses of the office.

"Okay, but make sure to let your mother know to sign out when she arrives." She reminded June before she made her move to answer the call. June nodded again, and watched as the secretary disappeared behind the mini maze of aisles and doors. She straightened her book bag, headed towards the exit and before she pushed past the door, she took one last glance at a place she would never return to.

"Don't go!" Trina lunged after June and reached to grab her shoulder to prevent her from leaving.

She crossed through the door's threshold, and could feel a slight touch of warmth and a weight lifting from her face upon Ori's release. Everything changed again as the window to the living world's present closed. The hand that reached out for a shoulder grasped nothing. A second glare of white light, once again blinded Trina's vision. Within seconds, the image of the girl in the letterman jacket faded with the light. Her sight adjusted and she anticipated the breeze of open air and view of the high school's parking lot. She was taken by surprise at the familiar territory she stepped into. The stale air was lightly touched by dust. She heard the yawning drone of hymns in unison. The aisle of the building was lined with cushioned pews of wood that led to white double doors. She knew this place. It was Elmwood Chapel, a small church that her family frequented on Sundays.

Trina stiffened, and found herself atop the steps on the far left of the pulpit. Initially, her nerves prickled with embarrassment; she stumbled into the church mid-service. She could feel eyes rove at her from the podium at center stage, the piano on the far right and the pews. She became curious. Where were the people? There was the hollow, soulful tuning of a piano and chorus of a gospel accompanying it, yet she saw no one. When a deep voice made its boisterous instruct in leading the opening prayer, the hymns from an invisible audience fell to a wordless hum. Trina's head gave a perplexed tilt. She heard the man's voice. It was almost melodic and with a thick drawl of his "ahs" and "ers," she could have sworn that it was old Reverend Dennis Humphrey getting ready for his sermon. Her eyes flitted towards center stage, she half expected to see a man, wide-bodied and with broad shoulders, and a bald head atop a neck that rolled from the collar of his dark dress suit. But like the pews, no one stood at the podium as a disembodied voice spoke into the microphone. Trina felt intrusive standing on stage and uneasy at the bodiless scene before her, she thought it better to leave for her search. Caution led her down stage steps and ushered her through the aisles. Morning light pressed against stained-glass windows. Dust particles sailed along stagnant air and light in an easy float. She had barely moved down the carpeted path of lined seats before she glimpsed some strange illusion taking shape.

Trina spotted movement near the window of a back pew. At first, a faint haze drifted along beams of soft yellow. Then, wisps of smoke rippled among threads of sun rays. Pale trails knitted together like wavering ribbons of vapor. The misty strings formed what looked like arms and shoulders, neck and head, the cap and outstretched brim of a hat. The ethereal substance grew denser, and translucence gave way to flesh, cloth, and color. The completion of the mirage took the form of a woman dressed in her Sunday best. Trina's eyes lingered on the apparition. She felt as though she had been acquainted with her before. Trina could not recall a name. She guessed it may have been a regular attendee at the Elmwood Chapel who she had spoken to once or twice in life. The lady phantom, however, had skin that was much less weathered and a straighter posture than the stooping back that Trina vaguely recalled. The fact that the woman, as well as the church, was a manifestation from her life's memories did not surprise her. What had caught Trina off guard was the fact that the phantom acknowledged her presence.

Seeing the dark eyes peering at her from beneath the brim of a white dress hat made Trina freeze in place. She was distracted from the search and lingered too long in memories that would waste precious time. Not only that, but being noticed by shades from the past seemed unnerving. Then again, Ori's vision did lead her here and his reaction upon entering the church gave no indication of danger. The lady mirage smiled at her in welcome and beckoned the girl to take a seat next to her. The phantom seemed harmless enough, even friendly. If she could interact with a mirage, perhaps she could get a lead on the whereabouts of the lost soul.

Her trepidation dwindled and Trina continued her path down the aisle. There was more shifting of sunlight, and more shapes formed as other phantoms peopled the pews. By the time Trina found her seat next to the lady in white, Elmwood Chapel had a gathering of specters in trim suits and dresses, all with Bibles. At first, Trina worried about sticking out among the audience of well-dressed shades. The lady in white noticed her, and the glances she caught from some of the other phantoms as she made her way to her seat were unmistakable. With her braids swirled in an intricate updo and shirt and trousers that could be mistaken for a kurta and salwar, Trina knew she wasn't the most discreet looking spirit of the bunch. Nevertheless, the congregation seemed more focused on their Bibles or the sermon than her conspicuousness. It didn't hurt that the throng thinned out towards the back and she and the lady in white sat alone on their pews. Trina studied the crowd, wondered, and prayed for any sign of her little sister or the lost soul connected to her. She felt a nudge at her lap and Trina's attention turned to her seatmate. With the same welcoming smile, the lady in white happened to have an extra Bible which she offered Trina in a wordless yet courteous nod. Trina smiled, gave a gesture of gratitude, and sat the book in her lap.

A part of her felt she should take to foot or air by now to continue her search. Then again, she remembered what the Orishas told her. The abstract was the way to get where you wished to go in Limbo. Perhaps what she looked for was somewhere in this church, in childhood memories that she and June shared. Perhaps there was a clue or open door within the pages of the Bible. Trina glanced from the gold lettering of the maroon cover of her book to the open passage of her seatmate. There were verses on trust and comfort, words that spoke of God as a sanctuary and source of compassion. *Verses under Psalms,* Trina thought as she opened the covers and began her search. The pastor's sermon was a gentle muttering in the background of Trina's concentration. She skipped through the first few sections, landed on Ruth, swept too far to Isaiah then backtracked to Ecclesiastes and further. She fell on the book of Job and knew she was nearing Psalms. Her sweep reduced to the turning of a few pages.

After this, Job opened his mouth and cursed the day of his birth. Job 3:1. Trina turned the page. *It is all one; therefore, I say, 'He destroys the guiltless and the wicked.'* Job 9:22. She moved through the section pages at a time and was sure to land on Psalms. *A whip may bring sudden death. And God will laugh when good people suffer.* Job 9:23. Trina paused, with a frown. The verse was profound indeed if not jarring, but that's not what was perplexing. She had glimpsed the verse before and was well past the prologue of Job. She should have reached Psalms by now. She did another sweep of ten or so pages. *He destroys the guiltless and the wicked. Cursed the day of birth. And God will laugh when people suffer.* Trina turned the page and stopped to read. *And God will laugh when people suffer.* There the words were in print and seemingly normal save for the fact that the abbreviated verse was written over and over again on the page. She repeated the cycle of sweeps and pauses only to be met with a page scratched in a large scrawling font of black ink marring neat print. *People suffer. And God laughs*, it read. Trina shivered when she felt the chill of alarm that neared an uneasy peak. Still, she dared another turn of the page. The giant, painfully red lettering was front and center of the page. On white paper and neat black print, the writing reminded her of scratches on skin. It read, *Suffering and God laughs.*

Just as swiftly as a dreadful epiphany rose in Trina, so did the warmth of the air and light dim to a cold gray. The melody of the sermon suddenly grew deep, warbling, and inaudible as though an audio recording had warped. There was a slight grumbling of shifting stone. Then, came the sudden rush of wind, carrying with it an anguished, distant cry. It was June's cry. Suddenly, the book that Trina held seemed to react to the passing wail. White paper and red scratches curdled to the color of ash. Cracks made its frantic climb from the center of the page. There was a loud snap as the book burst like a shattered stone. The break was sudden and unexpected. Trina yelped, jumped from her seat, and shielded her face. Luckily, the snap only propelled dust and pebbled debris. The dense shade and gale passed over the church and with it came the staccato burst of exploding stone. The commotion went as quickly as it came, and there was silence. Slowly uncovering her eyes, Trina's insides jumped, stunned at the bleak setting surrounding her.

Above her was a gloomy sky, the seamless overcast only interrupted by dark rings of distant treetop twigs. What was left of the roof was nothing but the jutting edges of a cupola and scaffolds. Shattered glass and broken faces of basalt were what remained of the walls. Trina was disturbed, not only because of the sudden devastation, but because of what she surveyed. There was no hint of white paint, sheetrock or wood or shattered pieces of fabric from the pew. The space, furnishings, width of the aisle, even the color of the place seemed different. From the fragments of the chancel sporting the statue of a broken cross to the near bare frame of the entrance, nothing of her small country church existed within the shell of a building. Elmwood Chapel, her place of worship during childhood, had been replaced in an instant by the shambles of a cathedral. And, with what she saw resting on the crumpled benches of stone that replaced the pews, Trina began to wonder if the ruins doubled as an open crypt.

Where the lady in white once sat, settled some strange mound. It was a drab mixture, a muddy blending of bone, dark blue, and gray. The way the mound looked with its slightly rounded, semi-smooth top rolled down into a bumpy mass reminded Trina of the melted wax of a wickless candle or molten marble because of its warped and partially glazed surface. Dried, viscid sheets like thick webs draped the lower half of the mound. She took a closer look at the cocoon, and noticed the open Bible resting at the fused surface that once was a lap. The Bible had turned to a splintered book of gray-like stone. A hand rested on one page and was covered in thick swaths of webbing. Trina inched closer to inspect the mound. Her expression darkened. The hand looked gaunt, almost mummified. Like an alarm, there was the sudden hiss of a rattle as the mound violently shivered, and Trina gasped. Her nerves were stung by the jolt of surprise as she nearly lost balance when she backpedaled from the shuddering sarcophagus. She stumbled into the aisle in haste and set off another shivering fit among the other sitting cocoons. The compel of macabre sights and sounds, pushed Trina through the frame of the cathedral entrance, and she left the broken chamber behind her.

She flew from the weathered porch, past a weedy stone yard and down a winding road columned by ethereal foliage. It was only when her nerves calmed that her flight slowed and allowed her feet to touch the ground. The agitated chorus of rattling was now replaced by another sound, that of voices. The slothful racket seemed to be some distance down the path. Taking a deep breath, Trina followed the muttering. She tread cautiously, and her hand clasped the pendant as she listened for any hum of warning. In the few minutes or so of her travel, the rambling of voices became clearer. *Are other spirits nearby,* Trina thought? She hesitated at first, until a familiar glow of cold blue twinkled through gates of twigs. Trina's heart surged. She hurried, skipping from a brisk walk to a quiet glide. Her eyes pierced through the entanglement of limbs and noticed a pocket of space, some sort of enclosure. The closer she drew in, the more twisted the road became. The further down she traversed, the stranger the wildlife appeared. Fuzzed fungi wrapped each other in bridged tangles. Drab stones or toadstools dotted in neon seemed to breathe as small creatures, some of which she glimpsed seemed a hybrid of reptile and insect, skittered about the heaving undergrowth. Moving closer to the enclosure, Trina soon found even stranger flora.

Upon hearing the clamoring of chatter, Trina expected another gathering of spirits traveling along the same path. What she discovered instead, was something that made her stomach turn. The trees that surrounded Trina as she approached the outskirts of the enclosure had faces. All of these ashen dendrites had sunken, milky gray eyes that blinked and hollow mouths that flapped. Those with a wider trunk sported multiple knots, each with its own pair of eyes, a bulbous nose and stretched, moving maw. Other stalks were crooked, so much so that some of the upper and lower jaws had been painfully contorted in a crosswise fashion. Still, these lipped orifices moved—their large, wobbling mouths—articulating speech.

Recalling what happened at the ruins, Trina was all the warier and slipped past the murmuring vegetation. The gibberish was almost mindless. Still, as she maneuvered past the stalks, the stretch and lift of each slacked jaw spoke phrases she understood. Some of the gibberish were repeated citations of some Bible verses she had either glimpsed back at the ruins or at prior other times. Other prattle almost let on with the semblance of a conversation. Maneuvering her way through the rambling woods, Trina would catch snatches of the exchange among the faces.

"Happiness is a choice, yes?" chimed one wooden knot.

A second bump jutting from a nearby tree then responded to the first knot by cheerfully declaring, "Yes, absolutely."

She passed a trio of low growths, and Trina could make out a conversation that almost sounded like the beginning of gossip. "Did you hear about... ." started one mossy looking stump.

Its sentence was cut short by a burled stool which replied, "Why it's such a shame, poor thing."

The third speaker, a deformed bulge with gray springs, then ended by saying, "That's just how it goes, I suppose." Trina moved on, and heard the same introduction from the incomplete chinwag of the trio as she left.

"Smile and the world smiles with you, cry, and you cry alone. No one ever said life was fair. What doesn't kill you makes you stronger."

These were some of the many clichés she heard weaving among more of the trees. Their recitation of banalities floated down past her ears like dying leaves from some distant branch overhead. Other mouthing gapes were at face level, and she could hear clearly as she walked by them.

"Really, not this again." Trina heard and barely glanced at a passing branch that mouthed the comment. "All this for attention. You're so selfish. The world owes you nothing."

Trina's eyes twitched, her insides cringing a little. The closer her advent of the enclosure, the clearer the blue light became.

"No one likes a pity party. You must enjoy this. Guys don't do tears, hon. You do realize that no one wants to be around when you're like this."

The words came from the three mouths placed on the zigzagging trunk of a crooked tree. Trina eyed the source of the cruel words, and wondered where such words came from. *Had June heard these words before?* She moved past the triple-jawed stalk. Trina was thankful that she finally set foot in the small clearing. Upon entering the open space, she noticed another talking tree. The lone dendrite was a wide-bodied tree with a full head of bare branches. Its eyes bulged lazily, and blinked from its squeezed cankers. Its nose was a large curling burl over a dowering mouth. And there, sitting near the base of the tree was a small figure wrapped in a blue glow.

Its legs drawn into a tight hug against its chest, the lost soul's head rested on its knees. The blue light emanating from zem dimmed. There was the sound of sniffling and every now and then, there was a movement to wipe away tears. Remembering the lost soul's resistance upon their initial meeting, Trina stayed her rush to comfort it. Instead, she made her silent approach, watching and waiting for the right time to engage.

"For I consider that the sufferings of this present time are not worth comparing with the glory that is to be revealed to us," the wide-trunked tree finally bellowed.

Trina frowned, the phrase sounding vaguely familiar and she guessed it was another canto from the Bible. She would take advantage of the tree's murmurs, and use its voice to mask her steady steps.

"Godly sorrow brings repentance that leads to salvation," the tree rumbled, again. "And leaves no regret, but worldly sorrow brings death."

At the recitation of a second verse, Trina took another step. Aside from the occasional spluttering of the nasals and shifting of arms, the child did not stir in alarm.

"I form the light, and create darkness," the tree continued its deep declaration. "I make peace, and create evil: I the Lord do all these things."

Small shoulders quaked. The child's sniffling stopped and zeir posture stiffened upright. A sharp, loud angry fizzing of air pushed through teeth, and in the midst of the blue glow, there was a small spark of crimson. Suddenly, the lost soul leapt to zeir feet and lunged at the tree. The phantom pounced at the trunk and latched on to the tree's lower lip. The hands that seemed too small held a surprising strength that ripped under bite from cheeks. The wrench of the jawline was so severe that it peeled the elastic bark from mid-trunk to baseline, and revealed the insipid inner flesh of stem under the blood orange of thick sap. Trina gasped. Her aghast matched that of the groaning tree. She sprang forward and attempted to arrest the child in a hug to quell the lost soul's outburst.

The child let out another harsh hiss, bucked at the closing in of arms, and spun around. "You, again," the lost soul snarled.

Just as the child phantom was poised to flee, Trina's posture shrank, her hands raised in capitulation. "I'm sorry, I just... ." she stammered, her mind scrambling from the bewilderment of witnessing the child's outburst to trying to find the words, hopefully, the right words, to keep the spirit from fleeing. "I know you're in a lot of pain, you and my sister both."

"Quit following me!" Alex's words pushed out through teeth in a low, threatening growl. "Go have your fun torturing somebody else!" What little rising strength the child phantom found in the fleeting heat of annoyance quickly fell under. In Limbo, sadness and guilt were acute ailments that could sap any spirit of vitality. Between the arduous travel and evading the assault of evil spirits, the fit of rage against the drones of the dendrite was a foolish spending of precious energy.

"Please, Alex," Trina entreated once more. "We mean you no harm."

"We?" Alarm now flashed across Alex's face as zeir eyes shifted from the female spirit clad in white, to the space surrounding her.

"Me," Trina's expression lifted again. She was thoughtful and welcoming. She leaned slightly forward, and her hands clasped the centerpiece of her necklace, a trinket fashioned into a rich, earthen mask. "And Ori, and others. The Creator sent us to help, to save you and June both."

"Save us?" The lost soul uttered. Zeir posture slackened as zeir sense of danger faded. Still, there was an intensity about the child phantom's face. Guarded apprehension fell to a staid mask of tenseness. "Like angels?" Alex asked, the small quivering of lower lip slightly broke the phantom's stony mien.

"I'm an ancestor, an Egun if you want to be more specific. Ori and the others are Orisha." Trina smiled and attempted to build some friendly rapport with light conversation. "If you prefer us to be, then in a sense, we are angels."

Alex's mouth trembled, struggling to speak through pangs of sadness. "My yana told me about angels once. She used to trust them and the God who made them. When you died, I tried to be an angel for her."

"You are her angel, Alex." A thoughtfulness veiled Trina's gaze as she smiled. In spite of her efforts to mollify the pangs of grief, the lost soul's gloom became too thick for even the slightest amount of comfort to penetrate.

"When she found out how the world was, the pain got worse. She kept telling me that she wanted to go where I was." Alex paused. The memory of their talks rushed back. They had meetings in solitude through dreams whether awake or sleep. Their sliver of peace that used to be their time of calm was marred by the creeping invasion of the blue. Tears flowed through June's pleading and Alex's fear. The phantom's recall sharpened the spikes of despair and clogged the lost soul's throat. "I didn't want her to come here and so," the phantom admitted, and tried to swallow down the ball of pain in zeir throat to continue. "I pushed her away. I thought I was keeping her safe and happy with her family."

Trina's mouth tightened into a dejected knot. She felt the weight of the lost soul's remorse and sadness. "You were only protecting her."

Alex gave a slow scornful shake of the head, and knew that the only thing that managed to happen was for June to be pushed out of reach. And now, she could neither hear Alex nor Trina, especially when she needed to hear them the most. Guilt clenched the lost soul's eyes and mouth into an anguished grimace. Then, as the lost soul's eyes shifted, zeir woefulness turned to venom.

"Gehenna trees. Ugly, aren't they? Manifestations of careless words and thoughts. Many of their speakers are trapped in these petrified forms."

Trina's brows jumped. She followed the lost soul's gaze and her eyes first fell on the disfigured dendrite, still grumbling and bewildered. Its open wound, some minutes old, dried slightly from exposure, and made the blood orange sap more viscous. Then, her eyes roved over the stretched and shrinking mouths of the trees populating the gray forest. She couldn't help but inwardly shiver at the revelation of the lost soul's words.

"Their words are poisonous enough to kill, you know, even before they form as those spiteful trees," Alex explained with a bitter tone edged with irony. "And to think that many of them flourished in the one place that June thought she would feel safe."

Trina frowned as she contemplated the lost soul's words and tried to fully digest all she'd seen. She recalled her brief stint in that phantom place. Of course, there was the trepidation of her sudden intrusion mid-sermon, of being acknowledged in a place that was nothing more than a shade of the past. But even in her heightened vigilance, warmth eased in. There was a sense of welcome and comfort. Sights, sound, and smell brought back the nostalgia similar to her memory of her old home. Then, came the jarring transformation from lulling refuge to an unnerving sepulcher. Warmth and white gold rotted to stark cold and gray stones. The visage of familiar specters becoming twisted and discordant. There was a numbness of disbelief, confusion, and the jolt of fear. At that moment, God's sanctuary become a den of dismay and fear. There was a reason Ori led her to the memory of Elmwood Chapel and it was to know disillusionment.

"Searching for help and only finding harshness and apathy. Looking for peace, but offered judgment and the dread of more pain. After what she's been through, her hope must be broken. Being by her all this time, even when you couldn't reach her. You must be at a loss, too," Trina uttered the words almost to herself. Eyes growing attentive, the subtle lines of callousness that hardened Alex's face melted and for the first time, she could sense the lost soul completely abandon zeir need to fight or flee. "Both of you are in a lot of pain, believe me when I tell you I understand. The best is yet to come for both of you, but not like this."

"You seem to mean well." Alex's smile was faint and brief as it quickly dissolved under a grim resolve. "The life that your Creator made hurts too much. Even in death, pain and fear seems to follow. Just leave us to find our peace."

Sympathy and dejection dimmed Trina's eyes. She wanted to reach out, to console, but as she moved forward her steps paused upon seeing the child's slight recoil. The lost soul was about to run away, again. What could she do? How could she show a wayward spirit that the one who sent her was not another problem stacked against zem or an enemy who would prey on zem? How could she convince the lost soul that the Creator was on zeir side? She struggled for the words she desperately needed to make her earnest plea. The lock of silence that arrested her was only broken by the vibrations of her medallion.

Trina's posture stiffened, and eyes scanned the area. Nothing of a threat presented itself in the clearing or among the cluttered trees, at least not yet. Prepping for an imminent attack, light energy flickered throughout her sacred tattoos. "It's not safe staying here." Her dominant hand crossed discretely towards the opposite shoulder over skin markings that resembled the sharpness of darts. Trina briefly released her hold while they were still in the short lull of inactivity, and offered her right hand to the lost soul. "Please, there's not much time."

Wariness made the blue spirit's tiny feet inch away, but indecision prevented retreat. Tentative eyes stared at the Egun girl, and suddenly flickered elsewhere past her. Trina suddenly read surprise and fear on the child's face. Amid the mumbling of words came the sudden sound of a guttural rumbling. Trina pitched forward and captured the lost soul in a rolling dive. In her tumble, she glimpsed a black blur and flung darts of light at it with her free hand. She heard a sharp whine, felt the light graze of the black thing shave past and then heard a heavy thud as the hurdling object fell short of its pounce.

Trina recovered her footing from the roll, but remained in a guarded crouch. Alex, once reluctant to take the Egun's hand, now trembled in the crook of her arm. Tiny hands clung for dear life to the white fabric of her shirt. With the small spirit burrowing zeir eyes in her shoulder, Trina looked at the dark heap. It had a tail and four legs, and appeared to be some sort of animal. Its shaggy, quill-like pelt was pitch black. From the way the creature landed, its face was hidden, but judging from its growling, Trina assumed it to be a dog. Then, with bristling and trembling shoulders, the beast raised its head and turned to them. Trina's eyes widened and her mouth went dry as the wolfish snout crinkled, its jaws grimaced to reveal a maw filled with white daggers. Like a giant piece of rounded, burning coal, the hungry beast's single eye smoldered. The black dog shifted to gather its feet. Before it could make its attempt to stand, Trina flicked her wrist, and tossed another dart at the dog. When white light struck the fiery sphere, the dog's head jerked back then fell forward as the rest of its body slumped lifelessly to the ground. The fire orb faded to black before the beast's shape sank and crumbled into a dark stain on the forest floor.

"Get out of here!" Without wavering her watchfulness of her surroundings, Trina relinquished the child from the cradle.

Alex's reluctance quickly broke upon hearing another snarl. The lost soul took flight upward and narrowly evaded the rush of a second blur as Trina sliced at it with one of her arms laced in a razor, sunlit lining. The strike immediately seized the second black dog in mid-air, its ocular furnace blotted out as its shape burst into nothing. With legs squared in defense, and arms poised, Trina searched, waiting for the next attack. After a short survey of her surroundings, she noticed the mob of black shapes and several infernal dots speckling the gray forest. Barks and growls came from all directions. A scream and the rattling of branches forced Trina's attention upward to find that Alex had never made it past the canopy.

Black twigs and ropes collapsed upon the blue glow. Arms and feet thrashed against the ensnare only for more of the branches to creep to reassert their hold. Mixed in with the cries for help was an ominous guffaw. Within the slivers of the break and collapse of limbs, she saw black-winged, wide bodies and gleaming pairs of crimson. Trina jumped and her own wings carried her up and up. Upon breaking the forest canopy, she reached for the blue light and clawed at the frantic writhe of tendrils and when she could, she wrapped her body around the lost soul as a shield. Amid the chaotic squirming of limbs, she saw strange black fowl overhead. They looked like owls, although they had bulging red eyes and teeth-like serrations that lined their pronounced, hooked beaks. Their talons were powerful and set open. Their bodies were wide and more than large enough to carry both Trina and Alex. A flock of the monstrous owls formed above them.

Trina winced at the scratching of canopy branches and turned to eye the conditions below. The pack of black dogs now covered the forest floor. Some paced and looked above. Others clawed at jabbering stalks. Quite a few of them had gathered a foothold into the bark and to Trina's dismay, they moved further up the trunks. If their climb continued to be successful, it was only a matter of time before the dogs reached them, that is, if the owls didn't get them first. Trina kicked wildly. Her arm curled around the lost soul in a protective hold now constricted in a twisted sling of wood. Her free hand flailed and sliced at limbs that quickly replaced themselves. Eventually, what was free and fighting became bound and immobile. The sight of the owls as they closed in was the last thing Trina saw before black shoots covered her eyes. At that moment, Trina felt a shuddering, then a lurch, and next the loosening of wooden bindings.

With her eyes under the blindfold of limbs, Trina relied on her ears. There were frightened hoots and death screeches above and the barks and yelps below. There was a collective snapping of wood and low whirring. Sometimes, she could feel the light touch of heat near her feet, thigh, and shoulders. As soon as one hand was released from the binding of branches, Trina tore off the bundled blindfold of twigs. Surprised and puzzled, she wasn't sure what to make of the thing hovering next to her on the canopy. The strange being looked like an animated sculpture of silver fashioned in the likeness of cupid. This caricature of an angel was armed with a sword small enough to almost be considered a dagger or short sword.

He was not alone, for Trina glimpsed a second cherub with a bow and arrow. In a brief suspension of time, the bairn archer aimed at the forest below and launched several rapid volleys of shining arrows before flitting out of sight. Noticing that the flock had long since scattered, she discovered the gathering of demonic owls had already covered some distance. Still, many of the birds dropped out of the sky as they failed to out fly the pursuit of a spiraling streak of what looked like lingering lightning. Though its shape looked faint in the distance, Trina could make out the source of the silver streaks to be a third cherub flinging at the stragglers with a whip.

"Are you all right, miss?" the cherub swordsman's voice sounded shrill, but friendly. As the silvery moppet beamed at her, Trina smiled, still puzzled, but relieved. "One moment, please."

Trina was given little time to brace herself, let alone think before a fourth cherub appeared directly above them. In one arm he toted a curving antler, decorated with carvings and was as silver as his body. The cherub threw back his head, raised the horn to his pursed lips and began sounding the instrument. The horn's call was resounding, and caused the sky to quake and the air to rush in a rioting updraft. Trina hunkered down and held tight to the child phantom that burrowed in her arms for shelter. A great rip of thunder made the bleak sky roll and the bundling of clouds spiraled then parted as a mouth to a tunnel. When light shone down, Trina looked up to see the gateway that the great horn's call had summoned. The way was fully opened and the cherubim gathered at the portal's entryway. The swordsman lingered behind. Turning to both the Egun and the lost soul, the cherub smiled as he beckoned them to follow. Trina hesitated at first, both awestruck at the structure and wary at the overall situation. Her uncertainty only shirked by the greater need to press forward. And at that moment, the only means in which the journey would continue was by entering the light at the end of the tunneling gateway in the sky.

Chapter 4

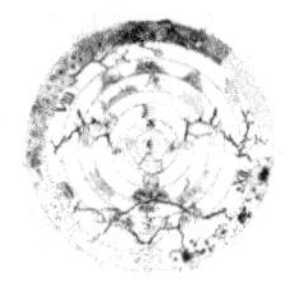

Trina paused. She found it far easier to catch the pace of her heart than her memory. From the dark forest to sky tunnels and now a town, she scarcely remembered the cherubim escorting them to some pedestrian plaza. The child still burrowed zemself in her chest and arms. Trina's measured breathing calmed her shaken nerves somewhat even as the lost soul still trembled.

"Are you hurt anywhere?" the swordsman chirped; his face drawn with concern. The cherub's small wings carried his infant form in sprightly flits about the young spirit and her companion.

"Alex?" Trina's inquiry came through a whisper while readjusting the lost soul in the cradle of her arms. Fingers of one hand softly strummed the wild curls of the child's scalp. The palm of the other hand gently patted the small spirit's back to calm the rapid thundering of zeir heartbeat. With zeir face still hidden and pressed against her shoulder, Trina felt the lost soul's head knead slightly in affirmation. Reassured that Alex was unharmed, Trina turned her attention back to the cherub. "You saved us. Thank you."

Grooves of his eyebrows and cheeks shifted upward as the swordsman's mien brightened. "You are welcome ma'am, but it was quite a miracle that we caught you passing through when we did." The cherub twittered, and his fluttering suddenly halted in a hover to level at Trina's shoulder. "The Gehenna Forests are dangerous, especially of late. It is certainly not a safe place for travelers to pass through, let alone for children to wander."

Trina read the quizzical look on the swordsman's face as an invitation to share her story of ending up on such a treacherous route. Perhaps, it would be advantageous to explain and possibly enlist some help on their journey. Still, there was something that held her back from speaking, something that she noticed as she lowered Alex from her arms. It was the pendant at her chest, warming and still humming its urgent warning. Trina inspected it and wondered why Ori's alarm continued even after they left the dangers of the forest behind them.

"A good luck charm?" the swordsman asked.

Trina glanced from the bold mask of the pendant to a baby-faced angel whose raised eyebrow conveyed a heightened curiosity towards the medallion.

"A guide," she corrected him, still at unease. "Someone to warn us whenever trouble's nearby."

"You have a keen alarm. The Gehenna Forests aren't the only places infested with evil spirits nowadays." A somber tone tinged the swordsman's laud of the pendant. "The four of us have been working overtime to keep those pesky fiends at bay from invading Angel Town. We've even had to make our patrol of the outskirts more frequent."

Trina's head jerked back slightly as revelation struck her. "So, only the four of you make up the Silver Guard?"

The swordsman's smile broadened, and he answered with a thorough nod. As she watched the silvery sprite arch his back, his tummy puffed forward with pride, Trina couldn't help but crack an amused smirk.

"As the strongest, Mayor Gold has charged us with the duty to protect the citizens of our fair little town. We may be small in number, but rest assured, nothing gets past the Silver Guard," the swordsman chirped.

"Mayor Gold?" Trina repeated. The named piqued her interest, especially since the words triggered another rush of vigor that colored the cherub's face with starstruck admiration.

"Oh, our Golden Angel. The most magnificent, the most powerful. He is our protector, a leader of Angel Town who rules with benevolence." As the swordsman sang praises, he fluttered about Trina and the child hunkering at her side. Suddenly, the cherub made an abrupt halt, his elation dimmed as a thought occurred to him. "That reminds me. I'm still curious as to why children were wandering the forests by themselves. Are you lost?"

"Not necessarily."

Trina paused and her thoughts vacillated between the unknown warning of the pendant and the prospects of gaining support on their journey. Then, the slight sting of tiny nails prickled through the pants leg and made her look down where the child stood. Zeir little fingers tightly gripped the cloth of Trina's pants leg and Alex's face stayed burrowed at the outer thigh the whole time she and the cherub conversed. Trina thought of the child's fear and considered the recent danger that resulted from traveling alone. She decided it better to divulge the truth.

"My sister is about to make a terrible mistake. This lost soul is the key to finding her. But with all that's happened, with all the obstacles still ahead of us, I don't know if we'll make it in time."

The urgency she had forgotten since their arrival, surfaced again. It reminded her of Ori's last vision of June as she left the school. It made her wonder how far her sister had progressed and dreaded the possibility of there only being hours or even minutes left.

"I see. A lost soul?" the gaze that had been measured and attentive throughout Trina's explanation melted into a sympathetic one as the swordsman's eyes lingered on the small spirit at her side. "Very well." The cupid's belly swelled once more, this time with a dutiful certitude. "I will make a request to Mayor Gold to seek an audience with you. He will no doubt have a solution to your plight."

Trina's eyes widened. She was hopeful. Admittedly, she thought the cherub's praise of Angel Town's protector had gone way beyond the point of sycophancy. The swordsman's cartoonish nature alone would have kept her from taking anything the cherub said seriously. Then again, the cherubim had made quick work of the demons in the Gehenna Forest. Recalling she and the lost soul's rescue per the Silver Guard had given the swordsman's words merit. Thoughts of having an ally, especially as one as powerful as the swordsman's claim, had made the graveness weighing down on Trina's heart a bit lighter, and she was thankful for it.

Before Trina could open her mouth to share her gratitude, the swordsman smiled warmly, and raised one hand in gracious decline.

"No thanks are needed, miss. It is the duty of the Silver Guard to help those in need. Now, I must inform the mayor post haste." The rapidly fluttering tiny wings raised the cherub and carried him upward. His departure was briefly delayed as he turned towards them to impart one final message. "In the meantime, make yourselves at home. Demon activity has made our citizens more cautious than usual, but they will be glad to tend to your every need.

Please, take whatever comfort and rest you may." Trina nodded, accepting the cherub's offer.

With that, the swordsman winked, gave a farewell salute and slowly rose above them. Trina returned the departing gesture with a wave and watched as the swordsman took flight above the level of urban roofs before flitting out of sight.

"Is it gone?" Alex's rasp brought Trina's attention back to earth. The child's face inched out from hiding, zeir eyes scouring the air for the whereabouts of the gleaming cherub.

"And hopefully, he will come back with good news from this mayor he's lauded about."

A brief survey of the quiet plaza still earned a disapproving head shake from the lost soul. "I don't like this place. We should leave, now," Alex urged.

Gruffness edged the lost soul's tiny voice. Stubbornness tightened the expression of the spirit's face. The gaze that peered up at Trina was as demanding as the lost soul's insistence. Despite the curtness, Trina could feel the cloth of her pants leg squeeze under the grasp of tense, small fingers. Her stance was slightly off-kilter from the weight that hugged her outer thigh tightly. She could feel the slight tremors of fear. The corners of Trina's eyes crinkled and her mouth raised in soft curls.

"Still scared?" she asked.

Alex's eyebrows jumped before the glowering mask of stubbornness returned. "Keep trusting everything you meet and you'll get eaten."

"You're still with me, aren't you?" Trina smiled, unfazed by the retort.

Surprise flickered across the lost soul's face again. The realization of coming to rely on the company and protection of another briefly caused Alex to stall before grumbling, "Strength in numbers."

Trina nodded, "Which is why we are asking for help. The more people to join us, the safer we'll be. It never hurts to have allies."

"This is a waste of time," Alex griped.

"Think of it as using our time wisely. Besides, we need the rest. We might as well have a look around."

Alex made no objections to what Trina proposed, and only huffed as a final complaint. The lost soul fastened to Trina's side and moved to keep with her steady steps. When she finally took notice of her surroundings, she found herself in the center of a tawdry settlement.

Angel Town. The name sounded contrived, as though invented by a cartoonist, or more aptly, some contractor for an amusement park. Then again, getting a chance to take a better look at the florid setting, the title seemed fitting. The place had features of a metropolitan square with an old-timey feel. Where they stood, three-storied brownstones speckled the U shaped arcade of shops and eateries. A large fountain made up the artistic centerpiece of the town plaza. The municipal court of even, paved stone, provided generous walking spaces to store walkways and to the patio of a shop/restaurant to the far right. With three sides of the square lined with buildings and narrow alleyways, there was a one-way street separating the arcade from a wide, red-bricked structure. The street likely led to cross-sections through other parts of the town. Though Angel Town certainly had the fixings of a metropolitan area, there was something odd about it. That something made the place reminiscent of the kiddie resorts she and her family had visited in places like Orlando or Anaheim.

The fabric of things seemed too clean in Angel Town. Features like awnings and roofs seemed exaggerated. The slight wear and bristle seen in the shaved wood seemed flawless and smooth. The grittiness and rough grooves slightly marked concrete and stone absent. One shop closest to them, *Amerotto's Jewelry* it was called, seemed fashioned of some synthetic blocks of vivid yellow instead of built of somber blonde brick. A street lamp nearest them looked artificial and not in a way that paint covered metal. Curiosity probed Trina to touch the neck of the sidewalk light. Strangely enough, her hand slightly sank in a material akin to something thick and spongy like clay. When she pulled away, it briefly left an impression where she'd touched it. Trina stifled a frown, careful not to stoke Alex's anxiousness any further as her gaze studied every window, bench, and door. The more she observed Angel Town, at least its arcade, the more the town impressed upon her that it was an imitation. It was like a replica of a town, an attraction that served as a rest stop or gift shop area at theme parks. She half-expected the township's tottering mascot to stumble out from somewhere to greet them.

On cue came the soft roll and clatter of running wheels. The sound drew Trina's eyes to a far corner of the square on the opposite side of the plaza fountain. There, a peddler and his cart strolled into view. He was a tall man, burly with a bib apron that fell over a protruding keg of a belly. His head swayed in tune with his merry shuffle as he hummed. Though not quite the character mascot she'd pictured, his happy-go-lucky demeanor, rounded stature and cap did make him quite the caricature. Then came the children. They appeared seemingly out of nowhere, and rushed towards him as he parked his push trolley of goods. More of the square began to stir. A couple walked out of the jewelry store romantically locked arm-in-arm. A trickling of walkers peopled sidewalks. In one of the brownstones a window slid open, its occupant's eyes brightened, smiled and waved, delighted to suddenly spy two guests visiting their town. Others took notice, and either reacted the same as the brownstone resident or casually greeted them with an easy smile, a nod of the head, or a tip of the hat. Alex remained pensive and watchful, and sometimes hugged close to her leg when the greeters' address seemed too forward for tolerance. Trina smiled in return. The citizens seemed pleasant and welcoming, but the attention only made her self-conscious. They stuck out like a sore thumb, after all, for all the citizens of Angel Town were bronze.

Hats, shoes, blouse, dress, suits, and uniform. Eyes, skin, teeth, and hair. All were matched the same alloyed hue of tan or orange-brown. Fine, well-articulated lines distinguished the body from clothing. Much like the members of the Silver Guard, they looked like living breathing statues of metal. And as angelic denizens of an angelic town, wings sprouted from their backs. Trina remembered how small the wings of the silver angels were. Somehow, they were still functional, still carried enough of their weight for long-term. She took note of the bronze angels, like their differences in the body to wing proportion. Unlike the silver ones, the bodies of the bronze and copper angels were similar to that of the typical human. In comparison to the wings of the Silver Guard, these same appendages on the bronze and copper angels seemed minuscule and useless. Recalling what the swordsman said about the strongest as the city's guards, the flight worthiness of the silver wings, the decorative nature of the bronze and copper wings, Trina wondered if there was a hierarchy to this town. Thinking about this made her even more curious about Mayor Gold.

A shadow loomed and brought in a sensation much colder than a chill. Its advance was sudden and quiet. The touch of its crawling growth jolted Trina from musing to a stark awareness. A reflex action threw her to stagger to an about-face. She clutched the still shivering medallion. The owner of the shade, a hefty man, made of bronze, dressed in an apron and a cap, stared down at her with a smile. "Why, hello there."

It was the peddler, the first citizen of Angel Town she had seen besides the members of the Silver Guard. Any reply or utterance of surprise caught in Trina's throat. Up close, the peddler seemed much taller, his height draped the shadow over her like some dreadful cape. She forced the troublesome lump down, and managed to nod in greeting.

"You look famished," the peddler sang. His eyes crinkled nearly to a close. His cheeks arched the wider he smiled, and made the chubby face look like a mask that belonged to a clown or a teddy bear. Then, as though rehearsed, the bronzed dealer slid across the cart's sign and merchandise, and recited his advertising spiel. "Gordon's Goodies are the delight of the town. Candies for the kiddies. Treats for the guests. How 'bout something sweet for free?"

The smile she conjured was strained. For some reason, the name Gordon hung heavy in the ceiling of her mind while something unsettling scratched at the basement of consciousness. Perhaps it was his great stature, or the subtle strength of his paws and long, meaty arms. Perhaps, she was still trying to recover from being startled so unexpectedly. The man had been clear across the street and suddenly there he was, behind them. She had heard the cart as it rumbled on the other side of the square earlier and yet she scarcely heard it upon his approach. Then again, she had been distracted.

Trina was hit with another jolt. She glanced down at her side and only a receding streak of blue light remained. A swift cut of the eyes over her shoulder and she glimpsed what lingered of a quickly dissolving trail. A tail of blue light zigzagged through the plaza, past street lights, and past the fountain. Dismay and relief hammered at her insides and noticed that the head of the blue streak disappeared past the building arcades, and fled down the one-way street.

"Alex, wait!"

Trina ignored the timid gesturing and long gaze of the concerned peddler. She hopped backward and created distance. A second skip and she unfurled her wings of light and hurried to fly after the blue streak. Trina frantically searched. Her hopeful cries showed no signs of Alex slowing down. She followed the staggering trail of light and prayed not to lose sight of her ward. Her inner pleas finally were answered when the short-lived chase ended down an alleyway. The ball of blue light halted in front of an orange and white striped barricade. Trina hurried her approach, the frantic beating of fear only calmed upon seeing a small, familiar figure with wild dark hair, dressed in a gown.

Relief washed away the overwhelm of distress, enough to allow room for reproachful impulse.

"Strength in numbers, remember! You can't just run off on your own like that."

Trina's scold did nothing to break Alex's gaze from what lay ahead. The other words of reprimand she had were soon swept aside by dry rustling and the dim stir of wind, that beckoned her to what the lost soul saw beyond the warning barrier.

Sandwiched between two buildings, and fenced off from them was another world, a dimmer world. After all that Trina experienced with Limbo's many gaps and diverging spaces, this contrast before her indicated a threshold of some sort. On the side where she and Alex stood, the sky was clear. Across the barrier, muddy gray sharply cut off the firmament of sunny blue-white. Below, the flawless asphalt of the backstreet ended at the cordon and a walkway of worn brick began. The eroded path led to the ominous shell that was the forefront of the gray world. It was a wide, archaic structure with dark windows as its eyes and steps led to the main door. Taller than it was wide, Trina guessed that it had about seven or eight floors at least. The pinnacle reached a story or two above the red bricks that columned the alleyway. A little more than halfway up the neck of the building was a terrace and an archway to view the other side. Just underneath the pinnacle's roof was the pale broad face of a clock.

"A clock tower."

It was a freestanding clock tower at that, one that seemed very old. Trina looked at the clock tower and was reminded of one of her outings with her parents. She, her mother, father, and sister took a guided tour of one. She remembered going on the terrace similar to the clock tower before her and looking out to a lake at the other side. She even remembered being in the clock's turret, a space that seemed decorated with large gears, thick ropes, a bell, and other parts. The clock tower from her vague memory of the living was a marvel when she was a child. The one on the other side of the barrier gave off the same eerie vibe as a funeral home. Complete with the black skeleton of a dead tree and surrounded by murky air, Trina wouldn't be surprised if the clock tower was the rumored haunted house of Angel Town.

Trina felt a familiar nestling at her leg as Alex returned by her side. Another dry rustle and cold breeze came through. Sailing on the wind, a dead leaf suddenly appeared and Trina guessed it was from the distant black tree. Beyond her initial notice of the leaf, she barely paid any mind to the wayward frond. Then, when the leaf brushed her ear, she heard something carried by the wind. *A voice?* It was faint and very far away, but Trina was sure it was a voice. When the wind raised the same sound again, Trina stiffened. Her eyes searched and she wondered if the source of the sound came from behind the barrier. A tiny spark of light suddenly appeared from the archway at the top of the tower. It winked, shimmered and waned as though the light were being manipulated through a reflector. She trained her focus on the archway and strained to see the distance. She hoped to gain clarity on the spark's source. For a third time, the wind raised, the faint voice rang and Ori jumped.

Trina and Alex flinched at the medallion's agitation. Over time, the wearer had become complacent to the constant warning hum. Now, the stone face's erratic bobble thundered against her chest, Trina wondered if Ori was angry. She wondered if her inattention had displeased her guardian and the way that the pendant knocked and tugged against the hold of her necklace, Trina feared the worst.

"I'm sorry, Ori. Please," she whispered. Desperate fingers clasped around the medallion. "Please, what am I doing wrong?"

In response, Trina felt pressure resonating from the pendant. The push against her palms and fingers were airy and gentle. Obeying the nudge of the medallion, Trina released her grasp. The stone face lifted itself from her hands, and rose as her heart sank. As she thought, the medallion would abandon its unworthy wearer. Its levitation halted at her forehead. Then, mimicking the winks of the distant spark in the archway, Ori wavered side-ward. His stony-self glittered, his movements caused parts of himself to shine brighter than the gleam of a diamond or mirror. Alex and Trina watched. Both marveled and puzzled by the wordless communication between Ori and the faraway spark. The contact was brief, however, after a near minute the spark stopped and Ori dropped, and returned to a semi-inertness. The wind and the distant call quieted to a doldrum.

"Get away from there. It's dangerous."

Startled by a man's voice, the pair whirled away from the warning barrier. A taxi car, or more like a caricature of one, was parked some paces behind them. Standing next to the open door of the driver's seat was another bronze angel in uniform. Compared to the peddler, the cabbie was of average height and build. Overlaps of bristling lines made up his trimmed mustache and thin eyebrows. A few, finer contours touched the corners of his eyes and thin cheeks, showing the age of a man possibly in his late forties.

"We saw some blinking lights over there, someplace past the clock tower. There were noises too, voices I think," Trina explained, and pointed up at the clock tower's terrace where the archway showed the gray beyond.

"Will-o'-wisp, probably. That may be reason for the light you saw," the cabbie replied. "Banshee or some other phantom could've made the noise you heard. Whatever the source, it is likely not anything friendly."

"This is a part of Angel Town, isn't? The Silver Guardsman said they've kept the town safe." Trina's brows furrowed slightly when she remembered the conversation she had earlier with the cherub swordsman.

"And that's very true all thanks to them, of course," the cabbie answered. Momentarily lifting his chauffeur's cap, he scratched a small area of his scalp with the same hand before tilting the hat towards the cordoned off zone of gray. "There was a venture not so long ago to build a public clock tower and make further expansions to Angel Town. Because of the rise in demon activity and reports of evil spirit sightings, the area was condemned."

"How did you know we were here?" Alex spoke suddenly. The awe at seeing the clock tower and Ori's reaction had long been replaced by vigilance. Ever since the taxi's arrival, the lost soul had placed the driver under the microscope of suspicion.

"There was quite a commotion in the square about two newcomers who suddenly up and left. Everyone was concerned," the cabbie explained. He was obliging and unflappable even under the intense study of Alex's solid, black eyes. "Some of the children pointed to where you'd run off to and I followed. And where you ended up, it was a good thing that I caught up in time."

For Trina, the taxi driver's answer seemed satisfactory enough. Still the small hand that gripped the tips of her fingers told otherwise. They seemed to hold her in place, but not because of the strength of restraint. Though the lost soul wore the mask of mulish distrust, the clasp that tightened around her fingers expressed anxiousness. Trina smiled, and her eyes fell at her side as she thought to knelt down by Alex's side. She paused suddenly, and her gentle smile fell into a confused glower of concentration as a smoky waft touched her nose. It was the delicious scent of meat and spices and seasoned potatoes. The aroma was so rich that as it delighted the nose, it coiled around Trina's gut until a loud growl rattled her abdomen. The nose drew in a silent inhale of shock, and her eyes jumped wide as her hands flew to the flatness of her still protesting stomach. It was not unheard of for spirits to eat. In the dwelling place of her fellow Eguns, they would indulge in this mainly through an active reminiscence of family gatherings at dinner or a pastime outing to lunch. In a sense, the Egun ate food made from memories; mostly out of remembrance of past lives or curiosity if one wanted to experience flavors not even known to the living. Since her crossover into the spirit realm, she had never felt the hunger twinges she experienced now.

Alex's brows shifted in surprise and then in annoyance as the smell of cooked food set off another roar of a rumbling stomach. The cabbie's mouth twitched. Seeing such reactions from the two, must have been amusing to the bronze angel and eventually the chuckle he stifled managed to escape. He read the look of confusion on Trina's face, and the cabbie collected himself.

"Well, even us spirits get hungry from time to time," he said, and pressed a button to unlock the doors. Then he motioned with an inviting gesture. "Hop in. You ought to try Harper's Place if you haven't. Finest dining in all of Angel Town, if you want my opinion."

The smell of cooked food made Alex less reluctant, and led the two to find a place in the taxi's back seat. During the short ride, they learned that the driver's name was Mr. Rousseau, he was a regular at Harper's Place, a visitor who frequented the café enough to know the people who worked there and the hidden specials of their eatery's menu. An obliging enough stranger, Trina told him a little about their quest when asked. Like the swordsman, the cabbie was sympathetic, and assured them that they came to the right place and that the mayor was the right person to see. Except for the gruff insistence of being taken to the airport or driving beyond the town borders, Alex said little. And then, as the driver sadly informed them of the absence of an airport and discouragements in venturing beyond the town's safety zones, the lost soul sulked in silence.

Within minutes, the taxi arrived at the square. Mr. Rousseau parked at the restaurant doubling as a knick-knack store, when he was met by a wiry woman with a hair styled in a bun, dressed in the work clothes of a restaurant worker. As she held Alex in her lap, Trina watched the pair of bronze angels. She noticed their small wings that flapped every now and then as they shared a joke or two. The cabbie called her Mari Elle and the lady hostess presented herself as such when the cabbie finally introduced them. Soon after the taxi departed, Mari Elle escorted them in.

"Patio seat or in-house, dear?" Mari Elle asked.

"Outside is fine." Trina's answer made the hostess clap in delight.

"Excellent choice, especially on days like today." Mari Elle then leaned in, cupped one hand around her mouth as though sharing a secret. "Why, you might catch me out here on my lunch break," the hostess joked.

Politeness made Trina join in the titter. Shortly after she took her place at the table for two, Mari Elle returned with two cups of water and two plastic booklets.

"You take your time with those menus and feel free to pass the time looking around. Orders are on the house for guests. I'll be back around to check. Enjoy!" Mari Elle sang. Alex's hardened stare at the hostess was met with a friendly smile and wink as she hurried off to other affairs behind the restaurant's doors.

Trina sat upright at first, and glanced over her shoulder where the hostess had disappeared. Then, she turned to the strumming at her chest, and took hold of the pendant. A tug of war went on in her mind. On one side, there was the vibration of Ori's alarm. The stone's shuddering was constant, a steady prompting that seemed to say be watchful and be careful, danger is near. There was the one instant of nervousness with the peddler and the clock tower at the impasse, but nothing of perilous consequence came of it.

Eventually, Trina let go of the medallion, and leaned on one elbow that rested on the table. With her head perched in the palm of her hand, her eyes meandered beyond the patio's enclosure. More bronze angels were out and about the square, shopping, visiting or enjoying a walk in the noon sun. There was a bronze angel, a squatty old man, who struggled to keep the reigns on a dog that tugged at his owner's leash. Trina thought it funny to see the dog and its owner with matching tiny wings. She thought it even more strange to see such a mundane scene play out in the afterlife.

The aroma of cooked food hit her in another wave, and interrupted her musings. It nudged her to eye the menu placed in front of her. A hollow clink of glass drew her attention to the sweating cup of ice-cold water. She reached for the cup and took a sip. It was cold, refreshing, and it quenched a thirst Trina did not know she had.

"Do you care about yana or not!" the shrill of discontent shattered the ease of midday, and demanded that Trina wake up from her leisurely stupor of people watching.

The harsh words rattled her out of laxity, and struck her heart with a hollow twinge. It pinched her mouth in a slight grimace. "Alex, of course, I do." Dejection's gaze met stern, black eyes that peered over the horizon of the table across from her. "Sometimes, getting help takes time."

"I should have taken care of this on my own." Frustration darkened the lost soul's stern mien into a disheartened glower. "I would have made it to her by now and she wouldn't be by herself."

There was a sadness in Trina's gentle smile. "You have to give things one more try, even when times are at their worst. Until the two of you take that to heart, you're stuck with me."

Alex's head shook before ze looked away. Ze knew the lost cause in that promise. "The Dead End is the only peace for us now."

Trina gave a quiet sigh as her expression sank. Now it was her turn to be frustrated. At first, she thought there was progress. She thought the two were companions throughout their journey and Alex would not only come to rely on her but, share the same hope she had. It seemed, however, that the negative field Alex held up as a wall still stood and for the first time, forbearance and optimism wavered against it. The lost soul seemed resolute. Still, this was no time to give up. Determination emboldened Trina's own resolve, and shoved aside the niggling fear of failure. Instead, her thoughts searched for more ways to try to reach whatever little hope was buried in hopelessness. More than anything there was a word, something that the lost soul said that prompted her to ask more questions.

"Hey new kid!" the chirp caught Trina's gaze a little beyond the shoulders of the chair the lost soul sat in. Alex spun around, followed her gaze, and flinched at the sight of little bronze faces beaming back. In their preoccupation, the two had barely noticed the band of children that clambered in their direction. Now, a small crowd of curly heads and ball caps, butterfly ribbons and pigtails had formed.

"We're looking for more people before we start our game. Want to come play?" it was the same voice that greeted them before, a bronze angel with the renderings of a freckled-face child with two or three missing teeth.

For a brief moment, as Trina observed the bronze children, she was reminded of the metal statues she saw planted in municipal spaces. When alive, she saw the still-life decorations, posed in glee and play in the green lawn of parks or in front of libraries. Unlike the tranquil sculptures she had known, however, there was a restless element about these bronze angels. There was something too eager about their grins and about the way their tiny hands clung to the bars of the low Belmont fence. It made Trina feel a twinge of uneasiness, a sensation that showed more intensely in the lost soul.

Since the request, Alex had not spoken, only stared. With a stiffened posture, and chin drew into chest, the blue spirit appeared to brood. It was a bluff at intimidation, Trina knew, and she could see the slight crinkling of anxiousness about the lost soul's eyes. Finally, Alex scooted from the seat interlaced with iron to patio floor, turned and glanced up at Trina in passing while walking towards the doors of the restaurant's interior.

Trina stood, and left only a glance and the contents on the table behind as she joined the lost soul's side. "Taking a look at the shop?" she asked.

"Looking for a key out of here," Alex corrected.

The hollow ring of the mallet against metal cup signaled their entrance through the threshold. Once inside, they were greeted by a nod from Mari Elle and the lingering fragrance of scented candles. Save for the quick acknowledgment of the hostess, Trina remained on watchful guard. Wherever Alex ventured, Trina trailed close behind all the while taking in the well-managed clutter of her surroundings. She spied a gramophone and a vinyl record player. Porcelain dolls congregated along wall shelves or sat among miniature tea sets. Figurines and knick-knacks displayed along tables, stands, and sills. There were grandfather clocks and faded pictures in antediluvian frames. Show vases and bowls, plate sets and stitched dining clothes, old-fashioned coats and hats on holding racks. From the cashier's counter towards the patio area to the display pane and double doors of the main entrance, erstwhile items were situated among shelves or amid ensembles of secondhand furnishings.

Trina kept the blue glow in periphery following the lost soul's lead into the maze of shelves where there were more objects that were either parochial merchandise or artifacts of yesteryear. Alex was small, and easily moved about the forests of ledges and sills, but for Trina, the jutting of toy limbs and wild sprigs of fake, potted plants, made maneuvering through the aisles a tight fit. Still, she managed to slide past rows of mirrors with outlandish borders, and past a collection of trinkets extracted from kid's meals and cereal boxes. She moved past a line of defunct magazines and books out of print. Her elbow accidentally clipped a slim, paper cover. The thin clap of paperback hitting the floor, sounded. Trina retraced her steps, backtracking to retrieve the book and place it back on the shelves. Upon laying eyes on the item, she paused, blinked first in disbelief and then a second time to make sure that what she stared at was not an illusion. Even as she knelt down to pick up the object for a closer look, she half expected her eyes and mind to correct what she saw as the illustration and title.

On the cover of the picture book was a drawing of a little girl with dark brown skin standing on a patch of grass. She wore a green dress with white polka dots that coordinated with the white barrettes snapped locks of thick, braided hair. She was patched on one elbow and her forehead had band-aids. At her feet, she was missing a shoe. One of her hands balled in a fist against her mouth and her large, black eyes stretched wide as they stared side-ward at something out of view. Trepidation formed a dry coating in the walls of Trina's throat. There was no doubt who the little girl in the illustration was. Looking at the bold lettering of the title overhead, Trina swallowed, and forced down the feelings of foreboding as she read, "The Girl with Marble Black Eyes."

She dared to separate the book covers. She flipped past the blank sheet of white, and carried onto the next page. "Now here's a little girl, with thick braids that curled, and large black marbles for eyes." The meter of words were bold and large enough that they made up three lines on one page. On the other side was a lone illustration of the girl from the front cover. She had both of her shoes and no band-aids. She was smiling, calm, and sitting in a sandpit playing with toys. Trina turned the page and another illustration took up both pages. At the forefront of one page was a close up of the little girl's face, who looked up in surprise as though being called. The eyes of the girl in the drawing had also changed, as the deep brown and the white were blotted in black. Trina knew only one other person with the strange stigmatism. Sometimes, when there was a rise in June's emotions, the pupils would only dilate to the point of blotting out the iris. In extreme cases of excitement or distress, the darkness bled beyond the borders of the iris, and engulfed the white sclera in solid black. The later of the disorder was reflected in the drawing, and though it was difficult to determine with the expansion of the pupils, Trina guessed that the little girl noticed the three distant shapes that approached from the other page.

When Trina leafed through to the next scene, fear clenched her heart. The drawing of the little girl playing alone in the sandbox was not a mere illustration in a picture book. It was the scene of something that happened long ago, an incident that happened a year since Trina had passed away. On one of their outings, their parents had decided on a change in setting that day by going to the playground other than the one at their elementary school. For the short minutes that she was out of range of her parents' watch, three boys noticed that June was by herself. Trina may not have been next to June in the sandbox that day, but she was there watching. The prickling touch of goosebumps climbed up her hands, wrists, and arms with the turn of each page. Sounds resurfaced from memory as those horrifying moments played out in still reels of pencil and paint.

The picture first showed a little girl playing alone. She had not noticed the presence of three older boys nor did she realize how close they had approached until she felt the small flick of a pebble at her shoulder. For a brief moment, she searched for the source and realized too late that the wandering of her eyes prompted by the sudden startle was the trigger. The trio murmured among themselves. They were shocked and curious, at first. They talked about her eyes. The girl kept her head down, and pretended not to hear the comments as they turned to jeers. In-crowd jeering turned to open heckling, and more pebbles being thrown. Then a rock grazed her forehead. Before long, the little girl fled. With the last flips of the pages, images showed the little girl stumbling, losing one shoe. The last picture showed the little girl finally gaining footing, her legs stretching in a desperate lunge to outpace the pursuit of three boys much bigger than her. Her face twisted in horror and distress, the girl's arms drew around her face as a shield from the assault of rocks, sticks, and laughter from bleating faces. On one side of the page bold lettering read, "The boys shouted, 'Witch!' threw rocks and sticks, and she ran, fearing she'd die."

"Excuse me?" The sudden intrude of a small voice shook Trina from the deep read. The startle loosened the book from her hands. She looked down to where the book fell and her eyes met with the bronze face of a little girl. "Sorry?" the bronze girl said, as she stared up at Trina with long drawn eyes until she bent down to retrieve what had fallen. "Are you going to buy this?"

Trina paused and tried to settle her nerves. A puzzling furrow of her brows formed as she strained to process what she saw. On the cover, a rosy caricature of two cherubim at play replaced the little girl in June's image. Its title now read, "Angels at Play on Sunny Day." Trina's stare lingered at the book's contents a second longer before a head shake sent the bronze girl on her merry way. Trina watched the angel disappear around a shelf corner and was hit with the sudden revelation that the blue glow was out of her sight.

Where had Alex gone? Trina quickly maneuvered through the aisles and called for Alex as she went. No response. No sign of a wild-haired figure in sad lights. An abrupt symphony of musical clinking threw her in a run towards the front of the shop. Upon arrival, she found several miniature carousels and music boxes cluttered along the large display windows of the shop's main entrance. Mechanical dancers spun in place. Toy musicians swayed in stiff poses with those that sat on sills and swung gangly, coiled limbs to the sound of the instruments they played. Aluminum animals marched in circles. Trains curved along tracks. And, then some distance, on the other side of the window, Trina thought she glimpsed the kick of a foot. She moved to get a better angle through the mess of toys that had sent a jolt of panic through her nerves.

It was a girl with hair twisted in a braided in a faux hawk, dressed in a gymnast's leotard. Trina remembered the design of a yellow comet that streaked across the dark blue, something that no one would have seen under the giant forearm crushed against the girl's stomach and hips. With her legs in a furious flail, the upper half of her body pitched forward as her hands dug into the meaty arm to pry herself free. It was another memory in June's past, another instance where a predator found a hole in the vigilant guard of her parents. June was ten at the time, and there were complaints of a man roaming the area where she and other girls took tumbling classes. When approached, the man claimed to be part of a fundraising event. The day of June's near abduction now played in real time outside the windows of Harper's Place.

Daddy didn't barrel out of nowhere as he had those many years ago, when he startled the captor to drop his daughter before he hurled a haymaker so swift and powerful that it obliterated the candy man's jaw. Instead, Trina crashed through the double doors of the main entrance. Upon exiting the shop, captor and captured changed, replacing June and the candy man with Alex and the peddler. Light energy charged the markings on her body in white heat as she burst forward in speedy strides. Dashes turned into hovering skips as the V-shaped lines on her back shined and the air carried her. White glow coursed through the lines and dots of her knuckles of the hand that was poised to strike. Her intent was to charge at the peddler while letting loose a volley of light quills. Something hit her mid-assail, something from the inside. An icy ball of space formed within her throat seconds before the pierce of pain in her stomach. Suddenly her vision wavered between clarity and blurriness. Vertigo came with the second stab of pain, and caused the light of her marked wings to flicker and finally fade with the faltering of her air charge.

What is this? Trina doubled over after a soft landing as the heaviness of the energy's drain and pain stopped the glide short of its destination. With a quaking hand, she gently placed her palm and fingers around her throat. The cold ball of air that lingered seemed to bring about a nausea she desperately wanted to purge. Though her senses were scrambled, the lagging of her hearing caught Alex's shout of concern, the shouts to get up and the growling protest that demanded to be let go. Between the bouts of blurred vision, Trina could see the blue glow and the fear that circled the wide eyes and gaping mouth of the child within. She could see the smiling peddler. His closed lips and eyes of his rounded mask held side by side with the face of the prisoner he held at the crook of his arm. Trina thought to shout for help until she saw the same blank smiles of the people who stood around him. A crowd had silently formed, all smiling, all unmoved by the lost soul's distress or concerned with the young woman doubled over on the floor. There was no comfort in seeing the familiar faces of the cabbie and the hostess in the crowd too for they had the same sinister, placidness on their faces.

With the way their heads crooked slightly upward and in one direction, Trina guessed they were waiting for someone or something. Whatever it was the crowd gazed in anticipation for, was somewhere behind her. The look of the buildings and the circled platform of the floor told her that the place that would be center stage for this congregation would be the town plaza's fountain. Before she even thought to follow their gaze, she spotted movement. There were giggles as low bronze figures maneuvered through the crowd. Right away, Trina recognized the children from earlier as they playfully weaved through the forest of tall legs of the town adults. As they made their way towards the plaza's center, some of them had a change in their upright gait. Their tiptoed running bent to a hunched scampering and then to a frantic scuttling like a spider. Terror crept in, and intermingled with nausea as Trina watched arms, necks, and legs stretched into crooked limbs. Twisted claws and gnarled paws scraped across the ground, and heads shifted into misshaped skulls. By the time the low creepers had surrounded Trina, the children were no more. Gaunt fiends with swollen bellies and distended extremities caged her in their small circle. Jack o' lantern maws and jaws disfigured by the crooked jutting of under bites opened, and spewed out a film of web-like strings to cover their prey. Trina tried to raise up or to even turn, but she could barely lift from her slouch on the ground.

"Perfect! Oh perfect!" went the merry singing of a shrill voice. "The timing of your arrival is most punctual, indeed."

"Swordsman?" Trina knew the voice before the silvery cherub hovered into her line of sight.

"Why so distraught? I bring good news. Wonderful news, in fact," the swordsman began his measured circle on the edges of the fiendish circle. As the cherub continued to relay his message, Trina's eyes could only follow as far as her head would allow her to turn. "No longer will the burden of this quest and cargo be yours to bear. The Golden One will deal with this plague that seeks to corrupt your sister's innocent soul."

Trina shook her head at the swordsman's fiery declaration and the hushed murmuring of agreement in the crowd. Confusion at the words of the cherub brimmed her eyes and in the small instant that her eyes flickered towards the lost soul, she felt dread. Whatever was going on, she had to buy some time to figure out their escape. "What did you say to the mayor? Whatever it is, there must be a misunderstanding."

Sympathy etched in the grooves of the cherub's silvery face as it gave a solemn head waggle. "Oh, you have been deceived. A child the lost soul is not. Its appearance lies to you. The Orisha know what a terrible thing that creature is. How awful of them to place such a heavy responsibility on a soul so pure. How shameful."

"You speak of deception, but I find it strange that you mentioned the Orisha when I said nothing of their involvement." Trina made her reach for the pendant as subtle as possible. She scoped her surroundings, and worked her limbs and senses to fire and, she silently prayed for Ori to provide an opening. "Looking around, Angel Town seems a slim disguise for whatever is hidden underneath."

"It is a shame that you feel poorly of our humble town, but it will grow on you in due time. Why everyone, is just beaming to know that you'll have a place with us soon." The swordsman's words made Trina's eyes meander from the fiends to the empty smiles on the bronzed folk. She thought about being trapped here and what it would turn her into and it washed a wave of goosebumps across her clammy skin. Still feeling sick, she prayed that her body and senses were strong enough for the uphill struggle she knew was on the way.

"Now, citizens … ." As the swordsman raised his voice he floated out of sight. Where he moved, the head of the crowd followed and settled on the fountain that was his stage and podium. "A wonderful privilege is upon us. The Golden Angel will soon arrive. It will be a blessing to witness the induction of our guest to Angel Town by the mayor."

"All hail, Mayor Gold!" shouted another trill voice slightly different from the swordsman.

"All hail, Mayor Gold!" the citizens chanted in unison. The cheers of their ruler continued even as the great blare of a horn interrupted their hailing.

Crouched in the web-like prison, Trina first eyed the circle of fiends. So far, the sunken sockets and mouths were agape at the activity above and behind her. She looked to the crowd next. An empty awe had also taken over the multitude and urged some to continue the chant while others like the peddler stood in silent awe. Trina's eyes zeroed in on the smiling, rounded mask, and her index and middle finger curled under thumb, and took aim. Slivers of white shimmered up the lines and dots of her fingers and knuckles but the power waiting to be released, stalled. She needed more room, more of the peddler's face to come into view, preferably the eyes. She needed Alex to know and be ready. Trina stared at the lost soul, and pierced through the unknowing until, for a wonderful second, their eyes met. Trina's heart leapt, and she had to stifle the smile and concentrate. She focused on the bridge of the peddler's wide nose, and the timing of his shifting. The second Alex's head tilted to unveil both of the peddler's eyes, Trina flicked.

Her prayers had been answered as both bullets of light tore through the fiend's netting. The first pellet of light stung the peddler's arm and loosened the grip of the arm while the second crashed into his face. The burly angel winced in pain, stumbled, and completely released hold of his captive as hands instinctively sought to ease the burns. Like the flare of electricity, somber blue flashed a sharp red as the lost soul let out a voltage of energy, and left the peddler with more than sparks of light to heal from.

Trina breathed, and drew her body. Her will pushed out faintness and fatigue as spikes of pure radiance light sprouted from her back to cut through the netted prison. The rapid beating of light wings eviscerated the webbing further, and sliced through members of the circle and repelled any rearward attacks. Arms and legs poised to spring upward for flight halted mid-curl as they buckled slightly, and shook. Another aching stab at her stomach and energy drain made her eyes widened both in dismay and strain through the shimmering onset of a blackout. Trina measured the drawing of her breaths, and her mind urged her body to make a quicker recovery.

A red light swam among the crowd like an agitated stingray, it's swift and brief figure-eight looping caused more confusion for the bronzed angels. Alex had bought her the time she needed. Vigor and lucidity returned for another exertive episode, and Trina pushed herself from the ground. She gained air and pulled herself out of reach of the clamorous mob, bound to the ground.

As Trina followed the red light in its retreat, she could see and hear the shifting. The cry of bending metal could be heard high over the monotoned murmurs of the masses. There were familiar faces among the sea of reaching limbs and warping bodies. Bellies swelled and necks extended from the normal length of their now bony shoulders. Stretched skin was drawn as tight as leather over sinuous arms and legs. Eyes and noses spread, and mandibles contorted into grinning maws sporting razors and fangs for teeth. Brassy shrieks sounded in tune with the distending of caps and orbital plates from skulls that rolled into deformity. Trina could see the taxi driver, Mr. Rousseau, and the hostess, Mari Elle, change like the others. At one point, she glimpsed the peddler. His transformation was more grotesque than the others. Multiple arms and legs sprouted from his head and barrel of a stomach. The face, burned from the light bullet, stretched apart like the bulking torso as the reaching hands found leverage to pull away from the mound that was the peddler's body. Before long, the collective transformation turned the slow lumbering of bronze into a scurrying reminiscent of a frantic pile of spiders.

Trina shivered and shook herself away from the awful mesmerize of the changing townsfolk. Her vantage point was much higher from the ground. For her, at least, she was out of reach from the fiendish horde. She took a quick survey of the fiendish horde below and spotted the lost soul leading the stampede, meandering through pockets of pursuers. The red light tread down a familiar path, the clock tower. Trina decreased altitude and followed the red glow all the while firing volleys of light to clear the path of fiends. Ori's violent tremble warned her before the rearward advance of a shadow. Trina summoned a saber of white shine from the outer ridge of her forearm, whirled around, and dragged the weapon with her in time to meet the downward swing of a long, silver blade.

It was the swordsman on the offensive. He came at her with a fencing barrage. The facial grooves that at one time sported expressions of innocence now carved a menacing smile on the cherub as Trina parried to keep up with the fast and ferocious jabs of his sword. The first round of strikes and deflections halted with silver edge grinding against the hardened substance of light. Surprise rippled Trina's eyebrows at the weight that pressed down on her resistance. The swordsman was a lot stronger than he appeared. He was also cunning, for in the reflection of the swordsman's body she noticed the glint of arrows traveling at her back. Energy bloomed from the pendant in a powerful and visible vibration. Arrows and sword shattered in the enveloping field, and knocked the cherub further back into the air while Trina tumbled downward until she crunched into aluminum.

Her back ached as she crashed into the roof of one of the cars parked below. After she shook away the daze of stars, she was thankful that Ori had not only saved her but sent her further along the escape route. Trina saw no sign of the glow, and hoped the lost soul beat her to safety. She inhaled and crept from the dent of the hood to the concrete of the road. A more severe bout of lightheadedness discouraged her from flight. She would have to make it by foot, but luckily the clock tower was within running distance. She limped into a sprint, and proceeded down the turn of streets. Fiends that had straggled ahead of the crowd met her with a shrieking pounce only to be cut down by her white-hot saber. Trina paced herself. She ran and breathed steadily to keep the vigor. She gestured her hands in a gun-like finger point, and shot down other stray fiends as they noticed her from a distance. There was another faraway blare of the trumpet and suddenly the surfaces of buildings began to bulge and roll. Trina picked up the pace of her sprint. She didn't want to spare any moment to witness what would become of the agitated stirring of roofs, doors, and walls.

In view came the familiar jutting of buildings, the same pinnacled roof between flat tops. The opening and turn down the alleyway was within reach and its sight made her kick. The lightness in her heart she felt before turning the corner soon dropped to a grinding pit in her stomach when she heard the cry. She kept the speed up anyway, and moved around the corner of the back street. As soon as Trina entered the alleyway, she saw the source of the commotion. Alex had been ensnared in the wrappings of a silver whip.

The fourth cherub calmly hovered in place, and waited for the lost soul to finally tire from its futile upsurges of red energy. When the silvery eyes of the whip wielder met Trina's glare, he smiled. She only managed one step forward before a flurry of arrows curtailed her advance. In her brief evasion of the arrows, the archer, swordsman, and trumpeter had arrived, and joined the scourger as they hovered together as a unit.

"Didn't I tell you before, miss? Nothing gets past the Silver Guard, not a soul." The swordsman's delighted hum carried the grim weight of truth.

Trina's eyes darted to the lost soul that was held hostage in the grips of a whip and realized that the angry red dimmed to blue again. The child's head lulled side-ward with eyes closed, not even stirring when Trina called. A quick survey over her shoulder revealed that the opening behind her had been blocked by the flailing gate of claws that sprouted from the surface of the building's walls. Behind her the exit was blocked, ahead of her, the cherubim obstructed the mere steps it would take to crossover into the clock tower. Alex had been captured.

Trapped, Trina took a deep breath, and gathered what little energy she had left to make a last stand. If resigning to her fate meant self-sacrifice, she thought it better to make it an effort to free the lost soul from its bonds. Fate had other plans as a gale rushed in, and carried a voice with it. Like before, the wind came from the direction of the clock tower.

"EPUELE!" The distant caw cut through the whirring of air. Trina's expression perked, first at how audible the sound was. Her next surprise came with the sudden appearance and upheaval of trailing plants. They were strange looking vegetation that were both misty and nearly white as though clouds or steam swirled around them.

Roots crawled quickly along the surfaces of buildings and halted the growth and sprouting of claws from alleyway walls. The vines came next, and shot out like spears and chains. The creeping tendrils broke through the ranks of the cherub. To Trina's good fortune, one vine pierced through the whip and released its hold as Alex tumbled from its grip. Taking the opportunity, Trina sprang forward, and caught the unconscious lost soul before she passed the barricade.

Crossing the threshold, Trina could feel the touch of coolness as the grayness of the sky and air fell upon her. Holding Alex in her arms, she hurried down the path of brick and the burning in her legs made her stumble once or twice. She tensed her back, and summoned her wings to carry them only for fatigue to stifle the effort. She kept sprinting. A head over shoulder's glance showed that the threshold was now covered by vines, but not completely. She glimpsed something forming on the other side from which she had escaped. First, she noticed the merging of hands, feet, and wings. Her eyes lingered on the writhing silver, and she thought she recognized some features of the cherubim that converged into one another to create a giant, floating sphere.

"To the top!" the man's distant cry tore Trina's eyes away from the threshold behind her. "To the top of the tower! Hurry!"

By the time Trina had reached the steps of the clock tower, the thunderous ripping of roots echoed from behind her. She broke through the door. *Climb up!* The words from inside her urged her steps along, and spurred her rush through uneven wood floors that heaved as though breathing. *Up!* She climbed up the first few flight of stairs, she still felt the floor breathing under her feet and soon took notice that the walls around her seemed to shift to the same rhythm. Her stomach felt queasy, and the hair on her head began to prickle. *Keeping going! Up!* She continued, her legs pushed over steps as her pace slowed slightly. Upon reaching the next floor, her periphery glimpsed smooth pink that peeked from missing spots of gray.

She took a closer look, and nearly screamed. She realized with horror that there were pulsing walls of flesh where wood or mirrors or pictures were missing. *Up!* Fatigue dragged at her legs, and she cradled Alex closer as she continued to push her way up another floor. When Trina approached the landing, she noticed patches of smoky root among the room's debris. The sight of the roots kept her calm and her attention away from any other morbid objects hidden within the area. Trina continued to move upward, trumping on the steps she had found in a slow, agonizing march until she reached the last room. She made it to the top floor, but her burning muscles and the loss of what to do next caused trembling legs to buckle under her. Suddenly the tower rattled. Trina gasped, and fear informed her that something huge had landed on the tower. Walls shivered then grew still as the measured creeping continued from the tower's foundation upward.

Cradling Alex close, Trina's eyes frantically searched for an escape route or hiding place. Before she could find such refuge, the giant eye hanging outside of the window found her first. The moment her terrified gaze met the ogle of the giant eye, Trina braced herself. She expected the fatal burst of a monstrous appendage shattering through window and wall to claim both her and Alex. Instead, she heard the man shouting again, but this time his voice was closer and right over the roof. Aside from the man's taunts and the monster's squawks, there was stillness.

The eerie calmness was short-lived, however, as the thumping of a tussle entered the exchange. Voices and growls raised. There was a loud rip of wood as the tower's floor suddenly swayed. Before long, the severe tilting gave way to a tumult of sound and gravity. Chaos was a cacophony of roaring, rushing air, and blurs of gray and wood. Trina's insides dipped with another shifting in gravity as the room was pulled upward. Swept up in the disorder of things, Trina felt disoriented.

"Your hand, child! Up here!"

Trina looked up when she heard the call. At some point in the chaos, the roof had been removed. Where the covering had once been, a man's silhouette stooped over the ledge with one hand stretched out to receive them. Trina reached up with one hand, and strained towards a distance she clearly couldn't reach. Smoky tendrils snaked over the cloud's jagged ledge, slithered down, and coiled around her arms and waist. When both she and the child were secure, the vines pulled them up until the silhouette's arm had tugged them the rest of the way.

"BACK!" the resound of her savior's voice matched the strength of the thunderous crack of divine force that crashed forth from his wielding of a splayed staff. Trina staved off the near collapse from exhaustion, and stumbled around to face the commotion at her back. The roost she had found pulled farther and farther away from a structure of colossal size. Though vague because of the continued stretching of distance, Trina could make out a shadowy, cetacean shape with a sunken, glittering hull for a back shimmering like lights of a city. The sight of an ever-stretching expanse was dizzying and the vastness between ledge and edifice was similar to the gap between moon and earth.

Trina gasped in disbelief at the other thing she saw in the brief aftermath of the conjured thunder. Sailing backward from its reach of the ledge was a winged humanoid, an angel. The powerful expulsion did some damage, and marred the angel's golden visage with sparse splinters of black cracks. There was a second creature made of silver, its thorax a snarling human's face melded on all sides by insect wings, segmented legs, and a reptile's tail. Trina shuddered, briefly remembering the large eyeball that ogled her from the window and how it took on the same color. Greater damage was done to the silver tetramorph for its form shattered completely when caught in the path of hurtling gold. Mouth agape, Trina barely heard her rescuers hums of relief as she watched the shapes drift fast and far until they were mere specks lost in the void.

Chapter 5

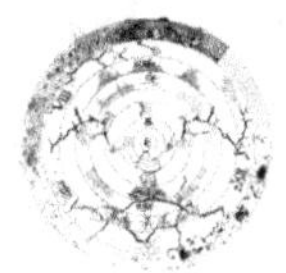

Nausea and the strumming ache in her stomach were enough for Trina to sweep hesitation aside. Lips that twisted in aversion soon pursed the rim of the bowl to down the dark fluid. It was bitter and grassy. The stuff almost reminded her of that liquid chlorophyll that her father used to and would still drink as part of his supplement regimen. She remembered when her dad let her taste the stuff when she dared. She could only describe the flavoring as being bitter and green, but not as pungent or wild compared to what she currently drank. She could imagine that the stuff in the bowl might also be green, but with the all-pervading bluish hue, it was difficult to discern a clear color. Whatever the liquid was, it was as smooth as water. It's warmth made the honey brown of her cheekbones blush. The liquid heat was soothing and it melted the cold in her throat and quelled the stomach stabs. By the time the bowl was empty, all of her ailments had vanished. Trina now felt invigorated and left with the cleanness akin to the green stuff her dad had given her.

"Feeling better?" the old man's grin showed teeth that were white and perfect. There was a sincere warmth in his expression, not the empty placidness or hidden hungriness perceived from the bronze and silver angels. Still, Trina felt the urge to distrust him. Even as the liquid cured her system of the icy poison, she quietly scolded herself for being willing to drink from the bowl. Considering what she and the lost soul had experienced, Trina should have been more cautious. After all, if Limbo was crawling with demons and evil spirits out to get them, who was it to say that this friendly old man was a soul-snatching devil in disguise. Then again, there was something familiar about the elderly stranger. Not only that, but Ori had been calm ever since they hitched a ride with their rescuer.

Trina handed off the bowl for the old man to take. She shook her head and smiled as she watched him with guarded eyes. "Thank you um, mister… ."

"Mr. Eleri will do, young lady," the old man finished her sentence, tipped his head and lifting his fila cap in welcome before he took and stowed the bowl.

With furrowing brows, Trina's head tilted upon hearing the name. Thoughts churned like the hushed turning of gears, nuts and earthy cords set about the contraption of a vehicle that Eleri fashioned. She took note of his attire, the fila cap, his shirt, a loose fitting buba, the large robe covering it, the agbada and the roomy trousers that were his shokoto. She flipped through the files of her memory in search of the old man's name. Her eyes lit up as the name Eleri brought to the forefront of her mind the other monikers associated with it. From the names down to the Aso Oke ensemble, it all started to make sense. Even the energy she felt that emanated from the white cloth of the old man's clothing, the sense of power and calm that belonged to Obatala, further confirmed what she supposed.

"You're here with the other Orisha too?" Trina could barely stifle her astonishment, especially when the old man answered with an easy smile and a steady head bob.

"Why, of course. It is part of my job as diviner, after all," Mr. Eleri smirked. "Besides, we were getting worried about you and how things were going. Thank the Maker that Osumare and I crossed paths with you and Ori."

Trina's eyes squinted. She was confused at first until she gazed at the staff. Carved from some opaque gemstone, the neck of the cane meandered then straightened at the head where outspread wings flanked the face of a snake. The vitality hidden within the stone rod felt somewhat similar to what rested in wait in her pendant. Trina smiled up at the snake's head and could perceive that something invisible smiled back. When she thought about all that transpired, her eyes fell on the lost soul still unconscious in her lap. The thought of her near failure as a guardian caused both her head and smile to fall.

"Never take food from strangers. The oldest trick in the book and I fell for it." Learning never stops, even when one's soul did cross over into the afterlife. In the Valley of Ancestors, a lot of lessons were told through stories. Some were shared directly in remembrances of tales passed down from different cultures while others came from secondhand murmurings of what they gathered from schools they attended during life. From the abduction of Persephone to the warnings about faery food, Trina remembered several tales where characters were either warned of or faced the consequences of eating strange foods in even stranger lands. It seemed simple enough to avoid, especially when one was forewarned ahead of their destination. Traveling to Limbo, taking this kind of precaution should have been a given, and Trina assumed it would be easy since her kind were immune to the sensations of hunger. The incident at Angel Town, however, proved otherwise.

"Don't lose heart," Mr. Eleri assured. "Everyone making it out okay is the most important thing."

"The smell, that hunger, and thirst. It all hit me out of nowhere." Trina shook her head. She still remembered the rich aroma of roasting meat. "Ori and even Alex knew, and it flew over my head. If it weren't for you, Mr. Eleri… ." Her voice trailed off. She did not want to state or think of the awful possibilities of what could have been.

"Mistakes happen, even to the most careful. Considering you were literally in the belly of a beast and managed to make it out with your soul intact is not something even us Orisha could claim." Mr. Eleri's tone and gentle demeanor grew dark. The old Orisha's change in mood and last sentence ran a chill through Trina's being. She was speechless, and wondered what he had meant by being in the belly of a beast? She did not have to ask as Mr. Eleri read her expression instantly from only a glance. "That son of a devil lives up to the wicked legacy of his lineage, especially when it comes to deception. He must have found a leviathan whose size and strength he could manage and killed it. The preta likely ate the carcass of the wretched creature hollow."

"Preta?" That was all Trina could utter as the mere mention and thought of the potbellied fiends made her throat turn dry.

Mr. Eleri nodded, and continued his explanation all the while steering the climbing vehicle of plant, wood, and vine. "The ghouls you encountered in that farce of a town were the hungry spirits of the most wicked in life. Their hunger was so ravenous for souls that only demons of exceptional strength can tame them. Likely, he trained them, using them both as actors and background in constructing a trap. Everything else, the buildings and sky, the smell and the sense of hunger, the thirst, and the water that poisoned you, all of it was an illusion of his making."

Trina swallowed and recalled the praises of the cherubim and what she could make out of the creature that Eleri expelled. "The Golden Angel?"

The Orisha's face suddenly curled as though he had tasted something displeasing and sour. His head gave a measured waggle from side to side. "An incubus. Narakai, the descendant of an overlord and devil. The worst kind of hell spawn to have at your heels."

Trina, fell quiet as a heavier sensation of dread touched her skin and seeped into her nerves. After what she had heard here and there about Limbo, she had anticipated some danger. On a plane rumored to be on the edge of damnation's gorge, it was not unusual to encounter maligned entities. Stray demons encountered in Limbo were no doubt deadly but were minor in ranking and strength. Archdemons let alone devils were never permitted above the edge of the abyss or so she thought. "Isn't something that evil supposed to be placed somewhere else?"

Eleri nodded. "But in some cases, they're stored in short-term prisons designed to further deplete their strength before the final transference. Somehow, this one got out."

The old man's eyes narrowed and he gazed inward. The gears of his mind turned and sifted through all of the possibilities of how such a circumstance could occur and that he needed to inform the others. A fleeting glance at the small spirit in his companion's lap conveyed the unease he felt. "Like the others, he'll be after the lost soul. He'll be persistent, but the knock I gave him should slow him down. Between that and this maze, you and the lost one have a bit of a leg up in your journey. We'll see to it."

Trina took a deep breath, letting Mr. Eleri's words of assurance sink in to quell her growing anxiety. She looked at the lost soul, zeir eyes still closed even as she removed a stray strand of hair from across zeir face. Now that she had settled down, her attention drew towards her surroundings. To say that this new environment of Limbo was strange was a severe understatement. It was downright bizarre. Everything was washed in shades of blue. The climbing coach that the three sat in crawled across a whitish surface that looked rough to the touch.

The more she examined the ground that the cart walked on, the more it reminded her of bleached piths of coral of matter or inner bone. The strange road was giant, its curving hinted towards an overall tubular shape. With the climbing coach's many legs creeping up the road's vertical curve, Trina had the impression of riding on the back of an insect that travelled up the branch belonging to a tree of immense size.

As far as the eye could see, there were more pale branches connecting to one another like cancellous tissue. A dusky firmament could be seen between the spaces of the ascending network. With the setting's ghostly glow, Trina half expected to see a moon or something of its likeness hidden somewhere in the great above. Instead, she caught the occasional electric ripple of hot pink that stretched its quivering rings across parts of the dark indigo before completely vanishing. Where she was, the tube-like passage was too wide to lend a view of what might be the road's trunk. Trina's eyes strained outward and searched the lower half of the environment, yet the utmost base of this blue matrix remained a mystery.

"Talk about anxiety-inducing," Trina said, in awe of such a staggering landscape. "How could anyone ever find their way around or even out of this place?"

Eleri's lips crept upward in a gentle smile. "Working through the Marrow can be onerous. Still, there's always a trick to things even tangled mazes like this one."

Trina's eyes jumped slightly upon hearing the name of the blue plane. She thought of the designation of the scape, and how microscopes rendered strands of hair on the scalp or inner parts of the body or cells into otherworldly environs. The more she thought of about this, the more the name fit with its setting. "What brings you to the Marrow?" she finally asked.

"On an errand, same as you," Eleri answered. His eyes focused in front of him for a moment to check the progress of the climbing coach's movements. The walking vehicle completed its upward climb of the first branch and now proceeded in a horizontal trek. The Orisha only settling back in his recline when he was sure the coach found a rhythm in its floating leaps across small gaps. "Ever so often, interims appear, giving way to rims of sleep. Osumare and I have an appointment with a seer." Then, with his head slightly tilting towards her, Eleri flashed a wide grin. He winked, his voice rasping a little above a whisper as he said, "The sleepy head is likely napping at his favorite fountain."

The corners of Trina's mouth lifted a little at the old man's jest. Only when she thought of her own sought-after destination did her smile fade. For the longest, following the whims of the lost soul's trail had been her only guide. But, something happened in Angel Town, something that she felt had the answer.

When she thought of her time spent there, her loss of where to go next gradually gave way to a nagging at the back of her mind. The answer she sought was at the cusp of remembering. She kept searching, digging into the recesses of her memory until, finally an answer surfaced on her lips.

"Dead End?" Trina's absentminded utterance made the old man flinch. His calm study of the climbing coach's travel suddenly rattled by a disquiet, but, in her musings, Trina barely noticed. "I don't know if it was only an expression or an actual place, but the child mentioned it earlier. Maybe it's a lead?"

The subtle sliding of Eleri's eyes landed on the lost soul and lingered where the spirit rested. Something much deeper than sadness rippled across the old man's face before he averted his gaze to close his eyes.

"It is a place where souls go to die."

"What?" Trina blurted out. Her mouth set agape and her eyes stretched long. When she somewhat had a handle over her initial shock, her face clouded over both in confusion and concern. What did he mean by a soul dying? The Orisha's words seemed convoluted, or perhaps more than anything, enigmatic. She did not understand what he had meant. Still, there was a graveness about him and his weighted words that washed her being with the prickly sensation of dread. It made the air lock tight in her diaphragm, and left Trina waiting with bated breath for the old man's explanation.

"Souls are eternal, but there are ways that souls can meet oblivion. The Dead End is such a place that welcomes those wishing to fade. Any soul planting themselves in that place are erased," Eleri answered. His tone was calm but weighted with the heaviness of his message.

"So then they… they'll disappear?" Trina stammered. Her voice quivering as tears clutched her throat. Her efforts to stay composed and clear-headed tested as thoughts of the worst rushed through her mind.

Eleri gave a slow nod, his thin lips stretched to two somber lines. "The many life cycles they've had under those seals, each hardship encountered without one another stacked upon the last. It must have taken its final toll on them. Their soul must be as tired as their bindings are worn if they are longing to fade away."

Trina's entire mien pinched in confusion. *Seals? Bindings? Many life cycles?* Eleri's words echoed in her mind as other thoughts spun in a crazy whirlwind. For a moment, she fell silent, and her gazed turned inward as she searched for order in the inner tumult. Thinking and rethinking, the rushing finally slowed as one discrepancy in the Orisha's words drew to the forefront.

"Their soul? You speak as though they… ."

"Are one?" Eleri interjected. "The sister you've known and were raised with, and the lost one resting in your lap are two halves of a whole."

Dazed by a revelation too surreal to digest, Trina could only look down and think. The blue spirit barely stirred since the rescue and still held fast to slumber even as Trina's slender fingers smoothed slivers of zeir thick, wavy hair.

Raising her gaze to the blue scape, she still saw the upward rise and crossing lattices of strange stems. Markers of where they had been and where they were going were still indiscernible, at least to her. The only notable change in the Marrow were the cell-like globes speckled throughout the scenery. These flesh-like orbs spun in levitation in some of the wider spaces of the lattices. In the brief quiet, Trina wrestled to piece her thoughts together. There was a sliver of doubt, a small, but still unwelcome inkling of uncertainty in the intentions of the Orishas. More than anything, the revelation left her with a need for answers. Suddenly, she was reminded of the parting message left by one of the cherubim.

"Back at Angel Town, the swordsman said things about Alex. He said that the lost soul was not what ze appeared to be," Trina said. Her eyes were dispirited and glassy as she looked up at the old man.

Eleri stalled, his lips tightening into a guilty bow. He could feel the weight of disbelief imbued in her stare. He sighed, and prepared himself as his gaze met hers.

"Their soul is very old. Its age surpasses that of the world where you and your ancestors once dwelt. It is primordial, even in the sense of the overworld that I and the others were born into."

Trina blinked. Her head slowly swung forward and her mouth slightly parted. More words went over her head while others knocked the wind out of her. For a second or two, she fell quiet, and concentrated on trying to accept what Eleri had divulged. The only words she could find were from her recollection of events in the false city of angels. "He also said that the Orisha had placed some sort of heavy burden on me. What else have you all been hiding?"

"So much to explain," Eleri breathed. "Perhaps I should start from the beginning. A little bit of the start was what the Creator told me," The Orisha said and smiled softly. "The rest, I remember." Suddenly there was a stall as the old man's eyelids crunched together. His spindly fingers massaged the stress from his brow and to keep at bay the sharp pain as his memory worked to draw near something dangerous he had buried deep into his subconscious.

"Mr. Eleri, what's wrong?"

The crinkled eyes of concern soon stretched wide in alarm when Trina noticed the frantic crawl of white slivers rippling like lightning through the Orisha's cloudy gray hair.

"It's fine," Eleri whispered. His hand was raised in gentle assurance. Trina was still alarmed, even as the Orisha began visibly to relax and the white streaks disappeared. Though reluctant, she stayed her movements, ready to hear the old man's tale.

"Before space or time existed, there was only the Creator who sat still, alone, thinking. After a countless period of meditation, it was decided that three sets of children would be made. When the Creator let loose his thoughts, he fashioned the Aeonicsphere. It is the eternal. It is what some deem the afterlife where heaven and hell exist. When the Creator opened his eyes, light leapt from them and we, the first set of children, were born." Eleri's expression softened again as though remembering happier times from the past. "Back then, there was only heaven. The first of the Orisha were more than what we are now. We among other beings were a more complete form of ourselves. We were Aeons. There were scores of us, more than there are stars in all the skies of the material plane. At our birth, we spent most of our time exploring the Aeonicsphere and our gifts. We bonded with our Creator and each other."

Her curiosity piqued, Trina's eyes crinkled into narrow slits. The name she had heard often among the Orisha prompted her to ask, "So then, Olodumare is the Creator's actual name?"

Mr. Eleri smirked. "The Creator has many names and had an all-pervading presence so close that its voice could be heard."

For a brief moment, the start of the story brought Trina out of brooding. The old man's description alone left her feeling a little awestruck and, in her mind, she could almost see a vast space suddenly filled with extraordinary beings. Admittedly, the sight of Eleri's cheerful reminisce of the past also lifted her mood. Still, there were things about the story that she had yet to understand. Hanging on to the Orisha's every word, her sense of awe changed to curiosity, as the old man's mien went from wistful to quizzical.

"When the Creator moved for the first time, the second birth happened. The Creator's rise and steps shifted apart places of creation that were still dark," Eleri continued. "Somewhere in the distance, hidden in the largest cleft of the dark were the second set of children. Far-flung from the first-generation throng hid the greatest crevice of the dark, a place later named the Black Dive. Nestled there was a being so beset in consternation it not only refused to emerge, but its intense indecision nearly divided its mind in two."

"Was that my sister and the lost one, back then?" Trina could tell from the dimming of the old man's tone that she had guessed right, even before he answered with a head nod.

"For the longest, it was known as the Second Born. The Creator was aware of its apprehensiveness at suddenly being. A welcoming committee of sorts was sent to the Black Dive, hoping to coax it out of hiding. Some of the Aeons were not as keen in dealing with the Second Born's reticent nature. Still, there were the nurturers of our camp, that tried." Eleri's chuckle interrupted the somberness like the sun breaking through clouds. "Yemoja frequented the Black Dive more than most. She barely had any luck getting it to break the surface of the watery dark, let alone get its name. Still, she, others and I remained patient and hopeful for its interaction, the Creator most of all. Especially with preparations for the birth of the third generation, we looked forward to the joyous occasion. We never imagined that disaster would force our first meeting."

Trina's stomach tightened. Only once did her eyes leave the storyteller when the lost soul moved slightly in her lap. She felt as tense as Eleri's eyes looked, and for some reason a small part of her thought it better for Alex to stay asleep through the old man's tale.

"Somewhere along the line when plans for the third generation was underway, some of us went astray," Eleri continued. "It was the wish of the Creator that his children take part. While many of us gladly took on the responsibilities delegated to us, others felt differently. There were those who formed ideas of rulership while the more disgruntled ones coveted the task of others. From arrogance and jealousy to greed and cruel curiosity, vices caused a rift between us. Factions were formed, that pitted Aeon against Aeon. Accord dissolved completely, and the first war began. What many mentioned in religious texts about warring angels and devils were abridged versions of events, an echo of the battles between Emanators and Corruptors."

"Are you an Emanator?" Trina asked.

"I was." Eleri answered. "In the beginning, we fought only to stop the conflict. We were much stronger than our misguided brethren, and with every victory, I was sure they would come to their senses. I underestimated how stubborn the Corruptors were. As the Emanators became more focused on order and control, more so than restoring the harmony, they too lost sight of things. When they could no longer hear the Creator's voice, I and others splintered off into mediating groups to relay messages to stop the war. With all the noise brought by the fighting, we had no idea what we had sown."

Eleri paused and winced as he was hit with another bout of headaches. His dark gray set to rippling again with an even more frantic dancing of white streaks. Trepidation coursed through Trina's veins, not only from witnessing what ailed Eleri but because for a brief moment, fear flickered across the old man's face in the seconds he glanced at the sleeper in her lap. With measured inhales and exhales, Eleri did what he could to ease the episode as he continued. "It started with the trickling of tears, then a distant crying no one bothered to hear. The calamity that came upon us was the first storm. At the eye of this storm was the first monster, the Divine Monstrum. It destroyed Emanator and Corruptor alike; its terrible wrath tore through the eternal. Even the combined forces of the remaining Aeons weren't enough to stop it. Eventually, the Creator intervened and forced the Divine Monstrum into a deep sleep, split it into two, and kept it in stasis."

"And the Second Born?" Trina asked with bated breath.

"A victim of our war. The Creator restored the broken remains of the Aeons. As survivors of the ordeal, we were fearful and confused at why the monster was spared. The Corruptors' other ventures were found out later. The conquest of the Black Dive was one of their exploits. The consequences of our inaction and what the Second Born suffered under their regime was its transformation into the Divine Monstrum. Further investigation of the war's aftermath discovered another casualty."

As Eleri spoke those words, his eyes hooded in shame. After a few seconds of silence, he managed to speak through his guilt. "Under our noses, the Corruptors stole excess materials that the Creator produced to form the third generation. When the war started, the nurturing of this material to completeness, halted. The Corruptors took the stunted substances, and degraded it further through experiments. Traces of life were salvaged from the rubble the Corruptors deemed failures of their works. These vestiges were what remained of the third generation, the Mortalis. The harsh system they were trapped in was a realm that greatly dwarfed the eternal, the place often thought of as the physical plane, the Nous Submateria."

"Submateria? The living world!" The eve of revelation knitted Trina's brows until it dawned on her what Eleri's explanation meant. "Then, the humans, people, we're the Mortalis? We're the third generation!"

"Humans, animals, even those that consider themselves immortal, all Mortalis," Eleri confirmed, then continued, "Beings of impermanence existing in a system that one would describe as hellish. At that point, things were delicate as we proceeded in working with the Creator to make repairs. Direct extraction of the Mortalis or destroying the system would result in their destruction. Instead, we tempered conditions the Corruptors made by modifying their system in addition to a process that, would gradually restore the Mortalis to what they were meant to be. This gradual process is a restoration program of sorts."

Trina forced an airy chuckle of disbelief. "I have the feeling that the whole life and death thing was part of this process."

"And don't forget rebirth," Eleri chimed proudly as though pleased with a student who solved a riddle or understood a lesson.

"I still don't understand," Trina shook her head. "Why didn't you tell me before, in the beginning?"

Eleri's smile faded again. His inward gaze conveyed his worry and his search for the right words. "Conditions surrounding state of affairs is more pressing than you can imagine. My peers and I gathered in council. We reviewed every twine of fate, all of the scenarios played out by your grandparents, your ancestors, us, and all of its results. Even when the one golden outcome revealed itself, proceedings had to be handled carefully."

As the Orisha spoke, Trina could feel the gravity of his words. The mixing of unease and hope shaded his eyes, and his prolonged pause of silence had arrested her in a consternation that set her skin to prickle.

"Believe me, child, our intentions were never to mislead you," Eleri said as his eyes met hers, his voice apologetic. "Had your family found out the true nature of your quest, they would have jumped in to take your place and rightly so. We had even quarreled among ourselves about how best to protect you, about administering the rite even as the fates showed that our efforts would end in failure. But seeing your strength throughout, you have proven time and time again that you are the Light Bearer. You are the only one who can succeed in carrying out the Raising."

Trina frowned. What was a Light Bearer? More importantly, what was this rite that only she was meant to fulfill? She had many questions that she did not have to prompt the old man to answer.

"There is more to the restoration process. Just as the Creator had plans to save the third generation, the same intent was for the Second Born," Eleri explained. "The stasis the Creator made to still the Second Born was short-term. To extend its inertia, the Tri-Hold was formed. The complex binding had three key parts. The first two bindings, the

Tether of Reincarnation, and the Tether of Space/Time, slowed the convergence of the two halves and kept these parts separated. The third component was the Seal of the Mortalis, a binding that grounded diminutive form of the halves to the Submateria."

"That doesn't make sense," Trina blurted out. "Why have something so dangerous embedded in something so fragile?"

"Because of a greater threat. During the restoration process, we had remedied a great deal of the damage caused by the Corruptors. Still, many of their devices remain. The greatest instruments of their subjugation, are the Archons. In every era, an Archon arises in the Submateria. In the past, the Mortalis have successfully defended themselves, but the Archon of this current age will be an enemy they will not overcome alone. The Second Born is the only sure victory the Mortalis have but even with it, the risks are high." Eleri chuckled to himself at the bleakness of the two options. "A fate worse than death awaits them, should the Archon be left to his own devices, but oblivion is sure once the bound one is loose. But in the Miracula," he said with a smile, "are four Heotrons to wield the forces of the divine and three Light Bearers to pierce through the darkness. In these seven souls imbued with powers cultivated by Aeons and the All itself, there is hope. The Archon will emerge, and the Tri-Hold will not hold forever. Through you and the other six, the Submateria can be saved, but not if the Second Born disappears."

As Eleri said this, he placed a hand on Trina's shoulder. "When the time comes you must send it back from the brink. Only you have the power to perform the Raising."

Trina was scared. Even as there was comfort in the hand placed on her shoulder, it was small compared to the task set out to her. Still, she was determined. She would not turn back even if she could. With everything left to lose, she had no choice, but to try and succeed.

✳✳✳✳✳✳

Losing herself in the surroundings of the Marrow was a welcomed respite from Eleri's attestations of creation, fate, and destiny. Beforehand, Trina loathed the thought of being dragged into the monotony of traveling through a seamless landscape. But, as she found peace in distraction, she began to notice the subtle changes in topography. By the end of the old man's narrative, their trek went into a convenient path devoid of blocks of verticals in the matrix that the coach had to climb over. It was a one-way route like a cleared trail through rising, clusters of pale blue stalks. From looking upward, Trina felt more like an ant on the ground of a grassy lawn than a traveler walking through a forest. The expansive base of these shoots tapered slightly in width as the trunks rose to the firmament. Polypores large enough for two people to stand on were shelved at the near height of the stems. Sometimes the shelves presented a strange show, an ethereal menagerie of shapes dancing across a lofty stage. Things familiar and not, faded in and out of the platforms like fleeting reflections from a window of a passing car. Eleri called what Trina had witnessed minor rims of sleep.

When an hour or so had passed, the timberland of blue shoots lent itself to another web with fewer junctions than the last. The introduction of new terrain brought about new and stranger structures. Levitating between the largest gaps of webs or the complete disconnect of the junctions were sphere-like objects. In contrast to the pale shoots and webs, the globes took on a murky color of blue. Trina could feel the pulse of humming in the air more than she could hear it. Aside from the quiet tinkling brought by the wisps of the minor rims of sleep, the hum of the globes was the most noise she had heard.

"Doing all right, young lady?" Eleri asked, finally breaking the tense silence between them.

Trina nodded, although looking at her lap, the worry she had somewhat buried in her survey of the Marrow had resurfaced. Save for a shifting here and there, Alex's eyes remained closed for most of the trip and that left her concerned. Being in the Marrow, it was hard for her to keep track of time and the more they wandered through the network, the more she wondered about the progress of their travels. "How do you know where you're going, Eleri?"

"The scent of lilies," was Eleri's simple answer. "It is faint, so I gather we are getting close."

"I don't smell anything." Trina sulked, partially finding her glum statement and wish ironic considering what happened the last time she followed her sense of smell. "Am I even going the right way? You may be headed to where you need to be, but I don't know."

"The lost soul knows," Eleri assured. "The little one feels even more urgent than you, yet ze rests. Sure, that ze is heading to zeir other half, ze is likely conserving what little energy ze has left while still moving along zeir path. I imagine that our journeys are headed down the same path."

Trina had hoped so. She wrapped her palm and slender fingers around the mask of Ori, and prayed in silence. Half an hour into the sparse webs the climbing coach had traveled to one of the lone cliffs. In view of the passengers and driver was a globe. Trina scowled. Up close, the globe took more of the shape of a cell or particle that was gaseous and fleshy. It seemed uneven with areas of its surface that was wavy and throbbing. Its cloudy color swirled as it spun in suspension.

"Feel that pull?" Eleri noted.

Trina did not have to nod to agree. With her pendant, the tugging at her curling crown and other loosely tethered objects that beckoned the globe, it was obvious that there was some form of gravitation at work. Curiosity crunched about the old man's eyes. Superfluous tendrils around the climbing coach found their use in creeping around passengers and driver as a security belt.

Suddenly, the old man acted on his dare, commanding the coach to jump from ledge and into the gravitational pull. Heavy for the air as the coach seemed, the vehicle and all its contents held together and stayed in orbit. He had to time it right. He let the coach spin a few times in revolution before shouting another order to disembark on the opposite ledge. Between Eleri's cackling of success and the coach's rough landing on to the other side, the breaking of a long sleep was inevitable.

Alex sat up with a start. Wide eyes stared at Trina in surprise but soon grew spiteful at the sight of an old man, a stranger. "Who?" Jagged slivers of red sparked from the lost soul's bristling, faded as the short burst of fight gave way to lightheadedness.

"Careful." Trina caught Alex's shoulders in mid-slump. Weakness trembled through the lost soul's shoulders, and she helped to support Alex's readjustment in her lap. "Calm down. We're safe."

Trina's consolation did little to assuage the lost soul's hostility. Alex glowered at the old man steering the coach and then turned accusatory eyes on the guardian and pointed at the driver. "Who is this man?"

"Mr. Eleri, at your service." The Orisha greeted Alex with the same smile and tipping of the hat as he had with his introduction to Trina.

"You don't have to worry about him, Alex. He's good." Trina reassured.

"He's no different than the cabbie as far as I'm concerned." Alex sneered and gave the driver the once over. "Wouldn't be surprised if there was something else underneath that old man covering."

Trina's eyes darted from the lost soul to Eleri. The old man kept cordial and composed, even as black eyes bore into him. Still, she could not help, but think of what the old man told her of the Divine Monstrum. The glimpse of fear she saw on his face was real and she imagined that same fear was now hidden underneath his calm exterior.

"I doubt Mr. Eleri would have cured me of the poison the angels gave me," Trina reasoned. "He was even nice enough to let you sleep."

The lost soul's posture stiffened, suddenly remembering the ordeal at Angel Town in detail. Alex recalled the sickly pallor of her skin and the lameness of her flight. Now, however, her skin color returned to normal and by the way she smiled even her energy level seemed fully restored. Knowing this put Alex somewhat at ease. Even so, the lost soul returned zeir wary glare on the old man. Tight-lipped, the daggers shifted from the driver then to the splayed-top cane as though searching to uncover what they hid behind their seemingly harmless appearance. The pointing of those daggers only shifted in direction when Alex's ears perked.

"What's that noise?"

The others heard it too. It was an airy popping sound. The faintness of its volume connoted that it was a considerable distance away. Eleri gave a curious furrow of the brow. Usually he would steer clear of any disturbance, but as he followed the scent of lilies he knew that his path was set where the noise took place. When no tell-tale signs of danger rang from Osumare or Ori, he continued to steer towards the sound. After a few surfs of the globes and moving from web to web, the network of tissue became cavernous. For a time that had entered an area completely hooded by whitish blue matter. The ceilings covered by tissue and holes marked some of the walls, still lent some view to the blemishing indigo outside. They maneuvered narrowed passageways and different levels of shelves. With every mile, the airy pops increased in clarity until the party arrived at a scape similar to a valley.

The first thing they noticed was the arrangements above them. Whitish blue tissue took on a mesh-like shape with gaps too wide to form a roof. Globes dotted the area, and hovered near table topped buttes and jagged pillars while others suspended themselves throughout gaps and disconnected areas of mesh. The second thing was the dark liquid-like matter speckled throughout the scape. The substance incrementally flailed outward from pale rock before recoiling from rapid reach. And the third were the gaunt and faceless shapes that peopled the land.

The grayish things had rough skin like dried paste or pulp. Some took on slouching humanoid shapes while others took on a more abnormal form. The strange things were placed throughout the area, and there seemed to be some organization, some method to their arrangement.

Upon first glance, one would have mistaken the area for some macabre exhibit, an open space gallery where crude sculptures made from the dried remains of chewed bone assembled into scenes. As the party continued a cautious trek through the valley, however, they noticed that the apparitions could move.

Within moments of embarking in the valley, Trina's eyes found the source of the airy popping. Before when she had heard the rapid pops, she had no idea that the sounds mimicked gunshots until she caught sight of a lumbering assemblage of slow-moving apparitions.

A scattered procession of humanoids walked or crawled in unison. Some of the shapes were the size of human adults while others were smaller. Their sluggish escape painfully matched the marching rhythm of a bigger apparition that pursued them. Their pursuer was a towering behemoth with four long legs attached to a wide round core. Topping the long neck beckoning towards the procession was a faceless head that was only distinct because of its small size and the barreled spigot protruding from it.

Trina wondered if the peculiar thing was an animal or machine, at first. The nozzle, she soon found out, must have been some sort of firearm that puffed out rapid shots of air and sound.

The subsequent reaction of the procession below was a collective trembling, a shattering of parts until the humanoid form was destroyed.

Upon the complete devastation of the procession, the machine paused the firing of its weapon and steps. During the machine's short respite, the bodies of the crowd rebuilt themselves only to start the scene of flight and destruction all over again.

"I've never seen anything like this." Trina shuttered, staring at the repeated performance until the lingering unease pried her eyes away. "They seem more like shadows than ghosts. Are they like what we saw earlier?" she asked, referring to the brief reveres of the minor rims.

"Scars act out their traumas here," Eleri answered. "The Marrow is a network for the innermost. Certain areas like this valley are where some of the more painful things are buried."

All fell quiet as Eleri continued to steer the crawling coach across the bleak scape. More of these half-living scars were seen. Like the procession, some of the faceless sculptures moved in replay of events. Some conveyed grotesque metaphors of torment through poses while other crouching shapes shed flakes of gray as they shivered. Another more resounding push of air called Trina to focus in on movement at a distant periphery.

The end of a disconnected mesh slanted downward, its table faced diagonally towards the valley floor. Though a considerable distance away, Trina spied movement on the downward facing table. It reminded her of the walking she had seen earlier, only the propulsion of air and dust from center outward was the cause of destruction. Situated near this particular mesh was a globe. Its gravity kept the walkers grounded on table as the scene of marching, destruction, and revive carried out its cycle.

Several miles passed before another sound broke the silence. It was a murmuring sound, soft and electric. Trina frowned, not sure if she heard the buzz of static or the distorted sighs of quiet sobs.

"Yana!" Alex called, and perked at the sound before abruptly dismounting from the coach.

Trina soon trailed after the runaway spirit and tried to catch up. Crooked figures and rocky fragments littered an uneven path as she followed. Her attempt to make up the rest of the way by flight was suddenly postponed by some strange sound and activity slightly off path. To her right was the swift upward thrash and fall of dark substance. With the dark upheaval came the same electric crackling and distorted burble. The burbling was inaudible and Trina could have sworn there was a voice in the warped sound. Curiosity pressed her further to maneuver about the debris until she found its source. Huddled figures scattered about a small space between a low pillar and a natural arch that thinned a rocky mound. Trina's face turned sour at the pool of dark sludge that three of the figures sat stooped over. Having a closer view of the ooze, the color seemed the darkest color of blue instead of entirely black. In undulation, something reminiscent of pixels glittered from the dark stuff the same way cinders gleamed from under the coat of molten lava. Voices hissed from the bubbling and sparks of peppered light, and caused Trina to hover above the pool without thinking.

"Too close!"

Eleri's caution was cut out by the unexpected eruption of muck. Trina's senses were scrambled. The muck felt as though liquid pixels mixed with melted plastic splashed against her face and enveloped her head. In between the flicker of white noise were images. The changing of each image felt as lopsided as the muck that tumbled over her eyes. The first vision was a close up of a talk show. On the television were two white men, bald and with black shirts sitting side by side as they were being interviewed. Tattooed on their heads and arms were swastikas and other white supremacist symbols. A swift transition to the next image showed her mother cradling the child versions of Trina and June in her arms and lap. She suddenly registered the image from memory. In the comfort of their old home, a mother tried to explain to her young daughters what they had just heard and seen all the while trying to console them. She remembered being scared and confused at that moment, wondering why people would despise her and the ones she loved because of their skin color. Being on television and in the comfort of their mother's arms, the hatred she and her sister witnessed seemed far away.

A third flash showed six broad black letters on white page: "Nigger." The next image showed a teenage girl in a basketball jersey of navy blue in green trim. Her light brown hair was bunched in a messy bun and her red face twisted in spite. Her mouth spit out at June the same words she saw etched in her textbook. The words that left a twinge in June's stomach in History class, and sometimes English, had knocked the wind out of her and her scoring streak one game night.

Other images assaulted her eyes and ears in rapid succession like the swift surfing of television channels. The visions were of photos, viral videos, and news broadcasts. They were of black men, women, and children. Each victim alternated from portraits of normalcy and content to the witnessing of their pain, their last breath, and sometimes worse. The next transition showed a solitary light from a projector screen washed over portions of a darkened classroom. A man, head crooked on a twisted neck, dangled in display to a grinning crowd below. In the classroom, most of the faces were cloaked in the dark. Two students within earshot and eyesight giggled among themselves and one of them mouthed the word "rag doll." Daze and disbelief collapsed into aching that gorged the throat with tears that could never fall. Instead, the last image showed June alone in the restroom stall, as she dealt with the brunt of the pain that culminated into the wrench of the gut so awful, she vomited.

When the last of the sludge sluffed off, so did the experience of June's memories. Trina found herself keeled over with one of the sculptures away from the pool. She was disoriented and it took her time to register the hands that gently ushered her to a steady standing.

"You all right, young lady?" Eleri asked.

Trina didn't feel okay, but she nodded anyway. With her nerves finally settled, the strength in her legs returned, and her heart rate slowed to a normal pace. "Something in her past." She breathed. "It was awful."

"Some of the scars still bleed," Eleri answered. "The sooner we leave, the better."

Trina shook her head in definite agreement before both hustled along the path to find their wayward companion. A brisk jog and a glide and the two quickly located the third member of their trio amid a small circle. Surrounded by crooked statues with imposing postures, Alex knelt next to a figure folded in a fetal position on the ground. Sadness tightened the lost soul's face, and a tiny hand rested atop the lying figure's scalp as though comforting it.

Seeing the body of the curled figure striped with dark and glittering streaks made Trina's stomach turn slightly. She inched cautiously towards the lost soul, and held out her hands. "Come on, Alex, we have to go."

The lost soul only looked up at Trina with scrunched eyes then back at the curled figure. Reluctantly, the blue spirit lingered a second or two longer before finally obliging to Trina's request. Then came a distant flash of a color out of place in the plane of the Marrow. Eleri's eyes caught sight of the yellow spark descending from one of the ripples of the firmament some miles away, before it disappeared. Ori trembled and Trina froze.

Alex gasped, and the lost soul's eyes stretched wide in alarm. Trina glimpsed the lost soul's twisted expression, and strained gaze beyond her shoulder. Another electric splash swept over her sight like a curtain. Craterous blue and gray gave way to soft light flickering over black. The near quiet basin populated with walking scars now came alive with the pulse of music and the crowd of a night club. And as Trina spun, anticipating the attacker, Alex's warning cry was replaced with June's.

For a moment, the assailant was one of the guys Nico, their cousin, had beat-down in one of his brawls. Humiliated at being out-muscled, the guy tricked the unsuspecting June into an outing only to face whatever form of retaliation he had planned. Instead of Nico stepping in with a swift jab of his fist, Trina fed him a palm full of shredding light. The hit connected and as the vision of the night club and assailant fell away, her eyes found the collapsing of a mouth under the crushed skull of a crooked figure that crumpled to the ground. One of the posed sculptures had moved and formed a maw to spew the blinding sludge to initiate a sneak attack.

The once still circle of statues began to stir and close in. An utter of surprise from Alex prompted Trina to look down. The curling figure lying on the ground now had a mouth that stretched open, and its arms moved to grab the lost soul. Something thin and black, a barb perhaps, was wedged in the side of its arm. A swift side step and Trina obstructed the curling figure's reach before stumping a hole in the hollow shell.

The standing figures surrounding them also had black barbs lodged in their skulls and were on the move. With a few quick sweeps of light laced arms and legs, she cut down other staggering statues closest to her. The sudden spring of vines whipped forward, and laid waste to the rest of the circle.

"On!" Eleri's voice spun Trina and Alex around to find that he had already hailed their ride. The old man had only to urge them once as the two rushed to board the coach, and as the many legs strummed in a rapid run, the land around it seemed to wake.

The riders noticed more of the figures moving towards them. Working their extremities loose from atrophy, the sculptures' movements picked up speed. Vague limbs half-submerged in the ground grasped at their passing in an attempt to trip up the cart's legs.

Alex hunkered between driver and guardian, frightened, but watchful of the lurking and the specks of black that dotted their surroundings. Eleri and Trina worked together and used projectiles to curtail the crowding further away while they cut down nearby obstructions with a light blade and cane. It was only when their cart ran out of range of the figures' menace the two settled back in their seats.

"I thought that those scars were just shadows?" Trina panted, confused. "Now, it's like everything suddenly notices us and attacks us."

"Those black quills did it. They came out of nowhere," Alex replied.

Trina recounted what had just happened in her mind. Her puzzled frown brightened in revelation as she recalled the thin black pins at the circle where the figures came to life. There were more sprinkled here and there along the path on the agitated land. Now that they were out of range of the rousing, the path before them was free of the barbs.

"This is his doing," Eleri growled. The lines of his face already strained by concentration grew even more tense as a disdainful scowl dawned his mien. "That devil found us sooner than anticipated." His harsh glare melted into an inward gaze of turning thoughts then flitted to the child-like spirit cowering in the seat before turning them outward. "We're going to have to pick up the pace. We will have to find an aperture at the major rim, or at best before then."

"An aperture?" Trina repeated and crinkled her eyes to a squint.

"The wrinkles that show every now and then in the sky," Eleri explained as he referred to the pink-laced ripples above them. "If we can find one closer than those we've seen, then it's your best bet in escaping."

"I am here, pure one." A man's warm hum spoke suddenly, seemingly appearing out of nowhere.

Trina and Alex gave one another puzzled glances before their eyes searched the surrounding rush of the cart.

"Do not fear me." When the gentle voice spoke again, its all-pervading nature made it impossible for the riders of the coach to pinpoint.

Eleri was all stubborn and grit as he ignored the call. He gestured the straps of the vehicle to accelerate its travel. There was a collective gasp as the glimpse of a sunny spark appeared. It glanced the driver's side, and like the rearing of a bewildered horse, the coach bucked backward. The wooden legs lurched, and stumbled, but quickly recovered with a side step. Eleri continued the advance until another dart of yellow caused a near topple. Eleri switched directions and tried to regain the speed the coach once traveled. The yellow was too fast. It darted in and out, to stop the coach before it could pick up full stride. Eventually, the light moved so swift that there appeared to be several. The heads of driver and riders whirled, and the coach shuffled about in circles as the light corralled them to a halt. Successful in causing enough caution in the driver to hinder the coaches progress, the source of the fleeting light zipped into view. Settling in a hover in front of them was a golden orb. It began to shift. It unfolded and stretched its round shape as it morphed.

"The burden you carry is no longer yours to bear."

As the man's voice hummed, the arms, legs, and wings fashioned themselves from within the orb. The shape of a tall man with large wings gradually slid into wholeness. The feathers of his wings, his muscular yet lean physique were well-defined on the surface of shining gold. His features were handsome and near perfect save for the one cracked line of black that splintered from one shoulder to the opposite side of his waist. In spite of the wound Eleri had given him, the Golden Angel held out his arm in welcome. His smile was as distinctive and clear as the rest of his features.

"They have told me of your plight. I am here to bring salvation."

"Out of our way, devil!" In his shout, Eleri raised both his cane and invisible burst of energy that the Golden Angel dodged with ease.

"Did you not ask for my help, Trina?" asked the Golden Angel, while he circled the coach in his hover.

"You call absorbing those wandering in that trap salvation?" Trina retorted, the frown on her face mirroring Eleri's scowl.

"We meant no ill will in enacting such extreme precautions," implored the Golden Angel, his face softening with regret. "One must be vigilant, especially against the more dangerous elements of this life."

Trina's eyes twitched, and took note of the slight venom in tone of the angel's final words. Alex burrowed in an attempt to hide. Trina spied the hint of a glare in the angel's eyes as he looked at the lost soul, and stepped in. Taking one hand to aim, she let loose a volley of light with a flick of her wrist and like before, the Golden Angel dodged them.

A sympathetic glower formed on the Golden Angel's face as he shook his head. "The old man, misguided. The lost one you harbor, a monster. Do you know the consequences of blindly following the Orisha? Your parents will face the horror of what will become of their only living child, should you carry out their errand. Let them be spared of that terror."

Trina's defensive posture suddenly relaxed. Aggression melted away from her face as the Golden Angel's eyes met her eyes as he spoke. "Rest assured that what I offer your sister is neither torment nor to be forever lost to the void. I offer a true peace for her soul."

For a moment, Trina seemed hypnotized. His words and even the tone in his voice caught her off guard and for a few moments her need to listen outweighed her desire to fight. The tiny fingers of the lost soul that hugged her leg seemed to be the only thing that kept her grounded. There was a reason she had come this far, and with the knowledge that Eleri had imparted on their journey, there was much more at stake. Besides, Trina could read between the lines, and whatever spell he tried would not be enough to woo her into compliance. "It's not time for my sister to rest in peace yet, besides I'm not about to let a demon have its way."

Dissatisfied, the Golden Angel shook his head as his frown turned sorrowful. Then, his eyes fell on the small figure wedged between the guardian and Orisha. "Being what you are, I know there is still some good in you. Surrender yourself to me, and she shall be warmly received."

Trina placed one hand on top of the small spirit's head, both to comfort and to discourage any inclination in Alex to take up the demon's offer. "Leave Alex alone and go back to Angel Town," she warned.

"Hah!" Eleri squawked. "A forked tongue seems to serve you little, Narakai."

The Golden Angel frowned and there was a subtle jump of shoulders at the sound of his true name. The taunt, announcement of his true self and the failure of his persuasiveness did what Eleri hoped. The old man took hold of the cane, and channeled his energy to combine with that of the Orisha hidden within it, and swung at his target. Caught off guard by his name, the masquerading angel failed to react in time to defend or evade.

Eleri's strike proved definitive and compelling enough that the demon's golden form burst apart like shattering glass. Wind rushed outward post concussive blast and the boarders of the coach shielded themselves from the gust. Trina flinched as something grazed her wrist and she could have sworn that she glimpsed the outward spreading of thin black shards. The Golden Angel's visage was no more, yet the air sounded with an all-pervading chuckle. All pretenses dropped, as a cool annoyance echoed around them.

"Very well," Narakai sighed exasperated. "Perhaps the mimes of agony can be more persuasive than I."

Eleri took hold of the reigns, and seized the opportunity to make an escape in the middle of the demon's attempts to stall. Trina caught sprinkles of black along the pale blue path. No sooner had the crawling coach made its rush then came the tremor. Humanoids and bulkier shapes seemed to increase in number, and passing them there was an onset of movement. It did not take long for the statues to stir again and to take notice of their passing prey.

The rousing increased worse than before. The driver of the coach pushed to perform his best steering skill as the land itself closed in on them. At grasping limbs below, Eleri pulled the coach to sidestep or gallop over the lowermost hindrances. When crowds began to form a blockade, Eleri swiftly adjusted by switching directions or using pillars as leverages of evasion. Humanoid mimes went from lumbering to running lunges, and spewed up dark sludge in a last-ditch effort when the coach swerved out of arms' reach. With the Orisha at the reigns, Trina took on the task as marksman. She dispatched outliers of the clambering with the darts of light to clear the path. For a time, this arrangement of defense kept them well abreast of danger until a cleaving missile nearly cut them down.

What hurtled at the heads of Eleri and Trina was hardened tissue fashioned in the form of a sickle. From the right of where the projectile originated, Trina spied a galloping bulk. She swiveled her head, and her nerves stung with an unpleasant jolt at what she saw. Giving chase was a mass of appendages and heads atop running legs that could only be described as spider-like. The dreadful chimera's legs tried to outmatch the speed of the coach but kept falling short of pace. Failing in its attempts to catch up, one of the chimera's arms began to stretch and its hand and wrist slowly morphed into the deadly scythe hook that nearly struck them before. Trina was quicker to the draw, and let loose light daggers in rapid succession until the chimera halted and stumbled out of sight. More of the chimeras came and flanked the coach in an attempt to fail it mid-run. Eleri's steering and the speed of the coach proved superior. He outmaneuvered the many-limbed amalgams in the foot race. Then, came a hurtling cleaver from the rear. The single firing of the projectile suddenly signaled a rain of the sharp objects.

Alex screamed. Trina could not help but do the same and thought it a miracle that Eleri managed to keep the objects from reaching them. Still, the Orisha could not evade forever and as the hooks chopped at parts of the coach, it was only a matter of time before the vehicle itself was cut down. Trina's eyes whirled around in search of a different route. Her heart jumped. Her frantic survey landed on an arrangement of land forms, globes, and disconnected mesh close enough and in alignment to make an alternate path.

"Your left!" Trina's voice raised over the commotion of fire, and directed the driver towards the new route.

Eleri's head turned slightly, and he saw the new route and abruptly cut the coach. In making the sharp veer, he signaled the unfurling of what was left of the vines. The cords were thick and long enough that the swift sweep of the creeping plants caused the line of chimeras to collapse at their heels. The topple made a heap and slowed the horde. The coach continued its gains in widening the gap, leaving the chimera further behind as the horde fumbled to recover their gallop. The coach's wooden legs strummed with ease and speed over rocky terrain, over ragged stumps of litter and finally up the first footstool that jutted from the lower body of their chosen pinnacle. With the climbing dexterity of a spider and the vines acting as leverage tethers, the coach scaled the spire in quick timing. Like a grasshopper the wooden brougham took a great leap and covered the final feet at the tower that put trio and ride into the globe's gravitational pull.

In mid-orbit, Eleri surveyed the alternative path of pillars and disconnected meshes. He made a note of the tables and hooks of each landform, of the four globes situated between them. His eyes traveling beyond the final globe and there was a gap between the basin of the valley and a suspended formation of passes. In the near horizon of the formation, bright, smoky rings of pink rippled outward before dissipation. Ethereal things twinkled on the smooth surface of the long strips of land floating still in the firmament, and Eleri beamed at finding the long sought after major rim.

"Nearly there," Eleri gasped. "Only breaths away and we're clear."

Trina had seen the smile rise on the old man's face and in following his gaze, glimpsed the islands of land in the dark during a passing revolution of the orbit. But there was still danger. There was lumbering atop the tables of the land forms, movement that all three knew were the mimes in reenactment.

Adding to the risk would be the loss of the carriage and succumbing to the horde should they fall short of gravitation's pull. Still, the short cut was a risk worth taking.

Eleri counted the timing of the orbit's revolutions. At his warning, the two riders hunkered further in their seat, and braced themselves against the shift. When they reached the top of the globe's rotation, the coach jumped, and seemed to glide from the propel of gravitation's throw. Trina could feel a dip with the gradual fall of the carriage, but it ended as long wooden legs settled onto small, flat surface of the first pillar. The first attempt was an easy landing. Eleri steered the coach, and circled the small space before making the leap towards the second globe.

Used to the timing of the orbit, the driver's jump of the second globe was easier. The landing of the upcoming surface would prove to be a trickier landing. It was a disconnected mesh, severed in a downward facing plain similar to what had been seen earlier. Spying the surface from a closer vantage point, they saw the slow-moving humanoids marching on its flat top. Like before, there was the upsurge of air, the scattering of pieces, and the rebuilding. Eleri waited, and timed the jump as the recent increment of blast of air faltered. The coach propelled itself from the second globe and glided upward, landing on the mesh's top among scattered pieces. Trina tensed. She felt Alex press closer to her side as scattered pieces scuttled about in a scramble to regroup.

Eleri's expression grew stony with concentration, and he maneuvered the coach about the rush of limbs. Sure of his position for the gravitation of the third globe, Eleri commanded the leap of the coach well before the completion of the mimes' converging parts. Pulling up from the march and away from the next upsurge of air, Trina relaxed, and felt as though she could breathe again. Then, came the second explosion.

The third globe ruptured shy of their gravitational embark. Chaos was the scattered rush of blackness and stars. Senses frayed by the sudden burst, it took time for Trina to notice that sound was stolen from her. The more the dark material of the globe dispersed, the more the vividness of the ether swept away the environment that was the Marrow. Upon being fully enveloped by the guts of the smashed globe, Trina found herself in space. The first thing she noticed was Alex and the colossal shape that Trina guessed was a space vessel of some sort. Its flesh-like alloy shined with an eerie glow, the vessel loomed at the small spirits back like some sinister planet.

Fear stressed the lost soul's face, as a tendril-like grappler looped zeir waist. From Alex's futile pry at the twisted snare to the backward tug of recoiling tendril, every movement seemed slow and weightless. Then, there was anguish in Alex's eyes as ze looked and reached for something past Trina's shoulders. Focused on the rescue, Trina pushed forward, her flight sluggish as she swam against the unbalanced shifting of wavering gravity. Within reach, Trina wrested the stem of the space grappler in one hand. It was only when she worked to pry at the restraints that she glimpsed behind her to see the focus of the lost soul's anguish, the silent devastation of a shattering planet. Just then, Trina realized that she was experiencing the trauma of Alex's past.

Trina continued to tear at the restraints, but the cord held fast. The rush of the globe's debris thinned , the clarity of the terrible craft wavered, and partially revealed the winged-figure of Narakai's shape within. With one hand, Trina grasped the cable, resisting against it to slow its drag. Like the coursing of electricity, she surged burning heat of light up the space grappler's stem. Just as she hoped, the sting of her light jolted the lost soul loose. With the dissipation of the globe's scattered parts, the sluggishness of space waned and Alex gradually pushed through the lag. Trina pulled at the tug of the grappler and let out another blast of blistering light to distract the dark shape until the blue streak that was the lost soul sped out of sight.

A sharp yank dragged Trina through the dissolving illusion of space, into the fading image of the eerie craft. She could see the harsh glare of bright solid eyes on the finely fashioned shadow of the demon's dark form. The space grappler Trina found, was the slithering projection of something serpentine laced into Narakai's arm. Before the full retract of the coil drew Trina into a choke hold, her palm masked his eyes. The two spun in a spiraling air dance. Trina lit up the demon's eyes with the burn of energy. He let out a sharp hiss, pained and angry. She had hurt him.

Next came the powerful lock of a claw around her arm, a sudden whiplash from the outward yank and the speedy carry of air. Trina felt the hard crash at her back and the frantic scratching of claws. As she looked upward in her daze, she saw the crowd forming over her. The circle of gray, featureless faces stretched open and sludge spewed out from each maw.

Trina's eyes suddenly drowned. There was the wash of white noise, and suddenly she could vaguely make out the hurried passing of a plastered ceiling overhead. Faces with mouths and noses draped in surgical masks surrounded her, and there were sounds, a distant pleading and the closeness of urgent chatter among the masked. She strained with every breath, and pulled with great effort to inhale, the chest that sunk deeper with every exhale until the compression of weight on her chest became too heavy to lift. Lungs drew in air harshly before Trina gave in to a severe bout of coughing. Released from suffocation's grip, her vision cleared.

"Easy now. One breath at a time." The Orisha instructed.

His free hand supported the back of the young woman's head as she sat up. Once the faintness of the daze passed, Trina slowly stood to her feet. Between Narakai's violent toss into the pack of mimes and the blotting of her senses under the crowd's pixelated bile, Trina scarcely knew how or when Eleri retrieved her. She only knew they had made it past the final globe, that some miracle kept most of the coach intact and Alex was nowhere to be found. Her head whipped around, her eyes flitting between alarm and bewilderment, as she questioned her surroundings.

"We're here at the major rims. It is safe," Eleri answered after reading the young woman's expression.

"And Alex?" Trina asked. She recalled what the old man mentioned earlier and the last image she had seen of the lost soul's flight.

The corners of Eleri's mouth rose and briefly broke the glower of concern. "The lost soul managed to breach the Marrow well before the demon did. Narakai's prey is out of reach, for now."

"To where?" she questioned.

The proud smile the Orisha wore fell to worry again. His head hung low as his fingers did a contemplative strum of his cane. "What lies directly beyond the aperture, I do not know. But you know where the lost soul's destination will be."

Trina nodded knowing the Dead End, the place where unfortunate souls disappear, would be the answer. Her questions of how to get there were soon answered with the change in Ori's reverberations. The pendant began to levitate. Its visage was laced in the heat of white as it beckoned outward. Positioning itself at arm's length and right above Trina's eye line, a white beam projected from Ori's forehead.

A light line expanded into a circle, and the spiral of light created its own rift that bore a tunnel through the firmament of the Marrow. The small doorway led to a space yet known, but somewhere deep down she felt that the path before her was the right one.

"I think Ori's lead is a good place to start," Trina said, assured in the guidance of the pendant.

"One thing before you go. If you find your sister's soul planted in that place, do not despair. So long as her eyes do not fully open, you still have time. Remember, her eyes must never fully open in the Dead End." At Eleri's warning, Trina nodded in affirmation. Her turn to depart stopped short, however, when the old man held up an index finger in a waiting gesture. "A second thing. When you approach the crossroads of your journey look for the name Elegba, and he will help. Dealing with him can be tricky, and he goes by many aliases. He used to have a red and black hat. Should he give you the runaround, ask about the color of his hat. Refer to him by Eshu for good measure. Do this, and you are sure to persuade him."

Trina frowned, unsure about the reasoning, but gestured in obligement to follow his instruction. After the impartation of advice, Trina moved towards the light until she disappeared beyond its rift. Sure of her safe passage, Eleri turned to the ethereal twinkling of visions around him. His feet followed the lead tap of his cane. Eleri walked to one dream in particular that had his attention. It was the lingering revere of a fountain with petals of lilies sprinkled about the surface of the water. A creature rested at its base, his hooved legs furled under supple form, his head crowned by a single antler. Parked in front of the sleeper, Eleri released the hold of the cane and allowed the splayed staff to levitate just above his forehead.

"Messenger, listen. I Orunmila, the Witness of Fate, bring Osumare, the Spirit of the Rainbow." The old man's introduction caused a stir of light and wavering color from the cane. Soon after, the clear outline of a man bloomed from the staff, his arms outstretched to mirror the splayed top of the vessel he currently inhabited.

"Behold mortal, I Osumare, am Quetzalcoatl. Take heed to my warning and instruction, this is the Plumed Serpent's Prophecy, and these are the three signs." The inner being of the staff hung like a heavy mist over the sleeper and fountain. Touched by the reverberation of Osumare's voice, the creature shivered, and lifted his head from the bow of sleep.

Chapter 6

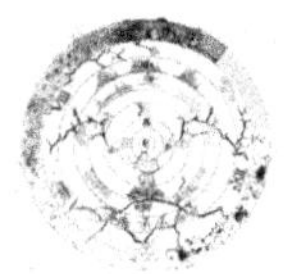

Trina squinted at the blinding white light that pinched her eyes. In the space of the light portal, Trina scarcely knew if she were flying or walking towards the tunnel's end. The only thing that kept her grounded in the space was Ori's hum that urged her forward, and the fear of becoming lost in the whiteout that kept her eyes ahead. Eventually, she noticed a dull circle in the stark white. Moving closer, the aching of her eyes subsided. The clarity of her sight pulled into focus the blur of a curtain raised over a wooden sill, that slightly revealed the sash unit of a wide window. Upon passing the ingress of the white portal, Trina found herself in an all too familiar place from her childhood.

The room was a mixture of beige, off-white, and pastels. Pink and turquoise were the Murphy valances and pleated draperies of the room's two curtains. Trinkets and framed photos lined the horizontal window sill and trim right above framed headboards. An aisle's worth of walking space separated the foot of the king-sized bed from the room's main dresser. Mirrors sided a thirty-two-inch Sony her grandparents received some Christmases ago. Littered on either side of the box set were traces of what they left behind, a tie, harmonica and flat hat, a jewelry box, silk scarf, head model and antiquated cosmetics. Dust gathered somewhat on the maple and on the gray screen of the TV, but Trina could tell that the surviving children of her grandparents had kept maintenance as they passed through from time to time to reminisce. The bed had been the only thing disturbed, its quilts ruffled, a cushion missing from the pair of pillows. Trina heard sniffling. On the other side of the bed closest to the wide window, there was movement. With the thin peeling of laminated paper, there was the low sound of shuffling and she briefly glimpsed a braided scalp peek the bed's horizon.

Trina tread closer, toeing each gentle step as though the footfall of a spirit could still be heard in the living. Moving down the short aisle, childhood memories flooded in of when they used to play hide and seek. The farm had a lot of great hiding places and indoors, their grandparents' room was a popular hiding spot either in the closet, utility pantry, or in places around the bed. Back then, she would find fidgeting socks half-concealed under the bed or hidden players hunkered down in the spaces between the bed and the window. Where the space was used as a camp-out in the past, June now used it as a temporary refuge while thumbing through pages of a photo album.

Back resting against the side of the bed, June's curled legs served as a table for the splayed covers and pages of their thick book of family pictures. Trina approached the slouched figure from behind and craned her head. She gazed past June's shoulders and noticed the first set of pictures. Polaroids, some which were faded, showed all six members of the Jettis family. One picture showed her grandparents, posed in an embrace in the back of a pickup truck as they smiled at the camera. Trina saw them age when she was in the living world, but in the couple's portrait, the two looked as young as they did when they crossed over into the spirit world. In another photo, two sons and two daughters of the Jettis household were in their late teens and wore dusted blue jeans, short sleeved shirts, and cowboy hats. Hips swayed, and arms interlaced with shoulders, as the four grinned from ear to ear. There were other photos of her mother, aunt, uncles, and their cousins in their prime as they struck silly poses or were caught off guard in a photo shoot.

Trina moved closer and got a better angle of the person who stared at the photos she cradled. June's nose looked blushed and puffy and glowed even redder after blowing into a wad of tissue paper. There was a distant, glassy look to her eyes. No tears would fall, but the stress of the lump in her throat translated to the darkness of her pupils that completely flooded over the dark brown of her iris.

June sniffled, and Trina's lips tightened in a dejected knot. At that instant, Trina wished she could wrap her little sister in a bear hug so tight that the sadness would suffocate. Instead, she found room on the top of the bed and sat near June's shoulder. She looked at the pages of memories with June.

"They look really young, don't they?" Trina chuckled and couldn't help but smile as she looked on.

June's mouth quivered and her mouth grimaced as the corner of one lip struggled to curl upward. Trina's eyes crinkled, but before she thought any further on the reaction, June turned the page again. There were four more photos, this time of her, Trina, and their generation of cousins. In one photo, three children stood side by side on the front porch dressed in Sunday clothes. Lined up in the order of age, Trina stood on the left as the oldest. Nico, one of their cousins, was younger than Trina by three years. June stood on the right and was the youngest at that time. All three held hands, and Trina and June smiled, while Nico's eyes rolled upward in embarrassment. June sniffled and gently placed her fingers over her older sister's image and stared. The smile she tried to make faltered, and the grief inside her sapped any ounce of contentment. June took her time with the next couple of pages, and struggled to unearth happiness from underneath the heaviness of depression with every photo Trina was in. Eventually, the photos of her older sister ended as the pages fell on another set of more recent photos.

For the next set of images, the Jettis siblings, their other relatives and peers were middle-aged adults while old age had touched the matriarch and patriarch of the Jettis household. Since Trina had passed, Iggy, Nico's half-brother, had joined the family, becoming the youngest member of the trio for a time before other young relatives joined the ranks. June flipped through the pages again. They showed children growing tall and adults growing old. Still, these photos were of good times in the past where the Finleys, the Jettis family, and other relatives got together for holidays, summer breaks, and weekends. Family vacations, clips of sports functions, and other significant events were all captured in pages of pictures. When June's eyes fell on a particular group photo, she paused. Relatives, both distant and closely knit, posed en masse for a family reunion photo. It was the last family reunion that her grandparents attended. Later that year, their grandfather died from a stroke. Death claimed their grandmother in her sleep six months later.

June blinked and tried to swallow down the pain as she stared at the family portrait taken three years ago. A flicker of winces flashed across her deadened expression and forced her to turn the page. In the next set of photos, there was one of her father, mother, and June dressed in formal wear. Taken June's freshman year, Mr. and Mrs. Finley had attended a function where their daughter was inducted into the honors society. The event was a special occasion for the family, and a rarer occasion for the school in that June was one of the few freshmen with the grade point average to make such an esteemed group. Trina had glimpsed that night and was as proud as her mother and father were. The three celebrated with a movie and dinner that night.

Trina's eyes intuitively fell on the same photo that June intently examined. Fingertips placed over the proud, puffed out chest of a beaming man standing on June's right. Her fingers traced across her own grinning image in the middle of the woman standing at her side on the left. The woman, her mother, had looped one hand around her daughter's arm, her weight slightly leaning into her while her other hand pressed against the handle of a cane. Like her father, her mother wore an equally pleased smile across her lips. For a time, June's fingers rested on her mother's shoulders. The attempted upturn of her mouth tightened and quivered. Her fingers went from her mother's shoulders to her cane. The smile she tried to make broke completely. Her face crumpled as the upheaval of emotional misery forced her head to drop as she gave way to a cough and hiss of hard sobs. Trina frowned. She felt her own heart ache and in her want to comfort, she placed a hand gently on June's bowed head. At that instant, Trina's phantom touch formed a conduit, and opened a floodgate of sensations, emotions, and thoughts.

The watery sting of blocked tears laced her eyes and tear ducts. The round gouge of dim fire trapped in the walls of her throat. The looseness of her stomach and the sinking ache of her diaphragm was so severe that it felt as though someone crushed it under the heel of a boot. The icy grip of numb held her wrists, and squeezed out the anxiousness that dripped down the ends of her trembling fingers. The same chilling spasm drained strength from the muscles of her legs and ankles. The thoughts clouded between a dwindling hesitation and a growing finality. And then, there was the plan.

June did what she was usually good at, doing research. She was careful to cover her tracks of internet searches as she gleaned information from documentaries and books. She had paid close attention to when her parents worked. She studied the pattern of when her mother, aunts, and older cousins frequented the farm. There was the razor in her pocket and the sleeping pills she procured from her complaints of having insomnia. They had been stockpiled for months. Except for a few things, almost everything she needed to follow through was already prepared.

In that brief moment of contact, Trina knew that at least ten or so bottles were in one of the dresser drawers, hidden underneath the folding of old clothes. Everything Trina now knew and felt made the breath she seized form a gasp. Air trapped in the cage of her lungs and her mouth was agape. As both hands flew up to clasp the circle of shock, it closed. With her eyes stretched open, Trina gazed down at the girl whose head curled in the enfolds of bent arms and legs. June's shoulders shook even as the sobs subsided into silent pulls of air. The tears that June could not spill instead rolled down Trina's cheeks.

"Just ... just don't move." Trina stammered and hoped with all hope that June could at least feel what she could not hear. "It'll be okay, June, just stay there." Trina outstretched her hands to calm June. Trina backed away almost as slowly as she raised to stand. Her eyes stayed glued on the broken girl huddled on the ground and feared that she would disappear should her eyes go elsewhere.

Trina needed help. She silently prayed to Ori, to anyone to come help. Answering her inner pleas came a movement and brightened space out of the corner of her eye. Trina dared to direct her full attention to what had been in her periphery. Normally, there was a utility pantry adjacent to her grandparents' bedroom and across the hall. Instead of the pair of old washer and dryer cluttered with clothes and detergent, there was an open space. It was an office area complete with shelves, an L-shaped office desk and a leather rolling chair. A coffee table sat between a couch and two cushioned chairs for visitors to use during parent conferences and interviews. An organized mess of papers, notebooks, and writing utensils decorated the desktop on the main desk. Award plaques, paintings, inspirational banners, and photos bedecked walls and cabinets of the space. Other articles, books, a glass apple, plastic knick-knacks, hinted that the office was somewhere in a school. As soon as Trina recognized the room as the principal's office, the front door to the suite opened.

The first person was a woman with a short, hippy figure that fitted trimly in a black and white dress suit. From the signature cinnamon hair just past shoulder length and wide smile, Trina knew right away that it was Ms. Lacey Parker, the freshman assistant principal. On one side she held a water bottle in hand and cradled a notebook in the crook of her arm. Using her free hand, Parker stepped aside while holding the door, and allowed the principal to come through. Trina marveled at the sight of the second woman who shuffled through with a cane and paper bag. Today she wore an olive pantsuit and pearl blouse. These days, she had her black hair styled in a tapered curly cut.

"Momma?" It never failed for Trina to get misty-eyed, every time she would check on her from afar. And now, as she drew close to the dark honey-toned woman who set her bag on the office desk, it was hard for Trina to fight what was welling up in her stomach and throat.

"Thank you, Lacey," Mrs. Finley said. She did not hear the pleas of a ghost. Instead, she grabbed hold of the water bottle Ms. Parker was nice enough to carry. With drink and bag on the office desk, the principal moved the sliding chair to the space at the workstation where she made room to eat. Famished, she took the breakfast burrito meant for a morning meal from the bag, and proceeded to take bites from it for her late lunch.

"Those boys were at it again and you-know-who is headed this way," Parker warned with a sarcastic tone.

"Um," Finley nodded, her mouth muffled with food. Then, she swallowed and with her third bite down, she answered, "Just ten minutes."

"All right, Debbie Deb. I'll catch you in 20," Parker chimed and winked before she exited the office.

Finley smiled, thankful that in the midst of the bedlam of the school day, she was able to find some peace and time to eat. She enjoyed a few minutes of sereneness and her meal as she sat in the quiet of her office, unaware of the presence that hovered behind her.

"Mom?" Once again, Trina's calls fell on deaf ears. Fear gripped her knuckles and caused laxness to quake at the joints of her fingers. She was at a loss, desperate for a way to communicate, desperate for more time. She prayed to Ori for an answer, but could not hear his voice. In a wish to feel some comfort of her own, Trina slumped over her mother's shoulders in a hug as tears spilled from her eyes.

"Please, Mom. I don't know what to do." Trina's plea was hoarse. Her lungs were shaken and heavy from grief and dread. "June's going to die. Please, help us."

Finley still did not catch the sounds of imploring nor did she feel the squeeze of her deceased daughter's hug. But something happened. As the woman's wandering eyes suddenly focused on a long-ago photo of two little girls. There was a pause in Mrs. Finley's eating. Trina straightened and recoiled from the hunched over hug as the woman sat upright in her chair. The few seconds seemed like minutes as she stared at the image before taking the prized memory in her hands. It was a photo of her two daughters dressed in diva costumes. Their beaming faces were decorated with paint as a substitute for makeup. On top of their heads were plaits tangled with messy ribbons and barrettes. Their feet were almost non-existent as they wore their mother's over-sized heels. Melancholy shrouded her eyes as Finley stared at the photo and a soft smile twitched across her face. Suddenly, the corners of her mouth fell as sentimentality was suddenly touched by a wrong feeling. Focusing in on June, Finley could not shake the sinking in the pit of her stomach. Upon seeing her mother's worried frown as her thumb lightly caressed June's image, Trina knew that her own distress had somehow bled through and reached her.

Trina's heart nearly leapt from her chest. That tiny emergence of hope was snatched away from her, however, as thoughts of a password, a will, and indecision inserted itself into her mind. The residue of June's thoughts still lingered in Trina's being. Whirling around, she now saw that June had moved from their childhood hiding place to the edge of the bed. Trina marched from the principal's office to a bedroom and moved across the aisle between the bed and dresser.

Trina looked over June's shoulder. In her hand, she held a photo she had taken from the family album. In the photo were two boys who had just finished playing a pick-up game of basketball. The older of the two wore a black skull cap with long matching shorts and a black T-shirt over a thick body on the verge of shedding baby fat. On his face, he wore his signature "too cool" scowl and arched eyebrow. His right hand held a green water bottle while the other arm hooked around the forehead of his half-brother in a headlock. His captive, a younger boy who still had a baby face, but had grown some in height, wore a navy-blue jersey over a white T-shirt. Hunched over and slightly off balance from his half-brother's headlock, a goofy open-mouthed smile stretched across his face in mid-laugh. They were their cousins, Nicholas Marshall Lawrence, and Iggy J. Howard. For most of June's life, especially when Trina passed, Nico and Iggy had kept her company.

To send or not to send. That was the decision June vacillated between as she replaced the photo in her hand with her iPhone. Hunched over the device, she pulled up the closed group text where the message would only be shared between her, Iggy and Nico. She typed in her password in the text message line, then paused. She rehearsed the plan over in her head for months and still she was not sure whether it was the right move or not. On her laptop, she had left her suicide message, left something to give away to everyone she could think of. To carry out the plan without causing alarm and without interruption was another matter.

Sending her password to Iggy and Nico seemed the perfect avenue to take.

She was close to them and they were like her own brothers. They were far enough away that even if they had suspected something was wrong, it would be too late for the two to interrupt. At least in a physical sense, her cousins would not be able to intervene, but as June thought more on the "what ifs," she hesitated. Then, again there was a chance that the two would call her parents should they suspect something was wrong. *Perhaps*, June thought, *I should leave the discovery of my will to the authorities.*

Trina shook her head. She felt her sister's tortured thoughts as they skittered about in her own mind like frantic ants. June's thumbs trembled over the electric keys, and her watery eyes stared at the nine characters she had typed into the send space. Leaning over June's shoulder, Trina's face hovered next to hers. "It's okay to call. It's okay to talk to someone," Trina whispered.

"Ready to roll, Deborah?" the sound of Ms. Parker's voice threw Trina into a whiplash as she whirled around towards the office.

"Coming," Mrs. Finley answered, reluctant to part with her photo and from her seat, at first. Then, as she rose, something rectangular and electronic fell from her pocket and into the seat. It was her iPhone.

"Wait!" Trina called out to her mother, as she strode through the bed and dresser aisle before stopping at midpoint. Trina felt as though she were being pulled in both directions. To her left, her sister sat alone and on the verge of finalizing her suicide. To the right, her mother was in the midst of gathering her things and was about the leave the room unaware that June's only lifeline had slipped from her pants pocket.

Trina spun around towards June's numb and slouching figure that stared down at the phone in her hand. "Call her."

For a moment, June stiffened. Trina's urgent voice translated into a small doubt that kept June frozen in place. For a moment, Trina could sense hesitation and hope hung in her throat. "Call Mom, please!"

But, as quickly as the thought of calling her mother entered her mind, June shook her head and pushed away the fleeting thoughts of reaching out. Trina watched, helpless as June began to set her phone aside, and fixed herself to stand. Her things gathered, her mother's hand now rested on the handle of the office door.

"Stooooop!" Trina's panic and frustration reached a fever pitch. The stress of powerlessness culminated into a force that seemed to hit her mother and sister all at once. It halted her mother at the door and forced her to turn around and look across an empty room. It startled June from her resting place at the bed. The jolt of sound made her jump and in the process of lifting up and spinning around, her hand pressed hard on the phone and caused the device to fall face flat on frieze carpet.

Everyone paused. Trina glanced from her mother to her sister, but she was not sure what to think as both their eyes seemed to focus in on her. The tense stillness only broke when Finley let go of the door handle, turned around and slowly toed back towards the space of the office.

"Everything good, Deb?" Sensing the principal's arrival had stalled, Ms. Parker doubled back to the room.

"I don't know, I… ." Mrs. Finley's head slowly shook, at a loss for words. "Did you just say something a while ago?"

Ms. Parker shook her head in response and frowned. "Everything all right, Mrs. Finley?" This time, the assistant principal's playful chime changed to genuine concern. Her eyes draped with worry as an inexplicable graveness drained Mrs. Finley's cheeks of color.

Trina's eyes stretched and her heart hoped that was at least a good sign. A shuffling at her back pulled her attention towards the other side of the bed. She turned around just as June stood up from retrieving her iPhone. Agitation and dismay flickered across her face, and her eyes flitted from the place where Trina stood, to the hallway. Nervousness that someone had entered the house made her frazzled. Flustered, her thumbs quickly danced across the screen. June swallowed and her hands loose with bad nerves, caused the device to tumble from her hands before her swift stride towards the aisle.

"June wait!" Trina called. Her arms reached out for the girl marching towards her, but fell on nothing as she moved through the embrace and beyond. In June's passing, Trina felt the transference of thought. It was an image, the final item critical to the last piece of June's plan. It was an old key, one that fit to an antique lock of a wine cabinet in the kitchen.

Trina spun around and glimpsed the heel of a tennis shoe disappear around the corner. Trina hustled in pursuit and expected to catch the back of her sister in her travel down the hallway, but found the path empty upon turning the corner. Dismay washed over her and her eyes searched the space of the entertainment room. No one sat on the couches of the entertainment room nor were there signs that anyone had taken the stairs to the upstairs bedroom. Wondering from right to left, the back door to the guest room also seemed undisturbed. Then, a sound of an electric chime followed by the subtle sliding of doors drew her attention to the pathway that led to the kitchen. Trina frowned and the noise caught her off guard. Such sounds seemed out of place in a house made entirely of wood. There was a low murmuring of voices and steady footsteps landed on linoleum. It came from the dining room and family area.

Trina hurried past the entertainment room and into the kitchen. First, she glanced towards her left where the stove, sink, refrigerator, and cabinets were. There was no sign of June and thankfully no sign that the lock on the wine cabinet had been broken. Next, she turned to the entryway towards the dining and family room. To the left of the room, there should have been a long walnut table lined with matching chairs surrounded by furnishings decorated with family portraits, shaded lamps, and china dishes. The adjacent family room, the bookshelf on the far side of the room, the piano they played on, the couches and cushioned chairs where they found their presents on Christmas day, all were gone. What stood in place of the dining and family room was the inside of a dingy gas station.

The electric chime sounded again, signaling the entrance of a teen who swaggered through the glass and metal sealed doors. All of five foot ten and broad-shouldered, his stature was squatty and somewhat wide. His routine of weight lifting and basketball had trimmed and hardened baby fat into muscle. Normally, he dawned a skull cap, but today he wanted to show off his fresh fades from a haircut he received an hour earlier. A black belt fastened baggy, crisp blue jeans, and his shirt was a white wife beater. By the way his shoulders and cheeks glowed on his high yellow skin, it must have been sunny outside. The boy's eyes slid towards the counter and gave a head nod towards the cashier. He surveyed the man behind the register and realized he leered suspiciously at him in return. The boy decided against using his fake ID for a drink this time and opted for a snack and a soda.

Trina instantly recognized it was Nicholas. She followed him as he slid through the chip aisle. She knew Ori had brought her to her cousin's stomping grounds of Louisiana.

"Nico, can you hear me?" Trina asked.

There was no reaction as the boy settled on the top row. His fingers and eyes sifting through pork rinds then hot chips before he was alerted by a buzz from his iPhone. Nico put his search on pause, reached into his pocket and gave a confused smirk as he looked at the screen. The upstart jolt of Trina's heart fell into a rapid pounding as she saw June's text message. The first line read:

SBc@9w@r3.

Trina looked on, not having to urge Nico to answer before he strummed a message back on the line.

"Lol! What's this? Blerd code?"

Nico typed in jest at such a strange message.

There was a pause, then three dots flickered. Finally, there came the second message. It read:

I'm good.

Trina's heart fluttered when it registered that the text message was the rushed response June made before she rushed from the room. "Everything's not okay, Nico. Call her!" Trina urged.

Nico did not respond to Trina's earnest plea but he did frown. Something about the message seemed off. Not only that, but it was unlike June to call him at this time of day. By now, June would be in the middle of class, a place he knew he should be. Likely, there were rules on cell phone use, and June would always abide by it unless something was wrong.

"What up fam? You good?" Nico typed, but there was no response.

 "Call her!" Trina repeated.

After waiting a few seconds for a text that would never come, Nico looked through his contacts, pressed on June's information and put the phone up to his ear. He waited, but there was nothing. He called a few more times before leaving a voice message for her to call him back.

"Call our mother's cell!" Trina demanded.

Her heart lifted, both surprised and delighted when her cousin scrolled through the call list to pull up Deborah Finley's number. Trina was sure that he would make the call. She rushed out of the store, backtracked down the hallway, and prayed the whole way as she rushed back to her grandparents' bedroom. When she arrived, relief washed over her to find that her mother was not only still in the office, but had found her iPhone.

"Hey, Aunt Deb! What's up?" Nico murmured from the receiver.

"Busy," Mrs. Finley sighed. "Although I should be asking the same question since you're NOT supposed to be on the phone *in school*."

Trina could hear Nico titter albeit nervously on the other end before quickly changing the subject.

"Say, is everything all right? I got a weird text message from June earlier."

"Text message?"

Mrs. Finley's thin black eyebrows furrowed and it reminded her of the sinking pit in her stomach that seemed to linger. "About what?"

"Don't know, some code or something? Hold on." Nico's voice fell silent, and he hung up the phone as he forwarded the message June had sent.

Pulling her own device away from her ear, Mrs. Finley watched the screen. A looped blip signaled that the message had been transferred. Trina watched her mother study the screen, the expression knitted in concentration immediately fell to a mild panic as she recognized the characters on the first line as the password to her daughter's laptop. She looked at the time signatures. She knew there was a zero-tolerance policy on cell phone use at June's school. Not only that, but the timing of the messages indicated that they were sent just as the athletic period had started. Alarmed, Mrs. Finley immediately dialed the number to Dixie Grove High School's front office.

"Hello?" Mrs. Finley paused, both hands clasped tight around the iPhone, tense. "Yes, Ms. Scarborough, this is Mrs. Deborah Finley, June's mother. I wanted to... ."

Mrs. Finley fell silent as she listened. On the other end of the line the receptionist's voice was placid, yet concerned when she asked how Finley's daughter faired with her nausea? She hoped that a rest bit at home would help her recover. Mrs. Finley shook her head. Composure and panic were in a tug of war within her as she insisted that she had not retrieved her daughter from school at the start of the day. Preoccupied with the dread and the conversation with Scarborough, Finley scarcely noticed the assistant principal step in until she abruptly ended the call.

Trina's insides tossed in an exhilarated fever of hope and dread, as she watched her mother rush to gather her things and relay the news to her colleague. There was hope, that as her mother dialed her husband and every nearby relative that June would be stopped in time. But as Trina held some inkling of light that her intervention would work, there was also fear. It was a fear that Trina shared with her mother about June's whereabouts. A fear that they may make it to her too late. Wanting to see the situation through, Trina fixed her steps to follow her mother's rush out of the office. There was another noise. A sound pulled Trina back from the space of the principal's office and into her grandparents' bedroom. She had heard the sound only once, but it was enough to draw her attention back to the farm.

"June!" For a moment or two, there was silence as Trina began to search the bed and bathroom. Then, she heard the steady drag of hollow metal as it scraped across a rough surface. It was an eerie sound like a water pail, perhaps something heavier, grinding across gravel. Trina paused, her ears primed to the silent air until she heard the hollow dragging again.

Trina's eyes fell on the narrow stretch of hallway leading to the kitchen. The change was a slight one, but she began to notice the light of the sun as it dimmed. Her gaze fell on the entrance to the kitchen, a wooden door with peeling off-white paint , its window covered with thin curtains. Trina stared at the graying shade of the window. The hollow grind rang. A flash of a silhouette passed the window.

"Wait!" Trina shouted and her steps fell in a brisk walk, but slowed to a halt for a moment. The subtle dimming was now more pronounced and rendered the gray-white of the sun to deepen to a dark hue. Shirking the trepidation felt by the darkening, Trina continued down the hall with caution. With every step, gray faded to gold, gold deepened to ember, and ember darkened to scarlet. When she finally reached the door, Trina paused. She watched and listened. Nothing passed the door. The grinding of hollow metal ceased, but she could have sworn she heard distant whooping and laughter. Trina took hold of her pendant and when she was sure that Ori's stone face was still, she took hold of the knob and pushed through. Her feet sank into the fine, grainy soil of black sand. Her eyes stretched open at the scenery before her and Trina's mouth fell open. What was before her looked nothing like the front yard of her grandparent's farm.

Chapter 7

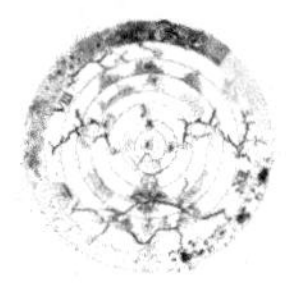

For a brief stint in Trina's childhood, travel guides became a thing. Her mother and grandparents began the spark. When it came to preparations for family vacations, her mother sifted through stacks of travel manuals. Granny May and Papa J would peruse through destination magazines, and have a spirited conversation about what they read from the magazines or saw on television. They made an event of looking through travel guides on rainy days and sometimes before they went to bed. Trina, June and the other grandchildren gathered in the back room among the spread of magazines and photo books. Their conversations were outlandish, and their imagination fueled boastful claims and curious musings about continents and countries and habitats.

Eventually, Trina adopted the leisurely activity as a solitary hobby. The reading of these magazines or brochures were sometimes difficult mainly because of the vocabulary she had yet to master. Still, she loved the photos of theme parks, museums, cities, and nature. Trina loved photographs of places near bodies of water. People always seemed to have fun in those kinds of photos whether they soaked up the sun on beach towels or posed in mid-play at the bank of a lake. Strangely enough, Trina was reminded of these vacation photos as she cautiously meandered towards the bank's edge.

Towards the right and some stretch down the curve of the bank, she spotted a pier. Even further down the bank and past the port, the land rose to a bight. The lift in land formed a bluff of sorts. Trina spied movement along the bank and saw a small gathering at the top of the cliff. Inside, she felt an uneasy tug with every measured step. Ebony sand, or perhaps ash from the powdery crumbling beneath her feet, made up the bank's soil. Even the reedy vegetation that reached up to her knees could be mistaken for being black instead of dark, charcoal green. Dressed in white, Trina stood out like a diamond among coal while she walked along the black land. Her clothing was not the only thing that made her conspicuous.

The laughter Trina heard earlier once again rang through her ears. Both hilarity and chatter sounded clearer since her walk from what should have been the front yard of the farm. She turned towards the bluff, and her eyes landed on the vertical's flat top in time to see a skeleton run into a somersault dive off of the cliff. She heard a mirthful whooping before the diver splashed into what looked like lava. More pale-framed figures loitered on the cliff top. Others lounged about, and conversed among themselves while the few that had cheered on the diver bragged about the stunt they would perform when it was their turn to make the leap. Skeletons at play was a strange sight to see and hear. Though their leisure seemed harmless, Trina learned her lesson the last time she stumbled upon a seemingly innocuous place. Besides, the whole deal of skeletons moving about in a scenery with more than a touch of the infernal was enough to keep her on guard. Trina preferred being as hidden as possible.

She looked to her left and there was not much else. Black sand stretched the length of an empty bank. Save for the white specks that moved on the decks of vessels that sailed in the distance, there was no one. Ahead of her and off center, Trina spotted a mess of pilings parked on the edge of black and watery ember. Trina walked closer and studied the arrangement of debris. Judging from the curve of the sides that met to a point on the face of the object, the base of the pilings was the hull of some sort of boat. Stacked on top of the boat to make up a roof and walls were scraps of wood, metal, and perhaps bones. Trina looked at the makeshift shack, and thought to take temporary shelter there. Better yet, she could use the vessel to search for the lost soul, that is, if she could ever figure out where to look.

Now within a few feet of the shack, Trina prepared to board the pile, but froze from the sound of a sudden racket and a tottering boat. Banter traveled from the pile as the owners of the voices stumbled from behind it. Like what she had seen on the cliff, the duo were skeletons. One of the boney phantoms had thick cones of metal jutting from the top of its skull. The spikes lined the center of its crown in the fashion of a mohawk. The index and middle fingers, big toe, and middle toe, were clad with jewelry that may have been sharp rings or metal claws. Thin dark traces intricately etched in certain places of its ribs and trailed down to the arm and leg of one side like a tattoo. The spike-headed skeleton's partner seemed shorter and had wider shoulders. The tips of its phalanges were painted black. A large, jutting pair of swirling metal reminded Trina of giant corkscrews and looked like crooked horns that branched low on either side of its skull. Metal hoops that pierced the scapula, ilium and a corner of its eye socket and mouth were connected together by chains.

Trina paused with her eyes stretched open. She was astonished at the sight of the pair that emerged from behind the boat. The two skeletons halted in mid-action, their voices silenced the instant their eyeless sockets fell on the newcomer. Trina's initial shock waned to a tense awkwardness as the boney specters stared at her for nearly a minute. The uncomfortable stillness only broke when the mandibles of the two skeletons dropped open and swung like loosely hanging trap doors. Before she could venture to say a word or prepare for confrontation, the skeletons ran. White branches of arms flailed, and their legs stumbled over one another in a hurry towards the boat shack. Her anticipation of their retreat or retrieval of a weapon, turned into confusion as she watched the frantic removal of loose scraps that crowded around the makeshift hovel.

Witnessing the spectacle of the specters wild cleanup of the vessel was like watching some panicked, out of sorts dance. The music of the clumsy waltz was the tumbling of wood, metal and lightweight trash. Upper bodies fell forward and lifted back in off-kiltered heaving of metal sheets and boxes. Windmilling arms tossed lumber and trash, and feet kicked cans. Most of the litter cleared, both skeletons scrambled towards the shack's opening. A few times, their hurriedness and off timing caused crashes between the skeletons. As she listened to the clatter of bones and watched the wordless negotiation of who would make entrance, it produced a tickling in Trina's stomach that nearly escaped in sputter through her lips. Finally, it was decided that the spikey head would enter the shack. As the spike-headed skeleton emerged from the recesses of the shack with a sign, his horned companion fixed himself from the recent fall. By the end of the spectacle, both skeletons stood on either side of the sign they had posted across the shacks opening.

The spike-headed skeleton stood posed, the bundle of bones that was one of its hands anchored on its slightly dipped pelvis. The fingers of the other hand curled into a fist, the white knot raised to a gate of teeth as it cleared its throat. Then, straightening its vertebrae and flexing out ribs, the spike head whisked out its hand in presentation of the scrawled lettering of the sign. A man's voice matched the melody of a circus ringmaster as he announced, "Welcome to Spike and Curly's Rowing Business."

"Gondoliers, *extraordinieres*, at your service," The curly horn interjected and bowed. His emphasized tone and slapstick altering of the word *extraordinaire* was an intentional misspelling to rhyme the term with vocation.

"If there's a place you need to go," the spike head began. With one hand hooded over sockets and knees slightly bent the top half of the skeleton twisted in a slow turn from right to left as he pantomimed someone in search.

"We'll take you to and fro," the curly horn finished. He turned one hand downward, and moved it in the same direction his partner had twisted. His index and middle finger mimicked running legs.

"We put our thinking skulls together." As the curly head spoke, he took fist to scalp, and knocked on it to sound a clip-clop. "And get to sculling across someplace better."

"Patronize us, and we'll ensure, indeed, that you'll reach your destination, guaranteed," the spiked one said, his finishing statement signaled that he and his colleague would bow to end a surely rehearsed advertisement.

With furrowed brows, Trina continued to stare at the skeletons still modeled in genuflect. Her mouth quivered as her lips tried to fix themselves to express how mystified she felt at the performance, but there weren't any words. The only thing she could do was gawk, shake her head, and wonder *what in Heaven, or on Earth,* or more aptly, *in*

Limbo had she been an audience to? Her silent confoundment must have lingered too long for it shook the skeletons from their poses. Their heads moved, first to look at their potential customer and then to one another. Their postures straightened and relaxed. There was another awkward silence between the three. Trina kept an eye on the gondoliers and listened to the reactions of the pendant, all the while wondering about her next course of action.

The gondoliers watched Trina and waited for a response. Finally, the two turned their gaze towards one another again, and shrugged.

"Uh, hello?" The spike head uttered as he ventured to take the first foot forward. When Trina took a step backward, the skeleton halted. "Heeel-Looo!" the spike head shouted, his pronunciation of the greeting slow and exaggerated. Then, he raised both hands in a nonthreatening gesture and the spike head moved again. "I-am-get-ting-off-of-the-boooat!"

As the spiked one measuredly announced, he made a steady dismount from the vessel. The curly horned skeleton remained on deck, shifted nervously in place, and watched his shipmate make his cautious advance. As the spike-headed skeleton came closer, Trina listened to her pendant. So far there wasn't any danger hum from Ori. She stayed in place, but stood at the ready.

"Hiiiiii!" the spiked skeleton greeted once more in the same loud, drawn-out fashion. "Iiii-Spiiiike," he said, and gestured to himself with both bony thumbs. "Heee-Cuuuurlyyyy." Spike's gesture was as exaggerated as his speech when he leaned slightly, and pointed both index fingers towards the horned skeleton that watched from the boat.

"Yeeeessss!" Curly added and nodded slowly. He raised his index finger towards his sternum and repeated, "Iiii-Cuuurlyyy!"

"Okay!" Trina nodded. The lines of her brow knitted together. She was confused as to why they spoke to her as though she were a three-year-old.

"Cooiiiinaaaage?" Spike's drawn-out delivery of the word held a touch of rosiness. His thumb, middle and index fingers rubbed together in a symbolic intimation of payment of dollars and cents.

Trina blew out a nasally puff of air, exasperated. "I can understand you, you know."

Spike's vertebrae arched, his head jerked back, and both skeletons' mandibles dropped open again. When she saw grooves suddenly appear at the tops of Spike's eye sockets, Trina was taken somewhat off guard by the bone's malleability.

"Oh, wow!" Spike uttered both impressed and slightly embarrassed. "Pardon us."

"Uh, sorry about that." Curly stammered. "We assumed that, well, you're quite different from what we see around here."

"No worries," Trina waved off the misunderstanding. "Still, you need money here?"

"Moola makes the underworld go 'round.'" Curly jested, and descended from the boat to join his shipmate and the newcomer.

"We take coins, preferably the ones you were buried with or any you've found on the way here will do too," Spike said.

"Sorry," Trina answered and shook her head. "Didn't think you needed money when you were dead."

"Oh!" both Spike and Curly grumbled in unison and their boney shoulders slouched in disappointment. The letdown quickly turned to a sly interest as Spike tilted his head and index towards Trina's amulet. "How about that for a boat ride?"

By this time, Curly stood at Spike's side. His demeanor suddenly brightened as he too, turned his attention to the broad face that hung on a chain. "Looks neat. A trinket like that would go a long way here."

"Yeah, it's something Samuel would like." Spike agreed as he briefly turned towards Curly.

Trina recoiled slightly, and with a discouraging head shake, she clasped her pendant. "Ori's not for sale. Besides, where ever I need to go, I'll fly."

Uncertainty twisted Spike's skull and vertebrae in an odd angle. "Taking to the air can only get you so far down the Running Pyr, lady. Trust us, it'll be safer by boat."

Upon her advent, safety was her top priority, and she was more so preoccupied with staying unnoticed than exploration. Ori's alarm had yet to sound, and since the gondoliers posed no threat, Trina relaxed her guard, and took in the fullness of the scenery. The bed of land which she stood upon gave way to a vast channel of liquid fire dotted by drifting crafts. Other banks edged the molten waters, that formed the base of high walls of eroding black rock.

From her vantage point, the smoldering course seemed to form the tail end of a "S," the remainder of its path hidden from view as it curved around wide columns of land. Lying beyond the dark walls some 10 or so miles down the river's passage was some sort of structure. The edifice was asymmetrical with trapezoidal features. To Trina, the mountainous structure reminded her of some oddly shaped anvil. Unlike the burn of the fiery river, the edifice emanated a goldish light and compared to the landforms that surrounded it, the structure seemed man-made like an ultramodern building. Every now and then, emerald twinkled from the dark crust that topped the roof of the edifice.

Trina's eyes narrowed into a puzzled glower. Gazing inward, some of the questions whirling around in her mind involved the nature of this place called the Running Pyr. Since her travels across Limbo, Trina wasn't a stranger to strange places.

Still, there was something oddly contradicting about this waterfront. Its black land, channels of lava, and smoggy sky made the place look hellish. Yet from what Trina could observe, the inhabitants seemed to find their paradise here. Aside from her musings of the Pyr and what the inhabitants were, there were other more important questions.

Namely, she needed to find clues, any lead she could, to find the lost soul and get back on course of her trek. In order to do this, Trina thought it wise to get some information about the area. She turned to Spike, and thought to start off with gaining some answers about the safest way to navigate the Pyr. Before she could utter a word in question, Curly's sudden gasp interrupted her.

"Noooo!" Disbelief drew from Curly in an exaggerated sigh. The two hollows narrowed in great effort to see something in the distance. His skull and vertebrae leaned in the direction of his strain until recognition snapped back the pate and ladder of bones. "No way!" he shouted, and his sockets stretched beyond its normal size before his skeletal frame reeled.

"What?"

Alarm colored Spike's tone. Trina could tell he was as confused as she was while he watched Curly snatch away his gaze and hurry towards the boat's shack.

"My god, he was serious!" Curly shouted loudly over the rustling of riffraff that cluttered the inside of the gondola's hut.

"Who Rodney?" Spike asked.

Trina tried to make sense of the exchange and her eyes shifted from the rummaging within the shack to reading the expressions on Spike's face. She recalled the line of Curly's gaze, and turned her attention skyward. On the bluff, the skeletons no longer took part in leisure and playful diversions. Instead, they all stood at attention, watchful of what lay beyond the cliff. Something they saw caused an uproar among the gathering. Their bewildered chatters rose from them as some of the skeletons rushed to the cliff's edge and pointed towards the direction of the edifice. Trina followed the direction of the jabbing pointers and noticed a blinking fireball in a steady soar towards the edifice. As she took note of the winking spark, she also observed the movement of dark specks that inched from its float about the perimeter of the structure's roof towards the advancing spark.

Catching sight of the commotion, Spike also found the source of the uproar and joined Trina in her strain to see clearly the airborne spark in the distance. Behind them, the sounds of rummaging ceased, replaced by scrambling footsteps and the hurried clattering of bones.

"See for yourself, dude," Curly announced, and passed off a pair of binoculars from his hands to Spike's hands.

Briefly distracted by the hand-off, Trina watched Spike as he raised the field scopes to his eye sockets. Suddenly, the skeleton jerked backward, his bottom jaw nearly dropping loose from the rest of his skull before it swung back in place. "The challenge isn't worth it, Rod," Spike rasped. His body tilting side-wards as though his vision were overtaken by the sway of virtual glasses. "Ooooh, turn back."

"What challenge?"

At Trina's inquiry, Spike turned to her and handed off the binoculars. She raised the scopes to her eyes, and she could now see clearly the converge between the winking fireball and stray fragments of dark specks. She set the lens of the binoculars on the spark, and her eyes widened. The spark was nothing but a fiery discharge from some contraption that she could only describe as a scrap rocket or plane which was piloted by a skeleton with flight goggles. She saw the overhanging gray that covered the sky and Trina assumed the specks to be particles of ash.

Through the binoculars, however, the dark specks looked to be a thin swarm of objects which had even, pointed features like squares. While there was a large collection of the squares hovering about the edifice, a small cluster of these objects separated themselves, and fanned out to the outskirts of the larger cloud. At a certain point, the small cluster halted. When the impending rocket seemed to almost meet the cluster, Trina noticed a stark yellow twinkling bounce among the cluster. The sour light darted among the squares before it stretched into a laser that struck the rocket and immediately caused the aircraft to explode.

Trina flinched, her mouth agape as she watched the falling inferno before she lowered the binoculars from her eyes. "The pilot he ... what just happened?" she stammered, dismayed at the sudden demise of the rocket's pilot.

"Cubrocarns," was Spike's simple reply.

"The very reason why flying is a no go," Curly added, and lifted the binoculars from Trina's limp fingers. "Well that's going to be quite a deficit, Rod will have to climb out."

"Yeah, but with the way things are going, he may get lucky and recover within fifty years or so." Spike said.

The bridge of Trina's nose crinkled. She was confused. "You talk as if Rod didn't get shot out of the sky and burn to death."

Spike's chuckle caused his teeth to chatter. "He may be really deep in the red now, but dead, he is certainly not. Not in the sense that you're thinking anyway."

"Like I said earlier, money goes a long way in the Pyr. The more we earn, the less constraints we have," Curly explained. "Supposedly, meeting our quota in coins means we move on to the next place, where ever that is."

"Right now, though, we're not in a big hurry to leave. Still, it can get kind of slow in this place," Spike continued. "For a while, it was nothing but dull moments until that blue sprite showed up."

"A blue sprite?" Trina repeated as her heart jumped with excitement. "Where did it go?"

"Last we saw it, that blue light landed at the Bazaar before it disappeared," Curly replied and gestured towards the trapezoid-like structure in the horizon.

Spike shook his head right before it dipped in a contemplative tilt.

"We thought it was a freak bolt of lightning or some weird discharge from a sick cubrocarn, at first. But the way it moved, there wasn't any way it was some outburst of energy. That thing was sentient."

"It was amazing," Curly chimed. "It came out of nowhere and zipped right through that swarm."

"The cubrocarns are territorial and good for getting rid of intruders. If that blue light didn't get past them, it got pretty darn close. Soon after, this 'Cube Challenge' emerged to pass the time." Spike stressed and threw up his boney hands to make air quotes.

"It's ridiculous when you think about it," Curly interjected. "If you can afford it, there's a safer way to the Bazaar by boat. If you earn enough, you can make it to the bank, at least. But with the challenge going on, everyone's trying get through by some other half-baked means."

"Alex." Trina murmured to herself. There was no doubt in her mind the blue sprite that entertained them with a spectacle was none other than the lost soul. Inside her stomach, hope and worry tumbled over one another while anxiousness danced about her eyes. "Did anything else strange happen along with the blue light? Any mentioning of a demon sighting, maybe?"

Both skeletons flinched, and their bones creaked as their jaws slightly parted. The word 'demon' conjured enough surprise in them that the upper ridge of their sockets arched. The two looked at each other, shook their skulls, and turned their hollows back towards the girl.

"On the matter of demons, no. I mean, not to our knowledge. You and the blue light are all the excitement we've had in years," Spike replied.

"Say, are you in some sort of trouble?" Curly asked.

Trina fell silent as she stared back at the two specters. Traveling throughout Limbo, she learned, could be tricky and to engage with its inhabitants, even more so. The few close calls she had was enough to make her hesitant to share any information let alone ask for help. Still, she could hear genuine concern in their voices, and despite being skeletons, there were subtle curls about their faces that conveyed worry. Trina held on to her pendant, and after a few more seconds of deliberation, she decided to risk it.

"My sister and the soul of another is in danger. I need to get to that Bazaar. I don't have any money to pay you with, but I would like your assistance. Is there a way I can earn some as quickly as possible?"

Curly and Spike exchanged glances, again. The ridges and crevices stretched about their faces, delighted that they had gained some business. But then, their hollows narrowed and bumps formed across eyeless rims with the knitting of their brows. Their postures stooped in contemplation as a dilemma occurred to them.

"Earning in your case is complicated," Spike finally spoke. "For us, it's sort of an atonement thing."

Trina frowned. She didn't understand. "Atonement?"

"Well, see we're Ennui spirits. Boredom led to our vices, vices led to unfortunate events, and the *fatal* results of these events ultimately brought us here." As Curly gave his winding explanation, his boney limbs flailed and ended with a sweeping gesture over the infernal oasis.

"Ferrying souls is our main means of making an after living until we reach the amount for our souls to migrate. But in your case, I'm not sure," Spike added. Then as boney tips scratched the side of his skull as unsure ripples spread across his gaunt mien, he said "Most of the time our customers come with coins or the like."

"Scavenging might be an option," Curly chimed in. "You could forage for items to trade, but that could be time-consuming."

Trina's head lowered as disappointment thinned her lips and shaded her eyes. The Bazaar was the only sure chance she had at finding the lost soul. She had a feeling, too, that the edifice may be the only other place holding the door to the next world. If that were the case, she would have to find another route, but where? She mulled over her troubled thoughts and barely noticed Spike and Curly as they shuffled towards their scrap-piled boat. It was only when she heard the racket of shifting that Trina looked up, and found the two dismantling and throwing debris from boat to bank.

"Getting ready to set sail?" There was a note of dejection in Trina's voice. She believed that since her case wasn't profitable, they would surely take their business elsewhere.

"Why, yeah. You're in a hurry aren't you?" Curly asked.

Trina's heart skipped again. She was surprised, but more than anything, delighted. "But, I don't have anything for payment."

Spike shrugged. "Eh, we're in a pretty good place, financially. And to be honest, we're not in that big of hurry for the whole soul migration thing. The whole to-do with money is getting Samuel to cooperate with us."

Trina's eyes narrowed, upon hearing the name again. "Is Samuel like a ruler among the Ennui?"

Another titter rattled through the teeth of the pair before Spike answered. "He fancies himself as much. He's the head ferryman and auditor of our sector. Anytime we want to travel to the Bazaar and beyond, we have to form a fleet. He has a deflector enchantment that allows for a certain number of boats to be shielded from the cubrocarn attacks. He can lead you safely across the channel, but there's a surcharge to join his fleet."

"Speaking of," Curly's announcement made Trina and Spike crane their necks towards the pier.

"Aahh, and there be the Perch," Spike jested. His lower jaw slid to one side while he exaggerated his Rs in a mock pirate's voice. "Welp, best we hurry so we're first in line." With that, Spike returned his attention towards the gondola, and picked up the pace to help his partner clear the vessel of unwanted contents.

Trina's eyes lingered on a broad watercraft that drifted towards the landing stage. By the time Spike and Curly finished unloading the gondola, the ferryboat parked. The gondoliers ushered her on board and set rowing oars to liquid flames and sculled towards the pier. They drew closer to the wharf and Trina took in the peculiarity of the craft that was Samuel's perch.

From a distance, it looked entirely black, but a closer look revealed there were a mixture of dark hues and material that formed the vessel. The words 'The Perch' was written in a bold, curling font in canary print, and jumped out from the ferry's onyx hull. The metal and other material of the ship looked dark gray, black or blue. Two drum-shaped structures mounted the vessel, and took up a great deal of deck space to give the ferry its broad shape. The drums seem melded together and they took on a unified and asymmetrical shape as one of the cylinders faced upward like a tower while the other laid down on its side. Blue-green showed through the dark gray of the drums and Trina could only venture that the cylinder structures were turbines, generators, or machinery of some sort. Also taking up the deck was a low, cone roofing with a wall that curved into a cylinder shape.

Initially, Trina assumed the small cylinder hut of metal to be another piece of machinery that was part of the ferry. But, as the metal hut began to unwind like the petals of a blooming flower, she was surprised by the collection of instruments that shifted into place. From the unfolding of metal came bulking material and small, sliding bits that reassembled itself into a circle of levers, buttoned panels, chained gadgets, and gears. Trina could sense that the circle of machines was a control center of some sort. At the center of the command counter was an actual perch where a white figure took roost.

As the gondola settled to park near the pier, Trina noticed how much the vessel dwarfed the ferryboat. The Perch was not so great that it was a massive ship liner and the gondola a mere raft. Still, the ferry was big enough that it could carry twenty passengers or even more without the generators, while the gondola could only make room for up to five or six. The ferry was bulkier, wider, and great enough in height to where Trina had only glimpsed the scalp of the ferry captain's skull.

After tying a rope to a pier leg to anchor the gondola, the three disembarked. Sure enough, she and the gondoliers were the first in line. The boardwalk was empty as they made their way to the ferry's entrance. The Perch's ingress overlapped the ledge of the pier, and the three crossed the bridge. Before they had even set foot on deck, Trina's eyes reflexively jumped at the sight of the Ennui spirit bent over his roost and circle of machines like a judge hunched over a courtroom bench.

"Hiya, Samuel," Curly sang.

"Long time, no see, Old Sam," Spike greeted.

He waved a boney hand as he approached the roost in a near-dance skip.

"Auditor!" Samuel's correction came out with the growl of a cantankerous old man. "You two would do well to greet me with proper address. Hmmm?"

Trina kept quiet, and made herself as unobtrusive as possible as she stood behind the gondoliers. Despite there being only sockets within Samuel's slightly deformed skull, there was an incline of vertebrae and cranium that suggested that her presence garnered his attention. Hiding behind two skeletons, even if it were for a false sense of security, did little to subside the inner squirming of unease. It was more than the disquiet she felt as surly words rattled from a parrot's beak. Trina studied the auditor. His features part human and part something else.

He had the arms, hands, pelvis and, for the most part, spine of a man. There were other parts where what was once human, melded with what might be avian or some other animal-like feature. The feet that gripped his roosting stand had five digits, but had the strong, sharp shape of talons. The talons led up to joints of human ankles then went up further to bowing appendages that were either crooked or simian. The skull was also human to a point. The bone structure around his nose and twin hollows, the place where his ears should have been, and sides of his jaws were human. For mandibles, however, a bird's bill made up the top of the jaw while a distorted under-bite seemed to pinch to a certain size to balance it. A long neck craned on too wide shoulders. And then, there was a midsection. Within a long humanoid rib cage seemed a disorganized knitting of bones and white fibers. There was something tucked away under the cross stitching of bones and fibers, and for the split second when Samuel would inhale, Trina swore she glimpsed the knot of a cog. She had not been in the Pyr long, and knew little of what was to be the norm among the Ennui spirits. Still, she had a feeling there was something different, something off about Samuel.

"Business or charity?" Samuel barked.

"Business, Auditor sir, and a favor." Curly raised both hands and pinched the air between his thumbs and forefingers. "A very, very small favor."

"You see, Ol ... uh ... Auditor," Spike stammered to smooth over the near error. His tone was both rosy and sympathetic as he began to implore his case to the judge on the perch. "This lovely lady here is on an important errand. An emergency, in fact."

"Did she pay?" Samuel asked, flatly.

"Well, people aren't exactly being buried with coins over their eyes, these days, sir. Funerary customs of the living change all the time," Spike remarked.

"And that's true, Auditor," Curly interjected, his posture meek in an attempt to appeal to Samuel's sense of authority while furthering his partner's cause. "We were wondering if you could make an exception, this time."

The great assessor let out nothing but a quiet hum while rocking his bottom jaw. Though his face was but a white carving, Trina perceived the irritation that hung about the curves and craters of his mien.

After an uncomfortable silence hung over them for what seemed like several minutes, Samuel raised one hand and snapped his fingers. On cue, the cluttered nest of contraptions that made up his desk, churned. The bridge of Trina's nose crumpled as electric shredding of paper reminded her of a cash register. Spike and Curly anxiously watched, as a pale strip of what looked like a receipt inched from a horizontal cleft of one of the machines. Within arm's reach, Samuel grasped the paper, tore the sliver from cleft and held out the white ribbon for whoever was brave enough to receive it.

"If you wish to be her sponsor, then you must make this endowment." Samuel said.

There was hesitation. Trina joined the two gondoliers in an exchange of glances. Samuel sighed, and eventually waggled the paper out of impatience with the pause. Spike shrugged, and bravely stepped forward as he volunteered to take up the receipt. He retreated back to his partner's side, and both Ennui crowded around to read the receipt. Trina craned her head in an attempt to steal a glimpse of what was on the parchment.

The scribbling seemed cryptic and unrecognizable, and she gave up. For her skeletal companions, there was a steady read through and then their jaws dropped collectively. The shock was severe enough that Curly's mandible quite literally fell to the floor.

"This…this is ROBBERY! It would take us two eternities to pay this off." Spike exploded in stammering protest.

Curly did a swift dip down and scooped up his lower jaw. After he fixed the bone back in place, he readjusted it. The hollows of his eyes stretched with stress as he spoke. "And, how are we supposed to pay off such a debt when our boat would be repossessed too."

"Traveling to the Bazaar is high, but what gives with this kind of price hike, Samuel?" Spike growled, as he crumpled the slip. His bones clattered as he roughly shook his boney fist.

"Tis the season of the Venetians or has that slipped through the little phantom matter that you do have left rattling in those *skulls* of yours?" Samuel's casually retorted. "Spots on the fleet are limited, the demand for them is high. To deprive those with the money to reserve a space in favor of munificence has no place in this line of work."

"It's not like we're asking for a first-class cruise or a trip down the whole river. All we ask is that you make an exception, just this once," Curly pleaded. "What if it's an emergency, she… ."

"Exceptions tend to multiply, gondolier," Samuel roughly interrupted. "She pays or you pay with the endowment delineated on receipt. Otherwise, you can go find charity elsewhere."

Curly's mouth parted, and the white rims around his eyes stretched in dejected ripples from the rude rejection. Spike's lower jaw scooted in irritation and the upper rim of his sockets collapsed into angry slants. After staring daggers at the indifferent Samuel who tended to his machines, Spike spun around, and swept one arm in an angry wave to gesture the others to follow. Trina dragged behind the Ennui in their slow march, and glanced over her shoulder at the roost.

Worry prompted her to clutch the pendant to try to settle her nerves. She may not have known the intricacies of the ferrymen's business, but she understood the break down in negotiations loud and clear. The dread of losing precious time tightened its grip at her core. Deep down she knew her only hope lay at the end of the pier and that hope seemed to drift away the further they walked from the Perch. She had to turn around, had to think and do something, but what? *Please, Ori*, Trina prayed. *Please, tell me what to do.*

The response to her entreat was an immediate calm that flowed from the amulet, in to her palm and throughout her being. It quelled the racing of her panic and cleared her mind which was mottled by her sense of being lost. Ori spoke to her. *Give*, he said. His word was perceived through mind only, but Trina felt what the Orisha spoke as clearly as she heard the murmur of a man's voice. Trina stopped in her tracks. The calm was still there, but what her guide suggested made her clutch the pendant to her chest and never let go. *Give*, he repeated. The overwhelming fear she should have felt seemed nothing compared to Ori's peace and certitude that flowed into her. Finally, she managed to pry away the fear as she unfastened the pendant from the clutch of her hands and chest. She looked down at Ori's carving. Under one eye of the stone face there was a glistening of grit, that twinkled like a diamond shard. Trina was certain the tiny glint from stone was Ori winking at her, his assurance that everything would turn out fine.

"Wait!" Trina's sudden break from silence caused the gondoliers to turn around.

Both Ennui exchanged glances as they sensed a soberness from their patron.

"Everything okay?" Spike asked.

The nervousness was still there, but after a deep breath, Trina finally responded with a head nod. "I have an idea."

Curly and Spike curiously exchanged glances again. Their wait for an explanation was only met with a gesture from Trina to follow. The two gondoliers shrugged, but quickly hurried behind the young woman as she returned to the end of the pier. As they approached the entrance of the Perch, they found Samuel as he still made last minute preparations before the all call for the schedule fleet. Even as the three rushed on to the scene to make an audience with him, the head ferryman barely stirred from his adjustments of dials and checking of the time.

"I would like to make a deal with you, Auditor. Do you barter?" Trina asked.

"It depends."

Samuel's response was casual, almost as though the three had never left upset from the rejection of the previous deal. It was only when Trina lifted the chain overhead to release the hold of her necklace did Samuel break from his calm indifference. Seeing the girl's movement from periphery drew Samuel from machinery to the one who stood before him with item in hand. There was a mesmerized almost greedy focus of the hollows in the strange skull as the ferryman zeroed in on the one item on Trina's person. He held out an open hand towards her. "Let me see that pendant."

Samuel's stare fixed Trina in place. It made her feel uneasy as though the ferryman would lunge at her at any moment. The impatient strumming of boned claws, prompted Trina to come forward and place the stone face in white palm. Samuel brought the necklace towards him and caressed its centerpiece in his hand like some precious jewel. The mandible around the skeletal beak seemed to smile with delight.

"Let's see now."

Samuel hummed, lifted his head, and straightened his neck until it was perfectly upright. Trina thought it strange that Samuel's delighted hum seemed to draw out in length and then change into a mechanical murmur. Suddenly, a bluish glow radiated from Samuel's torso. The tangling of bone and tissue inside of his rib cage began to shift. Trina could have sworn that within the entanglement of his rib cage she spotted the rotation of cogs and gears. Witnessing the jump start of Samuel's insides was akin to seeing an x-ray of some cyborg whose parts of man and machine twitched and turned within heaving lungs. Like a segmented spoke or rod, Samuel's neck stretched upward.

He swallowed, and pulled a glassy circular item connected to a chain from his rib cage, and caused the object to slide up his vertebrae to settle over one eye. Trina was left speechless as she watched Samuel inspect the pendant with the sinister looking monocle.

"An object of interesting quality," Samuel's mused. He was so charmed by the thing he appraised that his voice seemed to smile. "The energy is quite intriguing, almost as if it is sentient."

The three waited with bated breath and looked on as the Auditor did a final once over of the pendant before putting on the necklace. He turned his attention towards the gondoliers and their guest.

"A charm for a place in the fleet, correct?"

Curly and Spike's skulls did a number of swivels between each other and the patron that stood before them. After what Trina imparted to them about the pendant before their visit to the Perch, she imagined they looked as unsure as she felt.

Still, after a couple of seconds of lingering in silence, she nodded, "Yes sir, Auditor."

Satisfied with the transaction, Samuel's skull lulled in approval. "Consider yourselves the early birds of the Bazaar fleet. Prepare, and we will disembark within twenty minutes' time. Enjoy."

Behind her, Trina could hear the hiss of cheers between the gondoliers. Bones clattered as they celebrated with a gleeful hop and high fives. When Trina turned, she was greeted by the hugs of joints and arm bones. The three carried on in a stumbling exit from the pier as though they left a raucous happy hour from a night at the bar.

"You sure showed him, kid," Spike praised her.

"You saved us from going under," Curly thanked. "I think you left a good impression on him, too, and that's not easy."

"You may not know it, but you may have done us a favor in the long run. Impressing the higher-ups goes a long way in the Running Pyr. Still," Spike paused in mid-walk, and turned to face Trina as his cheerful tune turned sober. "I have a feeling you exchanged something for the trip that was far more precious than what he offered. Are you sure you're okay with this?" he asked.

Trina smiled, albeit weakly. She swallowed the uneasiness she felt, and knew now she was entirely alone. "I'll have to be."

******

Shortly after the meeting, the three returned to the gondola. After making last minute inspections of their vessel, Spike and Curly set their rowers for a suitable space in the fleet. At the ten-minute mark, vessels trickled in with the first blaring of the foghorn. It took little time for the meager gathering to swell in size and number. By the Perch's final signal, the radius of several hundred yards were filled with all manner of watercraft. An excited busyness replaced the quiet of the infernal waterfront. Caught up in the atmosphere, the gondoliers chattered among themselves, critiqued the condition of a nearby dingy, envied a far-flung yacht, and daydreamed out loud of one day owning a ship. Despite the verve of sights and sounds, Trina sat silent, thighs to chest, knees under chin. In her own head, she worried about her own troubles and seemed cut-off. There was a harsh screech when the megaphone turned on , but Trina barely flinched. Samuel made his lackluster instruction on the importance of staying within the deflector's perimeters and other rules of the fleet, but she barely heard his words. Nothing on the outside seemed to reach her, not even as the gondola began to follow the even pace of the Perch and other vessels.

"Holding up all right, kid?" Spike's voice seemed to break the spell and caused Trina to turn towards the pair in the middle of their steady scull.

"As fine as I can be, considering. Just a little nervous." Trina's attempt to downplay her feelings was more of a way to convince herself as much as she tried to assuage the concerns of the gondoliers. In truth, being a little nervous was a severe understatement. To keep anxiety from pushing her over the edge, she tried desperately to hold on to the calm that Ori left her with.

"Sam's a big meanie, isn't he?" There was a sympathetic tone in Curly's inquiry, and Trina had a feeling that his chide of the Auditor was an attempt to cheer her up.

Spike nodded thoroughly. "You'd think he'd temper his greed a little after ending up here, but old obsessions die hard, I guess."

Trina frowned, curiously. "Is there a story about him or something?"

"Sure is!" Curly sang cheerfully.

"Guy was a major collector in his past life. For him it was more of a sport than a hobby to pass the time, go through any means to collect rare gadgets and such. Supposedly, he got hold of some cursed watch or something like that." Spike crooked his head slightly over his collar bone, and glanced at the passenger who was now piqued by the story. "Whatever hex that item had on it, resulted in him being here and ending up like that."

Trina shivered a little when she listened to Spike's tale. She recalled how uneasy she felt in his presence. She was not familiar with the Ennui spirit's universal form, but she had a feeling he was atypical of the norm. The story was an interesting one, yet sudden. Trina had the inkling the pair attempted to distract her from her troubles and for the moment it worked. After hearing the story about Samuel, it was obvious how he was destined to enter the infernal riverside. Still, when she looked at the two gondoliers and thought about all that had recently transpired, made Trina even more curious. "Earlier you said boredom and vice ultimately lead spirits here, right?"

For a moment there was a pause, a stretch of silence that almost made Trina a little uncomfortable. Then, Spike tittered, clicked his teeth, and broke the silence. "Because we've been helpful and all, you probably don't think we belong. You're probably curious as to how we ended up in the Pyr?

Trina's brows jumped at the gondolier's eerie prediction of her thoughts, and all she could utter was a slack jawed "yeah" in response. Curly's teeth gave way to brief clicking, his head lowered, and his shoulders hunched as though they braced for something. There was another stint of quiet. Several seconds passed before the horned Ennui relaxed some in posture. Trina watched the two Ennui row, and waited as she listened to the soft, steady churn of liquid ember.

"It all started with a selfie, a prank, and a fire," Spike finally spoke.

"Spike, not again!" Curly's skeletal frame shivered as he let out an exasperated groan.

"Before I knew it, I was murdered, by this guy," Spike continued, and thrust his vertebrae and skull towards the other skeleton that hunkered in his stance.

"For the millionth time, it was an accident, Spike. An accident," Curly moaned.

"It was second degree murder," Spike declared, and there was a resolute stiffening of his spine.

"Manslaughter, at worst," Curly said next. "Besides, both of us got roasted, so consider it even, okay. Water under the bridge, remember?"

Spike held his words, while Curly desperately looked on. There was a more, stubborn stiffening of his frame. The mulish silence lasted for only a few seconds before the Ennui's frame deflated as he exhaled. "Fine, water under the bridge," Spike repeated before Curly reached towards him with one hand, and put the final touches of the reconciliation with a reassuring pat on the shoulder blade.

Trina looked on, a mix of puzzlement and shock on her face. She didn't know what to make of the two going back and forth, of the words shared and even of their sudden reconciliation. Even if they failed to divulge certain details of their past, the gist of how they got there was clear. A prank turned fatal freak accident where two friends lost their lives sounded tragic, but watching the two go back and forth in the aftermath seemed like some dark comedy. Whatever the case, it was apparent from Samuel's tale that every Ennui had a story and their own account of misfortune had made her see them in a new light.

"Ah, tourism is truly eternal," Spike jokingly relished. All the while he adjusted his sculling speed to slow slightly. The gondolier gave a brief nod of his skull, and directed their passenger's attention towards one edge of the fleet. "There be the ferryman's bread and butter, ladies and gents."

Trina stood up, turned around and craned her neck to focus on where the gondolier gestured. Along the edges of the deflector's radius came the first stream that converged unto the main flow of the river. She heard the butterfly laughter of women first. Their voices were silken, elegant and floated about the air. Towards the right, a rowing boat on the edge of the fleet slowed to a stop. A trio of apparitions on a stage drifted towards the rowboat. Their faces were masked, angular and white like smooth porcelain of fine china. At the center of the trio was a phantom, whose cowl or hair branched upward into several spiny horns, fitted around its white face like a crown. His robe was dark, and it billowed and seemed to be made out of night or dusk more so than silken cloth. Cracks or fine lines of silver and gold etched spiraling designs on the shoulders of his cape. The middle phantom was tall even without the spiked crown. His stature and overall air was masculine. The other phantoms flanked him, or rather nestled at his sides in a flirtatious cuddle, and held a height that seemed slightly lower than the crowned specter's shoulders. The specter on the left wore a shawl that shimmered and shifted between the colors of blue, green, and turquoise. The one on the right, wore a shroud of flaring red with swimming slivers of orange, light purple, and flecks of gold. The body length veils of the spirits looked more like thick, colorful fog instead of silk. The way their cloaks wrapped the curviness of their being, the jewelry adorning their heads, their makeup, and most of all their high flighty laughter told Trina that the flanking phantoms were lady spirits.

When the raft parked near the rowing boat, the rower, a large burly boned specter with a single horn on his skull, escorted the lord and his ladies onto the vessel. The gentleman seemed stoic although he did show some mild form of affection towards his fawning companions as the three settled in. Trina continued to watch the scene. She studied the vessel and realized that it was of considerable size. It was enough to fit the rower, his three guests and at least four more. She imagined that moving a vessel of that size alone would take work, but for the big-boned Ennui shuffled to his oars, he easily moved the boat back in pace with the fleet. A rise of chattering from male and female voices came as other stages and boats joined the fleet carrying more of the ethereal creatures with misty robes and white faces.

"What kind of spirits are they?" Breathless, Trina's words almost fell as she watched more of the fanciful spirits enter the ranks.

"The merchants. Pretty cool, huh?" Spike replied.

"Those were the Venetians, Samuel talked about. He calls them that because their faces look like those masks," Curly explained and glanced at Trina over his collarbone. "They visit the Bazaar from time to time. Sometimes they conduct trade with us for discount items on the outside. Even heard they donated some items for the deflectors."

"So, none of you've ever been inside the Bazaar?" Trina asked.

Spike sighed, the face of his skull blank and inward-looking in his brief pause to contemplate. "I imagine it would cost us some arms and some legs."

"And a soul," Curly added, with a head lull.

"Yes!" Spike agreed, giving an exaggerated nod of his skull. "Yes, and our boat and boat scraps, so nope. Never been. But since you're not bound as an Ennui, you should be able to enter free of charge."

"Yeah, just don't buy anything though," Curly advised.

Trina nodded and took his friendly warning to heart. She had already learned a hard lesson at Angel Town and did not want to make a mistake she would not bounce back from.

Going forward, she would have to keep a low profile and stay focused. Sitting down on the boat, Trina concentrated on calming the whirlwind spin of her thoughts, and tried to devise a plan and wondered if Alex was still at the Bazaar. As the gears of Trina's mind turned, she continued to observe the fleet as it transformed from the sober ranks of skeletons and dark vessels to a carnival of colors.

Silver, gold, and gems of all sorts adorned the fanciful phantoms' fingers, garments, and hair. Plumes of exotic feathers fringed the collars of robes. Tiaras, crowns, gaudy hats and headdresses dawned their heads. Some had folding fans, umbrellas, and canes studded with precious metals. Some hand cases were so big, that she wondered how the vessels could withstand the added weight.

In another disbelieving scene, she had even spied a table and two chairs mounted on a motorboat as two Venetians played cards. The sounds among them made her think of the murmurings one would hear from a crowd of aristocrats at a ball or gala. Glimpsing the details of their activities had also reinforced these ideas with an added touch of the whimsical. Watching the colorful procession kept the fear of Ori's absence at bay, but her anxiousness of the lost soul's whereabouts steadily stoked her impatience. Trina saw the nearness of the goldish structure and suddenly sprang to her feet.

"What's up?" Curly spoke up. He felt the shifting weight of the gondola as Trina stood up.

"I want to thank you two for taking me this far. Honestly, I hate that I don't have anything to pay you with. I'll have to make it up to you guys someday," Trina admitted.

Curly let out an awe sound, and the corner of his mandibles stretched upward.

"We ain't honorable, kid, just bored. Besides, interesting company and that deal with Samuel is enough payment for us," Spike said.

Trina nodded and the small smile she formed at their friendliness soon fell as her lips tightened to a sobering straight line. "As much as I appreciate your help, I think it's time we part ways. We're close enough now that I should be able to fly the rest of the way."

Now, it was Spike and Curly's mien that turned grave as they shook their heads in unison.

"Up there," Spike said, as he and his sculling mate directed her vision overhead with their boney indexes.

Beyond the invisible cordon of the deflectors, a cube-like object zipped into view. It halted above the crowd, directly over them. Trina studied the object's dark, yet metallic surface that gleamed when light touched it. Sharp and swirling lines etched on all six sides in an elaborate pattern. The cube hovered in place, and spun slowly in its suspension as though it watched them. Trina silently gasped. She was surprised when the middle of the cube stretched and its sides quickly shifted like a puzzle box when it abruptly flexed outward. The sides that once held together as a cube now changed its shape, and formed two pyramids of metals with their bases connected by sinew coming from a veiny, sphere-like tissue.

Soon after the sphere peeled away the shell of the cube, the knot of tissue glowed a familiar sallow color before it let out a rapid round of stark, yellow fire. With every contact from the fiery discharge, the invisible shield rippled, but stayed strong and intact, as the energy barrage was absorbed. The lone cube halted its fire and flit around the place where it had attacked like some confused insect. The cube did not leave. Instead, five more joined the loner that drifted from its swarm. Similar to how the loner reacted, the newcomers changed shape, peeling back their cube-like shells to reveal fleshy core before they fired at the deflectors as a unit. The shots were fierce and Trina's muscles tightened. She dreaded that the object might succeed in making a puncture. The barrier rippled and shimmered like very thick layer of glass. Nothing faltered or cracked. All of what was fired had merely been absorbed. The unit of six cubes stopped their firing and zipped over the spaces where they had shot. Two or three even threw themselves at the shield only to bounce backward without making a scratch. Eventually, the cubes lost interest and returned to the swarm. Trina knew then that the floating objects were the cubrocarns, the same things that shot down the daring Ennui from the sky.

"We're reaching the end of three miles and coming on two," Spike announced.

"Yeah, we will be there before you know it," Curly reassured.

Trina let out a puff of air, somewhat exasperated. Although reluctant, the demonstration of the cubrocarns' aggressiveness was enough to make her sit back down. Trina sat in a curled seating position again. Her chin rested on her knees, and her eyes stared at the looming Bazaar as the gondoliers continued sculling along. There was another screeching of the megaphone followed by the jaded voice of Old Samuel as he announced the closing miles and minutes of their approach, and advised all passengers to prepare for the advent.

Immediately, after the announcement, a buzzing of spirits gathered their belongings. For a brief moment, Trina turned her attention to the goings-on at the forefront of the fleet. On a yacht, she spied a barreled belly Venetian who held a pipe up to clasped lips. He posed as he surveyed their impending destination. On another vessel, a quartet of young Venetian spirits crowded around one another and gave way to giddy chatter as one thrust a folding fan to point at the Bazaar. Then, somewhere behind the front lines, Trina heard voices as they spoke words tinted with mild yet nervous disbelief. Trina stiffened, upright. When anxiousness turned to startled cries, her eyes scanned the area for the source of the disturbance.

What's going on?" Trina could hear Curly's questioning behind her as he took note of rising panic in the crowd.

"Wait a minute! What the… ?" Spike's voice wavered between distrust in what he saw and the rise of fear, just as Trina's eyes landed on the rowing boat she saw earlier.

The crowned Venetian stood ominous on one end of the boat, the edges of his dark robe reaching out like wispy tendrils. One of the tendrils grasped the lady Venetian in blue by her wrist. With her body crooked forward, her free hand reached for help as she struggled to pull away, but little by little, the black tendrils ensnared her. Screams of terror echoed from both lady phantoms as one watched the other become engulfed, and then, completely absorbed into the darkness of the crowned Venetian's robe. With paddle in one hand, the burly Ennui stood in a defensive pose.

The red lady turned from the crowned Venetian, and attempted to escape, but a quick jutting of the shadowy fringes soon snatched her in until she too had been swallowed by the crowned one's darkness. The only one left to stand before the crowned Venetian, the ferryman lunged at the spirit with his paddle, and his swing connected hard enough to the side of his opponent's face that the boat tottered, and tossed both combatants overboard as the vessel capsized. There was a collective gasp. Samuel's voice could be heard over the amplifier. What he said, Trina did not know. Her attention was wrapped on the creeping pool of neon green that spread from underneath the capsized boat. A loud crackle broke the air as the boat's black hull peeled where the neon made contact. Another startled cry rose, this time from the onlookers as a burnt skeleton suddenly broke through the surface. Blackened and partially melted bone of what used to be a hand and arm stretched skyward. What was left of the burly Ennui crumbled as his remains sank back into corrosive neon.

Trina's body uncurled, and she leaned towards the stern of the gondola as she noticed the climb of bright green over the color of ember. The harsh green began to expand further out and increased the pace of its reach. She watched aghast as ill-fated watercrafts buckled and eroded before sinking in its wake.

"Hunker down and hang on!" Spike shouted back, as he and his partner started to work the paddles.

Trina did as she was told and readjusted in her seat and braced herself. Spike and Curly quickened their unified sweeps of their oars, and pulled the gondola forward, faster and faster. They passed some of the other vessels, and noticed that the passengers and drivers also heard the commotion. Those much further ahead and on the front edges of the fleet seemed oblivious to the chaos taking place. A buzz of a motor caught her ears.

A jolt of panic stung the nerves throughout her body when the abrupt rush of fiery waves rocked the gondola after a near brush from a passing motorboat. The close call prompted Trina to turn sternward, as she watched for other incoming vessels while she kept an eye on the chaos that ensued.

Upturned hulls of boats sat just above the commotion and river's surface like jutting black crags. They groaned as they sank. Cloaked masks rose and fell as Venetians floated in graceful bounds across the tattered remains. Nimble and clumsy skeletons were also among them as Ennui skipped from quickly crumbling litter in an attempt to escape the corrosive neon. Swifter vessels rushed past the wreckage and one another, but there were some that dared to stop. Neon peeked the haste of the fleeing and the crafts that corralled the edge of the harsh green's reach. From the sturdier vessels caging the substance, there were flashes of energy fire from those with weapon in hand and from the vehicles themselves. It was clear they were either fighting the neon itself, or perhaps, attacking whatever rolled underneath its surface. Before the head ferryboat's nose eclipsed the scene completely, Trina noticed the strange, conscious movements of the soured color.

The Perch's foghorn blared in alarm. Samuel's voice over the megaphone was soon drowned out by the crowd's hysteria as panic reached a fever pitch. The race for the bank began. As more vessels sped past, the gondoliers quickened their pace in an effort to increase space ahead of the stampede for survival. In the frenzied rush, some of the crafts collided with one another. One such crash happened in their path of travel, but Spike and Curly skirted the debris with expert steering. The gondoliers picked up the pace, and kept the gondola balanced in the upsurge of waves while veering past slower vessels. Trina watch from the rear and signaled to the scullers the direction of oncoming crafts.

"Heading into the home stretch," Spike announced.

"Yeah, how's it looking?" Curly asked.

Trina held her answer for a moment. A quick peer over her shoulder, allowed her to look past the pair of skeletons near the bow and she could see the black lines of the bank. With land within reach, the true enormity of the Bazaar was revealed. Sparse specks twinkled and drifted from the darkened crust towards the flat peak of the goldish edifice as the fleet approached. Lungs filled with exhilaration at the sight of safety and anxiousness at the vast stretch of ember still left to go. Returning her attention sternward, the first thing she noticed was the rest of the fleet and the quickly collapsing line of what little space the gondola created to avoid being caught by the stampede. The broad, black shape of the Perch was among them. Displaced from its position at the fleet's center, the large ferryboat gradually carved its way through the river's traffic. It still trailed some five or six hundred yards behind the gondola and the first wave of the fleeing.

There came the sound of rapid popping. Flashes of energy seemed to come from somewhere, some distance behind the Perch and traffic. Then, a black figure suddenly cut into the sky. Trina's eyes widened and the exhilaration broke into fluttering pieces of panic upon seeing the black figure hover over the area of flashing lights. The thing that easily evaded the skyward shots of energy fire did not have a white face and spiked crown running into a midnight robe. Instead, the figure was bat-winged and held a lean humanoid shape. From its head, its eyes sparkled with the same menacing luster as the corrosive color that polluted the ember of the river.

The crowned Venetian that turned on his companions and the appearance of neon shortly after he was tossed overboard suddenly made sense. Deception and wearing different masks were this demon's M.O. Still, she was at a loss as to how her greatest enemy managed to catch up. Limbo was a vast spirit realm. The scape where she previously wandered, the Marrow, was as convoluted a place to travel as the other spaces of Limbo. Even as the apertures were portals that led out of the scape, there was little to no guarantee that several people traveling through them would end up moving to the same place. Yet, like what happened when she departed from Angel Town, the demon pulled off the impossible.

"What are the chances?" Trina breathed. Her voice shook with disbelief.

"Chances of what?" Curly did a quick glance at her over his collarbone, and from the sound of his tone, the Ennui could tell something went wrong.

Trina's expression darkened, and when she peeled her eyes away from the black figure that flit about the sky, she turned back towards the gondoliers. "Narakai's found me."

"Narakai, uh," Spike spoke as though he breathed through the brisk rhythm of his row. "Sounds like a demon."

"He is," Trina answered, before she fell silent. Her mind raced and she tried to figure out what to do next. She wished Ori was with her.

"Seriously!" Curly nearly shouted. "Wha…where is he now?" he stammered.

Hearing the boom of what sounded like cannon fire threw Trina's body in a whirl towards the gondola's rear. Her heart skipped and she found the black figure was now over the Perch. Narakai circled the ferryboat like a vulture, and likely looked for the lost soul or her. Extending from the deck of the Perch and trailing its airborne target, were a pair of artillery guns. The twin barrels jumped in recoil, slid forward, and let out another loud boom as missiles exploded from a gun. Smoke plumed above the Perch. The black figure disappeared under the explosion. Trina looked on and wondered if the projectile reached its mark. Moments passed without a stir in the artillery dust. Hope trickled into her heart, but crashed as a flash of neon jumped down from the artillery clouds like lightning.

The sound of rowing stopped as a great resound arrested Spike's and Curly's attention. Everyone flinched and felt the air shake. The bolt tore into the Perch, split it in two and threw it on its side. Its force was so great that a powerful shockwave rippled through the ember, and tossed nearby vessels into to a violent upsurge. Loud crackling crawled through everyone's ears as a jagged shimmering burst through the invisible dome of protection. A collective gasp rang under the dome as visions of the sky wavered between clear expanse to a firmament scarred by streaks similar to crooked lines on broken glass.

Dismay drew in Trina's breath. Behind her, she could hear the frantic utterances of the gondoliers upon realizing that the shield was collapsing. They started back at the paddle and their sculling became more vigorous as they fought to pull the gondola into an even faster pace. Trina flitted her gaze towards the Bazaar. There was still a ways to go and enough of a stretch that if there were any more hindrances, they would be caught in the collapse and left vulnerable. She turned back to the wreckage. A black figure flew forth just as the artillery dust dissipated. Trina's muscles tensed and she watched as Narakai made his careful survey of the fleet below. It would only be a matter of seconds before he would reach them.

Suspicious of Trina's silence and hearing the shifting of her movements, Curly glanced over his shoulder. The young woman's stance told him she was either bracing herself to fight or take flight. "What are you going to do?"

"I'm going to head him off," Trina answered. "I have to stop him, somehow."

"No bueno, lady! Look!" Spike gave a discouraged head waggle. Jutting his skull upward, Trina took it as an instruction to look above. The cubrocarns had been roused by the incoming fleet. Several of the cubes hovered *right* above the shield's surface as though they waited for the barrier to break. In the distant heights of the Bazaar, specks drifted away from the edifice. Some of the clusters floated downward in a threat that they would join the other members of the swarm that gathered below. "The airborne are the first they go after when the shield collapses."

The airborne. The words struck the spokes of an idea in Trina's mind. Wheels turned in her head and she looked to the sky. Narakai still in flight, covered the three hundred yards between them. Another movement attracted her eye. It was the deflectors' shield. Every now and then she glimpsed jagged slivers of white splinter across the invisible dome. The slivers looked dull, and reminded her of dented plastic or damaged thick glass. The strange scarring flickered into sight, its residuals lingered, shrunk, then disappeared altogether until the next flash of the airy splinters. She thought of the slivers of a failing shield and the demon's advent. Then, she had a question, one that made her wonder about the fleet reaching land and how the merchants were able to make it inside the Bazaar.

"What happens once you reach land? Is there a safe zone?" Trina asked.

"The cubrocarns stop attacking us," Spike replied. "Sometimes right when we embark on land, sometimes a little bit before."

"We feel vibrations when we get near the place. Makes our teeth chatter," Curly added.

Though his body rocked to the swift motion of his hurried sculling, Spike managed a thorough head tilt in agreement. "We don't know the details, but the merchants talk about the Bazaar releasing some sort of signal. After that, the swarm usually settles down. Why?"

Right then, a plan formed, albeit a risky one. Trina said nothing as she studied the white slivers and tried to catch the rhythm of when they appeared and dissipated. Then, she looked at the demon closing down the last stretch of distance. Her continued silence prompted both gondoliers to look over their shoulders. They saw Trina's wordless gestures to stay quiet and keep rowing. They also saw the black figure's advent and their skulls quickly spun forward without sparing another word. Trina turned to find Narakai, again. Her eyes trained on him as the ninety-five yards between them quickly wilted down to fifty, then fifteen.

The smooth heat of energy slithered from her lower back and up her shoulder blades. She pressed her hands together and curled her fingers. Her thumbs pointed up as a target guider while her index fingers pointed out like the spigot of a gun. Light filled the black markings that lined her arms and the back of her wrist. Heat and bright white finally culminated at the ends of her pointed fingers as she took aim at the black figure. Trina held the light, quieting its shine. Then, as Narakai was right above them, she turned up the spark. As she predicted, the dot of light suddenly halted the black figure's flight. The instant she felt his eyes fall on them, she fired. The first shot crashed into Narakai's shadowy body and temporarily stunned him. The second and third shot zipped past him and crashed into white slivers that streaked above the demon's hover and caused a breach in the shield.

The plan that Trina both hoped and dreaded would work, had worked. A cluster of angry cubrocarns rushed through the opening. As the gondoliers warned, the cubes swirled around Narakai like an agitated swarm of wasps. At first, the demon seemed to hold his own against the small creatures, and crushed some with a brush of his wings or burned others with his fiery green breath. The swarm retaliated with more intensity, and the numbers of the cubrocarns multiplied with every one of its members the demon destroyed. Before long, the demon's dark shape disappeared under the thickening cloud of the growing swarm.

Trina continued to watch as sallow light flashed within the spinning cloud. Suddenly the cloud collapsed on itself. Cubes crushed upon cubes as it formed a mound that dropped into the ember below. The distance grew between the gondola and the cubrocarn cluster. The last she saw of the collapsed cluster was the mound as it sunk beneath the surface of the river. There was no sign of Narakai, no sign of the fiery river turning bright green.

More of the cubrocarns trickled in. Another smaller swarm that entered the dome's rupture, began to fan out. Cubes that strayed from the safety of the group were easily dispatched by those armed with weapons or energy projectiles. Trina kept watch of the stern and shot down the few wandering cubes that ventured too close to their gondola. Another loud, drawn out crackle rippled through the air. The vista of the sky was marred by a web of white splinters so severe that it looked like glass on the verge of shattering. Trina's eyes jumped and her nerves stung from the jolt of alarm upon catching sight of what was left of the Perch.

Soon all of the fleet felt the same fear as she had upon the shield's total erosion as the last of the head ferryboat crumbled. Now completely exposed, all below could see the number of cubrocarns that had amassed in the sky. Yellow lights bounced back and forth in the large speckled cloud that made a slow descent. Spike, Curly, and Trina froze, and braced themselves for the electric rain of yellow energy or the funnel fall of a tornado swarm. A silent buzz hummed through the muscles that tensed throughout Trina's body. Aside from the subtle chattering of bones, the pulse of the air was so low that it could only be felt instead of heard. Trina remembered what Spike mentioned earlier and looked up. Relief washed over her upon finding that the cubrocarns had not only halted their descent, but the swarm was beginning to retreat.

With the danger passed, the frantic rush slowed. Still, the gondola kept its hurried pace until, at last, it reached land. As soon as the gondola found its place along the bank, Trina's muscles relaxed, and she could feel the tension release from her lungs.

The gondoliers huffed, puffed, and wheezed as they stumbled off craft. The slumped and staggering skeletons gave a fed-up toss of their oars, and stumbled several steps before they collapsed on to black grainy earth. The last of the trio to set foot on land, Trina floated from the wooden deck to the ground. Her cautious walk turned to brisk steps until she stood over the spread-eagled skeletons.

"Are you guys okay?" Trina asked. She saw the stretch and crunching of their rib cages.

"I think," Spike huffed between words. "I won't be bored for a hundred years or so thank you very much."

"Yeah," Curly wheezed. "Like, I'm sure we burned a thousand calories from that." Curly's comment made Trina chuckle.

The trip down the river had been dangerous. Yet, the two risked their well-being, for a person who had nothing to pay for their efforts. Her lips curled in a somber smile. She was thankful. "I really owe you guys for this."

"Ehhh, I told you, we got our hundred years' worth of excitement," Spike breathed with a lazy wave of his hand.

Waiting as the pair settled their breathing, Trina finally took note of her surroundings. Along the bank, a line of vessels from the first group had already docked. What was left of the incoming fleet gradually gathered at the edges of the liquid ember and black sand. Among those that just moored, she saw the mix of the disturbed and composed. In one huddle, two cloaked masks that were smaller in stature sought shelter under a taller pair of robbed spirits. Trina guessed that the taller pair complaining to a befuddled skeleton, were parents. Their smaller counterparts hiding at the knees of the pairs' robes were their children. Other times, she saw Ennui assisting merchants with their belongings. The white masks leaned towards one another as they chattered nonchalantly about what had transpired and seemed concerned with other affairs. Trina continued to watch, as all the merchants gathered in a parade towards the Bazaar's entrance.

From a distance, the Bazaar seemed to be a solid structure. She assumed the base of the structure was supported by the same solid substance she had seen at its peak. However, when she was finally within walking distance of the edifice's base, it seemed that the Bazaar was held up by a thick curtain of light. Fine robes and white masks amassed in a line that flowed into a ray of golden light. Trina looked on, somewhat hesitant to join the others as they disappeared into the threshold of blinding light.

"Look at what the tide washed up." Curly's announcement made Trina turn her attention back towards the bank. Her eyebrows rose, astonished at the familiar looking skull tucked under the Ennui's arm.

It was Samuel, or rather, what was left of him and by the way his hollows crinkled, he was more than a little disgruntled.

"Careful," Samuel snapped. He warned the skeletal arms that readjusted the hold of his skull. "It is unwise for subordinates to treat their superiors coarsely."

"And it would also be unwise for one without all of their faculties to make threats of any kind," Spike jested.

His comment to the bodiless head ferryman was a pointed reminder that the tables had turned on him. Trina smiled and joined the pair as they shared a good laugh. She stopped mid-titter, however, when her thoughts wondered towards the Bazaar. Samuel's return made her think about the transactions that had to be made with the fleet. *Were there other conditions she had to follow?* She worried.

"Is there a catch to getting in the Bazaar?" Trina asked, hesitating to join the merchants.

"Just follow the Venetians, and you'll get in easy," Spike instructed. "As for Old Sam," the Ennui bent down and his hands rested on the bones of his knees. His face now eye level to Samuel's skull. "Considering the state you're in, I'd say a bargain for a full body recovery is in order."

After sharing one last laugh, Spike and Curly said their farewells and wished Trina luck in the rest of her travels. She thanked them for all of their help and she joined the procession of merchants. Spike and Curly's banter drifted into her ears and she took one last glance at them. Witnessing their comical pestering of Samuel, made a smile creep across her face. Then, as her eyes did a quick sweep of the debris that littered the bank line, her smile fell. She felt a twinge of sadness when there was no sign of Ori.

Chapter 8

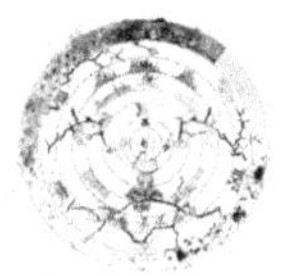

Trina passed through the ingress of the Bazaar and wondered if this is what it felt like phasing through crystal or diamond. The sound of faint, chime-like clinking overlay with the hollow, glassy crackling overwhelmed her ears. Her eyesight was engulfed by the glint of shifting gloss and the opaque shimmering of metallic yellow. What felt like minutes of experiencing the obscure soon gave way to coherence as she suddenly stepped into the interior of a market area.

Trina's head jerked back as she drew in a sharp breath. Like a lone stone embedded in the middle of a rushing stream, she stood still among the swirling of robes that swept past her. Overtaken by the enormity of the emporium, she barely noticed the greeting that echoed over the smooth chorus of the crowd's murmur. The Bazaar's exterior was indeed large, great enough in scale that it was the size of a mountain. Nevertheless, the inside of the marketplace seemed vaster still, as though the outside hid the expanse of a whole other region within.

One footfall shifted in hesitation to follow the other then stopped as her senses took in everything. Upon her initial notice of the floor, its surface looked to be carved from some pearl-like material. The glossy, off-white matter shimmered with the burnish of emerald, sapphire, and cerise. After a few moments of lingering, the floor's milky coat gradually began to fade. Seconds later, the color and texture of ridged pearl melted into a starry onyx. Every thirty seconds or so, the floor would seamlessly augment between chalcedonic shades and hues of dense light.

Lifting her gaze, Trina looked outward towards the spacious square. During her lifetime, she had made her fair share of visits to souks with her mother and grandmother. There was a shabbiness, but antiquated charm to the marketplaces of her childhood, with the cozy clutter of merchandises and paths to different booths that probed her interests to explore. What was a subdued charm of those open markets in her past life was the polar opposite of the shopping area where she now stood.

This otherworldly emporium looked like some avant garde mall. Shapes, both simple and complex, decorated the market floor. Abstract sculptures were well-situated about vendor stalls. Twin helixes columned the opening of outlets and their solid surfaces glistened in their slow spin. Interlaced mesh knitted together and formed the frames, spheres, cubes, and upside-down pyramids. Molten metal partially coated the frames of these shapes. By some strange trick of gravity, the molten substance flowed upward along the sides of these shapes. The metal-like liquid dwindled into drips and then disappeared when it reached the peak of each shape. Like lamps or hanging decorations, these levitating frames were suspended in rotation and were placed about the corners of seating areas, verandas and balconies.

What Trina spied thus far in the Bazaar left her as dumbfounded as its vastness. Everything felt too pristine and upscale, even beyond the standards of what could be found in the palaces of the most opulent in the material world. Considering the fact that commerce and compensation was the way of the Pyr, Trina felt nervous. Even standing in the aisles of the Bazaar felt expensive and she wondered if there were a price to be paid for being there. Eventually, thoughts of her mission broke through the nervousness and dared her to move. Without Ori's assistance, finding Alex would be more difficult. Still, there had to be clues on the lost soul's whereabouts.

Trina fell in line with the multitude of spirits that roved the vendor stalls. If she had thought the previous gathering of Venetians to be a carnival, the present collection of beings that surrounded her was an even more extravagant spectacle. In her steady scan of vendor stall activities, Trina's brows jumped upon seeing heads and elongated necks that shared the wide shoulder of one, amorphous body. The stretched neck of the heads craned then lowered and swayed like snakes as the specter scoured the items lined on the table. Three or four rows down, twin antlers crowned the bowed head of a gray, long-limbed being that looked more of a beast than a ghost. The crowd dwarfed this gaunt, gray beast, even as the cloudy thing sat in a crouch. Bones jutted through stretched, ashen skin, as the gray beast's head stooped down. Trina's eyes strained through the tangle of shoulders and heads and followed the gray beast's downward gaze and found one of the merchant spirits behind his booth. The spirit stared upward at the towering thing as the two conversed.

Trina continued to move about the colorful throng and searched. As she strolled, her line of sight wondered about waists and feet for any hint of pale robe, wild hair or the splayed, feathery, fin of a single wing. Nearby she spied spiked and yellow tufts that lined silken sheets of visible heat that smoldered the colors of oranges and reds. Among the elementals of fire, Trina also saw their other counterparts, beings with wispy tresses of wind and air and entities with wavy clear and blue strands that reminded her of oceans and rivers. Muscles tightened around her piercing gaze, and concentrated on the attempt to find any traces of a bright blue spark standing out among the swirls of fiery colors or blending in with cooler hues. Precious minutes passed of surveying the stalls and openings of outlets and when searching by sight failed, she turned to her ears.

Trina continued to move among the market strip and concentrated on sifting through the crowd's murmur. In passing, she heard many voices. Grunts and snorts that were a rude intrude upon her hearing sounded like the speech of pigs. Gibberish and other warbling seemed so warped Trina mistook the rapid screeches to be the noise of a tape recorder on rewind. There were utterances that sounded thin, airy, and soft to the point they could only be registered by walking next to, or through some of the phantoms. Every now and then, she caught something audible, something perceptible enough to be human speech albeit in a language she could not understand. Thus far, the only words Trina could recognize were those spoken by the announcer between fifteen- or twenty-minute cycles. Another toll of an electric bell rang soft but clear over the chatter. As scheduled, a velvet voice made its greeting and a nondescript apology for the recent disturbances and the inconveniences it caused. The announcement reoccurred often, and Trina soon relegated the broadcast to background noise.

"Hmph, inconvenience my foot!" The gripe carried the gruff and shrill tenor of an elderly woman. Trina recognized the language and walked in a pace that indulged her to listen further. When she heard the old "my foot" phrase, it made a corner of her mouth creep upward. She remembered the words as something her Granny May would say. "First that blue spark of whatever it was running amuck and then that whole business with the ferry fleet."

"Say, you're a Venetian, aren't you? Heard a convoy just came in not so long ago. Also heard that a lot of boats were lost." The second speaker was also an old woman although the tone held a more timid ring than the ornery trill of the first voice she'd heard. Of the conversation, it wasn't the gossip about the fleet, but the words "blue spark" that locked her feet in mid-tread. Trina's head swiveled and her eyes scanned booths within earshot until she landed on a trio cloaked in coarse and cloudy cloths. The three browsers had their backs turned towards Trina as they faced the vendor behind the counter, a smiling merchant who wore the conical cap and bells of a jester. Judging from the trio's stooped postures and the teal frail-looking claw that peeked from one of the browser's sleeves to rest on the knob of a cane, Trina guessed they were the owners of the crone-like voices she had heard. She moved closer and saw what else she could learn from the eavesdrop.

"That is correct, madam," the Venetian jester slightly bowed as he spoke. His tone was gentle and polite though a touched perturbed as he continued the tale. "Somehow a demon infiltrated our party and devastated quite a few of our vessels, even the head ferry boat. It was truly a frightening ordeal, especially when the deflectors failed."

"No doubt you had trouble with that safety hazard of a security system as well," griped the ornery crone. I can't tell you how many times those cubrocarns nearly did me in. You construct some half-baked security system that darn near vaporize its faithful customers yet a wayward bolt of blue managed to slip through and cause all sorts of havoc. Why, old Cloe here nearly got bowled over by that thing." As the ornery crone spoke, the exaggerated nudge of her forearm sent the left flanking member of the three to stagger sideways.

"As bullish as you are, it's a wonder they haven't caught you either." The third speaker, Cloe, Trina guessed, had a stately air to her voice, one that sounded thorny when she spat at the roughness of her companion. "But Attie has a point. A change is in order when it comes to the Bazaar's security system."

"A massive overhaul is what it needs." Attie, the ornery one spoke and waggled her index finger at the jester as she said, "I'd file a complaint and demand compensation."

"How awful! It's scary enough hearing about a demon sighting so close," the timid crone uttered and shuddered. "And I wonder what that blue spark was? Last I heard, it managed to reach the third floor near that gallery, I think? You don't think that was a demon too, was it?"

"Oh goodness no, Laci. Some odd will o' wisp probably, but no demon."

Cloe assured her and brushed at the air in front of her with a single, casual flick of her wrist. What one of the cloaked phantoms shooed away in disinterest, drew in more of Trina's attention. She glanced at the trio who still browsed at the jester merchant's table.

For a moment, she wondered if she should strike up a conversation. Then, she gazed up at the expansive height and levels of floors. She decided that the slivers of hearsay yielded enough information and Trina backed away from the crowds of the booths and towards the open area of the aisles. Sure that she had more than enough wing room, she hopped for airlift and took flight. She lifted over the heads of the crowd. She had reached the rim of some of the seating terraces above ground before the air began to bend around her. What she felt rolling over her wings, arms, and down her back was not quite air. The strange pressure seemed fluid to the touch, but without the trace of wetness that liquid tended to leave behind. It felt light in some crooks of her body then heavy in others, and the constant crawl of the energy bubble pulled her off balance. Her efforts to struggle against undulating air came to a quick end when the pressure wrapped her in a cushion of gravity. Suddenly tossed off-kilter in a sideways somersault, Trina's eyesight spun. She felt herself drop, and her arms and legs crunched into the rest of body to brace for the topple.

"We're sorry, but for air traffic control and your aesthetic pleasure, flying is prohibited. If you wish to access upper levels, please proceed to the terminals." The same voice Trina had heard in cycles over the loudspeaker sounded close and clear over the rustling of titters and puzzled chattering that surrounded her. When the caution repeated itself for a second time, Trina managed to lift her head and found two polyhedrons that hovered about. The two objects buzzed about her eyesight and were rails of gold with vertices and edges connected together to form a rhombus-like shape. Dazed both from the sight of the flitting shapes and the fall, Trina wasn't sure about the voice's source, at first, until she heard the automated drone for a third time as one of the shapes hung at her shoulder.

"She gets it, you half-baked wire hangers. Now SHOO!" Attie's reprimand came with a swipe of a cane that clinked against the golden frames and knocked away one of the polyhedrons.

"Goodness dear, are you all right?" As the other shape zoomed out of sight, the trio Trina had spied earlier now surrounded her. She drew in a silent breath of surprise, and saw their faces, or lack thereof, for the first time. Underneath their cloudy hoods was a black void. The only features that may have hinted at a face were the pairs of dots that shined white like hot coals. One had a gaunt, teal hand rested on a cane while the second held her pale hands together as the thumb and index finger fiddled with a dark jewel of a ring on her left hand. The third held a knitted craft made pouch and as she released a timorous hand from the clutch it held on the small purse, she extended it towards Trina in greeting. "I'm Laci."

Trina's introduction finally pushed through the stunned pause and she thanked them as she took hold of the offered hand. Thanks to Laci's grandmotherly nature, Trina's shock and unease wore off.

"Us honest to goodness paying customers suffer inconvenience and injury, but an invader or wayward phenomenon can get through willy-nilly. I've said it once and I'll say it again, a massive overhaul," Attie complained and gave the floor an earnest trump with her cane.

"Goodness child, don't you know not to go through those level barriers?" Cloe gently reprimanded.

"Sorry, this is my first time being here. A friend of mine was waiting for me at a gallery on the third floor. I was running a little late and thought I could take a shortcut. I had no idea there was a barrier." Trina felt a twinge of compunction in not being completely transparent, but she would have to be cautious. The crones seemed friendly enough, like the ferrymen that led her through the Running Pyr. Even so, her travels had taught her that ill-intent and any other dangers hid in the seemingly innocuous. Divulging too much information, especially without Ori's presence, was too much of a gamble.

"Well, there is the Camino's Galleria, I think, run by a mister Elba or a...uh mister Elga."

Laci's words fumbled. Her long, skin-and-bones fingers pressed against the dark of her mouth as she flipped through her memory in search of the right name.

Trina's eyes jumped open. Timing, Mr. Eleri's advice, and fate came to a rush and converged at the forefront of her mind. What the specter struggled hard to remember, Trina ventured an open, hopeful guess as she said, "Elegba?"

"Yes, that sounds about right," Laci nodded. "Still, going to that place at this time not knowing if that thing is still on the loose... ." her voice was laden with unease.

Worry weighed on the three as they fell silent. In the moments the trio paused, Trina felt her lungs tighten. In her silent prayer, she hoped their reluctance would not end on a missed opportunity to meet the only person who could help her on her quest. Finally, she heard a sigh as she noticed the slackened shoulders of relent from the specter anchored on a cane. "You enter that floor at your own risk, but you young ones have your own mind." Attie warned and waggled a crooked index at her. "At any rate, the least we can do is to show you how to get around. Hopefully, you'll gain your senses by the time we reach the terminal. This way."

With a mumble and a beckon to the newcomer to follow, Attie led the wade through the Bazaar's traffic. Trina kept in step with the crones' steady glide and remained watchful. There was a chance the lost soul may have doubled back to ground level. There was also the other possibility of danger hidden in the crowd. There was nothing of a child-sized figure emanating a blue spark surfaced in the sea of shapes and color. Luckily, in their walk past ten or so booths and stores, neither did the stir of violence. Congestion down the aisle eventually thinned, and eliminated the shoulder to shoulder cloister. Loiterers stood on the fringes and held conversations or picked a resting area from which to browse. Judging from the flow of traffic, there seemed to be a central point where spirits still on the move, convened. In spite of the traffic's confluence, there never seemed to be a backup or a swell. The crones headed in the same direction as the traffic flow. From what Trina could see in their advent, the central point and source of the seamless stream of spirits hovered above the multitude's junction.

At first glance, Trina thought the object hanging above them to be an ether chandelier or some other kind of ceiling decoration. Filed together in a cylinder cluster were bubbles or glassy rings dusted with the color of precious metals and laced with a coating that looked smoky and electric. The glossy orbs quavered as they floated into view from an invisible base and rose slowly upward and then disappeared when they reached the cap of its invisible confines. Neither string nor glass container suspended the orbs in their respective lines. There appeared to be a rotation as the bubbles that disappeared upon reaching the cap would soon reappear as it rose from the base. It took a long study of the object for Trina to figure out that it was more than ornamental. Blurred streams sprang from these orbs. The lines were so indefinite Trina wondered if she had imagined the air streaks that made their vague imprint between the spaces of the orbs and the crowd below. Trina was able to put two and two together as she watched the transparent lines, how traffic never backed up, and how the shapes of spirits she saw in passing suddenly appeared in the clear surface overhead. In a sense, the orbs collected in a cylinder were the elevators that allowed spirits to move from ground level to the Bazaar's other floors. This was the terminal.

"Give me your hand, like this." Trina did as Laci instructed and held out her hand as the crone took hold. The teal hands felt cool and fragile. Trina barely moved. Using her palm to hold Trina's hand, the pointer of Laci's other hand trailed a nail over the back of it where the joint of index and thumb met. "Normally, you purchase these from the Bazaar via mail request. But, in our visits you learn a trick or two. There." Laci stopped the tracing and her spindly index curled back and soon after a small, boxed symbol stamped in gold appeared on Trina's hand.

"Just follow that old saying about the Romans, child. 'When in Rome, do as the Romans do.' Hold your hand up to the terminal, like so," Cloe said and pointed in the direction of some of the spirits who raised appendages in the air and disappeared soon after being struck by streams of the orb. "You're looking for the third floor. One of the gold orbs should get you there."

"As for us, we're going straight to management," Attie announced. "Now you be careful. No more bonking your head on ceilings, you hear?"

Trina smiled, nodded, and thanked them for their assistance before the trio spoke their final farewells. She turned away from the crones and managed to catch a snippet of the ill-received response from Attie's declaration. Before complaints among the trio devolved into an argument, Trina moved closer to the junction. She raised the hand with the golden stamp. There was a stall which lasted five seconds, and then sixteen. Suddenly, Trina felt a light pull, a touch of static. The traffic and scenery of the ground level vanished and was quickly replaced with a room or chamber that made Trina feel as though she were inside a bubble or elevator. The floor underneath her feet was level and looked like marble coated with specks of gold, something Trina thought was surprisingly normal. A curving wall of watery glass surrounded her and stretched to the point whatever was on the outside was severely distorted. Her posture stiffened, and she backed as far away from the walls as possible for fear that any slight contact would cause the chamber to burst. Her efforts of zero contact were in vain, however, as everything in the room shattered. Specks of gold, windows, and flooring scattered and the chamber dissolved further into nothing as its pieces expanded outward. Upon the chamber's complete dissipation, the expanse of the third floor came into view.

Trina was disoriented and her feet moved in a steady shuffle. Before her was another vast court lined with outlets and more abstract sculptures. She inched away from the concourse in a slow spin. When she completely turned an about-face, she paused. White lettered lights showed in a fanciful, curling font. The French-styled characters of the sign formed the words, "Camino's Galleria."

From where Trina stood, the store looked empty, and except for the masked flashing of something electric and hidden, the lighting of the galleria's lobby looked dim. The outlet seemed closed, yet there were no gated shutters that blocked the opening. Trina continued to scan for any signs of life, and her cautious steps forward paused for a moment upon reaching the opening's edge. First, she eyed the retail counter that curved until both ends met to form a circle. The counter was mostly open space save for three rotating item racks placed about its smooth acrylic top. No one met her at the open space towards the front of the counter or stirred when she called out to make her presence known. She took a deep breath and finally crossed over from the pale, natural lighting of the third floor's open court and into the shade and incandescent haze of the galleria's interior.

What she stepped into looked like your run-of-the-mill gift shops that one would find in the living world. The retail counter sat at the center of a room. Shelves lined along walls seemed to curve the same way the counter did, and gave the lobby a circular shape. Now that she was fully under the threshold of the shop, Trina caught sight of a sign hung over the retail counter. It was an illustrated cut out of the sock and buskin symbol, an outstretched arm with directing fingers as its banner.

Trina's eyes first landed on the grinning mask of Thalia, and followed its pointing finger towards the right of the room. Snacks, toys, joke books and games filled the shelves on the side of the room situated under the mask of comedy. Next, her attention fell on Melpomene. Eyes traced from the crumpled glower of the mask of tragedy, down the long, wavy arm and index. There were somber paintings, books titled with plays of misfortune and heartbreak, clothing that was chic, but reminded Trina of articles that people wore during funerals. The merchandise of comedy and tragedy eventually met their end towards the shop's rear.

A sign that read "personnel only," situated itself above a door at the back and center of the room. Nothing was exceedingly antiquated or avant-garde about the place, which came to somewhat of a surprise considering what Trina had seen. Of course, it had its own modishness and captured the ambiance of some artsy, out of the way eatery or local shop.

Trina turned her attention back to the retail counter. Curiosity about the muffled flashing from recesses of the counter drew her to the desk's open space. Behind the counter seemed to be another level of table-like ledges tucked under the top ledges of the counter. The source of light came from a television set, an old CRT that showed the pixels of a retro video game circa, the 80s. She was about to move away from the front of the counter, but froze when she heard a rustling. It was the low sound of shifting cloth and a quiet scrape of metal pegs from a chair being nudged. Black fabric peeked the horizon of the counter's open space, then came the rounded crown with its short black rims. The bowler hat rose until fingers, and a pair of eyes crept halfway from beneath the surface.

Dark eyes popped wide and fearful with a gaze that crawled. As soon as the wary pair landed on Trina, fear turned into surprise and then relief.

"Oh, hello there, miss."

Trina knew the owner of the bowler hat was a boy before he stood up. Judging from his height, voice, and baby face, the boy had to be at least ten or eleven. His fluffed, outward branching hairstyle reminded her of horizontal antlers.

Initially, Trina figured the top of an afro crunched underneath the hat, but judging by the way it settled, she was beginning to wonder if the boy's hat hid a bald scalp. The rest of his ensemble, or from waist level up, at least, was a black frock coat over a white dress shirt and suspenders. The shoulders of the coat were slightly frayed and too wide, and the way the sleeves folded over the elbow and crook of his wiry arms indicated the coat was a few sizes too large.

The boy soon stooped halfway across counter and finger-less gloves fit the hands splayed across the surface.

"So, what will it be today, eh?" the boy smirked with a flirting twitch of his eyebrows. The fear that fluttered his voice earlier was gone. "Let me guess. A girl on the cusp of womanhood on the search for love everlasting? There is romance in tragedy and trinkets, too."

"No." Trina declined.

The boy shook his head in agreement. His face crunched in disapproval. "Me neither, a bit too heavy for my taste. I'm more for light entertainment, myself. Comedy's always good for a laugh and curios, too."

Trina shook her head. "I'm looking for Mr. Elegba."

The boy's eyes jumped wide with surprise again. In one quick movement, he jumped and twisted his hips and used his arms to hoist the rest of himself to sit on top of the counter. His trousers were patched and checkered black and white. The flooded pants swished and the toes of his tennis shoes tapped together. "Ahhh, you're looking for the manager, yes?"

Trina nodded, then paused as she studied the boy. "Are you, Mr. Elegba?" Under normal circumstances, she would not have made typical assumptions of a young boy behind the counter of an empty shop. Circumstances were different in Limbo. In keeping company with Ori, Eleri, and Osumare during her journey, the Orishas were more than what they appeared. If she were dealing with the trickster of the bunch, making normal assumptions could mean walking right past the answers.

"Call me E., sweets," the boy said. He didn't deny, but he also didn't quite answer her question. When the boy gave a mischievous sneer, Trina spied a metallic glint from the silver plates that covered his teeth. "He's been out and about conducting business here and there. Perhaps, I might be able to help. Relay a message from you to him, maybe."

Trina paused, as she studied E. She had the sneaking suspicion he was dancing around her questions. The reluctance veiled behind him being seemingly hospitable, but it also suddenly stoked the onset of Trina's urgency for a quick resolution. Nevertheless, she would play along. She continued to tell what she knew in the hope that answers would be found.

"I'm looking for a spirit, a child-like soul covered in blue light. There were sightings of a blue sprite or spark. Rumor has it that it was last spotted on the third floor entering this shop. If you were here, then you must have seen it."

E. grinned and his silver grill was in full view. His eyes slid toward her with a twinkle that Trina was not sure carried impishness or spite. "Ah, so it's information you want. We've got plenty of that too, although, information can be quite expensive."

Trina frowned. She was confused and taken off guard by his response. "All I want to know is where the blue sprite went. It costs to have a simple question answered?"

"Oh, but of course it costs, doll," E. sang and spun around until his back was towards her before he slid off the counter. Then, as he took the chair hidden behind it, he returned to face her, sat down on the chair, and scooted forward. "A question based on a rumor can be simple, yes, but a rumor is anything but. The simple truth of something could be say, someone accidentally breaking something, but rumor through hearsay can end in vandalism."

The boy's hand gestures became animated as he continued to explain. "Going through the mouths of the grapevine takes a lot of footwork, lots of interviews, and lots of documentation."

Trina's lips tightened. She understood the point E. was getting at in his explanation of the work behind equal exchange. She sighed and relented that, for the time being, she was at the mercy of his game. "Expensive how?"

"Nothing much," E. said and leaned back in his chair. "Just a few errands on a few floors. I've got a list of items to make things easier."

"Fine, but I'll need to get stamps to get to those floors." As proof, Trina moved closer to the counter and held out her arm to allow E. to see the lone stamp.

For a moment, the boy's head flitted from the golden mark on the young woman's arms and then at a face expecting to receive. Brows stretched in a questioning arch, E.'s mouth went crooked as one corner crept upward. His silver grill flashed and let out a single, airy sputter as though stifling a laugh. "Well if I had them, then what would be the point of asking you. I'd just do it myself."

Trina's wrist dropped along with her heart. "Then, how am I supposed to get to other floors to complete the errand?"

"You managed to get this far," he shrugged. "Just do what you did earlier to get you here. Taking shortcuts can be a gamble, I'll admit. You may have to put your soul on layaway with some specters, but you might get lucky, again. There are some good-natured spirits that will lend you some stamps free of charge. Of course, you can always go the standard route and order some stamps, but that can take some time, a year at most."

"I don't have a year or a week or maybe not even a day." Trina sucked in air and stopped herself moments before she exploded. With eyes clasped shut, she finally scaled down her heightened emotions. "Know what, I think?" Trina spoke in a tone that was muted, but laced with the edge of frustration. "I think the blue sprite did come through here and the sight of it sent you running under the counter."

E. gave another shoulder shrug. He was unfazed. "Maybe I did see it and maybe I didn't."

"Know what else?" she asked, as the sharpness in her voice grew. "I think you're not telling me everything about who you are either. You're Mr. Elegba, aren't you?"

"Or I could be an Edgar or an Edward or an Ethan. Last I checked, E. was at the start of those names, too."

E. slumped further into a recline, and tipped his chair back in a slight rear on two legs while he plopped his own on the counter. Crossing sneaker over sneaker, E. stuffed one hand into a coat pocket to retrieve a deck of playing cards.

Trina stared at the boy as he shuffled through the card deck. His demeanor was seemingly carefree while Trina steadily sank in the quagmire of desperation. "I need your help. It's a matter of life and death. Perhaps even more than that if my sister succeeds."

"Those are the stakes of existing or choosing not to, sweets. Anyway, all this serious talk is a downer." E. shuffled the cards a few more times and with the dexterity of a magician, he thinned the stack into a fan. He held out the splayed cards in one hand. E.'s eyes glittered with a mischievous charm as they met Trina's. "How about a game, eh? Go fish? Blackjack?"

Trina's mouth parted slightly and her stunned gaze soon drew long. Eventually, disbelief turned to disdain, and her mouth twisted in disgust as she slowly shook her head. "Elegba or not, you're callous."

Her insides churned between the boiling that roiled at the boy's nonchalant nature and the sinking disbelief at his careless reply to her pleas. Still, there was a small part of her that had hope. A small anticipation that her reproach would gouge whatever semblance of a heart the boy had, garnered enough guilt that it would prompt him to provide some assistance.

"Uh, never mind," E. groaned with an eye-roll. "You're getting too testy to talk to." With that, the boy lifted his shoes from counter top. As soon as his legs disappeared behind the booth's horizon, he dragged the chair until his back faced her.

Trina's lips tightened to the point where the corners of her mouth felt sore. The onset of tears burned her eyes and her gaze lingered on the figure that lined up cards along the table to play solitaire. Not once did the boy look up or fidget under the pierce of Trina's gaze. She got the hint, but where could she go? Without any stamps, Trina was stuck on the third floor. Other than the name Elegba and rumors about the lost soul, there were no other leads. Anxious, Trina rose with her hand up to her chest to clutch the stone out of habit. When her hand clasped air, she was quickly reminded that her guide was no longer with her.

Feeling stuck, she thought about Ori and the old man. What she wouldn't give for Ori's presence or Mr. Eleri's advice. Anxiety threatened to turn into full-on panic and Trina looked to her memories. She thought of the calm Ori left her with at the pier. Thinking about Mr. Eleri, she remembered his easy-going nature and his words. It was then that she felt the itch of a looming answer. There was something Mr. Eleri shared with her before she left, something about Mr. Elegba.

Like hands in a frantic grasp for something to hold on to, her mind raced. Trina circled part way around the counter until she could see the faces of E. and the cards he dealt. Her eyes wandered over the files of solitaire, and studied the patterns painted over white. The color green jumped out at her from the symbols of tiles and hearts. For a second or two, she lingered on the cards of tiles and hearts. She thought green was an out-of-place color for such symbols. From the counter she began her amble about the store. After a quick survey of one shelf, she paused on a band wrapped around the crown of a top hat. Trina's brow furrowed. The color blue felt somewhat off-key against black. She moved over to a rack of greeting cards and browsed through a few until she came across one, she assumed, was for a Valentine's holiday. Pink and white hearts decorated the inner and outer cover. It seemed normal enough, but something about it got her into a habit of looking for all the hearts in the room. The more she found, the quicker Trina's insides danced. Of all the drawings, embroidery, and plush items of hearts, none had the color commonly associated with the shape.

Continuing to study the merchandise, she examined the cap, stitching, and logo. Drawings and figures of clowns had yellow, green and blue makeup against the face paint of white. She looked among the jewelry embedded with gems. Among the cooler colors of gems there were hues of light rose, a touch of pink and some orange bordering on yellow, but never a shade too close to red. Then came the blemish and most obvious piece of evidence. It was a broach clasped around the tassel of a scarf. Trina was no specialist of minerals by any means, but she knew a ruby when she saw one. There was no rich blush or deep and fiery hue normally displayed by rubies. In fact, there was no color at all. Instead, the broach appeared oddly washed of color, not quite gray, but as if it were an object pulled straight from an old black and white film. The revelation made Trina feel a little light-headed. The initial stun was soon replaced with clarity, as the last piece of Eleri's advice rang like a bell in her head.

"Interesting shop." Trina's voice hung in the quiet and for a moment, she worried that the boy would continue with the silent treatment until he took the bait.

"Elegba's big on presentation," was E.'s boast. Not once did he raise his head from the solitaire's deck. "He was going for a bit of Bohemian and a bit of chic. Wanted to create an indie shop/café ambiance so customers would linger. Nice, eh?"

"Nice enough," Trina nodded before she continued. "But, it's missing something," she said, as she bide time with a roundabout stroll that would eventually end at the front counter.

E. tittered and flashed a silver smile. "You suddenly an expert on how business is run, now?"

"Not at all. I'm not trying to tell anyone how to do anything." Trina gave a verbal backpedal, but all the while her steps lead her to hover near the desk. Now and then, her eyes shifted from the shelves lined with merchandise to the black hat crowning the boy's bowed head.

"Nonsense! Share! We value customer input, here." E.'s playful caw rose from behind the counter and encouraged the young woman to follow through with her contribution.

Taking E.'s words as a beckon to return, Trina's gradual hovering between desk and floor took a more direct course. Her circling steps barely increased above the pace of an amble, a tiptoe of speed as though not to raise suspicion from making steps too hurried and eager. "I can't quite put my finger on it. It's just an observation of something I've noticed ever since I got here."

"Oh, really now," E. uttered. The slight head tilt he gave matched his quizzical tone. "And what would that be?"

Trina returned front and center at the counter and leaned forward enough for hands to splay the table top. "Well, if presentation is everything, like Elegba said, then everything associated with the store should reflect that motto, right? For instance, employee attire." The response to Trina's words was an agreeing hum. With his back turned to her, the boy not once raised his eyes from the game of solitaire, even as she shifted and leaned further forward to replace her hands with her elbows across the table top. Trina carried on lightly, talking in a tone that was even and accommodating. Her gestures were somewhat animated as she worked towards the proposition of an idea even though the person she spoke to could not see her. "Camino's Galleria is supposed to give out an artsy vibe, correct? Why not have the uniforms advertise that? The overall suit is a nice touch, but, maybe, do something a little more creative like a half and half hat that's black and blue or black and red."

"Come again?" The charm deadening and cheerfulness faltered from E.'s inquiry. "What was that about my hat, now?" The boy's voice steadied and he tried to stay composed, but there was an edgy tone underlying it.

"Nothing to be upset about, Eshu." Trina made a casual and intentional slip. "Just, why not have a hat that's something like black and red?"

Thin cardboard abruptly erupted in a splutter. Trina flinched. E.'s slouched back stiffened upright. For some reason, both words and air caught in Trina's throat. Warily, she straightened into a stance and froze. The whole time she stared at the boy's back and read him. With his face turned away, there was no clear discernment of the boy's expression. Still, there was something about the silence that made her feel uneasy. The air suddenly felt weighty as though it took hold of her in a heavy-handed grip. Trina flinched again as the seat the boy sat in cried out an aluminum drag as he slowly stood to his feet.

"First, the attitude and now you've got insults." E. finally said. His voice was as calm as the air, but it carried a dark and deadly tone.

"I ... insults? No!" Trina stammered. "That wasn't my intent at all, E. I didn't mean… ."

"So now it was nothing?" E.'s voice turned hoarse and harsh. He sharply cut off Trina's apology before he slid into a low, venomous hiss. "You think runnin' around, making fun, messing with honest to goodness folk is nothing to you? Nothing but a game?"

"No, I wasn't trying to play any game." Fear made Trina's throat dry. The words barely crackled out of her mouth.

"Yes, it is!" E. hissed, again. "Nothing, but a silly little game for a silly little girl to play." Trina gulped. Trepidation hit her with a stinging jolt as she heard the boy speak. She caught something strange in the hoarseness of his voice. For a moment, she could have sworn she heard the cutting in of an octave that sounded too deep to belong to a boy. It was fleeting and slight, but enough of a change for Trina to take notice.

E. turned around to face her. His eyes pierced her and it seemed there was a glow under the hood of the hat's short brim. An electric sizzle sounded and the already dim lights flickered once. When the lights flickered a second time, it briefly raised the lighting to sallow brightness, darkened to black just as quickly, and then resettled into its original dimness. Trina gasped, and took a few steps back. In that brief faltering of light, she could have sworn she saw a thin black crawling across the boy's face just as white splintered briefly through tufts of black hair. Her heart thudded, and she took a few steps back as E.'s shoes scraped across the floor in his slow rock forward.

"Some silly little girl, probably bored," he said as his eyes fixed on Trina. E.'s anger rose steadily with the volume and vitriol. "Probably thinks it's fun, going all over the place, running her own mouth about things she ain't got business spouting." The lights flickered again as he walked forward. Trina took a few more steps back and made sure there was enough space between her and the counter. There was the phantom sound and feel of rumbling, a tremor that was so faint and tucked well under the air she could scarcely tell if she could actually feel or imagine the sensation.

"I'm in here runnin' my own shop, mindin' my own business and in comes a silly girl runnin' her mouth, stirring up bad things in my shop!" The sound that blared out of E.'s mouth was no longer that of a preteen boy but rather, a growl. The octave was deep, monstrous, and guttural. The rumbling now surfaced above the imagined, and became severe enough there was a collective clinking from all that was metal, glassy, and hollow. The rattling around her gradually grew as though a train was about to pass near or over the shop.

Fear at its peak, Trina thought to make a run for it. She looked for the opening. No sooner had she turned her head, she felt fingers and a gloved palm wrap around one forearm. She knew she had created space and that E. was still well behind the counter before she turned away. The feel of a grip on her arm was as surprising as its strength. Its yank easily sent her stumbling back towards the edge of the counter. She yelped, and her eyes stretched wide at a face she partially recognized. Lines weathered the youthful face until it was harsh and gaunt. Dark eyes that once glittered with charm shone with a glow of burning scarlet. Angry white streaks danced with the fury of lightning across black hair and made Trina's skin prickle with goosebumps.

"Whose gossiping sent you here to torment me, eh! Some yammering ol' witch? Some meddling ol' man? Who?" E. bellowed. The rattling turned to a severe quake. It blurred Trina's vision. Now and then, she could hear the clatter of glass through thunder. The fear and rumbling scrambled Trina's senses and nothing came out from the gaping 'O' of her mouth.

With red eyes flaring, E. raised a crooked point and snarled, "Answer, or I will yank out your tongue along with the meddler who told you what they shouldn't have about me and put it in a jar to add to my shelf!"

"Eleri!" Trina managed to shout through shock. "Mr. Eleri told me about you!"

E.'s menacing sneer gradually dropped. The quaking fell to stillness as irate anger relaxed. Just as recognition of the name dawned on him, something else did also. Awareness set in, and E.'s glare softened to a stare that lingered too long into Trina's eyes. The flash of the glowing red pair he saw while glimpsing his own reflection startled him.

In sudden recoil, E. released his grip and his eyes snapped shut as he threw his hands over his face in a shield. A frightened boy's yelp escaped an old man's visage as E. stumbled and his hat toppled forward while the rest of him disappeared behind the counter in his plummet to a clattering heap.

Seconds felt like minutes as Trina stood there and calmed the pace of her heart. Her mind tried to process the previous chaos while it attempted to negotiate whether or not she was safe. She froze when she heard a rustling from behind the counter. Fingers timidly pawed the table top, and both hands anchored themselves on the counter to hoist the rest of a body that belonged to an old man with hair covered in stark white. Despite his appearance, he still moved with smoothness although he paused every now and then as he groaned, and slowed when an ache tempered a lunge or a pull he overestimated. By the time he plopped down in the chair he had set behind the open space of the front counter, the old man slumped in its back support. He was spent.

Trina craned her head at the hoary-headed figure across the counter. "E. or which one are you?"

"One and the same, girl." E.'s titter came out in a croak. "Just many aspects rooming in one house. Elegba, I am and always will be. And, sometimes E. when I run the galleria or just for fun."

"And, Eshu?" Trina asked.

The inquiry forced E.'s brows to crunch in a forlorn furrow. Shame stooped his head and his eyes clamped shut like before when he saw the awful color in the mirror of Trina's eyes. His knotted knuckles pressed together in a timid ball in an effort to stop his tremor. "A part of myself I tried to leave in the past among other things I wish to forget."

Trina watched the old man, wary at first. After, the previous chaos, she was still on edge and she braced herself against any other unpleasant surprises. Her tenseness lessened when she heard what was once a monstrous growl, tame into a voice that was timorous and fragile. Even his appearance, the way he trembled and crouched in his seat gave her a lump in her throat. She searched the floor found the black hat, retrieved it from the place where it had fallen, and moved up to the counter. E. was startled by Trina as she suddenly stood over him, but relaxed when he saw she was there to return his hat. He thanked her and Trina gave him a welcoming nod.

Her eyes wandered to his scalp, and she suddenly thought of what she suspected was under his cap. She was partially right; it was a wavy buzz cut that was as white as the puffs that branched from his head. She half expected him to put his hat back on, but instead he held it under his curling fingers. He looked down at the hat and stared at it. His head waggled in a slow, sorrowful shake. His mouth was fixed in an effort to say the words, but like his memory that had a tendency to block out the image, the words of the hue he long desired stalled. "That color," E. finally said as he looked at one half of the black bowler hat. "It used to be my favorite color."

"I didn't mean to disturb you so," Trina apologized, then stalled. Part of her felt guilty for sending E. into such a state and even more for asking him a favor. Nonetheless, there was too much at stake, and too much time had passed for her to wrestle with her reservations. "Mr. Eleri said I would eventually run into you. E…Mr. Elegba, I need your help."

E. nodded and sighed as he closed his eyes. "I know why you are here. I know about the lost soul, your sister, and everything." E.'s eyes opened, but he stared hard at the table top as he shook his head. "The younger Orisha do not understand. It was expected that they would go along.

They were not what the oldest of us were. They do not know the horror."

"You were an Aeon, like Mr. Eleri," Trina said.

"Like Orunmila, yes." E. nodded. Then he shook his head and rocked. He was agitated. "Even if he did not see what I did, he saw enough to know better. How could he agree to this?" E. suddenly stilled himself and looked at Trina. He saw she was worried. "Young woman, you are still a precious child to us, no matter what state of being you are in. We see you as your mother and father do. We pray for your safety just as your grandmother and grandfather are doing right now. What Olodumare, the Creator, is sending you to do." E. could only shake his head, not able to finish.

"Mr. Eleri told me everything," Trina declared as an attempt to assuage E.'s disquiet more so than to ease her own anxiousness.

"To a point, yes." E. gave a great sigh and paused. He prepared himself to confess a weighty truth of his own. He lowered his head and looked at the lines of the table top. Finally, he found courage and lifted his head to face Trina. "Some of my brethren were at one time lost. In time they became the engineers of what many in the Submateria would call demons, wicked souls, anything evil. Archons are perhaps their pride and joy. What they were as progenitors of evil was far worse. At one time, I was one of them."

Trina shook her head. Her brows crunched together in confusion. "No way, that can't be true."

"It is true," E. admitted. His mouth drew tight and solemn. "I am a trickster through and through, but sometimes my more maligned nature surfaces. The part of me that is Eshu was a small fragment left over from my past when I joined the corrupted ones."

Trina grimaced as though the confession left a bad taste in her mouth. She looked at the old man with a gaze that shifted between despondency and reproach. "All of the terrible things they've done, the chaos it still causes now and you were a part of it? Why?"

"Enterprise," E. confessed again and he lowered his head in shame. He stared at his hands and clasped his hat. His mind was far-off. "During the war, I sat on the fence at first. I was an observer. Then, when I heard about their plans for the Black Dive, I got curious. When the Corruptors invaded the Black Dive, I joined them."

He shirked the guilt long enough to raise his head and he returned his gaze to the girl. His sad eyes looked into her accusatory ones. "I'm sure Orunmila told you that Olodumare cleaved the Divine Monstrum in order to properly bind it. The truth is he reopened an old wound, though it pained him to do so."

"An old wound?" Trina winced. She remembered what Mr. Eleri told her about the Creator creating the Tri-Hold. This new bit of information took her off guard. "What happened?"

"The Second Born was still huddled in the deep, asleep when we found it." E. stopped mid-explanation and swallowed hard as his eyes faltered from Trina's gaze. "Soon after, it was dragged out the blackness and was torn in half. The Corruptors had beaten and bound it. They farmed information from what still worked well, and tried to learn secrets that would give them an edge in the war while setting up post in the Black Dive."

Trina drew in a nasally breath. Tears laced her eyes and knotted her throat, but she pushed the lump down.

"And what did you, do?"

"Nothing." E. confessed. "I shared my misguided thoughts from time to time, but mainly I observed. I was intrigued by what adversity would mold it into. One day, somehow, it put itself back together. Everything we made to prey on it became its quarry. Eventually, it developed a taste for us. If the Black Dive still exists, I'm sure that bitterness leftover's still gnawing on the carcasses of the Corruptors." As E. explained, his visage looked, haunted. His eyes glazed over as the memory of wrath and destruction played back in his head like a projector screen. When he was able to snap himself from being drawn in by the waking nightmare, he turned to Trina, again. "Orunmila told you the Second Born became known to the Aeons as the Divine Monstrum. Another name was whispered among the Corruptors; the Crying One. The hatred it felt for us brimmed to the point it bled from its eyes. Those odd things glared at me like a pair of awful suns while I fled with what was left of myself. That memory alone robbed me of the fondness for some of the small things."

Sympathy for the old man's phobia and anger at his past inaction mixed in an uneven churn in Trina's stomach. "You could have stopped this, E."

E. nodded. "Not a day goes by where I don't feel regret. But what the Creator has in mind to resolve this is insane, let alone possible."

"Maybe for you it's impossible, but I won't stand by and watch like you did." Trina clenched her fists until her knuckles burned. The anxiousness she felt earlier was almost nonexistent in the face of her renewed resolve.

E. paused and shook his head for a moment. An exasperated chuckle escaped his mouth before his lips thinned into a fretful pout. Frustrated, the wrinkles of his forehead crumpled even more. "The Creator plans to use fire to rid the village of a wolf, and hopes you and six others have enough water to keep the village from burning to the ground." E. fell silent again and his head waggled with uncertainty the more he thought about the absurdness of the plan. His eyes settled on Trina. Warmth and graveness clouded his gaze. "You still only see the little girl you used to play dress and makeup with. As for that lost one, the one you've known only for a short time during your journey, you mistake its child-like form, when what you actually see is a creature at its lowest point. With every loss and pain they have experienced through the process of the Tri-Hold, its anger grows. After the Archon is dealt with, then what will the Crying One do next, eh? This thing won't stop till the devil's broke down, dead, and God's got a scar. With a grudge like that, what can seven mortals do?"

With every word he spoke, there was a weightiness, a conviction that strived to make her understand the gravity of the odds. Now it was Trina's turn to lapse into silence. Looking inward, her head bowed.

She reflected on the trickster's desperate warning. But she too thought of how far she had come and what was at stake. The life of her family was on the line, after all. Fear was a factor, but more than anything she was driven by faith.

"Right now, all I want is to protect my family. The Light Bearers, the Heotron, and everything else is all new to me. I don't even know what the full extent of my role as a Light Bearer entails. But, if the Creator believes in us enough that we can bring about the best outcome, then I am willing to take whatever risks."

"And you are so sure of yourself?" E. spoke, half with sarcasm, half with concern.

Trina's posture straightened and her head lifted to meet the old man's anxious glower. "Sure, enough to carry out the Raising."

For some seconds, E. studied her with a worried gape. Then, convinced she had made up her mind, he relented. "If that is the case, then … ." He leaned sideways to get a better angle for one hand to reach into the side of his jacket. No sooner had E. fumbled around in his pocket, his hand resurfaced, and he held up a puffed, metal disk complete with stem. "Should you find trouble in the Dead End, toss this at its feet."

When it was offered to her, Trina took the disk, and inspected both its stem and brightly wrapped paper. It reminded her of a spinning firecracker. Her eyes dipped as she tucked the trinket into her own pocket. As her head lifted, the glimpse of E.'s upwardly pointed head signaled a call to attention. "Light and fire. They are cousins, believe it or not. One shows the way and keeps you on the path. The other can be useful too, but it can be harmful if not exercised properly."

The old man's expression warmed. His smile was close-lipped and thoughtful as his index turned towards her. "There is a lot of light in you and that is good. But sometimes you must know what other people have and which one to use." The corners of his lips curled slightly and proudly. Then, as the smile melted into a more solemn mien, E. swung his index towards the back of the room. "It went that way."

Trina followed the line of E.'s eyes and index finger. The rear area of Camino's Galleria had changed. Earlier, the back of the shop was nothing but a wall with a single door with a sign that said the back entrance was exclusively for personnel use. Now, a black curtain covered the wall. Its length stretched from the shelves of comedy and tragedy. Sitting on top of the curtain's center was an arching signage reminiscent of the electric letters one would find along a Broadway marquee. Bulbs fixed inline of the French font raised the lighting of the store from dimness. The letters of the signage spelled out, "Expo of Darkness."

"Art installations are the bread and butter of this here establishment. The title's the theme. Look, if you wish. See if you can find where the lost one ran off to, but once you go beyond those curtains… ." E. cautioned.

Trina drew in a deep breath and her head gave a quick shake. "I know, thank you, Mr. Elegba."

"E., sweets." He corrected and smiled weakly then winked. "Good luck."

Trina smiled at him, then turned to the sign and the curtains underneath. She blew out another puff of air. Trepidation strapped her feet to floor and shirked away with the first step and then the next. She inched closer to the black curtain and the pitter-patter of a racing heart turned into thudding. Mentally, she repeated a mantra to stay brave and to keep moving. She kept walking and, all the while, the Orisha kept watch until she disappeared behind the black veil.

Chapter 9

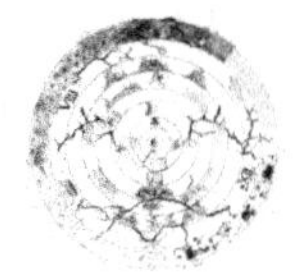

The darkness was dense and Trina was caught off guard by it. As tangible as the black curtain was when she lifted the flap to cross over, there was something about the darkness that stoked the uneasy imaginings of a fly caught in a jar of honey. Despite its openness, the stagnant nature of the space made the black a viscous thing that pressed in upon her mind and senses. It rendered her immobile and indecisive. She, the fly, sank farther and farther into the void without even taking a step. Elegba may have meant something else by there being no return, but the darkness on its own was enough of an impediment. While her body stood motionless, she mentally floundered against a rising panic and the mind fog formed from the complete blackout of her vision. Trina let out an exasperated sputter that banished the jitters from her nerves. Here she was in the throes of panic about being in total darkness that she nearly forgotten she was her own source of light.

Trina's heart rate dropped back to normal. She felt the corners of her eyes stretch and she could imagine them rolling around on a face wrinkled with annoyance. She concentrated and conjured up an inner warmth that began at her core and spread throughout. Light bloomed with the diffusion of warmth and before long, Trina was like a candle that emanated its gentle shine about a dark room. As the soft light completed its reach across every surface of the area, Trina gasped. She was in a chamber of some sort, a space with curving walls and arched ceiling that gave the area a dome-like shape. The chamber was of modest size, not cramped like a closet or even snug like the rooms of a house or an apartment. Instead, the encircled nearness of the walls and ceiling gave her the impression that the chamber was a showroom. Judging from the objects placed within the chamber, the space was a showroom for art.

With her mouth slightly parted in awe, her feet followed what her eyes drew in along the surfaces of the room. A fresco covered the walls and ceiling of the chamber like the Sistine Chapel in the Vatican City or hollows of some ancient gathering hall. Colorful, telluric plots and churning oceans stretched into rifts of starry black or firmaments both akin to and alien from the skies seen on earth. Figures and shapes that populated these images were marvelous and surreal. The fresco appeared fantastic and unreal, yet there was a texture to the paintings wrought with realism that told Trina of things seen with actual eyes rather than conceived from the imaginations of the mind.

At first glance, there seemed to be an overlap, a continuous stream of images that ran into one another. A longer study of the fresco, however, revealed an order. The circled link of the mural held several scenes where the end of one episode gave way to the beginning of another. These images told of a series of events that began peaceful but spilled into chaotic activity and ended in a state of ruin. There were several stories told here, but Trina was not sure what they were.

Nearing one of the walls of the chamber, Trina traced her fingers across one of the scenes. A subtle itching of recognition settled in. First, there was the vague feeling of something familiar about the fresco-like lost memories that dug their way to the surface. She pondered on what surfaced from the dark recesses of her mind. She would think of a single flower, and her eyes would find a painting of that peculiar plant that stood out from the rest of the landforms. She would think of some lone animal odd among its fellow fauna and would find its likeness on the wall. There were more of these thoughts of a single living thing that grew of a place, yet was alien among its peers. The strangest thing in imagining these lifeforms was not only seeing them in the murals but what she perceived. All of the lifeforms singled out in the fresco, seemed to be one being in many forms, that lived through many cycles, and suffered many hardships. Its existence ended from many catastrophes. In trying to make sense of what she intuited, there was one thought paramount, a longing, a search for the pair and a place to call home. Then came the breakthrough, an understanding. The scenes painted across the walls and ceiling told the story of Alex's past lives.

Though the scenes of the fresco that ran along the walls were new to her, there was one segment of the fresco that jumped out. It was a scene towards the dome's summit. The painting was an image of a diminutive being, dragged through the expanses of space. Though the small figure had an alien form, there was enough humanness about it that Trina could discern the head looked where its limbs reached down at a trio of planets that shattered to pieces. She could tell where its waist was and that it was ensnared by some tendril-like grappler that was connected to a bulking body that was either a spacecraft or a monster. She had seen this scene, albeit briefly in the chaos that occurred in the Marrow. Her eyes could see the tragedy as clearly as her mind registered it. The lost soul's last reincarnation held hope. The other half that had been missing was within grasp. A peaceful place ze could call home had been found. Everything Alex yearned for was suddenly taken away by a tyrant that brought the catastrophes of war to the doorsteps of zeir haven. The results of such a visit ended in Alex's abduction, the severing of the ties to zeir other half and the loss of zeir home.

Trina felt the rise of a knot in her throat and swallowed to fight it down. She finally withdrew contact from the surface of the fresco, then she turned to the other piece of artwork. A pedestal sat at the chamber's center. Suspended in place a few inches or so above the pedestal's platform was a stooping rag doll enclosed in an armillary of two, uneven metal rings. Thick metal spikes pierced through the doll in all directions, and held it in place of the rings' steady rotation. Approaching the armillary, Trina studied the doll caught in the crossing of spikes. The doll's lopsided posture threw its messy string of dark hair towards the side of its slouch with some strands that dangled with the revolution of the rings. Now in front of the pedestal, she noticed the places where the spikes had punctured dark brown burlap to the point where more white stuffing showed. White fluff partially puffed from where a mouth would normally be stitched in a smile, or in this case a frown. One of the buttons hung loosely, and made what should be a pair of buttoned eyes uneven.

Staring at Alex's likeness made the lump in her throat harder to fight. It may have been a prop for the purpose of display, but the doll's state was enough to summon an uneasy ache. Suddenly she had the urge to readjust its eye, to mend the places where the stuffing was open, better yet to unhook the doll from the spikes all together. There may have been rules about tampering with the displays of the art installations, but Trina did not care. She reached up and took hold of the doll. The flash across her mind was violent. It was a mental whiplash. The vision flickered with the harshness of a camera that snapped bursts of light that burned into her retina before its fading spark stretched warped images over it. There were several of these flashes and each harsh burst revealed flickers of shapes. Jagged objects, some metal, some of other substances, all looked sharp, restrictive, and intrusive. They were instruments of experimentation. Cruel eyes on the faces of monstrous figures watched from some distance away. Indistinguishable speech warbled in the noise that carried an industrial sting like electricity or sizzling fire and clanking of metal. A shrill cry for help tore into the chaotic noise, and a tattered appendage suddenly waved into view and attempted to shield itself against the terrible instruments. Something metal passed overhead. A reflection gave glimpse of a cowering figure, damaged by the violence of those probing machines.

The dreadful vision vanished as quickly as her hand recoiled. Trina nearly stumbled backward and her throat screamed with the air her lungs pulled in. Tears trickled down and her eyes crunched together. She tried to shut out the horror she had felt and seen. A hand flew up to her mouth and clamped down on the impending sob. Tears had already seeped through, but any moment there would soon be a flood. The uncontrollable wave of emotions was only intercepted by the distant dragging of something hollow and metal. Alarm forced down any ache that threatened to climb out of her throat. Trina did not want to take the chance of attracting potential attackers, therefore she quieted her light and receded its reach from the walls and ceiling until it gathered at the fingertips of her right hand. Her left hand cupped over the light candles of her right hand and further masked the show of white shine. Motionless, she listened closely for stirrings in the dark.

With every nerve of her being locked in stillness, she felt as though she would turn into another art piece to compliment the chamber. Murmuring and the soft clicking of loafers broke silence's span. Trina's narrowing eyes were her first parts to unfasten from the hold of immobility. The sound was near, not close enough to be in the room directly at her back, but near enough for her to tell that someone or something was passing by. There was a clinical nature about the monotoned drone and muffled clatter of steps, and it reminded her of something one would hear at a trip to the doctor's office. No matter how mundane the sound, Trina had to proceed with the utmost caution. Sensing its distance, she dared to look over her shoulder in a cautious swivel. The rest of her body followed the turn of her head and Trina unsheathed the fingertips of light. The black curtains that served as the entrance to the art showing were nowhere to be found. Instead, there was the rectangle of an open ingress that led to someplace dark.

She could suppose or worry as to where such an entryway was headed, but that would lead her nowhere. The scarcity of time said she could not afford to linger too long. Urgency led her step by step, while caution kept her senses open. Upon crossing the threshold to leave the fresco chamber, Trina half-expected to step out into a hallway. She was caught off guard by the blink and sizzle of fluorescent light the instant she set foot in the next room. Like a sleeper coming to wakefulness after a long nap, the light flickered a few more times before it settled into a constant run. The cold glow of pale lighting made the space look and feel sterile. With linoleum flooring and slap brush plastering for the walls and ceilings, the room was basically a white box. Its insipidness forced Trina to blink and rub away a wilting dryness that made her eyes itch. She spun back to where she had first entered, and the ingress was gone. There were no doors anywhere; no way out of the white box. Her eyes swiveled in search of an exit, and a rising panic shuddered under the somnolence that gradually set in her mind like frost. Then came another sizzle and a flicker, not from the lights, but from the brief images of furnishings that populated the box.

Fixtures buzzed in and out of being like a bad connection on a television monitor. First, she glimpsed an executive chair behind a heartwood desk. On the opposite side, were two guest chairs set side by side. Honorary plaques and paintings hung about the walls while knick-knacks, engraved items and writing utensils decorated the work station. It was an office of some sort, perhaps a meeting room between practitioner and visitor. In another phase of flickering, the polished features of an office gave way to a scene set with more industrial equipment. There was a wall cabinet and a sink. Another cushioned guest chair camped against a wall with a magazine holder at foot, and a roller stool next to a family practice table. It was an inspection room. These objects were transitory and they alternated between the furnished sets of the therapy office and the examination room. Trina's brow jumped. She noticed movement and the appearance of three vague shapes added to the scratchy images of the therapist's office.

Trina's eyes strained at the shape behind the executive desk. Electric fuzz proportioned to the height of a man, entered from one end of the desk and moved towards the seat. There was a blip in the image and a split second of clarity revealed that it was indeed a man, a practitioner dressed in formal work attire, who maneuvered his way towards the executive chair. No doubt this man was the therapist. More intermittent blips of clearness delivered snatches of human voices. There were words of welcome, and a name addressed in greeting that Trina immediately recognized. The instant she heard the name, Mrs. Finley, the fuzz that took up the pair of guest seats, settled. She glimpsed her mother momentarily stretch her arm across the desk to shake the therapist's hand. In the other seat, the twelve-year-old image of her younger sister sat slouched.

"June! Mom!" With an unwavering gaze, Trina's voice was barely above a whisper as she approached the guest chairs. Of course, neither her sister nor her mother stirred. Like the wavering fixtures, the likeness of her loved ones were nothing more than electronic mirages installed as art pieces in a gallery. Even so, Trina could not help but place a hand on her mother's shoulder. Contact with the electric fuzz made her nerves itch with a sensation akin to the feel of one's limb falling asleep. For a brief moment, there was density in the fuzz before it yielded under the weight of a hand. And then came the worry, the rapid running nerves of urgency, the sinking feeling in her stomach. The mind's eye held clear the image of her mother's hand as it held a young girl's arms marred by the keloid of old scars. Next came the vision of her mother's face with her eyes stretched wide with dismay. A knot formed in her throat as the sight of the scars caused her heart to tumble down. She pulled the twelve-year-old June in a hug. Another vision showed the tears that clung to the corners of her mother's eyes in June's presence. They fell freely in front of her husband as she told him what she discovered. The sadness and dismay worn by her mother in the previous vision now dawned on the face of her father. There were words exchanged before husband embraced wife in a hug, and his strong arms tried to shield her from emotional pain. After the quick succession of the visions, her sight returned to the white box.

Trina took deep breaths and attempted to settle down the uneasy mix of her mother's consternation with her own. After a few moments to gather herself, Trina moved to the side where June sat. Trina stood there and stared at the much smaller cowering collection of fuzz that sat in the chair. She had to find answers, had to keep moving forward, but how? Trina rummaged through her mind and struggled to make sense of the puzzle she found herself in. Her thoughts bounced back and forward from the time spent in the last chamber to the blinking image of a therapist's room. The answers were right in front of her, but somehow, she had to make sense of things and find an order that led to progress through the gallery. When she touched the fresco and the doll, things were revealed to her and a passage led elsewhere. Things were also revealed when she made contact with one of the electric mirages. Was interacting with the art installations the key to moving forward? She did not know, but perhaps this theory was worth testing.

Trina lingered on the blurred image of her little sister as she sat in the chair and remembered the brief solidness of the fuzz. She thought of how the fuzz injected her with the view points of the chair's occupants. The idea that flashed in her head seemed random and unfounded to work, but Trina acted on hunch anyway. She stood at the place where June sat with her back turned towards her mirage as she timed the flickering objects. When she caught the fuzz in clarity, Trina sat down. The density of the chair's electric mirage held her in place. Trina was surprised when the fuzz did not collapse seconds before her weight settled on it. A bleariness struck her and made the inside of her head feel as though it were stuffed with cotton. The vision that buzzed over her eyes was a closeup of her sister as she sat stooped on the examination table. Details of the vision were fogged by blur, and there was the low, slowed warbling of speech. A sudden shift in image brought a change in perspective, and Trina could suddenly see through June's eyes. The image of the person who sat in front of her was out of focus, but Trina could tell it was a woman in a white doctor's coat. The voices may have been muffled and the words indistinct, but Trina perceived clearly the nature of the exchange.

"Feeling better?" the doctor chimed in, her head front and center to observe the patient.

"Okay," June answered in a voice that was either unsure or slothful.

With her head tilted down, the doctor scribbled pen to pad of what she heard and visually observed in the patient. When the scribbling stopped, the doctor looked up from the notepad as she asked, "Seeing or hearing any more things that aren't there?" She looked up from her notepad.

"No," June answered again with an even tone.

Just beyond the doctor's shoulder, Trina saw a child standing behind her. She knew it was Alex standing there with zeir body bent slightly forward. Zeir shoulders, arms, and legs tensed. Though the detail of the face was blurred, she heard Alex shout and beg June to listen to a voice she could no longer hear.

Like a swimmer who broke through the water's surface to meet air, Trina felt the muddled vision and the cold fuzz of bleariness fall away. The shroud of what she saw may have passed, but a gloom lingered. The more the fuzz cleared, the more Trina understood the connection Alex sought after life cycles had once again been severed. Trina realized the gravity of what she had witnessed. She sighed and tried to rid herself of the weight that impressed on her heart. There was no time to mull in melancholy. As she wrested herself from the gloom to look around the room, she noticed a dark, open frame carved into the wall of white. Her guesswork on interacting with the art pieces to move along the path seemed correct. She stood away from the flickering seat and walked towards the new-found opening.

Before she departed the white box, she cautiously peeked from the ingress's frame and held up her light-tipped fingers to a space she knew was dark. She made a quick study of what lie beyond the white box and she found faint traces of light that dimly showed in the black. Other frames lined the black in rows that hinted at parallel walls. Even before stepping out, she noticed the flooring from the traces of light that trickled out from the chamber to path. Together, the floor and the row of frames created a corridor. To where it led, Trina did not know. Ahead, it was pitch black. For all she knew the thick darkness ahead stretched into an endless void or ended at a solid wall.

Eyes and ears surveyed the dark corridor. Trina completely stepped out from the white box to the dark corridor. Her fingertips held up like a guiding candle and her footsteps moved along in a steady pace. For every room she passed, there held an art installation fashioned in both simple and surreal imagery that likely conveyed some emotion or memory from June or the lost soul's past. Trina scanned each entry frame and hoped that among the art installations she would glimpse anything that hinted to the lost soul's whereabouts.

When she passed the sixth row of rooms, a flash of a cool glow a few doors down caught her eye. She paused when she glimpsed the light, and drew her eyes to focus on the spot of the glow's initial wink. The flash showed itself again and revealed that it was a blue light. With wide eyes, her excitement carried her footfall at a faster pace towards the direction of the blue wink. The glow flashed a third time and with it came the airy sifting of breaths from quiet sobs.

"Alex!" Trina's brisk walk turned into a jog, then she sprinted and hopped into a glide. She quickly covered ground and she arrived at the frame where the blue light once flickered.

"I'm right here, Alex! Where...?" Trina stiffened. The words jumped back in her throat as one foot rocked back. Her jaw slackened and her eyes peeled wide in a baffled gawk as she tried to make sense of what she saw.

The chamber seemed small, maybe the size of a single bedroom within an apartment. In the middle of the room, a light hung low from the ceiling. Directly under it she could make out a headless neckline and shoulders, glances of a knee, hands, wrists and elbows. The texture of these parts bristled in some areas and smoothed in others. The dull sheen of their surfaces reminded her of old nickel. By its immobility, Trina guessed that it was another art piece, a sculpture. The model was positioned low to the ground. From the glimpses of its leg, she assumed the statue sat cross-legged on the ground. Its upper limbs slightly bent upward as it anchored out, almost conveyed an overwhelming futility of halting the mass of dark chiton that clamored from its headless neck.

Despite her heart thundering to the pace of a gallop, she could barely hear the rapid beating above the symphony of clicking. Trina watched the dark infestation spew from the headless statue. It swirled about and matted floors, ceilings and walls and caused her skin to bristle. From the overlap of legs that strummed in a frenzy to tumble over dark bodies, she could not tell what the creatures were. The way they scuttled along the walls and the floor reminded her of spiders or roaches, yet there were times they went airborne. She could only assume they were some sort of insect. As a cluster ascended from the crawling floor, and swam pass the statue in a squirming vortex, she heard another airy sob.

"Alex? June?" Trina craned her head and searched to find the source of the sound. She pushed aside feelings of overwhelm from the sight of the swarm and she inched closer to the opening. She stopped at the threshold and her eyes scoured the pulsing room.

"Alex, are you in there?" Trina called out again. A sniffle and a blue spark jolted her attention. On impulse she leaned forward and took hold of the opening's frame. Her excitement turned to dismay as she saw blue light spark from the sculpture's neck. The sound of sniffling and airy sobs was a trick of sound. It was an illusory effect from the intermittent sparks of light that let out a muted noise and mimicked the voice of quiet weeps.

Running limbs swept over the fingers that clung to the opening's frame. The contact sent Trina's mind in a reel and her sight was seized by another flood of visions. No sooner had her mind's eye settled on the peaceful image of her mother and little sister in the front seat of their old Camry, then came the hard rock of impact. A shrill shriek rang out with the squeal of rubber across asphalt. The color red flashed at the window of the driver's seat milliseconds before the burst of crushed metal. Glass shattered and splashed over her mother's shoulders as she lurched violently sideways. The car horn blared over panicked cries from a little girl whose mother was unconscious. Her hips and legs pinned to the seat, her upper body crumpled over the armrest. The next image came in quick succession. It showed a hospital bed where her mother lay motionless, eyes closed, her body supported by a mask and tubes. Her father sat in the waiting room and held little June who couldn't seem to stop shivering. Her mother finally regained consciousness, but remained bedridden as she reunited with husband and daughter.

June's eyes glued to her mother. Her mother and father's attention were fixed on the doctor who had joined them. Their expressions were sober as he made a report. Countless scenes depicted surgeons crowded around an operating table and more scenes showed her mother as she struggled in rehab. The last image was of June as she sat in a corner of their old room, legs folded with her knees tucked under her chin, and her arms hugging her shins while she rocked in place with her solid black eyes blank and sad.

The visions faded and Trina found there was a considerable amount of space between her and the room with the headless statue. She cradled the hand that made contact with one of the crawling things and she trembled. Even as the vision vanished, she found it hard to slow the rapid rapping of her heart against her lungs. Her nerves tingled so badly that at any moment, she thought they would scuttle out from beneath her skin like those things in the room. As difficult as it was to calm the lingering panic, she willed herself to do enough to where she could reflect.

What she saw was a memory. It was supposed to be another girls' day out. Her mother and sister were on their way to the mall until the hit and run. Aside from knowing that it was a red truck that caused the wreck, no one was able to identify the offender. It was a blessing that both June and her mother survived. Still, after countless surgeries and grueling recovery, their mother was still lame. Even after she fought to stay alive, the pain and the disappointment, their mother came out with a smile and stronger than before. From what Trina witnessed and felt, however, it was apparent that June was still haunted by the ordeal. Trina could still feel what June did. She felt the despondency of knowing how fragile her mother's life was, and the powerlessness of not being able to relieve her suffering. She felt the dread most poignantly. She thought about such an awful emotion and looked back at the room. She wondered if all what crawled in the chamber held dread tied to a traumatic event?

Trina slowly backpedaled and tore her eyes away from the crawling room. She finally hurried along her path. She moved down the corridor in a brisk walk and she passed the one door that was away from the room of the swarm, then a second, and a third. It was the fourth door down and across the hall that the hiss of breath and flare of crimson light halted Trina in mid-step.

The light itself did not forcibly hold her in place, but indecision did. The lost soul, the clue to zeir whereabouts or the entrance to the Dead End could be hidden in that room. Still, something radiated from that room, something that locked her in hesitation to pursue the matter any further. She let out a sigh to gather her nerve and her mouth drew into a determined bow. Trina willed herself to turn to the light's source. With her steps measured by caution, she peered into the opening. Crimson light let out in a thin curtain that gradually grew in intensity the closer she approached. She paused momentarily, and her ears caught a low sigh or exhalation barely above the quiet. When the fleeting sound was heard no more, Trina took only a single step closer. She still stood at the corridor's edge and outside of the red room's entrance.

The first thing that caught her eye as she scrutinized the room from the hallway was another color. It was green. A chalky neon glow clashed against the room's bright red and the lime-coated objects dangled from thin thread attached to the ceiling. She focused in on the dangling shapes, and made out the bodies of rigid plastic under the powdered clumps of neon coating. They were action figures covered in lime paint, all bound by thread and hanging either by the neck or torso. The macabre decorations weren't the only objects in the room. A pedestal settled at the center of the redness. On the pedestal was a miniature aluminum truck, pierced through the roof and pinned to the platform by heavy iron scissors. Trina swallowed and uneasiness crept under her skin. She studied the toy truck that was cruelly stabbed through and through with the scissors. Aside from the haunting glow of the dangling action figures, the crimson light overpowered every other color in the room. Still, Trina had a strange feeling that the toy truck was red, just like the one that caused the hit and run crash.

There was something wrong about that room. It had a feeling of something menacing, but hidden. She wanted to look away, but her eyes transfixed on the podium. The red light seemed to draw her sight closer to the object on the podium, even as she stood petrified outside the entryway. The air hissed beneath the quiet, again. The sighs echoed in her ears and rose to a brooding almost spiteful susurrus. Among the indistinct chorus of harsh whispers came voices and words she did recognize. The onset of voices sounded far-off like a faint echo. They were young children's voices. The first voice warbled through tears. The second voice sounded much older, his tone was confused as he asked if everything was all right? The second voice said a name, Iggy.

Right away, Trina was able to discern the voices. The second voice belonged to Nico and the former, much younger one, belonged to his step-brother, Iggy. There was an exchange of dismay and confusion between them. The squeal of wheels and sound of a crash interrupted them. Footsteps ran. Her mother's shocked inquiry at the calamity rang out. Heels clicked in a hurried run. Nico's speech high with dismay, wondered about the commotion. And then, Trina heard her sister's name. Nico questioned why she ran towards the chaos and what she held in her hand. The image of the truck and scissors neared to a view as Trina heard his tone rise in alarm. His demands to stop quickly reached panicked shouts that called for Aunt Deb.

Trina clamped her eyes shut and wrested herself from the trance. She nearly stumbled to a heap in the process of shifting in recoil to escape the red light's reach. All was silent, but the remnants of alarmed cries still echoed in her ears. What Trina heard from the red room loomed over her like an ill-boding glare from the opening. But, as her body moved away in aversion of the dreadful crimson, she kept at bay the ponderings and implications of what she heard and saw. Right now, her only concern was to find the lost soul and get away from that room as quickly as possible. Trina slowly backed away from the red glare and opening, and only turned away when she felt safe enough to do so.

She continued down the dark corridor and her eyes roved from room to room from the path. There weren't any signs of the blue spark. Her hearing strained against the silence as she listened for the hollow scrapes of metal she heard earlier. Suddenly, she stopped and her posture stiffened as her ears perked at the high, forlorn whine of an instrument. Trina's brows leapt and her head swiveled in search of the distant sound. When she heard the instrument again, she began a closer scan of the openings that lined the hall. A glint of gold suddenly appeared and broke the black void at the end of the hall. The sunny twinkle touched Trina's eyes and forced her to wince from the slight sting of its touch. For the brief moments it took for her to rub the soreness from her eyes to adjust, the more the curtain of light stretched into the darkness. Acclimated to the new light, Trina found that the golden rays of the late noon sun extended a path from the open door to where she stood.

Initially, Trina was reluctant to follow the light. After what she had experienced in her tours of the previous rooms, she wondered if another horror or possible danger lay in wait for her. And yet, there was a soothing nature about the light, a warmth that reminded her of the comfort of her old earth home. Finally, she spread her wings, lifted from the floor and glided towards the light and warmth that beckoned her approach. When she reached the light at the corridor's end, she was momentarily blinded by the glare of the sun. Trina blinked away the shine to adjust her eyes, and the first thing she noticed was the smell. It was an old familiar aroma, a hint of dust and old wood mingled with the scent of pecans and leather. The image of the backroom at her grandparents' farm appeared in her mind before she saw it with her own eyes. It had the same red and brown commercial carpeting and wood laminate wall with a yellowing flush light at the ceiling. There was the long guest's couch against the side wall and a single person bed opposite it. The RCA television set where Papa J watched his football and basketball games was still there. The chair was different. Granny May's rocking chair had replaced the cushioned and yellow armchair in front of the television.

After a quick sweep of the room, Trina walked over to the rocking chair. She smiled a little, when she noticed the flower designs against white on the padding her grandmother added to make the seat more comfortable. She looked at the objects settled in the rocking chair's seat and immediately trained on the mouth piece of rectangular, metal plates. Trina let out an airy chuckle. She remembered the echo of a doleful tune in the dark corridor and knew she had found the right place. She stooped down to retrieve her grandfather's harmonica, twirled the piece in her hand and inspected it. Then, she admired the reedy instrument and she placed her lips on the mouthpiece. The mental flash was instant, and Trina saw June puff a feeble tune from the instrument as she did.

The fleeting image of her little sister made Trina pause and catch her breath. *She's been here*, Trina thought. Her sight pulled her back into the space before her and Trina carefully surveyed the room. Aside from the replacement of her grandfather's chair, there were other changes in the room. On the left side of it, there were other hats and coats on hangers, knick-knacks on shelves and other items that did not belong. When she looked towards the right, there were other items, mostly photos framed on walls, set on the old RCA, propped on a tucked away coffee table, and laid out on the ruffled sheets of the single bed. She returned her gaze to the seat of the rocking chair and took note of the photo that sat in the white and flower cushion. It was a family portrait of sorts, a photo taken of her, her sister, and their parents during childhood. Her mother and father flashed a smile of perfect whites while she and June's beams were dotted with the holes of missing teeth. From their loud colors, shorts, and trademark accessories, Trina could tell that it was a vacation photo taken most likely at a resort.

She sat in the chair and stared at the photo, wistful at first. She did another scan of the room and noticed something else. To the right of the room were photos of aunts and uncles, cousins, and distant relatives who had yet to cross over. She examined the items on her left and twirled the harmonica in her hand. She reclined in the rocking chair. Suddenly she remembered the dread of the crawling room. She thought of the brief flash of June with the harmonica, and the feeling of her heart sinking. She thought back on her own journey and her thoughts lingered on what she felt and saw when she found June huddled at the bedside of her grandparents' bedroom. It was at that point that the revelation hit her. This room was a shrine.

She stooped forward in the rocking chair and held the framed photo in both hands. Trina stared at the grinning family of four. Then, she realized June mourned the living before they passed as much as she did those who had crossed over. At that moment, Trina sat with a desperate ache. She wanted her sister beside her and wished that her words could pierce her ears through the sadness to say everything would be all right. A familiar, grinding ring broke the silence. It was the same hollow dragging of metal and judging from its rumbling scrapes across gravel, it came from the front yard's driveway.

Trina stood up, ears to the air, and legs stretched across the floor to swiftly cover the length from rocking chair to door. She exited the back room to cut across the entertainment room. Her sweeping strides shortened as she scooted through the narrow aisle between the coffee table and sofa. She stepped over an ottoman impeding her path and nearly stumbled. The chill of goosebumps rippled across her skin when a murky cast rushed across the windows of the room and blotted out the warm peach glow of the sun. The shrouded sky happened suddenly and made Trina shiver even though she had yet to reach open air. Its swift advent and quiet settling seemed little like clouds brought in by the gust and more like the ushering of an omen. The air rang once more with the grind of hollow metal, its toll as near as tires that crunched over driveway gravel. Trina hustled across the entertainment room, down the hall, and into the kitchen. By the time she burst through the screen door and onto front porch, her ears caught the distant raise of a voice.

"Hello! Is anyone out here?" Trina shouted with a pant. Her head swiveled in a frantic search of the yard. There was no one in sight. There wasn't any response. She only heard her own ragged breaths as they disturbed the silence when they tried to calm the rattling of her lungs.

She swore to herself she heard people nearby. Trina stood in the quiet and listened. Around her, the air dampened slightly. Judging from the graying pink of the air and its heaviness, Trina anticipated the smell of rain and earth. Instead, her lips quivered, caught off guard by a bitter, chemical scent that made the roof of her mouth feel dry. She sniffed and identified the light waft of ammonia before it was overtaken by the more pungent mingling of odors.

Trina stepped away from the porch and her eyes fell on the ground as she heard the stray pitter-patter of what she thought were droplets across gravel. Immediately, she spotted a bit of white that stood out among the dry dirt and pebbles. Her eyes studied the speck and she moved closer, then froze in place. Her brows jumped when she identified the bit of white. Trina swallowed hard as she knelt down to pick up the pill capsule. The air felt stagnant and the sky held the rain and wind, just as the breath held in Trina's lungs. In spite of the doldrums, she heard something that drifted to and from her ears. Trina's head wildly whipped before briskly jogging a few steps or two towards the side of the house. She saw no one, but there wasn't any mistaking the voices. It was the second time she heard the voices. Their passing was brief and faint as the last, but she knew the owners of the unison call. Their father was here, somewhere. Like her, he searched the farm. Desmond Jettis, one of their uncles, had joined the search, too.

Another pass and go of an echo sounded again. The disembodied voice was distressed and it crackled. "Where is she?"

Trina heard the sound of despair in her mother's voice and swallowed down the aching knot in her throat that began to form. Now and then, she heard murmuring about finding June's backpack in the house and her bike in the yard. There was other talk about the state of the house and about the text message that Iggy and Nico received. Calls were made to June's phone, to coworkers and relatives, and to the police. Trina could hear them speak, but not once did she see them in mid-rove of the yard or house. Their voices were impossible to pinpoint almost as if the sounds they made were carried on the backs of the wind. Still, from what she heard, they were on the right track. That gave Trina a small hope to cling to while her heart thundered with dread.

She thought of the pill she found in the driveway and doubled back. She started from the place where the pill was found and moved along its path. The odor returned. The farther along she progressed, the smell grew more pronounced. She analyzed it. The scent was more of a rank, overpowering mix of fusty, brackish water, and the sickly-sweet aroma of something fermented. She continued along the driveway and heard the pitter-patter that signaled the clamorous fall of rain. There was no dot on her skin from the rain. Instead, she found that the sparse sprinkling of pills ran a light trail from the front yard tree to an empty bottle. Trina followed the trail. The stink of brackish water took on another smell. Sodden iron. She reached the empty pill container and saw something that nearly made her heart stop. A few feet away from the bottle, a deep brownish red stain dampened the dry earth.

Trina shook her head at the stray spatters of blood at the end of the trail. Inside, her head roiled as compose fought against panic and disbelief fought against realization. The wrestling inside her head kicked up numbing fumes and for a moment, Trina felt as though she was going through the motions as she walked past the bottle, the trickled stains of blood, and stopped on a dry stint of dirt. Then came the ring of the hollow metal grind like a death toll that beckoned her to look down the driveway, past the dirt road that separated the farm from a field.

Across from the farm was a pasture. Every now and then cattle appeared from the wall of trees from the far end of the pasture to graze. A white and brown spotted cow was the most consistent visitor of the field and because of the animal's regular visits, a water trough was placed near the pasture's edge. Though the field was cordoned off from the road by vinyl post and rail fencing, the gates were low enough for people to easily bypass.

The drinking tank was still there. It was gray metal with a top marred by the brownish red stain of rust. There was an audience at the water trough. Three vulture-like spirits took roost on the tank's rim, and their frames moved within a translucent covering as they craned over the container. The fourth guest, an equine phantom with a form as ethereal as the vultures, trotted from elsewhere to join the other three to see what lie at the bottom of the water tank. Whatever the horse saw must have disturbed it, for it reared, and bumped the tank. The vultures hopped at the upheaval and shifted around the rim and Trina saw a bleeding wrist and a hand sink out of sight.

"No!" Trina gasped. Her feet pulled her forward into a walk and then into a run. "Oh, no! NO!" Trina screamed. Her legs moved into a sprint as she took to the air and flew. Her pounce on top of the trough caused the macabre spectators to flee into invisibility. The wind returned and carried an utterance of confusion, followed by dismay, shouts, and wailing. She could hear the ghosts of hurried scrapes and panicked cursing. Shouts for a medic haunted her ears. She could hear the frantic sloshing of water before she plunged her arms into the murk of blood and foam.

Trina flailed around the tank, desperate to pull June's head above water. The whole time she called in the same manner as the voices in the wind that pleaded for June to open her eyes. She reached still for any part of June's body she could find and her hands grasped on to her sister's armpit. With all her might, Trina pulled upward. Despite June's lifelessness, her body seemed to rebel against Trina's efforts. The more Trina pulled, the more her grip slipped from armpit, to forearm, and then down to her wounded wrist as though something underneath the trough tugged at June from the opposite direction. Trina gritted her teeth and her hands clamped down on June's wrist and she fought against the tug, even as the force seemed to pull her sister further under. Trina vowed to never let go, even as she too was pulled into to the tank.

Blood and water flooded her mouth and nose. A ruddy darkness obstructed her vision as the rest of her body felt the wet, icy submerge. Suddenly, the shallowness of the tank became a seemingly bottomless deep until her face hit air. The breath in Trina's lungs burst forth in a great inhale, and as tightly as Trina gripped June's wrist, her hands suddenly clasped the emptiness. Blindness gave way to sight. Gravity shifted, and her wings branched into full splay and caught the wind like a parachute to halt her drop.

Gathering her wits, Trina soon found herself airborne, miles high above the ground. Whatever sky she entered was in some other realm housed within Limbo, but it was someplace bleak.

Below was a scape of shells. Flotsam and jetsam cluttered the land the same way lush canopies dressed forests floors. Exposed ground dotted the wasteland. Plots of dirt were weathered, dry, and useless.

The patches of vegetation she did spy, were yellowing and low or were dark, gray creepers that constricted dead wood and fragments of what may have been buildings. An overcast bloated, but never relinquished a drop of rain as it bore down over the blood orange of a setting yet hidden sun. It cast an almost violet hue over the fuzz and crust of corrosion.

A junkyard was all that Trina could make of it as she first glanced the land below. Where she was and how she got there was the least of her concerns. Sometime between tumbling from the depths of the water trough and into the new realm, Trina lost hold of June's hand. She frowned and her mind strained to think. She tried to remember frame for frame all that had transpired. Whether she witnessed her sister drifting through the air in mid-drop to the bottom, she could not recall. As June sank to the base of the trough, Trina was temporarily blinded by the murky water. Could she have fallen from her grasp then? Had June hurtled down in a crash landing into the pile of junk, while she had been blinded? If that were the case, what would that mean? Would the dangers of her soul falling to the bottom from such a height in Limbo be tantamount to the fatality one would suffer in the living world?

Frozen in mid-hover, Trina's thoughts reeled from panic. Then, she heard a noise, the sizzling of static, and a quick transition to the sound of voices. It interrupted an utterance and cut in the middle of a sentence. There was an electric crackle and silence. Hearing the brief stint of racket snatched Trina from the onset of hysteria. She played back the noise in her mind, and it reminded her of a television set.

She thought more about what she heard, how it seemed like it suddenly turned on and off. Trina not only wondered where the television set was, but who or what had triggered it. The sound had been faint, as though some distance away, but not so far that her wings could not carry her there in quick time. The trick was to spot the source of the sound in this sea of junk, and her hope was that her search would be a fruitful errand and not a useless effort.

Trina glided and followed the direction where her ears had first caught the sound. She kept a hawk's view as she scoured the wasteland. Discarded things, some familiar, some unknown, made for strange and eerie markers that littered the land route. A giant-sized head, its face lying on its side and half buried in a shattered pile reminded Trina of an ornamental head belonging to some signage or architectural fixture of a toy store. She spied a broken Ferris wheel, dated models of planes and other erstwhile objects. Once, there was even a fragment of an ancient building she knew she had seen from somewhere in a travel guide or history book. Then, there was the unrecognizable. Pieces of architecture that were arcane, large esoteric instruments that appeared to be the spokes of an even larger machine lay among the ruins. Though rusted, their forms were bitten and worn by time. The ancient and unknown litter still held marvel. She looked at the unknown debris and wondered what hands fashioned the alien objects and how magnificent it must have been when the structures were new and whole.

She continued her flight path and saw more mountains of junk and more sparse scatters of trash. After she passed more mounds, strips of arid land began to appear. Speckles of broken cars littered the dirt and then came another gathering of trash that looked more and more like a dumping ground for cars. Before long, she came across a bare streak that formed a dirt aisle or road to cut through a heaping wall of automobile parts. The end of the road came at an open area surrounded by scraps and rails of rusted fencing that formed a ring. A truss-like structure mounted on a broad platform immediately caught Trina's eye. She studied the area below and noticed the sparse formation of car rubbish in the wide arena of dirt and how the vehicles seemed to face the wide structure. She returned her gaze to the truss and platform. The longer she looked at it, the more it reminded her of an outdoor screen. Questions whirled around in her mind. Was this place some sort of drive-in theater? More importantly, could the screen be the source of the sound she heard earlier? These questions made her hover over the clearing, and scan the place with a bird's eye view. Then, something else caught Trina's eye. Something made her heart skip as its dull wink broke through the drab setting of an abandoned drive-in. The twinkle of light was brief and weak, but as soon as Trina saw the blue spark, she made her descent.

Shoe soles scraped parched earth. In a steady revolve, Trina scanned the drive-in's vacant lot. Scattered here and there were the remains of cars she had spotted earlier. From the sky, the corpses of vehicles were easy to make out, but there were other objects that she could not discern until she landed. Now at ground level, she noticed the small things out of place even for the ruins of an outdoor theater. Old toys and other faded trinkets hung from tangles of wire and graying weeds reminded her of makeshift cenotaphs found at roadsides.

Trina remembered the dull twinkle of the blue light she spotted and thought to call on the lost soul. Her eyes scanned the area and her mouth fixed to cry out Alex's name, but she choked back any sound when a face in the weeds jolted her nerves. For nearly a minute, Trina paused, her wide eyes locked on the vacant gaze of a blank face that stared at her from one of the tangles. It was only when the face did not stir, that Trina's nerves unfastened from fear's grip. *Was that a statue?* Trina thought. Although still unnerved, Trina dared to move. Her breath drew in with a silent gasp and her uneasiness grew at the other things she discovered in her quick survey of the area.

Amid the wreckage were petrified shapes. Some of the shapes were as fragmented as the ruined architecture. The frayed pieces of the ossified were crumbled mounds of pieces scattered along the dirt. She glanced at the right side of the truss structure. Trina spotted a piece of debris the size of a house. The longer she stared at the hunk of debris, the more she noticed a face in its broken features as though it belonged to a giant statue. What was left of its eyes, mouth, and nose showed an expression that was vacant like the face she found in the tangles. This broken thing was not as innocuous as the tattered figureheads she spotted in the journey to the outdoor theater. Though hardened like weathered stone, there was something about its face that seemed corpse-like, and she quickly turned away from the staring giant.

Other fixed figures seemed whole, or at least, held some semblance of intact bodies with heads and shoulders. Waists and legs fused together in a trunk, their feet nothing but thick, gnarled roots tethered to the ground. Some blue-green encrust lightly coated stark gray like dried moss over stone. Perhaps what was most unnerving of all were what the fossilized all shared, melancholy carved with subtlety about the corners of lips and eyes. It was the convey of concession that struck Trina with the most unease for every time she lingered on the wilted lids of vacant stares, she thought of the way June looked, huddled at the bedside of her grandparents' room. She needed to find the place where she had spotted the blue light and soon.

She thought back on her bird's eye view of the ruined lot and turned her focus towards the left of the theater's truss. Trina maneuvered past statues and cars and studied every stump, every shamble of parts and wires, and every dark crook for glimpses of blue. She worked her way to the fringes. Twin pillars settled in tufts of cloudy vegetation caught her eye. Unsure, Trina tip-toed a few steps forward. The first thing she noticed was the height difference in the pair. The one on the right dwarfed its counterpart by several inches. The heads of the twin pillars bowed with their eyes closed. The pose of these statues was an odd difference from the others, and she frowned as she wondered about its significance. Her curiosity at the minor detail was fleeting, for as she inched closer to take a better look at the pillars' busts, her heart leaped. The twin pillars had the faces of children. Despite being molded into stone, with moss and long tresses of web-like vines that hung from them, the likeness of the taller pillar jumped out at her.

She sprinted into a leap and glided the short distance and landed at their feet. Trina settled her stance and looked up at the face of the left pillar with her suspicions confirmed.

"Alex!" The pillar did not stir, but Trina was certain the lost soul was trapped inside. With arms half-crooked upward at the elbows, she searched for cracks and chips in stone for any hint of blue light.

Light flashed from the direction of the theater's truss and Trina's head swiveled in its direction. The widescreen flickered. An electric buzz gave way to the rushed sound of clamoring feet, clanking instruments, and the signaling of a machine. The snowy fuzz of static soon settled on the image of men and women in white coats that swarmed a stretcher. Narrow feet dangled from the ends of the stretcher as a collective hoist to transfer patient from carrier to operating table took place. The scene jumped in point of view, and moved from the wide shot of the swarm of scrubs to the close-up framing around the operating table. Trina heard voices in a composed yet pressing exchange. The medical jargon tossed among the medical team went through her ears. The words she did understand rang with an awful echo in her mind. "A lot of fluid buildup in the lungs, a lot of blood loss, barely a pulse."

From another angle of the screen, Trina spotted the crossing of arms, gloved hands, and hospital items. Then her heart broke. June lay on the stretcher. Her eyelids were closed and her brown skin took on a deathly pallor that made her tone a sickly green. Trina stared at the lifelessness on her little sister's face and her mind made excuses to protect itself. *It's on a big screen, therefore, it's a movie. June being on the table, unresponsive, was not real. The emergency team were actors going about their blocking to clamor about room and table. The exchange between the team on how she was rapidly deteriorating, on what to do to get her stabilized, all lines.* The swimming inside of Trina's head convinced her of this for a little while, but the longer she watched, the faster the delirium faded. What was on the full screen was real.

The gorging lump that formed in Trina's throat suddenly exploded into tears as her hands clasped her mouth. Despite dismay and panic that ran rampant on the inside, her body locked in place as she too became petrified. The only thing that tore Trina's eyes away from the horror that played out on the monitor was a trace movement off screen.

She returned her attention to the pillars and gasped. The pillars had moved. Both of their heads raised slightly. The lowest of the pair sprouted upward. The top of its scalp had risen from elbow height to right under the shoulders of Alex's pillar. She looked at the face of the second pillar and swallowed. The face carved into the pillar was that of a little girl about five or six years old. Despite, the difference, she knew June's face at any age. Commotion and the blare of a flatlining signal threw Trina's attention back to the widescreen. It was an announcement that June's heart stopped. A command came next, a request for a defibrillator. Trina's insides churned as she watched the increased rush in organized clamor until there was another rustling of the earth. Now her attention was drawn back to the pillars. Her eyes bulged as the pillar with June's face pushed upward, its shoulders now even with its pair. In the background, Trina heard the shouting of the word "clear," and heard the blast of the defibrillator. The flatline signal still blared. The necks of both pillars rose even more erect. There was another shout of the words "clear" and with the second blast of the defibrillator, the flatline blare was interrupted by the steady beep of the heart monitor, and the twin pillars halted.

Trina watched the ordeal and was struck by a revelation. She suddenly thought of Mr. Eleri and the place he had mentioned. Earlier he spoke of a place where oblivion waited for the sorrowful who sought to be erased. The petrified shapes that populated the ruins, all with blank stares were not statues. Once they had been alive and had souls. Now they were empty shells. Trina knew then that the ruins of the drive-in theater, the entire wasteland of the realm she had entered, was indeed the Dead End.

Trina flinched when she heard another long continuous chime of the flatline signal and the bursts of the defibrillator. She saw the twin pillars' heads lift and their necks straightened. Closed eyelids of the stone busts shuddered. Her heart thundered and she turned her gaze to the blank faces. She thought of the old Orisha's words again, the instructions on what should never happen should her sister and lost soul take root.

When she remembered what the old Orisha imparted, panic stung Trina's nerve with a jolt. She turned her gaze to the pillars and noticed the lids raise ever so slightly. The only thing she could think of was to hold the pillars in a hug, clamp her hands over their eyes, and pray that the ring of the flatline returned to the skips of a beating heart. As though answering her inner pleas, the drawn-out chime of the flatline fell back to slow, rhythmic beeps. Movement underneath her palms stopped. She raised her hands from masking their eyes and she saw their upper and lower lids open into narrow, crescent slits.

"Alex? June? Can you two hear me?" Trina asked. Her voice tremored from the tears that hung in her throat. Trina stared at the stone busts, but nothing stirred on their blank faces. Her arms were looped around the shoulders of the pillars in a hug, and she lowered her head in alignment with zeir ears. The tears fell freely as she whispered, "Go back. Please, go back home where everyone is waiting for you."

Hugging the twin pillars, Trina could hear the words that circulated among doctors in what was relative calm. The pills had done their work in rendering her unconscious. They significantly slowed down the functions of her organs. The true damage came when her body slumped into the waters of the trough. June had been starved of oxygen for too long. Even as the ventilator slowed the progress of the shutdown of her body, there was severe damage to the brain. Trina let the tears flow and her arms tightened even as the press of stone caused the flesh of her biceps to ache. Alarm broke her embrace when she felt the fleeting pass of darkness disrupt the stagnant air. She backed away from the pillars and her eyes turned to the sky. Nothing dotted the heavy blue and gray of bloated clouds, but there was no mistaking it. Mere seconds ago, something fast had passed overhead. Trina recalled the swift blanket of the shadow's cast. It was something much bigger than her and the pillars combined.

With the muscles of her shoulders squared with her legs, Trina's feet moved in a slow pivot. She scanned the ruins and air above. She tucked a hand in her pants pocket and her fingers felt flat, aluminum plating. Nothing swooped from the skylines or rumbled from piled gates. She turned back to the pillars.

The crescent slits of the eyes widened ever so slightly since her quick survey.

"Listen to me," Trina urged and placed both hands on one cheek of both busts as though she were lifting the heads of the weary, too heavy to raise on their own. "I understand you. I understand that you're both in pain. You're both tired. Life has thrown things at you time and time again, but you have to hang in there. You have to stay… ." Trina paused for a moment and swallowed down the tears and tremors so that her words rang in a clear, desperate warning. "Don't come here. You don't belong here."

"I concur wholeheartedly." The sweet purr of a honeyed tongue hummed with a soft yet terrible rumble. "Lost ones, I know of a sanctuary for the peace you seek, a place far better than oblivion. Let me take you there. There will be no more torment, no more pain, and fear to cripple you." Trina whirled around and tried to pinpoint the source.

Narakai was there, but his voice floated about them. It was hard to discern where he was. She tucked her hand in her pocket again, and her ears tuned in to every rustle. Her eyes caught any movement. Light coursed through her body in a silent hum. The air changed. There was a subtle updraft in the stillness. The sudden touch of darkness and the light Trina held, burst from her being in a blinding flash. She spun around where she last felt an impending shadow and took hold of the trinket E. gave her. When the flash faded, Trina saw the monstrous form in mid-hover to where her back had been turned. In one swift motion, she jumped aside and tossed the trinket under the shade, all before the giant claw of a hand pounced unknowingly on the trap she had set.

Trina backed up to the two pillars to shield them as the impact from the trounced trinket let forth a burst. Contact was met with a powerful burst that repelled the dark shape. There was a monstrous utter of surprise. The concussive blast was powerful enough it sent the archdemon's shape sailing a ways up and outward. Simultaneously, something clear encapsulated Trina and the pillars. The archdemon extended his wings and caught himself in midair. With her back still turned to the pillars, her eyes fixed on the creature hovering in the horizon. Its body was dim as the thickest shadow with glowing green eyes. It was no doubt, Narakai, but his features had changed. Two sets of ram-like horns crowned his head. A gleam from an extra pair of small, sour dots rested above the larger, eyes that slanted and were portioned evenly about an altered scalp. His sleek, lean form gave way to a build with long, powerful limbs, broader chest and bulking shoulders. He had grown in size, not to the mammoth heights of the statues she had seen, but large enough that in comparison, Trina was the size of a doll. His wings grew into proportion to keep his body airborne.

For a moment, his wings kept him steady and in place. One moment he hovered in the air, and watched her. The next moment, he vanished. Nerves jolted by the sudden disappearance, Trina's frantic mind reeled. An electric crash and boom of reverberation sent her stumbling. It was more from being startled than impact. When the same noise happened seconds later, her eyes glimpsed the wide face and large hooks of black talons that pressed against the glassy waves and whitish squirming of some electric-like substance. With widening eyes, Trina realized what encapsulated her and the pillars was a force field. She also realized something else. Had it not been for the shield, she would not have known what had hit her with Narakai's first strike.

She held her breath and watched as the archdemon pressed against the shield. She prayed it would hold. The field did not crack or yield. Narakai flew rearward into the air with a swift wind, and growled in frustration as he hovered in midair. Certain that she was safe, Trina turned back to the pillars. The curtains of the top lids had inched upward slightly from the place where the bottom of the cornea should have been.

"Mom and dad cried when they found you, sis," Trina said, her eyes directed towards the carved face of the young girl. "They're crying right now. Everyone is. Whatever it is you're going through, they'll be there. Things we'll get better."

"Things will get better, but for how long?" Narakai's voice swam in the air around them again. Trina's head swiveled. The archdemon's form was as evasive as his voice for every time she glimpsed a dark shape circling them, he would move out of the corner of her sight. "Until the next hardship? Until the next tragedy comes? Until the next person she cares about dies? Until she is left alone?"

"No," Trina shouted more towards the incubus than at the pillar. Her head jutted in a sharp turn towards the voice and she wished the shield could cut out the poison of the archdemon's voice as much as it shut out the rest of him. She gave up on chasing the black shape. Trina returned her gaze to June's carving. She continued, "You won't be alone! As tough as the world can be, there are good people in it, people that will help."

"Ah, the goodwill of fellow man. A blissful afterlife in a heavenly realm has made you forgive and forget." A snide titter hissed through Narakai's silken voice. "Minutes must have been an eternity for you as you gasped through a closing airway. Time is precious, especially for a little girl struggling to breathe." The gentleness in the archdemon's tone almost sounded sincere as he spoke. "The hospital was only a few miles away, yet it took so long for the dispatchers to reach you. Tell me, Trina, where was the compassion and goodwill of others then?"

The words of the incubus took Trina off guard. The venom he spoke made her remember that fateful day. It was a fairly normal one, and she had felt fine all morning. They had a field trip to the zoo that day. It was towards the end of lunch when the onset of an asthma attack came. Her inhaler ran out of medicine. EpiPens and other emergency equipment would have been on hand at the school, but they were away at a park. The asthma attack was so severe that the hospital was called. Sometime after the event, after she had passed, there was talk from the people who witnessed the ordeal. Two men arrived as dispatch. They had been almost thirty minutes late from a drive that would have taken five minutes. There were rumors about the way they sneered at the frantic antics of panicked children and chaperones. Angry discussions held among fellow parents swirled about the men exchanging eye-rolls, the two scoffing at the melodrama of people from the "inner city." The way it affected her parents and sister hurt Trina the most. But she was all right. She had found her peace in the afterlife. Her only concern now was the safety of her loved ones in the living.

Trina wanted to tell the demon off, and she would have, but in the background, she could hear an urgent rise among the medical team. There was another scare as June's pulse dropped. They went to work and tried to recover her vitals, to raise them. There was some relief among the murmuring when they stopped the complete descent and managed to find some stasis of her pulse. Improvement of vital signs had yet to be seen. June's body still struggled and relied fully on machines. Amid the scare, the eyelids of the pillars inched upward underneath her pupils.

Shockwave after shockwave thundered in Trina's ears. Suddenly, her eyes were overtaken by a black blur as Narakai zipped in and out. With such blinding speed, the successive attacks the incubus made at the barrier looked as though there was a swarm of several assailants. Trina tensed at every hurtle and crash against the barrier and again hoped it would hold. At one point, a white spot lingered longer than normal and she dreaded that the archdemon succeeded in finding a weak spot in the shield. Eventually, the white blemish dissolved. To her good fortune, the glassy field stood against the battering. The blurs slowed and consolidated into Narakai's towering shape. Still in a defensive stance, Trina's scowl met the creature's unwavering stare. Contemplation hung the incubus still against the sky. Trina returned her gaze to the pillars.

She turned to the left of the pillars. She gently placed hands on either side of the solemn sculpture. Trina knelt down until her eyes were level with the stone carving of the lost soul. "Alex, can you hear me? Please, she needs your help. You're her other half, aren't you? You know better than any of us what she feels. She would not want her family to suffer like this." Trina knew there wouldn't be a response and any stir of movement put her on edge. Her only hope was that somewhere, the lost soul listened to her and her words would somehow get through.

"As much as she would want the pain to stop, you know that letting this happen isn't the answer. There is still hope, another chance that both of you can make it past this." Trina continued her pleas and her ears drifted to the background.

She glanced at the widescreen, and hoped her words registered. Nothing changed. "She doesn't belong here. Neither of you do. Please help us. Don't disappear."

"Continue? For what? To endure for crumbs of happiness? For the sake of completing a fleeting life span?" Narakai's hums floated in the air as the incubus made another circling round of the shield. "Remaining in such a hellish cycle is but cruel entertainment for God and devils. The lost soul understands more than anyone that the only recourse is exiting this chain."

Trina's eyes searched and attempted to find a hovering, black form, but could barely get a fix on him. Her mouth parted in protest when she heard the change. The feed on the vital sign's monitor altered and became irregular. A voice rang out from one of the emergency staff that June's pulse was dropping. And then came what Trina dreaded as the skips of electric chimes fell into a long, drawn-out blare. Busy calm turned into a rushed, deliberate effort as the medical team worked to bring the patient back from the brink. Horror stretched Trina's eyes as she watched them retrieve the defibrillator. The instrument was pressed against motionless lungs.

Someone shouted "clear!" and signaled the electric blast of the defibrillator. Nothing changed. There was a quick pause in preparation for another attempt. For the second time, the defibrillator settled on lungs. There was another shout followed by another shock. A skip interrupted, once, twice, before it fell into the singular blare again.

"No! You have to fight!"

Trina's mind reeled as she faced the widescreen. There was a third burst of the defibrillator, another interlude of skips, and for a moment, Trina's heart fluttered. Her hope was short-lived when the skips once more fell to the flatline. Flitting from widescreen to pillars, Trina noticed the eyelids of stone, shudder.

"Listen to me." Desperate, Trina's hands grasped the stone shoulders as though she urged the defeated to come to their senses. "You're right about the world. It can be awful. Sometimes it makes you question the creator of a world where there is nothing, but loss and painful certainties. It seems like everywhere you turn there are people that mean nothing, but harm or people that care less one way or another. You may think that leaving that world behind would make things better off, but it won't. Mom, Dad, everyone you care about. They need you to protect them from what's coming. If you leave everything behind, they won't stand a chance. Everything you love will be gone."

"It's no use pleading," Narakai's disembodied voice chuckled. "Neither of them can hear you anymore."

Trina visibly shirked the archdemon's fateful words with a head waggle. They were too harsh to accept even as the curtains of the stone carvings gradually rose. The only sounds that blotted out the echo of the Narakai's words was the blast of the defibrillator as it was used a fourth time. The flatline didn't waver. Trina's head rolled towards the truss as they discharged the fifth blast, then a sixth. The next calm that fell over the medical team was a solemn one. There was a final check of the monitor and for a pulse. Dismal murmurs floated among the gathering. Among the words heard were questions about the location of June's parents and an announcement for the time of death.

The bridge of Trina's nose crunched as her eyes clasped shut and let loose tears. It must be a nightmare. Everything she had heard, everything she had witnessed was a bad dream. It had to be. She wished it to be. She blinked away clouds of tears and felt instant regret as the monitor brought the stretcher into full view. With her head crooked sideways and her eyes closed, June lay motionless on the operating table. Seeing the image was a punch to Trina's core. The ache nearly made her sob. Instead, she gasped. She was surprised at the darkness that suddenly thundered down upon her. The ground under her feet shook with the archdemon's landing and she threw herself in a huddle over the pillars. A loud grind of crackling glass and electric frying overtook her ears. The field encapsulating her and the pillars wavered between a glossy clearness and shimmering dents of white.

Its point of disruption was the pressing down of a curling, black claw. With wings and horns that jutted at sky, the incubus pressed down on the small shield the same way a cat loomed against a glass bowl to stare hungrily at the fish trapped within. The dark hook gradually inched through and Narakai beamed. Any moment now, the shell between him and the savory souls would crack. When the shield still showed resilience, his beam tempered into an intrigued sneer. "Their will is gone, now. It is time to let go. Whatever hope or stubbornness you are clinging to will fail, as sure as this shield will break under my nail."

Trina hunkered down under the sizzles of buckling energy. Her own fortitude crumbled. Again, the words of the incubus bounced around in her head. What hope? Did he mistake the borrowed power of the shield as her own? At this point, the only thing that kept the enormity of grief at bay was either denial or survival. Even as a spirit, her will to survive was potent. Denial, on the other hand, was a chasm that quickly shrunk. Eventually, despair would drown her, given that her soul would not be devoured first. She struggled to prepare for the inevitability of both. Trina lifted her head. Words of farewell did not come easy. Instead, her mind could only take in the vacant eyes of stone staring back. Inside, her mind was as blank as the statues. No sooner had a calmness settled in than a familiar stirring from within occurred. Another echo bounced around in her head, a small impart hidden in her memory. Suddenly, two words sprang forth to the forefront of her mind. Light and fire.

The crackling of a shield that neared its limits rang through her ears. Head bowed, she concentrated. Trina took a deep breath and looked up. "So, you wouldn't stay for Mom and Dad? Not even for me?" Her entreat was timorous and the tone barely carried above a whisper as she stared at blank, open eyes. Then, she calmed the quavering in her voice and the tone of her broken plea grew heavy and almost stern. "I thought you cared enough to protect them, but, I guess, I was wrong. You're no better than the God that left you to suffer." Focused on the gray, Trina half-hope for something to stir. The stone remained still. Trina's head bowed in resignation as she heard another amused rumble overhead.

"To the devils go the spoils, dear," Narakai tittered. "If it is any consolation for your efforts, you will be with the rest of your family, again. I will personally see to that."

Head weighed in defeat, Trina could not see him, but she knew the incubus smirked. She could hear the hint of a smile in his words. Had she the strength, there would have been choice words, and the spark of anger would have prompted her to lash out. With despair creeping in, Trina could not muster a scowl.

A loud pop made her flinch and forced her eyes open. To find that the shield still stood was a small relief. Dents of white undulated between clear and marred and webbed throughout the protective encircle. From the staccato resound of glassy grinding, the shield would not hold much longer. There was the whine of crying energy, the increased clamoring of splintering glass. Then came the defining snap, a tinkling of something fragile being shattered, a grim hush in the shield's resistance. Feeling the expose of still air, Trina braced herself. The heaviness of a cast shadow pressed down on her, but the terrible wrest she prepared for never came.

"I...I can't move? Why?" Narakai's stammer was colored by confusion and fear.

Despair lost its grip and Trina looked up. Above her, the hand of the incubus froze and trembled.

"She moved! Doctor! She's moving!" The single utter of surprise and disbelief came from the full screen. Trina shifted her attention from the looming hand to the theater truss. Although her head was still crooked sideways, the horizontal portrait of June's face was in full view. With her gazed fixed on the screen, Trina's heart nearly skipped a beat when for a brief moment, she caught a single twitch break the mask of death. Then another twitch. Visible spasms rippled over closed lids before they made a steady lift upward. Puzzled murmurs among the medical team soon turned into a collective upheaval of bewilderment. Excitement rushed over Trina's skin in waves of goosebumps. She flitted towards the pillars and noticed that with the slow dawn of June's consciousness, the stone shutters of the busts began to fall.

Mesmerized by the gradual opening of June's eyes, Trina barely felt the stagnant air quiver. The vibration was weak and brief and its initial beckon went unnoticed. When blackness peeked from the crescents of an unfolding pair, there was another tremor. Its presence lingered and was felt not only from the slight unsettling underneath Trina's feet, but by the subtle clangor of the operating table and medical tools in the emergency room. Consternation trickled among the medical team.

Trina's exhilaration gave way to forebode. The wax of opening eyes revealed ebony tarns that cast a menacing sentience on June's face. The onset of a quake, the shouts of rising panic, the rise of a dreadful dawn on a waking countenance, was cut off by a blank silence that ripped across widescreen.

Trina rocked backward and glimpsed the pillars as their eyes closed. The trembling air went still. Motionless, Trina's heart was the only thing that thundered amid the quiet calm. Ever since the shattering of the field, Narakai had not moved. Was there a fear so powerful to freeze even an archdemon in place or was there something else? What force did the incubus senses pick up? Staring at the busts, she sensed something latent within the carved faces. Darkness seeped from stone like a lone stream of tears that trickled from each corner of the statues closed eyes. At that moment, she felt a jolt of dread as the mouths on the stone faces fell open. Faint shrills broke the silence. Was it a scream? The sound was far off. It had to have been carried from several yards, may be an echo of a mile. A low distant rumble sounded, intermingled with distant shrieks that seemed to draw nearer. Before Trina thought to ask herself whether or not it came from the statues, there was a blast.

Violent vibrations shot through her. Its rush threw her backward with the strength of a tidal wave. Pain jolted through her ears. A shredding agony rippled through her back before she went numb. At some point, she must have blacked out because of the brief blotting out of sight, sound, and feeling. She came to, seconds later, to howls of a banshee's choir that conjured an upheaval which tore at the air like a storm.

The earth groaned. Another burst grazed her skin with the explosion of glass and metal. Eyesight toppled over each other in her backward hurtle and she glimpsed the tall, crouching black shape crumple the same way paper did when the suction of wind dragged it out of the window of a car. The same time the demon's form disappeared from a ferocious whip of force, the theater's truss shattered.

Next, her sight rolled down to see dirt and sculptures drop under the opening of chasms. Her vision rolled up to the sky as the gradual set in of a hellish crimson bled over the dull shade of an overcast. Another blackout came and went, and Trina found herself in a mid-backward roll until she settled belly down on a quaking earth. Merciful shock that granted numbness and disorientation wore off. When she tried to spread her wings, she cried at the fire of a flayed back, peeled bare and raw. The projection of her own screams was completely blotted out by the legion of baleful wails. Wrath and an anguished roar that swelled, pressed against her ears to the point where she felt a pop. Had she happened upon the Dead End at that moment as part of the living, Trina knew she would have gone deaf. As a spirit, the cacophony persisted.

Noises unfolded. Guttural booms of some beast or cloud overlapped vaguely human shrieks. Deep rasps of grating cords overlapped the neighs of scratching strings. The thunderous whir of raucous air danced with the whine of electric, shredding notes. Trina hunkered down from the tug of rioting vibration and wind and managed to peek from the shelters of her arms. Giant shells shifted and sank while smaller fragments were swept away. Scars splintered the sky and matched the crooked crevasses of the ground as parts of the firmament crumbled. Even the fiber of the desolate scape buckled, slightly flattening in a wide stretch before it thinned into threads on the verge of ripping apart. Dissonance was an ever billowing, wrathful force that wrenched at the fabric of the Dead End and beyond.

Trina felt the sensation of the dreadful bear down on her own cells and the only thing she could think to do was crunch her head and limbs inward. What pushed from her lungs were overpowered by the echoes of a terrible yawn. Even as she clasped her eyes shut, the image of what she last saw burned into her retina. In place of where the twin pillars once stood was a twisted mass of orange, blurred by snowy, electric static. The spark of mallow and crimson twinkled high on its two portions and struggled to merge. Part of the shifting blur reached upward and extended a vague appendage towards what was left of the firmament before its great topple. It took with it the realm as it descended to whence it came.

Chapter 10

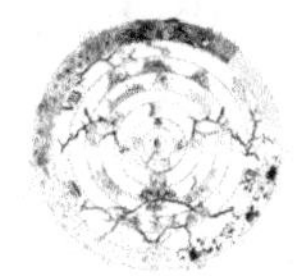

The cacophony ceased, but a lone shrieking still tore at the air. Thousands of needles of heat, breath, and terror, pushed out of a raw throat. With a mouth pried open, a high, stricken peal released in exhale, the explosion of sound only paused between harsh inhales. Trina's lungs ached. They heaved out and then crushed together. Their soreness was only overshadowed by the pain of her tattered back. Her knees tucked under her chest and waist in a tightened hunker. The whirlwind of wrath and hatred passed, yet Trina's head pressed onto the ground and under the shelter of her arms. Tufts of her hair and flesh of her arm were still in the grip of trembling fingers as her nerves jumped and her muscles tensed. She braced herself against the storm's phantom memory.

"You are safe, Trina." A man's voice, gentle as a heavy mist, tried to comfort her. Trina's screams finally fell to low, hard sobs. Her body and mind was fatigued, but still trapped in the horrifying moment of the Crying One's wrath. "Trina?" The gentle voice called out again, and this time reached out a hand.

"I'm sorry, please! I'm sorry!" Trina shrieked. Suddenly she flew backwards, startled from the solid touch of fingers on her shoulder. Fear outweighed the flayed wounds that tore deep in her shoulder blades as her hands and feet moved in a frantic backpedal. Still burned into her retina was the image of crimson and mallow beams fixed in a pair.

Broken colors and a fragmented atmosphere shifted about the odd and sinister lights that struggled to form a twisted likeness of a countenance and other unrecognizable shapes. The blur caused by the warping of Limbo's fabric spared her sanity from any knowledge of the monster's true features. Nevertheless, this disjointed vision was slow to fade. The lingering image blinded Trina to the man crouched in front of her with outstretched hands.

"I am coming towards you, okay?" the man announced. He cautioned the frightened Trina of his approach.

"I'll leave you alone," Trina's quavered, through tears. "I promise. I'll leave you alone. Just don't hurt me anymore." She froze with her eyes crunched shut to close out the image branded in her mind. The bulge and knots of large, powerful arms made her flinch. Her adrenaline dwindled and every ache and fiery sting of her wounds made her wince. The arms that pulled her into a hug moved gently to not cause her further pain. The initial shock and fear that came with the sudden contact quickly dissipated with the nightmare that clouded her vision. Gentleness silenced the sobs, but tears still flowed. With her energy spent from being tense for a long period of time, Trina loosened her limbs but found it difficult to stop shaking.

"Easy now. We are here for you, Trina," the man cooed and patted her on the back of the head. He swayed side to side as he cradled her. "Obatala's strength surrounds us."

Obatala? Trina's eyes flew open. She recognized the word. It was the name of an Orisha, a chieftain of the skies and of purity. Trina lifted her head and surveyed her surroundings. With her sight cleared of distortion, she surveyed a formless plane. Among the Orisha, Obatala was sometimes called the White One. Sure enough, her surroundings evinced the sky chieftain's nickname for everything was soft white mist and light. Trina felt as though she sat somewhere in the middle of a cloud where a veiled sun shined down on them from somewhere high above.

Her attention shifted to the one who cradled her in his arms. She wanted to know who he was but the question caught in her mouth as she studied him. The man was dark and muscle-bound. His head was smooth, even and free of hair. There was something familiar about his chiseled facial features, broad nose, and the gentle curve of his broad lips. Despite his stature, there was a placidness about his eyes that put her at ease. Then, there was the feeling of calm and reassurance she recognized back at the Pyr. She stared at the man's face a while longer and her eyes brightened.

"Ori?" Trina asked. She was still unsure until the man's lips slowly upturned in a thoughtful smile as he nodded. This time, tears of joy leapt from Trina's eyes as she swung her arms around the wide neck of her guardian. "I thought I'd never see you again."

"It will take more than a demon and infernal fire to get rid of me," Ori chuckled, but suddenly stopped as his placid mien darkened to a sobering one. "I have to admit, when Limbo began to collapse, I was fearful I would not make it to you in time. The Creator kept you safe, and I am so grateful." Ori pulled her in once more for another great squeeze. As Trina pulled away, she shook her head as the sorrow returned. "Hey, what's wrong, young one?" Ori consoled her and wiped away the running river of tears.

Trina's mind was thrown back into a chaotic whirlwind of emotions and memories. She thought about all of the realms of Limbo she had traveled to and what she had found there. She remembered Alex's tragic past and the present of June's anguish. She also thought about the evil hidden in wait to take over the Submateria and the lives and very souls of everyone, including her family, that were at stake. And most reeling of all, the monster she had awakened could destroy everything if not kept in check. The source of her highest anxiety was June. In one thought, there was the image of the sister she was raised with, a goofy, beaming little girl who loved cartoons, strawberry Pop Tarts and playing dress up. The thought went from innocence and joy to the gray face of emotional pain, blankness, and death. And then, there was the face that came after the sorrowful calm, the twisted visage of rage that flooded a hatred so powerful it brought Limbo asunder and nearly tore her apart. Reconciling these faces was a hard struggle that left Trina's mind as broken as her heart.

"I did something. I started something terrible, Ori." Trina finally croaked through sniffles. Her lips tightening into a quivering grimace. "The things I said, I just wanted her to live. I had no idea." Trina shook her head and struggled to speak. She thought about what she had unleashed. "I failed and now… ." The guilt was too much, and the sobs that knocked at her throat broke through again.

Ori gently drew Trina into his chest and arms. His lips let out a soft shushing as he swayed side to side to quell the quaking of her tears. "No, my sweet girl. I am proud of you. Very proud."

"We all are." A woman's interjection made both Ori and Trina pause and look up. Silhouettes suddenly crowded the mist. The dark hazes impressed upon the soft white were the shapes of people. The small gathering moved in unison and closed around them. The leader of these silhouettes, a woman, elegant and wide-hipped, wore a headdress of levitating rings and was wrapped in the watery white and silver of a sleek and billowing gown.

The corners of Ori's lips arched upward as the rest of the shadows revealed themselves. "Lady Yemoja, everyone, it is nice to see you've survived."

"Likewise, Ori," Yemoja greeted. Her full lips glistened with glitter as she smirked. Then, as her gaze fell on Trina, a relishing glow set about her eyes. "As for you, Light Bearer, you have succeeded where all of us had failed and survived. In the face of a demon and all manner of dangers, you showed courage. Through pain, fear, sadness, their inner struggles and your own, you persevered. And when despair threatened to drag them under, it was you who pulled them from the brink even if it meant daring to face wrath in its purest form." Yemoja's chest swelled with pride. With every word she spoke, her smile shined and grew like a waxing moon that gave light to night. The queen and mother of the Orishas was not the only ones overcome with awe and pride.

Trina looked at the familiar faces among the gathering. She saw Oya, a warrior Orisha and lady of wind and thunder. Oya was a woman who always carried herself with unflappable regal and charisma in short-lived meetings or with prowess and raw tenacity during combat. It was strange to see someone Trina admired suddenly look towards her with marvel. Next to her was Shango, the patron of power, lightning, and fire. The confident warrior who often wore a smile that either worked to charm or spoke haughtiness. Another fellow warrior who often accompanied Oya in battle had also joined her in his expression of marvel and disbelief.

Mr. Eleri flanked the right of where Yemoja stood. His beam was shiny and white. The Orisha who was an old man, could hardly contain his joy. Though Eleri was free of his staff, Trina noticed something familiar about the other Orisha who stood behind him.

Towering above Eleri was a younger man. He had shoulders almost as broad as Ori's, but he was taller in stature. His locks reached a little past his ears and though he wore white, his silvery aura laced the outline of his figure and shimmered with the thin sheen of the rainbow. Muscled arms folded over his chest and the man smiled and gave Trina a proud nod of approval. It was the young man's aura and her own intuition that made her recognize Osumare, the old man's staff that now took on human form.

"You did it, girl!" Eleri sang, and his slender hands gave a loud clap. His feet skipped mirthfully and Trina was sure he was about to click his heels together.

"That blast could be felt from all the way in the fields. It was bad. I thought the matter I was made of would shatter. Even the recollection of that frightens me, yet this girl took the brunt of it at ground zero."

Shango shook his head. His eyes narrowed while he remembered the awful reverberate that literally tore the sky apart. The fear of wondering where Trina was and whether they would get to her in time resurfaced. Then, as he looked at the young woman cradled in Ori's arms, Shango's confoundment and trepidation disappeared under a proud smile. "Perhaps she has the makings of a warrior Orisha like us."

Oya glanced over at her companion, then waggled her head in disagreement.

"She is much greater than that, even beyond the gifts of a healer. If this is the type of power a Light Bearer possess, it is an awesome one."

"Awesome enough to move the Divine Monstrum to break the tethers of Life and Death and Space/Time," Eleri chimed.

"But at what cost?" As Trina spoke dejection lay in her face and voice. For a while, the astonishment and praise of the Orisha kept the guilt at bay. But, Eleri's mentioning of the tethers to the Tri-Hold, brought her guilt to the forefront. "Because of me, Limbo is destroyed. There was much at stake and in trying to save my sister's life, her humanity was lost in the process. All I feel is torn." Tears caused Trina to crack. Her finger rose to wipe away a lone river running down her face and her voice was muffled by the lump that rose in her throat. "Elegba was right. I shouldn't have gotten involved. Maybe I should have left them in peace."

In the crowd, the faces of pride and amazement dimmed to sympathy as Trina could no longer stop the streams from falling. Ori's smile melted and pulled her close. He held her close in a hug, and tried to shelter her from her own sadness. Again, he swayed from side to side, and attempted to console the fits of sniffles and quiet sobs.

"No Trina, it was I who was wrong." A man spoke, and interrupted her sniffling and sobs. Her brows crunched in recognition of his voice. Her eyes set to search for the speaker among the crowd and stopped in one area of the gathering that began to shift. Among the shifting, Oya and Shango, stepped aside. They parted to let a sharply dressed gentleman saunter through. Like the others, the man wore white. He was of average height, with a thin, lean build and angular facial features that gave him high cheekbones. He had traded a black bowler for a white Scala Panama, an over-sized frock coat frayed at the elbows for a crisp structured suit jacket, checker patched and trousers that flooded for full leg length dress slacks, and tennis shoes for loafers. Right now, he was a striking young man, but there was no mistaking his identity.

"Is that you, Mr. Elegba?" Trina asked, still disbelieving at the dramatic change.

"Call me E., sweets," Elegba answered with a wink and with the same mischievous sneer of the boy who lounged at the clerk's desk of Camino's Galleria.

"You're late, Elegba," Yemoja said, half- teased.

"Thanks to the White One who worked on the outside. I was lucky enough to make it in one piece. But, there goes one of my streams of income." Elegba sighed and his tone was mixed with relief at surviving the Limbo crash and melancholy for losing his shop.

"I'm sorry, Elegba," Trina apologized. "I should have listened to the first advice you gave me.

"And I should've had more faith in your instincts and in the Creator's plan, as insane as it is." Elegba sighed again and bowed as he took off his hat. He massaged the knots of stress at the back of his neck and searched his mind until he found the right words.

He continued, "Sometimes, the way out of one's own darkness is to go through it. In stirring the Crying One's anger, you renewed June and Alex's will to fight. Because of your actions, you not only saved two broken souls but the lives of your loved ones among many others. With something to challenge the Archon, the Submateria may have a chance at a future."

"But even if that's the case, Limbo is still destroyed." Trina could not help but feel pangs of guilt. She knew Spike and Curly were among the casualties of an annihilated nether realm.

"Limbo is in shambles, yes, but not obliterated. Luckily for the nether realm and all therein, the Crying One's current state possesses but a portion of its destructive powers. Had it stirred with the strength it had as the Divine Monstrum of primordial times, it would be a graver matter." Eleri reassured her and his voice only darkened slightly at the mention of the consequences of the grim alternative. "Limbo and its denizens still exist, but the realm has been reduced and disorganized from its original state."

Yemoja nodded in agreement. "It will be near impossible in its fractured form to travel from stratum to stratum. But, Obatala's power extends from beyond the netherworld. His strength imbues our clothing and envelopes us." As Yemoja said those words, her hands waved down her gown before it waved outward towards the whiteness. Trina brows arched. She was amazed at the explanation and prompted her to finger check the white silk of her own clothing.

"A good thing, too. I'm sure you'll have quite the celebration upon your return to the home, especially from your grandparents," Shango interjected with a smile.

"She is due for some much-needed rest. After a bit of rest, there will be much work to do, but first our own celebration." Eleri threw up his hands and let out a single word of cheer. The crowd responded in kind and in unison.

Trina gasped. She suddenly felt herself rise in the air as Ori stood to his feet. A swaying dance and song swept through the Orishas who formed a circle around them. Yemoja stepped forward and joined Trina and Ori at the center of the circle. All around her, the Orishas danced. Their style was unique to who they were yet unified to an upbeat rhythm. Their voices raised in song and lifted Trina's heart, even if she could not discern the language of the words. Ori also sang and smiled, his sway matched the rhythm that surrounded them. Yemoja moved like the smooth slivering of a river, and as her hand raised in a wave, she summoned water to follow. The daze and awe of the celebration that surrounded Trina soon outweighed the fiery sting and deep ache in her back. And then, as the songs of the Orisha changed in tune, Ori raised his hands, and hoisted her up until she left his hands. The flow of the waters Yemoja summoned surrounded Trina. The pain of her wounds, both inner and outer, fell away. As Trina continued to rise in levitation, so did a new strength of light and hope. As the Orisha closed the song of her ascension, Trina's inner strength was more than restored. In place of branched scars where her old wings had been torn away, her renewed self found new wings.

Chapter 11

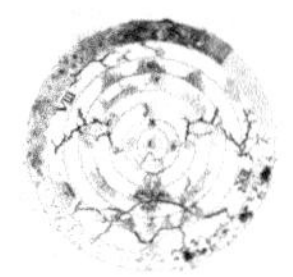

Two souls dreamed of falling down. They began like feathers that drifted to a slow drop. At first, they sensed nothing. Like the quiet void that surrounded them, their minds were weighed down in the heavy blackness of catalepsy. They were unaware of the fragments of the Dead End that sunk around them like debris from a shipwreck floating towards the ocean's depth. Even as the void shifted, the two souls remained locked in a state of unconsciousness. Eventually, space and time converged as a smoky banner cleaved through the spanning gap of darkness. The glow of its smoky haze grew opaque and under its contact, the shells of the two souls hatched.

Little by little, death's stony rind peeled away from the falling souls. The blue-green of moss bleached and withered. Gray flecks curled away from husk and left a trail that dispersed into the rest of the ghost world's sinking remains. Catalepsy gradually thawed. A half-sentience formed. On the cusp of consciousness, souls encased in shells could only dream in a fog. While they stirred, the gray of space/time thickened to a curtain that descended in the dark. Black shapes made fleeting appearances, and slid across the misty scrim like marionettes in a shadow play.

Like the subtle drumming of voices that carried throughout an audience, murmurs echoed with the passing of dark forms. The shadow of an animal with a strange crown danced. The fleeting image of the elegant creature vanished as soon as it appeared. A series of images of robed figures stretched across scrim then dissolved. In some instances, there were two or three, and in other instances, there were gatherings of many. Strange instruments and ornaments sometimes accompanied the forms of the cloaked ones. Their whispers were urgent and they ran together as they spoke of a looming portent. Among the sweeps and susurrates of the cloaked, the float of feathers quickened to the pace of leaves laden with blades of wax.

Another transition spread across a clouded curtain. Unyielding outlines replaced the shadows of cloaks. They were dark castings of massive turbines and rings. Even shapes that bristled, splayed into wings of metal or alloy. Cylinders of giant turrets jutted from their bases. Jagged edges of satellites and annexes revolved past expansive hulls. These images slid in and out of view. Each shape was partially shown as though pieces of a larger construct. The centerpiece of these images was that of a great barbican roosting on the fragmented and wavering substratum. The magnificent shadow of a spire at the center of detached and revolving ells told that the construct was either some great, floating citadel or a large ship set adrift in space.

"That vibration. It's weak, but there's no mistaking it. That ripple of force matches the same energy signal of the war's watershed. Could it be that Zodiac 9 is on Earth?" The voice seemed to come from the lingering silhouette of the hovering bastion. Though the words hummed clearly above the ocean murmurs, what was spoken could barely touch the minds still held in blackness.

The great bastion dissolved with another transition. Outlines of magnificent structures soon gave way to terrible shapes. Teeth jutted from gaping mouths and many-eyed shadows swirled against the scrim. Like black waves that turned in a violent tide, claws, menacing slants and jagged edged orifices tossed about in an amorphous mass with the slosh of low rasps and growls. Now and then, the upheaval of shapes showed some coherence in form. The disturbance in the wave reached up and the sprouting stream partially fashioned a singular shape of a beast before it collapsed into the black, yammering wave. In one great, sideways lurch, the wave shifted and stiffened into a crag with the vague portrait of a face.

"The Hand claims to be the most capable of us, but our Lord has yet to see the retrieval of Zodiac 9. Has your plan failed?" Mocks from a monstrous buzz came from the crag, a crunched snout atop a crooked maw. Though the awful vibration was articulate and clear, not once did the slackened jaw move to speak its ridicule.

"On the contrary, we now have Zodiac 8. It is only a matter of time before he finds it for us." The answer came from another voice. Unlike the baritone rumbling of the scoffer, the one who responded carried the thinner tone of a woman. Against the monstrous contest, it gently buzzed with confidence as the darkness changed once again. The shadow slid from its sideways profile to a center silhouette. The crag wilted down and morphed into a vaguely humanoid shape. Its arms held outward and what billowed from its shoulders were either wings or a hood cape. For the time it spoke and few moments afterwards, the silhouette held its place in the center of the scrim before being swept aside by another roll of shadows.

Like the speed of descending leaves that grew slightly heavier from the weight of a raindrop, the pace of the plummet increased. Peeling of the stony layers progressed.

Arms and legs lengthened as spirits aged. The more time returned to the falling souls, the more the shell mask of innocence wore away. Unconsciousness softened its grip, as some hazy sense of hearing formed.

"Quakes don't happen like that, not in Texas, do they?" With the timorous inquiry came the stretching outline of a woman whose hair was pulled back in a ponytail. Inside the translucent shade was a smaller, more defined shadow of the same woman clad in scrubs. Her head tilted upward; she faced another shadow of a coworker.

"It could have been the result of all those drillings." As the second shadow of a woman with a wider build spoke, the first line dissipated. The cross stretch of a profile loosely crowned with curly hair replaced the outline that vanished. "Besides, the important thing is that everything worked out all right. I can't imagine what a scare this must be for her family."

"A scare is right. You saw it, didn't you?" Words pushed out quiet and tense as the nervous shadow continued. and Now and then, her arms unfolded to express her uneasiness. "No heartbeat, no brain activity or pulse. Movement from gravity or a nudge I can dismiss, but dead bodies don't make deliberate turns of the head let alone open their eyes."

The curly headed shade ducked her head, hunched her shoulders, held up both hands in a motion to pacify the other shadow. A hiss of shushing quelled the rising anxiety and volume. "Not so loud, her parents," whispered the curly headed one. When signs of agitation somewhat subsided in her pony-tailed colleague, the curly head relaxed. "We've witnessed stranger things in the ER and plenty with bad endings. Let's just say what we saw today was a miracle."

"I don't know." With arms folded and braced tight against chest, the loose tassels of the ponytail shuttered. Head weighted by dread, she was only able to lift her gaze after she swept away the eerie reminiscence. "After that quake and those eyes, I can't...."

"Don't worry about it," the curly head interjected as her hands settled on the shoulders of the ponytail in a comforting pat. "Listen, I'll go check on them and finish making the rounds. Maybe you should rest." As the ponytail made a short, vigorous nod in agreement, the image of the two silhouettes slid from view. As the dialogue ended, the unclear murmuring slipped from the grasp of waking minds as the shadow of medical workers vanished.

Gravity's gradual touch added momentum to falling leaves. Gray groaned. Shells of binding husks and masks crackled against the knock of time. Stone faces stretched from ages six, to seven, to nine. After a certain point in the descent, the erosion of youth slowed, ages thirteen, ages fifteen, sixteen, seventeen. Black and the numb of mindless sloth receded like the shrinking of an ice block on defrost. A sensation set in and the touch of life was felt at the tips of toes and fingers. Knuckles ached. With the curling away of death's last layer came another sensation. It was a setting warmth that made its way through brittle peelings. It was the feeling of embrace of one hand that clasped over the hand of another.

Shadows that made measured castings across scrim suddenly swept the banner in a rushing stop and go. Silhouettes clamored. Speech toppled over speech in a collective chatter. At one point, the teeming noise ceased. The scurrying traffic of shadows slowed. In the settle, only two shadows appeared on the scrim. On one side of the banner was the image of an armillary. Two rings twirled at its center and the outer frame molded from an alloy to fashion a claw. At the top of the armillary and tip of clasping talons, a jewel twinkled. On the other side of the scrim, the profile of some great and sleek ophidian, laureled with spiny horns faced the instrument with inimical slants. What accompanied these images were two sounds. The first was the trilling verve that danced in the whistle of spinning metal. And then came another sound, a dragon's sighs. Over the guttural purrs was a chanting by a human tongue but in a language not native to man. On the scrim, the performance of a spell conjured writhing black lines. The tendrils leapt up, streamed outward and grasped until few became a multitude that rendered the banner black.

One hand wrested from the clasp of another and left one soul to descend alone. The sting of shock flickered at the sudden absence of embraces. It agitated the mind and caused it to shiver at the heaviness of somnolence and black. Awareness waxed at catalepsy's wane. Gravity bore down in full weight and a lonely leaf dropped as a single pebble. A falling soul that traveled from the surface of a netherworld neared spanning voids nadir. Reaching into the crests of a plane that breathed, the brow spasmed. Will tingled through fingers that worked against atrophy. A veil slowly rose.

The first thing June felt was the dry ache of bruised ribs. Next was the warmth. Fingers barely twitched in search of the first embrace now registered another gentle overlap of hands that cupped hers. Then, she heard her mother's voice. Her eyelids fluttered and, with great effort, pushed open. The face of a caramel complexioned woman came into view as the fog cleared. Ruddy traces and puffiness around her nose and eyes hinted that she had been crying. Lines of worry and stress slightly aged a face whose high cheekbones added a youthfulness to the middle-aged woman. As June's eyes gradually adjusted, however, her mother's youth seemed to return. Eyes stretched wide; the corners of her half gape trembled upward slightly as the weight of anguish left.

The plop of a grocery bag dragged June's eyes to the doorway. Shoes hustled as one of the approaching pair raced out into the hallway in search of other family members. The second person who stood in the doorway was June's father. Slack-jawed, a look hovered about his eyes that was difficult to pinpoint. Something almost like hope or joy twinkled through but seemed to be tempered by an expression akin to shock. Whether it was one or multiple emotions her father wordlessly conveyed, it seemed to drain him of strength despite the might poised in his powerful shoulders and arms.

June's stomach sank and she turned from the doorway. Her name was spoken again, and she turned to her bedside. Her eyes held in her mother's gaze. Seconds felt like eons. Within those moments, the joy that lit up her mother's face began to melt. After everything that had happened, there were still questions. Of all the "whats" that returned after the chaos ended, only one inquiry stood out. She fixed her mouth to utter it, but the single word "why?"caught in her throat. Instead, she leaned forward and extended her arms to wrap her daughter in a hug. June looked over at the doorway and she could see her father's head slouch as one hand covered his eyes. A knot formed in her throat and June's eyes grew blurred and glassy. When the tears from her own eyes could never fall, her parents cried for her.

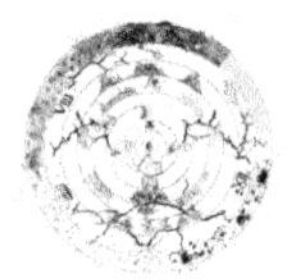

Aeonicsphere-Also known as the eternal, it is the ultimate and highest plane of existence. Heaven, hell or general beliefs of the afterlife is in reality the Aeonicsphere. Though there are negative pockets considered to be states of the plane equated with hell, it is mostly comprised of positive or heavenly states. The immensity of the Aeonicsphere is such that all the material planes and spiritual interims are but a speck. The vastness of this ultimate reality is only dwarfed by The Creator who gave birth to it.

Aeons-Aeons are the first born and the eldest of The Creator's children. Populating the Aeonicsphere, they are beings of immense power and knowledge that many mortals would view them as gods. Before the first conflict, they were the epitome of wholeness and harmony.

Archdemons-The term is more of a title for demons with above average strength, wickedness and abilities. This class of demon is extremely dangerous and has the might to lord over demon hordes and usurp dimensions.

Archon-Archons are direct offshoots of The Corruptors. In every age, an Archon would arise to bring calamity and suffering to devastate those of the mortal plane. Left unchecked, their terrible strength and aspirations to rule will reach beyond the material plane.

Avadon-It is the full manifestation of an intensely negative state in the material plane populated by demons, fiends and evil spirits. Avadon is not originally a domain of the material plane, but a phenomenon in which a dimension is completely overtaken by hellish forces. The name of the phenomenon derives from Abbadon, a being most believe was a devil or past Archon. He is the first of his kind to successfully establish such a kingdom. After being defeated, his kingdom was exorcised from the material plane.

Black Dive-The first domain of darkness in the Aeonicsphere that is the birthplace of the Second Born. Though invaded by Corruptors and visited by few Aeons, it is a plane still largely shrouded in mystery.

Cherubs-An infant-like creature with wings that many perceive as cupid or an angel.

Cherubim-It is the plural term for cherubs. It is also the collection of multiple cherubs merged into one form to create a chimera-like being.

Corruptors-Aeons warped by jealousy, pride, greed and other vices. They are the ones who gave rise to conceptions of devils and are responsible for many negative aspects of existence.

The Crying One-A moniker for the Divine Monstrum because of the black tears shed in its throes of rage or intense emotions.

Cubrocarns-Cube-like creatures said to be the security system of the Bazaar. They attack in swarms and are especially aggressive towards anything flying into their territory. Only a special vibration can control them.

Divine Monstrum-Cruelty from the Corruptors transformed the Second Born into the embodiment of wrath. Both a creature and a force, the Divine Monstrum's is the first monster and storm. Its terrible form has adverse effects on the mind and only its eyes are recognizable.

Egun-Commonly called ancestors; they are the spirits of humans that reside in The Valley of the Ancestors after death.

Emanators-Aeons who original upheld the will of The Creator, but later became preoccupied with maintaining a positive state through order. The idea of angels came from them.

Ennui spirits-Apparitions born from fatal accidents resulting in their own untimely deaths and the demise of others. These deaths were spurred by impulsive actions to alleviate boredom. In other cases, curses tied to a person's vices were the cause of their death and transformation. Being an ennui spirit is temporary in that the transformed can earn their way into a proper spiritual transmigration.

Epuele-A chain made of shells used for divination in the material plane. In the spirit world, however, Orisha can also channel their energy through it to wield as a weapon or a projectile.

Gehenna Trees-Careless words, thoughts and, sometimes, speakers trapped in the form of grotesque, murmuring trees.

Heotron-Four souls infused with divine powers directly from the Creator and Aeons, each has an affinity with the four elements of nature. Still, their powers go beyond that of the natural world. Among the Miracula, they are warriors and purveyors of benevolence.

Incubus-Male demons of lust that feed on the souls and carnal energy of women. Whether face-to-face or through dreams, they can use a number of illusions to lure their prey and siphon their life-force.

Light Bearers-The essence of the Creator and others of the divine emanates through with immense positive energy that their souls are of pure light. Among the Miracula, they are healers with powers that can combat evil, cleanse rancor and bring uncanny grace in the face of certain doom.

Miracula-Seven heavenly souls that are the precious children of the divine. Bestowed with the powers by the Creator and Aeons, they are the only ones who can defeat the Archon and sway the Divine Monstrum. Four Heotron and three Light Bearers makeup the Miracula.

Mortalis-The third set of the Creator's children, they are the lifeforms cycling through the impermanence of the Nous Submateria. They are often called mortals .

Nous Submateria-Stolen material fashioned into a low state of existence by Corruptors, it is a miniscule domain impermanence referred to as the material plane, physical plane or living world.

Orisha-A host of divine entities that command or embody various forces. They are recognized as deities or deified ancestors especially among the mortals of West Africa. Older civilizations view them as holy liaisons that maintain contact between the physical world and the eternal.

Preta-Hungry spirits who were either wicked or driven by greed and envy in life.

Second Born-An entity that lived and rested in the Black Dive. Unlike the teeming first and third generation, there was only a single form that The Creator knew would develop into pairs. Its original appearance has been forgotten and its true name unknown.

Sheol-A spiritual world and one of eternity's negative states. Souls and other apparitions exiled to this world of darkness are fated to wither into shades. Fragments of darkness from Sheol have been collected to use as jail cells in an interim called the Processor.

Sluagh-A cloudy swarm of evil spirits doomed to wander the spirit world.

Tri-Hold-Divine restraints designed to keep the Divine Monstrum in temporary stasis. The Tether of Reincarnation, the Tether of Space/Time and the Seal of the Mortalis are the fetters that make up the Tri-Hold.

Venetians-Also known as Merchants, these spirits are cloaked in extravagant wisps with fanciful masks for faces. They migrate to the Bazaar and other places to trade items both tangible and intangible.

Yana-A term of endearment used by the lost soul that hints to some past life connection with their other half.

Ze- The term is a gender neutral, third person pronoun that is the subject of a sentence.

Zeir(s)- The word is a gender neutral, third person pronoun that is possessive or a pronoun showing that something belongs to someone.

Zem- A gender neutral, third person pronoun that works as the object of a verb.

Zemself- A gender neutral term that can function as an intensive and/or reflexive, third person pronoun.

About the Author

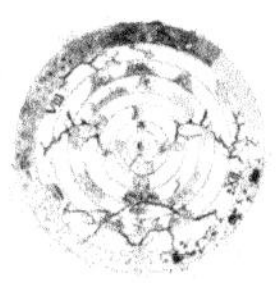

Diagnosed with one of the Autism Spectrum Disorders, communication was a challenge for W. L. Carol and writing was a grueling task. In her early childhood, she struggled with penmanship and spelling and often grappled with the simplest assignments for hours.

For the better part of the third grade, Carol shunned pen and paper until a resource teacher showed her the fun in painting her imagination across the page with words. Since then, she had a notebook and pencil attached to her hand as she embarked on a journey to become a published author. Before long, Carol went from scribbling tales in her notebook during elementary to completing articles and a thesis in grad school. Her love of sci-fi, horror and anything within the realm of fantasy fueled her passion for creating stories. When she isn't hunkered over the keyboard or notepad, she's watching anime, playing videogames or reading comic books or manga. Carol currently lives in Texas and enjoys a job where she works with a lot of books.